The Cannibals

The Cannibals

A Novel About Television's Savage Chieftains

KEEFE BRASSELLE

BARTHOLOMEW HOUSE LTD.

Publishers

FROM THE AUTHOR

To Mickie, who started my life and whom I worship and adore—to Rosana, my pride and joy and "Daddy's favorite little girl"—to Melisa, who captured my heart the moment I saw her, and who is probably smarter than all of us—and to the woman I love, my wife, Arlene.

To my mother, who taught me—to Mama, whom I loved and will miss—to Jo, who read—to Barbara, who typed and helped—to my "Loyal Opposition" with love: Ann, Gloria, Terri, Gene and Billy— plus Jane, who helped so much at the end. . . . And of course to *Chili Monroe*.

To Craig Kellem, who never took a backward step or even faltered —to Herman Rush, who kept his word—to Paul McGoldrick, who stuck all the way—to Big Jim K., who drank my booze.

To Fred Klein, who had the guts to buy, a rarity in the "Land of the Cannibals." With gratitude to Samuel Post, my editor and friend, who locked me into the Tudor Hotel and wouldn't let me out until I finished, and who took the abuse of my loneliness.

Especially to Allen, who schooled me—to Maxie, who showed me the meaning of friendship—and to Joe, Sammy, and Louie, who were there.

Finally, with great love for the "Sympatico" and honor they showed, to my Cousin Sal and my Uncle Joe, who never stopped believing in

"Keefo"

The Cannibals

Chapter 1

It was 6:00 P.M. All the sun worshipers at the Fontainebleau Hotel had gone to their rooms to change clothes. I sat alone at the far end of the pool area, a vodka and tonic in one hand and a half-smoked cigarette in the other.

For the first time in five years I was at peace. The giant orange sun was about three-quarters visible over a purple horizon. The breeze hummed soft background music for my reflections. Which were—the bomb was due to explode in just twenty-four hours.

Fifteen minutes before, I had been holding court in the Poodle Lounge. It was just starting to load up with all the painted, shopworn wives. The hookers were in their slacks and costume jewelry. The fat slob men were in the garish Bermuda shorts that exposed their skinny, gnarled legs—without any awareness that they were the topic of conversation.

Indeed, the one thing that the wives and the hookers agreed on was that they both hated the ugly bastards.

Away from the horseshoe bar, down into the far end of the room, sat the swinging crowd—the agents and sharpshooters who never paid for a piece of tail, and the little starlets who never sold it—but gave it away if they thought you could do them any good.

9

Collectively, they were all full of shit, although in their own codes of honor they considered themselves the only real people. And in those warped codes of honor, they were right.

I was trading gossip with these swingers when a hand tapped me on the shoulder. I turned around only slightly, because I had already lamped the bellboy heading my way.

"Telephone call, Mr. Bertell."

"Thanks, buddy." I slipped him the usual dollar bill.

Strolling over to a house phone booth, I cursed the sonova-bitch who would dare call me between five and seven. Anyone who knew me realized that between those hours I dug for gossip, so that I'd be up on what the hell was going on in my world.

I grabbed the receiver in that mood.

"This is Joey Bertell. Gotta call for me?"

"Yes, Mr. Bertell. Long distance from New York."

While waiting for the hookup, I lit a fresh cigarette. As I puffed, the *click* came.

"Hello."

The instant I heard that soft, calculated tone, I knew who it was. Also that it was important. That tone was never used on me unless it was—or unless someone was with him taking in the conversation.

"Hi, what's new?"

"I'm so glad that I found you. I wanted you to be the first to know that I have resigned as president of the network."

One thing about Jonathan J. Bingham. He sure as hell didn't mince words.

10

It took me two seconds to collect myself, but I knew he expected that—plus an indicative response.

"Well, Johnny, if that's your decision, I'm sure you know what you're doing."

"Joey, that's it." He spoke with finality.

"Good. Of course, it doesn't change a damn thing," I said. "We're still together, and we'll still make it work."

Now he paused.

"You're so right, buddy. It'll be bigger and better than ever."

"That sounds like the Jonathan I know. Now, I'll stay here over the weekend, and if you need me, call at any hour. And for Christ's sake, just know that I don't fade in the stretch. I start when the rest quit."

"You don't have to tell me that, pal. I always knew I could count on you. I'll give you a call tomorrow. I meet with the network on stock and severance pay. Keep it under your hat, and take it easy."

Click.

I knocked out of the phone booth and headed back to the table. Administering a mental pep talk, I grew two inches and walked with a slight strut.

The swingers at the table seemed oblivious to my departure and return. The trade talk went on. Across the room the freeloaders continued gorging themselves. The hookers were still hooking. The wives were still comparing minks. The fat slobs in the Bermudas were still out of the world.

They were now rewriting history and reliving great football

careers—although it was obvious that they had never played on any team unless they owned the ball.

I grabbed my check, scrawled my signature, and dropped a deuce for the waiter. I had to get out of the rat race, and right now. With a few casual exit lines, to which the swingers still seemed oblivious, I left and made my way to the pool area.

The orange sun was about all in the water now, but the day had just dawned for me, and it was whirling in my mind. Whoever wrote the "Best-laid schemes of mice and men" lines was one smart sonovabitch.

My thoughts were focusing on Jonathan J. Bingham. I was assuming the roles of judge and jury. The verdict was ready. Jonathan J. Bingham was guilty.

He was guilty of being weak—by standards he had set up for his own game and anyone who dared to play it with him. He was weak for folding up like a tower of Jello instead of playing his trump card.

That trump card was not mere creative genius, but the courage to make determinations and call the shots when all around him was chaos.

What had happened? In the biggest battle of his life he had made the wrong determination, hesitated to call the shot. The courageous general had let the enemy pull rank on him. He had become an ordinary private.

They say that self-preservation is the strongest human instinct. Maybe so. In the entertainment industry—the land of the cannibals—there are different rules.

THE CANNIBALS

The more human you are in the land of the cannibals the less chance you have of succeeding . . . or even surviving.

The stakes there are so high that you have to grab where the hair is short and pull like a bastard. You pull, and kick them in the balls. The more you pull and kick the more respect you get.

Treat a lady like a whore, and a whore like a lady.

Jonathan had made a career out of being ruthless—until the end.

In the beginning he enjoyed being feared. He loved being crucified with nicknames. He thrived on knocks and would have fits of depression if he felt that he was not the topic of conversation on any given day.

But toward the end of his imperial reign, he began to reach out for a little love.

Whereupon the powers that prevail in the land of the cannibals handed him his ass.

I took another swig of the vodka and tonic. Some tranquilizer! It made the think glands bubble like a school of hungry albacore. Another swig, another drag . . . I was back to the big question. *How did it happen?*

In a game you play for all the marbles, you are either a team man or a loner. Running the mile is lonely, but at least it's all your race to win. Playing football is a team effort, and you must have that line blocking for you, plus a couple of halfbacks standing next to you in case someone breaks through the line. But team man or loner, there are only two results. You either win, or you lose.

I once read a novel called *What Makes Sammy Run?* It was the best goddam book I ever read. It proved to me that there is a certain breed of guys who live for nobody but themselves and what they can screw out of you. They infest every walk of life and should be sprayed with DDT.

Too bad I didn't analyze that novel more carefully. It would have saved me lots of trouble. On second thought, I probably wouldn't have recognized the lice in my own life until too late. They have a way of disguising themselves—sometimes with gold-plated halos.

Which louse had bitten Jonathan J. Bingham? Was it one or two of them, or all of them? I put them into a figurative file box and began to sift their cards.

Could it be beady-eyed Chester Plan? The fawning Mario Colucci? Bryan Westgate and his "wife" John? (Fags are always dangerous.) Fred Tashley, the jaded agent? Leonard Morris, the alleged close friend and pseudo-intellectual, had to be considered. Tom Brady, whom I nicknamed "Ralph Restaurant," was also in contention, since he was close to Bryan Westgate, but he was hardly a serious prospect. It couldn't have been Joe Ballantine, because he had real balls. (I always liked Joe and felt he was one member of the team who could be trusted. Outside the team, he was a thief, but when he made a move, he did it with real class. I always enjoy watching an artist at work.)

There were so many candidates for the title of Top Louse. But as I mentally sifted the cards, I began to realize that it wouldn't be fair to sift down to one and award the cup. *Two* of the prospects were unique in crafts of double-dealing. After all, the Parasite of the Year Award must not be taken lightly. Yes, the cup must be bestowed upon two.

Chester Plan and Mario Colucci had won, hands down.

I was distracted by the tinkle of ice cubes. Mel, the waiter, was walking my way.

"I was just leaving, Mr. Bertell, and thought maybe you could use this." He had a glass.

I automatically reached toward my pocket, but he stopped me.

"No, thanks, Mr. Bertell. Have a drink against Castro." He handed me the drink, smiled warmly, and walked off.

I thought it over for a second and found myself chuckling. Mel, on top of being a great waiter, had a helluva sense of humor.

There is an old wives' tale that when you're sitting in the electric chair, your whole life passes in front of your eyes in ten seconds.

I wasn't sitting in the electric chair, and all I wanted to remember was a couple of years.

I chug-a-lugged the whole damn glass of vodka and tonic and started remembering. . . .

Chapter 2

New York in March can be nasty weather. The air gets through your overcoat, and each breath is like inhaling razor blades through your nose.

It was 6:30 P.M., and colder than Kelsey's ass. There was four inches of snow on the streets, and the wind was blowing skirts up to the eyebrows. Half the commuter highways were closed, trains and buses were running late, and you could get the President of the United States on the phone quicker than you could get a cab.

Thus I was walking to Louis and Armand's. My ears were like two frozen popsicles, and I still had six blocks to go. I didn't dig the food, but the drinks were great, and I looked forward to bowing for about fifteen minutes and shooting the bull with the fellows before heading for New Jersey to do a benefit.

Besides, in my mood, the snow was warm sand, the icy wind was a warm breeze that soothes your face just after you've stepped out of the ocean after a summer dip. I was a conquering hero.

"Joey," I congratulated myself, "you've done it again, you magnificent bastard! You came through and knocked them right on their cans. How can anyone deny you now? You are a goddam winner."

17

I was on top of the world and enjoying every second. I had just produced and starred in a pilot show that was going on the air. No more sweating. No more phone calls campaigning to get it in the schedule. The powers had committed themselves. It was locked in. Christ, it was a beautiful night.

I turned into the entrance of Louis and Armand's. Walking through the door were a couple of agents whom I really despised. I grabbed the door and held it for them. Screw 'em. I could afford to be kind. I even made a mental note for my secretary that when they called they were to be granted interviews. After all, why should I penalize them for being stupid? That disability was an occupational hazard.

"Hi, honey," I greeted the hatcheck girl, shucking my overcoat. "Never let this out of your sight. It's vicuna."

She smiled and gave a typical show business shrug.

I stood a moment and looked around the room. I had not failed to lamp the table when I walked in, but it was my style not to press. After a "sincere" amount of time, I "accidentally" spotted the group and sauntered over.

Half the hierarchy of Broadcast Corporation of America was there. Omar Cone sat in the chair facing me, his bald head beaming underneath a pink pin spot. As BCA head of production for both coasts, he rated the best seat. Among the rest were Herb Post, sales; and Bill Blackman, account executive for the big ad agency, and one of my best friends. Mario Colucci sat on Bill's right, drinking a crème de menthe and trying desperately to look comfortable, not like a recent arrival from Naples on a banana

18

boat. Unfortunately, he lost that bet. Filling out the table was Gottfried von Klung of the Tobacco Company's ad agency. We had nicknamed him "The Nazi," but he was probably the nicest and brightest of all Bill Blackman's rivals.

Omar was nearing the punch line of one of his famous stories. I slipped into a seat quietly so that I wouldn't step on his laugh, and I observed him.

Personally, he was a good family man. Gina loved his Rosalie, a really lovely lady, and Rosalie dug Gina. His only vice was throwing the galloping dominoes for strong stakes. Business-wise, his weakness was a lack of the killer instinct. This kept him from becoming a real power in the land of the cannibals. His likability protected him against eighty percent of the rats that feed on such languid imperfections, but Omar was doomed to fall. It was just a matter of when, and by whose hand.

Gales of laughter indicated that Omar's story had, as usual, scored. The pink pin spot did a lot for his smile.

Welcomes and pleasantries were now exchanged. I ordered my standard vodka and tonic. As always, I specified Smirnoff, which I had done originally because I thought it was chic, then continued when I discovered it suited my taste.

Gottfried raised his glass and gave it his pompous German best. "To Joey, TV's newest and brightest star."

"Gottfried," I applauded, "I couldn't have said it better. You have fine taste."

Bill Blackman chimed in. "I always said that Joey would make it on modesty alone."

He got a helluva laugh, which I didn't mind. Bill wanted only the best for me, and his rib had the undercurrent of sincerity.

Omar strove for a topper. "Joey, when do you plan on taking the network over?"

"Omar, my boy," I struck back, "at the moment you are doing an adequate job. Not great, you understand, but adequate. If you continue to keep your blunders to a minimum, I shall allow you to remain."

Everyone laughed. Omar beamed. Colucci made a feeble attempt to say something ingratiating and was generally ignored. He was a real pain in the ass. However, since he was Italian, I reminded myself to be fair and check out this neophyte ass kisser. If he didn't add up, I would cut off his balls. If he had any capacity for advancement, I'd make it my business to be the kingmaker on his next move.

At the far end of the room the captain motioned to me, then did fists to the nose and ear for a quick telephone impression. Were there any straight men left? Everybody seemed to be in show business.

I made my apologies, rose, and headed for the alcove behind the captain.

"Mr. Bingham is on the phone," he said as I passed.

I thanked him with a nod and picked up the dangling receiver. "Hello."

The soft voice. "Hello, buddy."

"How the hell did you know I was here?"

"I have my spies too," he answered. "Let's get together for a drink."

"I'd love to, but I have to do a benefit in Jersey. It's a promise to a couple of buddies of mine, and I wouldn't want to let them down."

There was a pause.

"That's okay," he said, "I'll drive over with you and we can talk in the car."

The tone was kindly but persuasive. I decided to take one more shot at ducking the meeting before asking if something was wrong.

"Hey, pal, I'd love to have you come over with me, but you have to be out of your mind to drive in this snow. Relax, grab yourself a couple of drinks, a broad, and a warm bed, and I'll see you tomorrow."

I crossed my fingers.

"Joey, you call the shot. I don't mind driving at all . . . or you can cancel out and we'll have dinner somewhere quiet. I want to talk to you."

His "You call the shot" was strictly *pro forma*. Nobody called his shots. By now my instinct told me that it was important, it was trouble, and it sure as hell involved me. I managed, however, to play it cool.

"Okay, you've got me convinced. I'll cancel out and we'll have dinner."

"Great," he answered, "where do you want to eat?"

"I'll meet you at Mercurio's in thirty minutes."

"You can make it fifteen," he replied. "By a coincidence, I'm at Mercurio's now."

The sly bastard! His conniving gave me a chill.

"You got a deal," I replied, and hung up.

I spent a few moments staring at the graffiti near the telephone. Something was up. What in hell could it be—what area? The evening had started magnificently, maybe I was making a mountain out of a molehill. Well, one thing was sure, I wouldn't learn it standing in a corner reading dirty sayings.

I tried to calm myself, walking back to the table.

"Who was that—Big John?"

I looked hard at Omar. He was either a mind reader, or else he was in on the play.

"That's who the man was," I answered lightly.

I looked casually at Herb Post to see if he was with Omar. No indication.

"How about one for the road?" I suggested, forcing myself to pick up the tempo.

Everyone was ready, willing, and able. I motioned the waiter.

"Another round, and bring me the check."

When the drinks arrived, I gulped mine, signed, and exchanged the quick good-byes.

"Call me tomorrow," Omar said as I was turning away.

"Right," I promised over my shoulder.

The hatcheck girl was solicitous with my vicuna and appropriately rewarded. I dove out the door into the wind and the snow. Next stop, Mercurio's.

At Mercurio's, the vicuna came off again and went into the hands of another promising type. John, the maitre d', practically brushed the girl aside to grab my hand. He was an oil pumper, and he was talking right into my ear. But I was in a kind of trance and could only concentrate on finding a cigarette in my pocket, lighting it, and inhaling.

I held the smoke down until it was ready to explode, then slowly whirled it out, along with my mental fog. I was back to normal and managed a smile.

"Right this way, Mr. Bertell."

I followed.

At the final left turn I spotted Jonathan. He was in the booth at the far end of the room, very casual, and in complete control of the universe. As I approached, I wondered just how long it had taken him to arrange the exact location and pose.

Jonathan had a flair for the dramatic, the impressive. I appreciated it, especially since I was the guy who had taught him.

I slid easily into the booth, shaking hands with him as I sat. I tried to analyze his grip for a clue to the situation. A man's handshake is infallible. You can tell the climate, the mood, and, if you have studied handshakes, you can sometimes forecast the exact subject of a conversation.

With women, of course, the grip is not that strong. That's one reason they can keep you guessing so delightfully. At that momentary reflection I promised myself to buy Gina a Russian sable if I had clocked this situation wrong. Christ, how I was rooting her—and me—in, but at that moment I had to quote odds of ten to four going against us.

While I was reflecting, Jonathan was taking charge. "Must be colder than hell outside. Order yourself a warmer."

The waiter was there. "Make me a vodka martini with Smirnoff."

The next few minutes were passed with small talk and the quick end of my cigarette. I tried three matches on another, but none lit. Jonathan smiled and tossed me a Mercurio's pack from the ashtray.

The drinks were served expertly. I gave Jonathan a quick toast: "Salute."

"Salute," he replied.

By this time I was losing my cool. And at the precise moment that I started to speak, the captain arrived with menus.

I almost took his head off. "Leave the menus. When I want to order, I'll call you."

Then, recovering quickly, I patted him on the back, smiled, and said, "Okay?"

These bastards can second-guess you to death. "Of course, Mr. Bertell. You take your time and let me know when you're ready."

I took another drag on the cigarette and looked at Jonathan. He had a slight smile, which struck me as patronizing. He had done nothing to make it easy, starting with his phone call at Louis and Armand's. I had it up to the hairline.

I gave him another four seconds, then looked him in the eye and got right to the point.

"I'm not a goddam fool—something is up. Get it out right away—and if it has anything to do with my new show going on the air, don't fuck around with pleasantries."

He had a fork in his hand and doodled on the tablecloth for a few seconds. Suddenly I knew that my instincts had been correct—and to my surprise, I felt sorry for him. Here was the biggest man in television getting ready to whack out his best friend. It wasn't easy for Brutus. It wasn't easy for Jonathan.

He looked up.

"Joey, I've got to pull the trigger on you."

I took that line and never quivered. I had sensed the maneuver, tightened my gut, and was ready with a counter.

Staring into his eyes, I had total cool again.

When I was a kid, some smart ass had told me: If you ever meet a lion, stare him in the eye and he'll back off. Now, I knew that Jonathan wouldn't back off . . . but I sure as hell knew that my silence was giving me points. I continued staring. Then I felt a surge of power as his eyes shifted and he reached for his drink. His sweat glands were working. I was not about to alter fate, but for this instant at least I had the edge on him.

He rearranged his position in the booth. He finally spoke, eyes still averted.

"Joey, it doesn't have to do with *Sandstorm* going on the air
... it has to do with its *not* going on the air."

I never relaxed my cold look. "Why?"

"The Chairman took it out of the schedule."

"There has to be a reason."

Now we were getting into the fencing contest. Sooner or later
I'd have the complete story. I held myself in check, because
Jonathan was going to tell it his way and from here on in he had
the edge again, it was his ball game. At least, I didn't want to
lose the mood I had succeeded in setting.

"You're right," he started, looking at me at last. "Jackie
Benson and QMA got to him."

That blew the mood—I couldn't control myself.

"What the fuck have that senile comedian and that shit-heel
agency got to do with my show going on or off the air?"

I gulped the martini and caught my second wind.

"I worked my ass off on that pilot. I used every friend I had
in Miami Beach. I turned over the Fontainebleau Hotel to your
network, with a thousand people working for free; delivered
every nightclub in the city for photography; even dropped an
entire marina in your lap. And now you sit there and tell me
that washed-up Jackie Benson, who hasn't the brains to lie down
and die, who doesn't realize he's further out of it than Joe
Miller's joke book, could force you to take my show off the air?
You gotta be sick!"

I ran out of second wind.

Jonathan was patient. He knew I was fighting on impulse and
should not be held accountable for the heat of my words.

"All right," he said quietly, "is it all out of your system?"

"Yeah, Johnny. I'm sorry—take your best shot."

He smiled like a big brother. At that moment he became as human as he would ever allow himself to be.

"It's this simple. Benson owns *Chessgame*. I think it's the worst show we have. All my guys agree with me. The three leads are totally embarrassing. We dropped it from the schedule and gave its time slot to your show."

He paused. My mind raced.

"We don't have Benson tied up for next season. And now, as awful as I think he is, we have a hole in the schedule that only he can fill, for the right program mix. We need him for his name."

With impeccable timing Jonathan spelled it out.

"He won't sign for next season unless we agree to keep that abortion *Chessgame* on the air. It's been on for two years, and he needs next year for ninety episodes—capital gains."

I fought back like a tiger.

"What about that cowboy star you forced me to give twenty-five percent of my show to? You told me the network had to find ways to make his bullshit company legal from a tax standpoint, and I had to give him the piece and form a joint venture with him, when he had as much to do with creating or producing *Sandstorm* as Mussolini."

My anger, expressed in jargon, plus the ridiculous situation, suddenly amused Jonathan. He actually laughed.

I should have been furious. But Jonathan had a way of disarming you. His charm was most effective when he turned it on.

Besides, I really admired him. It was a mutual admiration that had been built up over many years. We had seen each other up and down, rich and poor.

It was a classic case of friends from opposite sides of the tracks. He came from a wealthy family and went to the best schools. He was athletically trained, and though he couldn't punch his way out of a paper bag, he had the guts of Caranza and so was accepted by the guys. He formed his own tight circle of friends, however, and preferred a clique to the world at large.

In the world of business he was an acknowledged expert and an utter snob. He had a contempt for his opponents and at times would allow them extraordinary advantages, just for the thrill of demolishing them, like a Dizzy Dean or a Bill Tilden with a sadistic streak.

He had that control and that power. In the end the deal was only his deal. It was legendary.

Why, then, had he let this happen to me, of all people? I had come through for him personally, and his entire staff believed in my show. I became tigerish all over again.

"What the hell are you going to do with the cowboy?"

"*The Interrogators* is owned by QMA, and they're going to give him twenty-five percent of the show."

"Why can't you leave *Sandstorm* in the schedule and cancel *The Interrogators?* Twenty-five percent is twenty-five percent."

"Joey," he explained, still patient but getting a trifle edgy, "use your head. Don't you see the ball game is over? QMA and Benson, who hate my guts, went to the Chairman together.

28

THE CANNIBALS

They've been friends for years—Benson jumped from the other network and helped make us what we are today. So Benson can make us renew *Chessgame* by holding out on his contract, and also throw the weight of QMA on us. Do you know of any agency with more weight?"

"No."

"Well," he said, "at least you're beginning to think clearly again."

He sipped his drink and proceeded to another point.

"Joey, this is a move on me, not you. They're saying that I favored your show. But you're just a fall guy—it's the only shot they've got."

"What you're saying to me, in effect, is that those two impotent bastards and that octopus are doing exactly what they're accusing us of doing."

"You get an A for logic."

I signaled the waiter and ordered another round. For once, I hardly had stomach to drink it. I lit a cigarette. It tasted lousy also. I looked at Johnny looking at me, and we clocked each other.

"Johnny, I'm your best friend. But that's a two-way street. You have to be my best friend. I want you to answer a few questions. Answer them all, and without comment. Okay?"

"Shoot."

"Did Omar Cone and your entire staff commit *Sandstorm* to the air without one dissenting vote?"

"Yes."

"Did they sincerely believe it was a good show?"

"The best in the schedule."

"Rather than favoring me, didn't you, in fact, lean over backwards and make it even tougher for me? Didn't my show have harder standards?"

"Absolutely."

"Was the show sold out to sponsors?"

"Every minute."

"Did I let you down in any department?"

"No."

"Did I fail you personally in any way?"

"Joey, you were great in the show, and I was proud of you as a friend."

I stuck out my hand. "Johnny, you're off the hook. I won't do one thing to make waves for you."

He took my hand and shook.

With that handshake we both went back to the years when he, Bill Blackman, Clete Barber, Bill Burke, Jack Bolt, and I were pals. We were actually Musketeers. We used to drink together, go to ball games, "beard" for each other, and have great times.

We didn't have money at the same time. But when one had it, we all had it. In the beginning I had starred in a big picture, owned a piece of a Vegas hotel, and was winning big. Jonathan was with a local television station doing God knows what—but he was doing it better than anyone else could possibly do it. And, again the classic case, he had an insatiable desire to read.

He always had a book with him or in the back seat of his car.

Even then I knew Jonathan would rise from low man on the totem pole—and rise past me. He planned that rise with great thought and executed it with machinelike efficiency. His trademark was giving the credit for everything to his superiors—now his underlings. It was a meteoric rise, from low local man to undisputed czar of BCA-TV.

"Joey," said Jonathan, "I'd have bet my life you'd say that."

He seemed to be answering my thoughts, as well as my words and my handshake.

"*However*," I corrected his earlier remark, "the ball game *isn't* over. Just the first inning."

"I'll buy that."

"Promise me one thing. When we get last licks, let's nail those dirty bastards."

"You have my word."

"Whack them all out," I poured it on, "except six for pallbearers. That much I got coming."

He laughed at me again, then went back to business.

"Now, the network will pay you for your commitment, or put you into *Chessgame* as one of the stars and give you twenty-five percent of that show. My advice—take the money, because the show stinks."

"Deal."

"We'll still go into further development on your other show too, but that's window dressing. The program guys will be scared to touch you after this."

31

"That's a nice kick in the ass."

"Well, it's a kick you can clock. You know as well as I do that they all live in fear. They'll wait it out and see how the ball bounces before they move."

"Spineless straw men," I spat.

"Straw makes bricks," he countered. "And remember, without Indians you don't have any chiefs."

I began to sense there were wheels within wheels in Jonathan's plans.

"There are a lot of bent noses here, Joey. Consider Bryan and Joe on the coast. They were counting on your show to be done out there so they'd have another leg up on Chester Plan. You know the war that goes on between them."

"Did Bryan and Joe really stand up for *Sandstorm?*"

"Right down to the final bell. As I told you, everyone from Omar down. Sales was furious. And Chester Plan stood up for it because he hates QMA."

"In that case, I can't fault the team."

"Basically they all like you and resent the indirect attack on me."

"What's the next move?"

"Just let it die down. Play it cool."

"Nothing else—"

"Joey, let's not blow up all over again."

"Okay, okay. So what do I do, go over my deal with Mario Colucci in business affairs?"

"Don't waste your time with Mario, go directly to Vincent

THE CANNIBALS

Fisk. You've got BCA scared to death of what you'll do—use that edge."

Again I sensed wheels within wheels, but missed the point.

"They're scared, all right. It's like the fighter joke. 'Watch the referee, because somebody's kicking my brains out.' "

"Wrong joke," said Jonathan. He loved to be secretive and discuss tactics. He moved closer.

"The hole card is the G," he began, affecting my jargon. "Another agency blew the whistle on QMA, and the government wants to break them up under the antitrust act."

I began to see some of the pieces of the jigsaw puzzle.

"The Chairman is going to retire in a few years," continued Jonathan. "He would like people to remember his great gift to mankind—building the network. Fillmore, who's practically given up waiting for that retirement, has been campaigning for three administrations in Washington for a cabinet appointment. He'll have a stroke if there are any investigations into network practices. And believe me, pal, if the government ever starts, it'll unbuild every network, down to the cornerstones."

The jigsaw pieces now began to fit together.

"I see a few ideas have begun to roll over in that cunning mind of yours," he smiled.

I was flattered. "You have made your point."

"Not quite. We have information that *you* are going to be called by the government, Joey, to go before the grand jury on the QMA situation. If only we'd known it sooner, we wouldn't have made the Benson deal. . . ."

33

I leaned back, whistled, and grabbed for my martini.

Jonathan produced the final piece of the puzzle.

"Consider your position. You'll get your money, the network will owe you a big favor, and the only thing you'll be behind schedule on is that your show won't be on the air."

The puzzle was complete—but I didn't like the picture it showed. Despite Jonathan's interpretation of how I should feel, what I wanted most was still going down the drain.

Jackie Benson! If he had been in the restaurant at that moment, I'd have taken his mythical Stutz Bearcat and jammed it up his keister.

My emotions had gone from high to low tonight, and the pressure wanted some outlet. At this precise moment my eyes fell upon Jonathan's cufflinks. They were handmade replicas of the BCA trademark. Italian marble. Everyone in television from New York to Hollywood knew they were symbols of top management and power.

"Okay, Johnny, I buy the position. But you have to seal it with a favor."

"Name it."

"Take off those cufflinks. I want them."

He booked the bet. In a flash he got into the mood and made a ritual of it. The cufflinks came off slowly, first one, then the other. He handed them over as if he were King Arthur conducting a new knight to the Round Table.

The knight accepted his place with appropriate humility.

34

"Okay, Joey, you've had a rough time tonight. Let's order some food."

For once, the thought of eating turned my stomach, and I told him so.

"Then what do you want to do? I'll go out and drink with you, or take in a show. . . ."

"Johnny, I know you're being a good friend, and I appreciate it. But I've already eaten something very filling—one big, bitter pill. I'd be bad company for anyone tonight. To be truthful, I'd prefer to go somewhere by myself and drink, to let it all sink in."

"Joey, if I were in your spot, I think I'd feel the same way. I respect your decision."

"Thanks. By the way, why didn't those guys of yours tip me in? I was at Omar's table when you called."

"Not one of them knew what to say—or how you'd react. It was too important to blow, so I told them I'd do it."

"Christ, they played it the opposite way and really had me set up for the kill. Well, you can tell them I took it standing up."

"Standing up," said Jonathan, "and with class."

He reached for the phone that was plugged into the booth jack and dialed what I could read as the network number.

"Hello, this is Mr. Bingham. Get me Vincent Fisk at home."

I sat silent while he waited, and then he was on.

"Vincent, Jonathan Bingham. I just finished with Joey Bertell. . . . It worked out fine in the long run. He took it as well

as could be expected. . . . Of course he was upset. . . . We agreed
to pay him his commitment money and develop the other series.
We'll have no problem with him at all in regard to that other
thing we discussed. . . . I feel lousy about it, but that's this
business. . . . I'm sure you do. Tell him when you see him, because he likes you anyway. . . . Right, Vincent. I'm sorry to have
bothered you at home. . . . That's nice of you to say, but it wasn't
that hard. He did what I knew he'd do. . . . Fine. Good night."

He put down the phone and waited for my reaction.

"Couldn't have been better."

I stood up and shook hands. "Talk to you tomorrow."

"By the way, he said as I started to walk away, "I called Gina
and told her I had to talk to you tonight."

I stopped. "Thanks, but she doesn't need props to hold her
up. See you."

Before I knew it, I was outside in the snow, walking aimlessly
toward Fifth Avenue.

A block later I spotted a public phone booth. I entered,
fished out a dime, and made the call. Gina answered promptly.

"I just finished with Jonathan. I'm headed for the Hi-Ho
Club for a drink, and I'll be home later."

I didn't really listen for an answer, but hung up, opened the
booth, and continued walking. However, in the next six blocks
I had time to think about her.

Gina was a great broad. Gina was also a great wife. She was
approaching her middle twenties and looked like eight million
dollars. She also looked like she could easily borrow another

four. Gina had a face like Elizabeth Taylor, flashing black eyes and hair to match. On top of that she had a body that wouldn't quit.

Besides looks, she was a talented singer and knew show business in and out. Most important, she'd had that great Sicilian training as a girl. She was my broad, kept her mouth shut, did exactly as I told her to do and didn't bug me with questions. She had the brains to know she wouldn't have gotten any answers anyway. Gina was all mine and I knew it. She had the security of knowing I'd go through a wall for her and that in the long run we were building together.

We'd been getting along fine lately—only getting about two divorces a week. It used to be two a day. Some of our arguments lasted as long as three minutes, but most were shorter. In short, we were both hot-blooded and screamers. It was great fun and the making-up was fabulous. She also had infallible instincts. If she pegged someone as a wrongo, believe me, he turned out to be just that. Thinking about her made the cold air warmer.

I went through the door of the Hi-Ho Club, and it was like being in my second home. It was just where I wanted to be till I came out of my walking coma.

When I walked in, I got hit by ten handshakes and warm greetings from Carmine, Herman, and all the redcoats.

If you ever want to get a rundown on a guy and you're sitting in the Hi-Ho Lounge, watch the maitre d', Carmine, plus Herman and the redcoats. It never varies. They are cordial and polite. That's their job. If you've got some speed in you and have a reputation of being a right guy, you're welcomed like you were Ricky Pollard himself.

Ricky is fascinating in his own right. It's his club and he runs it his way. Nobody's big enough to push him around or get out of line.

Ricky and I had been friends for the ten years I had been in New York. I'd been introduced to him by friends, and that was good enough for him.

I started toward the bar and passed him sitting at the corner table. He waved and smiled. From Ricky that was a twenty-one gun salute and the Congressional Medal of Honor. I waved back and kept going.

I ordered my drink and it was set down at once with the message that it was "compliments of Mr. Pollard." I always wondered if Ricky was wired into the bartender's ears.

Up on the stage were some gospel singers that had the joint rocking. My foot started tapping and for a few moments I forgot my troubles.

Music has all kinds of effects on people, and with me it served as a tranquilizer. The drinks, finally getting to me, and the tempo of the lounge chatter were a welcome respite from the mental wars of the last few hours.

A redcoat tapped me on the shoulder and brought me out of my temporary Utopia.

"Some friends of yours want you to join them for a drink, Mr. Bertell."

I looked over and recognized a face out of Las Vegas. I signed for my extra drinks and strolled over.

THE CANNIBALS

My friend rose as I reached the table, stuck out his hand, and pulled me down in the vacant chair. "How's it going, Joey?"

"Great, Lou. How 'bout you?"

"Still twistin' and turnin'," he replied. "Say hello to Bob . . . Harry . . . Mousie . . . and Al."

We shook hands all around. Lou nodded to the waiter for a glass and poured me a drink. The Scotch tasted like kerosine after all that vodka, but what the hell's the difference when you're with friends.

"This is the greatest stand-up guy you'll ever run across," he announced with great pride. "Take a ticket on what I tell you. This guy's got big brass balls."

The four looked me over with impassive eyes and accepted the accolade with mute but friendly nods.

"How's the wife?" Lou asked.

"Great. How's yours?"

"Jam up."

After those formalities were over, we had a few more belts and cut up touches on friends of ours. I was getting ready to shove off when Lou had a thought.

"Harry is leaving for the Coast in the morning and had broad trouble. Do you need a cocktail ring for your wife?"

Harry handed something to Lou, who passed it on to me. I looked it over, and it was beautiful. I could already see it on Gina's finger.

"What's the mutuals?" I asked.

"Six bills."

"Any story?"

"Straight and worth triple."

I reached into my kick and peeled off six one-hundred-dollar bills and handed them to Lou. He, in turn, passed it on to Harry.

I stuffed the hoop in my inside pocket and shook hands all around. We wished one another luck, and before I knew it I was out on the street again looking for a cab.

I grabbed the doorman's eye and motioned. He understood and waved one of the cabs in line. I handed him a bill and jumped in ahead of about twenty indignant tourists.

I turned the key in the door and walked into the bedroom. Gina was taking off her makeup.

"*Sandstorm* isn't going on the air. I'm getting money instead and here's a present for you." I tossed the ring on the table in front of her.

I switched the channel to the *Late Late Show,* threw my clothes on the chair and hopped into bed. Looking at TV brought back the happenings of the early evening, and I took it out on the television set by just glaring back at the stupid movie.

Gina came back from the kitchen with a can of beer for me. I needed that like butter on a Jack Dempsey's cheesecake, but I took it from her without a word.

She turned the lights off and started taking off her clothes. I could see her body take shape by the light from the TV. I kept staring at the set, but I was watching her every move out of the corner of my eye, and it was better than the centerfold of a Christmas *Playboy*.

I kept wondering when she was going to ask for a complete rundown on the show and what I would do when she did. It was a choice between telling her to mind her own business, giving her a slap in the mouth, or getting up and walking out. Frankly, I was too tired for any one of the three.

I turned over on my side and with half closed eyes watched Boris Karloff pretend he was Mr. Wong. Gina slid into bed and lay motionless. After five minutes it was apparent she was not asking for the rundown, and there would be no aggravation.

She turned and snuggled up to my butt, and under regular circumstances I would have fallen asleep before bothering to get up and turn off the television.

However, the circumstances were not regular. My emotions, it seemed, were still looking for an outlet. Gina's nude body made me promise myself to talk her out of those hundred-dollar nighties. That warmth, and the skin smoother than Bergdorf's silk, did something to my shoulder blades. My nostrils picked up a perfume that could only be called "You Joey, me Gina."

She threw her arm over my shoulder and started rubbing my chest in the friendliest way. The circles got larger and larger. At the appropriate point, I turned over and welcomed her in my arms.

My six bills must have bought a magic ring at the Hi-Ho Club. Gina's body was quivering with delight.

"You've had quite a night, Joey," she whispered, holding me closer, "and now it's my turn. . ."

She and I both knew what it was to have something that not even the most ecstatic audiences of New York and Vegas put together could give you.

I wanted to chop her up, put her in a kettle, make a delectable stew, and eat her with a spoon. I would devour every part that wouldn't get up and run away.

Who knew or cared what tomorrow would bring.

The hell with Jonathan J. Bingham, screw BCA-TV, Chester Plan could drop dead, and I couldn't give a fiddler's fuck for Jackie Benson and his Stutz Bearcat.

Gina and I were alone . . .

Chapter 3

A droning in my ear lulled me into a narcotic sleep like a combination of LSD, "pot," and a few sniffs of "Charley."

The sleek DC 8 was winging its way from Los Angeles to New York and eating up the miles in an effortless glide that gave one the feeling of sleeping on clouds.

I was totally knocked out from the last four months of intrigue, plotting, and scheming, culminating in my appearance before the grand jury, which I modestly admitted to myself was a major triumph of truth, diplomacy, guts, and big, large, huge brass balls!

Bryan Westgate, the dear boy, head of programing for BCA on the west coast, had been delirious with praise as I walked into his office after my final session.

"Joey," he cooed, "you were absolutely marvelous. We're all so proud of you."

As I looked at his plucked eyebrows and watched his mincy walk, I cursed Jonathan under my breath for making me put up with this fugitive from a gay bar. I made a mental note that one day when I made my mark, stashed away my loot, and could thumb my nose at some of the vermin that infest TV, I would take a large, old-fashioned, black umbrella, stick it right up his faggot keister, and then open it up and pull it out. Then, for an encore, knock him on his ass. Just the thought gave me a nice feeling.

What the hell could he possibly have on Jonathan? Why did Johnny keep him on? Temporarily, at least, I would buy Jonathan's answer that he was a friend. Anything else was inconceivable because Jonathan was all man. But it threatened the organization I was building to have a violet in the middle of a dozen carnations. I had to solve the puzzle, and you could make a bet I would.

Dreaming on an airplane is a thrill second to none, because you see events and recall situations so vividly. All the pushers would be out of business if the potheads and hopheads would use planes for their trips. But those trips I never took. In my set you never told a woman your business, never balled a friend's wife or girlfriend, and, above all, never trusted, hung around, or even spoke to a junkie. Young in life, I found out that a junkie would turn in his own mother for a fix. When I was sixteen and wearing hundred-dollar tailor-made suits (earned from organizing the ticket takers at the Vermilion-on-the-Lake dance hall), I turned my best friend down on a loan he needed to grab a tube of H for himself. He ended up turning in his mother as a prostitute for twenty dollar stool pigeon money. From that moment on, I realized that in any business, any walk of life, it's dog eat dog, survival of the fittest. Everyone lives by the rules of the jungle, and TV is no exception. And in the TV jungle everyone is a cannibal.

THE CANNIBALS

The jet engines hummed an erotic tune as I twisted and turned in my seat. The "stewies" always locked off two seats for me, and I'd yank the separating armrest out of the middle, curl up and snuggle off to sleep.

The stewies are something. They have their own jargon. The wise asses that toss them phony baloney lines are called "stew-bums." But you can't con a stewie because they've heard it all. They won't take money, they'll return your gifts, and they're not suckers for the soft salve. But if you play it cool, tease them, talk baby talk, and don't immediately go on the make, if they ever decide to get "eyes" for you, the ball game is over and you better either relax and enjoy it or get the hell out of the way, and in my life I made it a policy to relax. Stewies trusted me . . . and dug me.

Twisting once more to get comfortable, I looked out of glassy, half-closed eyes trying to focus and get my bearings. Straight up along my unblurring line of vision were two beautiful tanned calfs directly over my face. The stewie had climbed onto my aisle armrest to get a pillow. Above the calfs was a pair of cute little white panties that covered the firmest little butt I'd looked at in a long time. It was delightful to see. I was mentally undressing her when I also saw two eyes staring down at me. Knowing what I was looking at and having finished getting the pillow, she deliberately moved her legs a little farther apart, gave me one last look, and stepped lightly down.

"Well, little boy, did you have a nice sleep?"

"Yes, little girl, I certainly did."

"I'm so glad you did," she teased. "I had my eye on you."

Little cute-ass was not about to ad lib me out of position, so I stopped her with, "And I had my eyes on you."

Her smile was delicious.

"How far are we from the magic city of New York?"

"We arrive in about twenty minutes, and don't you dare ask me for my number again, you bad little boy—I've given it to you three times and you haven't called yet."

I paused theatrically, gave her a lingering glance up and down to remind her that I had just mentally destroyed her and I knew she knew it, and said, "I never was in the perfume shop, but it looks and smells good, little girl, and you can bet your cute little *tushie* I'll call you in time."

That did it! She was now a Joey Bertell property. She looked at me happily and walked away. I watched her go down the aisle and laughed to myself at all the stew-bums that would give a year off their lives just to say the right thing at the right time.

"Ladies and gentlemen, we are beginning our descent and will be landing at Kennedy International Airport in approximately ten minutes."

That announcement brought me back to reality instantly.

Jonathan was picking me up at the airport for a full report on the West Coast and, in turn, had exciting news and plans that couldn't be discussed on the telephone. His flair for the mysterious was pronounced, and, as usual, his timing was impeccable. He knew Joey Bertell. Off a big success in California, money in my pocket from the *Sandstorm* fiasco, and everyone in my corner at BCA, I was ready to rip and tear. And one thing Jonathan J. Bingham knew about Joey Bertell—as he put it, "Point Joey in any direction and everybody better get the hell out of the way."

The wheels touched the ground, and before my little stewie could make her announcement, "Please stay seated until the plane comes to a complete stop," eight potbellied bastards with the big cigars and the J.C. Penney plaid shirts got up and broke for the door. It was easy to know who they were because they had the little plastic pins with their names on them. Bless their little hearts.

Walking past my little stewie and pinching her cheek, I said, "Gloria, little girl, I'm mad for you."

She winked back. "Joey, little boy, I'm mad for you, too."

I stole one more look at her wild body and made damn sure she saw me stare.

"The phone company will go broke on you, little boy."

"Oh, no, they won't, little girl, I just decided to become an investor. One of these days—" I gave her one last mental ball and stepped into the tunnel.

Walking through the milling crowd of waiting relatives, two-suiter in hand, made me wonder what Jonathan would have in mind. It was actually mental gymnastics trying to out-think him and clocking his next move. One thing was dead certain. Jonathan wasn't driving to the airport because he was thrilled with the Van Wyck Expressway.

While walking down the corridor, I spotted several people standing around a huge, electronic machine with lights blinking like a Times Square souvenir shop. They were ohing and ahing about how the robot's handwriting analysis had so accurately told them answers to their secret questions. Fumbling in my pocket, I dragged out two quarters and placed them in the coin slot. A red light blinked, telling me to sign my name. Having done this, I pressed the next button and you'd have thought it was a Saturn rocket taking off for the moon. The lights went berserk. After ten seconds of all this gaff, a punched card came out. I looked at the back to see who I was. In the first two categories, I was modest and introverted.

Stridng toward me in quick tempo was my chauffeur, George. It was *prima facie* evidence that Jonathan was somewhere in the building, probably in the bar, waiting for me. If George started stuttering, it meant I was correct. Just being in Jonathan's presence terrified him. It was my technique to make everyone connected with me terrified of Jonathan. The more terrible I made him, the more necessary my influence became.

Rushing up to me, George sputtered, "Mr. Bingham is w-w-waiting in the c-c-c-cocktail l-l-lounge."

I smiled inwardly.

"Thank you, George. Pick up my bag and wait in the car. If Mrs. Bertell calls on the car phone, tell her I'll be home soon. If Vera calls from my office, take only an urgent message and tell her I'll be in after I stop at the house. Understand?"

"Yes."

48

THE CANNIBALS

"Yes, what!"

"Yes, Mr. Bertell."

"George, you stupid sonovabitch, how many times do I have to tell you never to forget the *Mr.* We're not back on Canal Street stealing tires. And stop your goddam stuttering!"

"Joey, you know I'm trying."

George looked at me with those soft Wop eyes and I smiled. Twenty years we had been friends. We hustled pool, cheated in dice, rolled drunks, and balled every broad we could lay our hands on. George was like solid steel and could punch like a mule. I was always tough, but George was *really* tough. Once I became enraged and hit him the hardest punch I ever threw in my life. He went backwards over a table and flat on his back. The last memory I have in this two-punch fight was George getting up off the floor and charging me like an angry bull. My next recollection was of hazily staring out of two swelling lids, ice packs on my neck, ten strangers hovering over me in the bar, and George standing over me with tears in his eyes, sobbing over and over, "I didn't mean it, I didn't mean it, he's my buddy. I wouldn't hurt him for the world."

I opened one eye a trace and in a feeble voice said, "Get me a priest, I'm dying."

This really brought on the anguish. George sobbed, "He's the best friend I ever had."

I was enjoying my performance so much that I went even further. "Tell mother to forgive me for not being the son she wanted," I gasped.

George was now prostrate, beating the floor with his fists and in his agony groaning, "Why did I do it? I should have let him hit me."

That's what I wanted to hear. I jumped up and said, "You're right, you silly bastard, never argue with the master. Let's have a drink."

George stared at me as if he were witnessing the Resurrection. Suddenly he lunged toward me, wild-eyed and crazy. As far as I was concerned, this was it. I only hoped they gave me a decent burial. Grabbing me in a bear hug, lifting my body off the ground, he shook me from side to side like a bag of feathers. He was half hysterical. "Christ, I thought I killed you. My buddy, my buddy."

I looked at him now, in a two-hundred-dollar uniform and money in his kick and he was the same George to me. Dumb, kind to me, vicious to my enemies, but above all, loyal. At least in the outside world or "on the street" I never had to worry about my back.

Coming out of my dream world, I softened down and said, "Grab a drink before you get the bag—it'll do you good."

"Yes, Mr. Bertell."

I smiled at him. "Make it vodka so you don't smell like a brewery."

He smiled back very slightly, like old times. "Yes, Mr. Bertell."

I walked away.

Walking into the cocktail lounge, I spotted Jonathan. He looked like a million. Tanned from golf and fit from the gym, he was radiant . . . one helluva competitor.

THE CANNIBALS

I spotted two drinks on the table and realized this was about to be a great meeting. Whatever was to be, I was ready.

I stuck out my hand. "Hi, buddy."

Jonathan gave me his soft voice and a real smile. "Hi, old pal. Sit down, have a drink, relax, and then we'll talk."

My heart started pounding. I knew Jonathan's every move, his voice, his tone, each nuance of his delivery. This plan was going to be big. But I know he would sadistically make me wait for it until after I reported my successes on the Coast.

Jonathan sat confidently opposite me, studying *my* every move, his eyes slowly scanning my hair, to see if it was recently trimmed, my nails, the cut of my suit, and down to my shoes to confirm a proper shine. Evidently pleased at what he saw, he raised his glass in a toast. "Welcome home, to bigger and better things."

We clinked glasses and drank. I savored the vodka, swallowed, and sat back in my chair. As an actor, I mentally visualized us as two titans at a summit meeting convened for the purpose of cutting up the world. With me it was second nature. Having been born with a knife, I was now ready to join in the carving.

Deliberately I put my drink on the table. Regardless of which way the conversation went, it had to have an aura of showmanship. Without it, any speaker would lose Jonathan's respect and, by degrees, nullify any interest at all.

Respect, on my side of the street, was all-important. My people were brought up to suspect all outsiders, honor your mother, father, and the Church, and put in a special category your own wife and children. In another pigeonhole were men. A man is not a man just because he wears pants, stands up going to the john, pays the bills, or gets drafted. With us he must earn his name, over a period of time and wherever he goes. And when a man becomes a friend, to dishonor him is to dishonor yourself. Temporarily, at least, Jonathan qualified.

"I imagine you already have the bottom line," I started out easily.

Jonathan's eyes suddenly narrowed, the mouth tightened and became mean. There was no more charm. He was ready for business. This was what made Jonathan Bingham the most feared mogul in television. This is also what made him great. He left men like Paley, Stanton, Goldenson, Kintner, and Aubrey standing in his wake. They were real giants in the business, capable and respected, but Jonathan was a Goliath. Plus, he wouldn't make the mistake of underestimating a David. Nothing was too minute for J.J.B. He left nothing to chance.

"Start from the beginning and leave nothing out," he commanded.

"In a nutshell," I started, "the G dragged me in for a rehearsal. They told me QMA had to be destroyed, gave me the good citizenship speech, and in general tried to put words in my mouth."

I sucked in the cigarette, tasted the martini, and started again.

"I told them flat out that I was going to tell the truth. I indicated that my testimony would be helpful to their case but that I would qualify my remarks. I also put them on notice that under no circumstances was I going to hurt BCA or you, and if they had that in mind, to be on notice that I'd destroy them from the stand."

Jonathan listened intently. I went on.

"They asked me what I meant by destroy them, and I said the statement stood by itself. I told them to play straight with me, and if they were clever, they would get what they needed. However, if they shot me a curve, I'd turn them around. Johnny, I assure you, they got the message."

J.J.B. looked pleased and settled back more comfortably in his chair. "Did they ask about me?"

"A step at a time." I countered. "It's a good story, try it on for size."

Jonathan stared straight into my face, his eyes cold. He got the same stare right back. This was my goddam story and he was going to listen to it my way. If he wanted a messenger boy, let him call Western Union.

He wasn't going to make a "jocko" out of me in order to survive. In fact, that was the way to nail Jonathan. Never work for him, only work *with* him. And always fight back.

He settled back and waited. I took a sip of the drink and continued.

"They had one thing in mind, and that was to bust the octopus. I tell you this, Johnny, they have them cold. QMA has gone too far in their restraining of free enterprise. The thing that kills me is the rats that are putting them away are the two talent agencies that are their competitors. They're the ones that blew the whistle."

Jonathan stared and I went on.

"The key witness turned out to be me. My show *Sandstorm* had been firmly committed, actors hired, production companies set up. Yet through QMA's power they were able to turn BCA around by going to the Chairman over your head."

I took a breath.

"Johnny, nobody fools with the G. I don't give a goddam who they are. They gave me all kinds of inference threats, showed me secret affidavits and testimony. The stupid bastards lost me right there. Here was a secret grand jury probe into antitrust and everyone had a pipeline."

I paused a second and weighed my next words, "Take it from me, QMA has made a deal with the G."

"You couldn't be more correct. How did you know?"

"Some high-placed friends of mine are in on the stock swindle. It's for millions—if you want to go in, I've got all the dope and we can make a real score."

"Forget it!"

"Why?"

He was patient. "We don't want to be connected with it, for one thing, and for another, if things go right, we'll control everything anyway."

I jumped on that. "I'm glad to see you said *we*."

Jonathan frowned and became impatient. "If you're through being cute, continue."

I rolled with the punch and went on.

"Anyway, Johnny, I made up my mind to one thing. If they asked me certain questions that were rough, I was going to answer truthfully. For once in my life I had the ball; there was nothing in it but good for me. At the same time I'm not in the funeral business, so why should I volunteer to bury someone?"

I continued, pointedly, "The networks are the ones they're really after. Johnny, I never quite understood what you used to say to me about network control. They're the ones that screwed me. They're the ones that have a license to steal. They make racket guys look like Boy Scouts."

The corner of Jonathan's mouth curled ever so slightly in a smile. I picked up the instant impression that he knew everything I was going to say, was being tolerant and allowing me to report on areas in which he had already been briefed.

"So now you understand. Joey, these people are legitimate gangsters. All we have to do is play them at their own game and we'll knock their brains out."

He raced on. "They couldn't give a crap about anyone. The Chairman spends one third of his time in the Bahamas and one third taking bows for what I've accomplished; the other third he spends building monuments for his father whom he never liked anyway. When they invented the word toilet, they had him in mind."

I laughed. Not only at the insult, but because Jonathan was known to reserve any display of humor for special occasions.

"Between the Chairman and Dennison Fillmore," he went on, "it's the biggest laugh of all time—two con artists bullshitting each other. The Chairman keeps saying he's going to retire and Dennison Fillmore has kissed everyone's ass in both parties to get a cabinet job. The windup is the Chairman hates Fillmore and I promise you he'll stay on if only to screw him, and Fillmore has as much chance of getting into anything other than a china cabinet as Mario Colucci has of being president of anything other than a feast on Mulberry Street."

That broke me up.

"Christ, you sound like me talking."

"Hell, how else can you describe these people?"

He laughed. "Is anything funnier than brilliant Dennison Fillmore with his pea-sized mind inventing an audience reaction machine that we're stuck with to put shows on the air and in ten minutes you figure out how to rig it so that it says anything we want? Do you realize that if you were around a few years ago there would be no Dennison Fillmore?"

"With that name," I laughed, "Dennison Fillmore could have been my dentist."

It was fun unwinding with Jonathan. He never indulged for long.

"Okay, Joey, get to the meat of it, because I have some things to talk over."

"Here's how it went. When they put me on the stand they asked me to explain the *Sandstorm* deal from the beginning. I immediately threw in the disclaimer that I wanted it on the record that you and I were best friends but that, strange as it might seem, you were hurting me rather than helping. I also pointed out that every step of the deal was handled with your people and not you. I traced pitching the idea to Omar Cone and to Virgil Esty. I also discussed the West Coast situation. I told them that Bryan Westgate became high on the show and after the production department's approval it was decided that their facilities, after location, were better suited for production than New York. Clear so far?"

"Clear."

"I explained it was a 'step' deal. A step at a time. At any time BCA could back out—idea-approval, script-approval, cast-approval, budget-approval. It was like school, Johnny, and they asked me to explain jargon as I went along."

"I understand."

"I then brought them up-to-date on talent. Finest director, top-notch writers, and first-class producer. I emphasized that we had the finest creative people in show business in all phases and that we figured to come off with a fine show."

"Did you mention their names and credits?"

"With reverence."

"How did you handle getting the firm commitment?"

"Easily, and exactly as it happened. I said you and your staff came out to view products on the West Coast and had screenings from morning till night. I explained producers and stars are not allowed at these runnings because it is strictly a management decision meeting. I got a big laugh when I said they wouldn't want us to know how bad we were because it would be a waste of their time, and they wouldn't want us to know we were good because we'd demand more money."

Jonathan did not react. He was waiting for the bottom line.

"I described in detail Danny Carroll, our producer, and Chuck Feller, my co-star, and me sitting in the bar of the Bel-Air Hotel waiting for all of you to come back. It was easy to tell, Johnny, 'cause I remember we were sick with emotion. It meant a lot to all of us."

Thinking back on that night gave me goose bumps. I'd been drinking with the fellows, watching the clock and mentally throwing up. Jonathan must have had at least a speck of compassion: He didn't make me wait until the very end.

"Phone call, Mr. Bertell."

I'd jumped out of my seat and gone to the house phone.

"Hello."

"Joey?"

"Christ, yes. Johnny, I'm ready for the gas pipe."

"Relax, buddy, you're in!"

"You're kidding."

"No," he answered, "it was just great, and Omar thinks he's found a new leading man in you."

I started to answer, but he stopped me.

"Don't mention this call. When Omar and I walk into the bar, don't come to us, we'll send for you. Give him all the bows and thanks, because in all truth I didn't have to help a bit."

"One question," I jumped in. "Did you like it?"

"It's the best show we have in the schedule. Everyone agrees on that. I have to hang up. So long."

I remembered walking back to the table and looking at Danny and Chuck. They were ashen.

"Give it to me," Danny said. "Quick, short, and sweet."

I said nothing. I picked up my drink, sighed and smiled. We all toasted. Success is a special look.

Back to the present, I continued my report to Jonathan.

"In detail I described being called over by Omar Cone and you and Omar saying, 'Congratulations, Joey, you're in the schedule.' Also Omar shaking hands with Danny, telling him it was firm and the best show he'd seen. I also recapped Omar saying to Chuck Feller that he should 'move his family to California, because that's where you'll be working.' All in all, I detailed it exactly as it happened."

"All that is preliminary. The basis is restraint. How did the government handle you on that?" Jonathan was now intent on each word.

"I testified under questioning that in the fall schedule we were set to replace *Chessgame,* an extremely bad show. *Sandstorm* was firm for twenty-six weeks. Money and scripts were authorized and in production."

"Did you mention the show had already been bought by an advertiser?"

"Of course," I answered. "I also made it clear that they were mad as hell at the network for shoving that horrible *Interrogators* on them, and really furious for getting stuck with *Chessgame* again."

Jonathan listened intently.

"I went into minute detail. That Jackie Benson used to be a star in radio and was the first really big star to jump from a rival

network to BCA. That the jump brought him a special relationship with the Chairman."

I took a breath and a gulp of my drink.

"I jammed in the fact that he owned *Chessgame,* which had
been on for two years and needed the third year to get
ninety episodes in the can and complete his package for rerun
purposes. Also, I pointed out that Benson needed a production
company going to keep him out of a personal holding situation
with Internal Revenue. When I developed those money angles,
the jury looked like they were making mental notes to indict
Jackie Benson."

Jonathan smiled at that, because he despised Benson with a
passion. And not for any personal reason (or racial reason, as
some insiders suspected). It was just that Benson wouldn't die
gracefully. The guy was one of those no-talent hams supported
by characters and pieces of stage business.

Benson's format had worked for years, but now the public
was tired of it, and the ratings were way down. In short,
Benson had two chances even to stay on the air: slim, and
none. By a fluke, Jonathan had a hole in his schedule and could
use the tired name for one last season, after which Benson
would be led out to pasture, playing cards at the Hilldale
Country Club and smiling at his friends' jokes for a change.

So Benson had won a round with Jonathan, but he was
through with the big time. And when Benson was dumped by
Jonathan, he'd know he had been dumped by an expert. When
that time came, Jonathan would be on firm ground. He would

be arrogant enough to tell the Chairman exactly what he was going to do. He would get his jollies knowing that the Chairman wouldn't lift a finger to help Benson, once Benson had no value. That was one thing about the Chairman: bananas included, he was all heart.

So that was the background for Jonathan's smile.

"Anyway, Johnny, they followed a line of questioning to prove their case that Benson, through his QMA agents, forced BCA to reverse itself and accept two shows it didn't want. He went over the head of the president of the network and his entire staff, plus satisfied advertisers. Why cheat the public out of two good shows and give them two inferior ones? Simply to defraud the government out of taxes. How? Simply by placating an agency that was threatening to withhold creative talent."

Jonathan observed, "Exactly what I told you three months ago."

I went on. "Then they queried me on the big meeting at the Sherry-Netherland, where the heads of QMA laid down the law to the network with actual threats. I made a quick statement that I had no firsthand knowledge of the meeting but understood that it did take place, and in the context they described. They didn't press me."

"Joey, they had it cold anyway."

"Then, thank God, one of the stupid bastards gave me the opening I was waiting for.

"'Mr. Bertell, would you say you have been hurt by this action?'

61

" 'In what manner?'

" 'Did you suffer any financial or other kind of loss?'

" 'I received a substantial settlement from the network, but nothing compared with what I'd have earned if I had gone on the air and gotten thirty weeks' exposure and a better-than-even chance to be renewed. However, I do not blame Benson or QMA in any way.'

"I waited for that to sink in and hoped someone would ask for an explanation. The G attorney was too smart to get trapped, but a sincere little guy in the jury box, who had been trying to follow all the twists of the business, raised his hand.

" 'What do you mean, Mr. Bertell, when you say you don't blame them?'

"That was my shot to get the disclaimer on the record. 'Sir, in my business, the stakes reach fantastic proportions. We are betting lives to win pots. The rules of that game go back to the jungle: Kill or be killed; survival of the fittest. Sitting here now,' I told Mr. Sincere, 'I tell you that I have probably taken a hundred jobs away from other actors just because my name was bigger, not because I was better. If I were Benson or QMA, I would have made the same moves they did. As a matter of fact, I look forward to the day that I'm big enough. The name of the game, sir, is *win* . . . although I must confess that I'm getting punchy from losing.'

"That drew a huge laugh, and I asked Mr. Sincere if his question was answered. He said it was."

I looked at Jonathan and settled back. "That's it—end of report."

Jonathan J. Bingham, unchallenged boss of BCA, undisputed kingpin of the ratings war, and master tactician of the industry, stretched his gangling legs, corrected his posture a bit, and spoke, softly but pontifically. "Well, Joey, I think that's just wonderful. All the fellows on the Coast called it just like that. They agree that you handled yourself real well." He signaled for drinks efficiently. "We're going to relax," he purred. "We're going to sit here, have another drink, and then I'll tell you something I have in mind."

"That's great with me."

"Good. Did you have time to play a little on the Coast?"

I spoke with feeling. "No, dammit. I was racing here and there, especially downtown for the QMA thing. By the way, was I right that QMA made a deal?"

"Of course. The whole hearing was just a stalling tactic while they worked out the stock maneuver."

I rolled with that one. "Weren't they afraid of the government?"

"Good God, Joey, wake up. They *used* the G (as you call it) to put twenty points on both stocks when they divested. Free publicity in the *Journal* every day, word of mouth with every broker in the country. They're more powerful now than when they were together. They still sleep in the same bed."

"Some bed. I wonder if there's room for me."

"Joey, you don't need them anymore. You've come of age. Let me give you credit—you've learned this end of the business faster than I would have believed possible."

"It's easy when you've got a good teacher—"

"Bullcrap. I've tried to teach some of these imbeciles working for me, and they get a little more stupid each day."

"Johnny, I've always wanted to ask you, why do you keep those *jadrools* around when you know goddam well they have nothing to offer?"

Jonathan spoke like a friendly philosopher. "For one thing, good manpower isn't easy to come by. For another, Joey, remember that without them we don't exist."

"But there are too damn many chiefs, Johnny. Send me some more Indians."

Jonathan dug the metaphor. "When in doubt, charge forward boldly."

We both laughed . . . and I remembered Jonathan's first official act as president of BCA, when nobody knew him except "Lavender Lips" Bryan Westgate.

Jonathan flew out to the Coast and went right to the projection room where they were screening tests of actors for the lead in a new series.

He entered the room, spoke to nobody, picked an isolated seat in the front row, and stretched his legs out silently through four tests.

As the lights came up, the brilliant executives opened discussion about the merits of each actor. Still Jonathan said nothing, didn't even turn around.

"I like Joe Curl," Gray Cooper opened. "The others have good points. Larry White has looks. Craig Kelley's blond hair will appeal to the broads. But Rick Randall has nothing in my book."

"I agree with Gray," Joe Ballantine came in. "Joe Curl is no Valentino, but he has guts. Randall is weak."

"I like Curl," Bruce Wayne followed. "Anyone but Randall."

"But, *fellows,*" lisped Bryan baby, "we're on a cycle of blond-haired leading men. I agree that Randall is dead wrong. But let's at least consider Larry White. He's blond, too. The blond adds dimension." He sensed the passionate plea for a blond going out the window and called out, "What do you think, Jonathan?"

Jonathan J. Bingham rose. Majestically. Without turning, he stretched his frame, then his arms. He turned slowly, walked up the aisle toward the brain trust.

"Hire Randall." And continued walking right out of the projection room.

Meanwhile, the cocktail lounge waiter set two ice-cold martinis on the table and disappeared. I picked up mine. "Salute!"

Jonathan followed suit. "Salute!" An obvious silence followed.

"All right, Carl Cunning," I finally said, "what the hell else is on your mind?"

"Oh, that." He smiled. "Very simple. We're going to take over either UBC or World-Bond Studios on the Coast. How does that fit?"

"Loose. You're creaming UBC in the ratings now. And who the hell wants World-Bond? They haven't got one show on the air, and that professional Greek has stolen them into near bankruptcy. This nut can easily make the can—a lawyer friend of mine may just put him there if he doesn't bow out gracefully."

"Everything you say is right . . . but the trip you just took should give you the answer."

"Go on."

"Joey, in five to ten years the networks will be chopped down to size. You saw what happened to QMA—they're infants compared with the networks. The networks are getting more and more greedy, and they're getting too fat. The Justice Department will bust them like a grape."

"The networks do have the ball game," I conceded.

"The whole ball game, and more. The days of production companies making millions are over. We're now programming our own house shows. We have syndication rights and ridiculous rates. And I can assure you we'll start our own production and financing of motion pictures for television next."

I lit a cigarette and tried to absorb this.

"We've got the greatest weapon in the world: creative control. It's in every contract, along with a firm budget. We can force a producer to lose money just by being obstinate. That's too much power for the wrong hands . . . including the hands of the incompetents who work for us."

Jonathan was a thoroughly authoritative lecturer.

"On top of that, we can charge whatever the hell we want

for the time spots. Now you add it up. We own it all: time, rights, airwaves, production, and control of what the American public sees. How long do you think they'll allow this to go on?"

"The way you put it, Jonathan, not very long."

"Of course not. The real money will end up in the big studios. The little producer will be swallowed alive and become a thing of the past."

"I'm with you. The studio move I understand—then why UBC? You're with number one right now. Why change to number two?"

"Money, Joey, nice green money. Now is the time to make the move. You see, they don't even dream that they *can* get me to come over and run their store."

"Can they?"

Jonathan answered simply, "Yes."

"But Number Two. How can you be satisfied?"

"Easy . . . I'll make them Number One."

I cursed myself for slow thinking and tried to cover up. "How—with a wand?"

"Christ, it's so easy it's embarrassing. In the first place, UBC should never have been anything but the top network. They've got more resources than all the others combined. They're first in electronics, first in color, first in news. The only reason they're not first in ratings and popularity is because they don't have anyone to call the shots who has even the slightest conception of what the public wants to see."

"Maybe they don't buy the numbers game," I suggested.

"The Old Man thinks of nothing except numbers," said Jonathan. "Even though he's an inactive board chairman, he has the fierce pride. And he hates BCA."

Johnny measured his next words.

"The Old man is going to move son George in as head of the parent company. Frankly, it's a right move—George is a damn good administrator."

I told Johnny I'd met George a couple of times at "21" with Dan Talbot, and he seemed like a classy guy.

"I don't know how classy he is, but I could get along with him. As far as I'm concerned, George could take all the bows. I just want to run the ship my way."

I mused. "You've got it so good now. . . ."

"Good my ass." Suddenly Johnny was belligerent. "The Chairman's the cheapest sonovabitch alive. I've driven that stock to the sky and I haven't even started. He's got a million shares, and for openers I've made him a million dollars every point the stock goes up."

"Johnny, they're not imbeciles—they'll take care of you."

"You taught me a great expression a few years ago, Joey—don't forget it yourself."

"What expression?" I asked.

"Money talks—bullshit walks. Joey, the further away from the Chairman I get, the better I like it." Johnny was now free-associating. "As for the Dentist, I'm sick of him telling me I'm like a son to him. He doesn't fool me one second."

I broke in. "I heard a rumor the other day that he was the one who shot Lincoln." It was time to get back to the subject at hand, and I had to take charge a little, to put things in organizational order. "Okay, buddy, let me ask some questions and you supply the answers."

Jonathan was all business in a flash. "Right," he said.

"First, you've considered this move, and you want it, right?"

Johnny nodded.

"The whole ball of wax at either one of those two places?"

"Right. With UBC first choice."

"Naturally. Second, you want stock and autonomy."

"Correct."

"Third, what's my end?"

"Joey, you're with me, wherever we go."

"As number two man and head of production?"

"It won't work, Joey. You'll be executive vice-president and assistant to the president."

"With autonomy, and answerable only to you?"

"You've got it."

I sat back, sipped the martini, and let my mind race a little. "Do we bring the team with us?"

"Joe Ballantine will go anywhere I go. Also—"

I interrupted. "Don't tell me, I know. So will Lavender Lips."

Jonathan couldn't help laughing out loud. "Why the hell do you hate Bryan so much?"

"I can't stand piccolo players that use live instruments."

That was further than Jonathan wanted to go, but I was ready to let it go on all the way. "By the way, as long as we're talking about Her Majesty, here's—"

"Goddam it, Joey, we're talking about millions of dollars, a chance to build an empire, and you sit here like a high school freshman picking on the town fruit." Jonathan was livid. "Grow up!"

I went right into it. "Bullshit, Johnny. This isn't just how I've been raised or how I feel personally. I've warned you before and I'm not going to stop now: This goddamn fairy, someday, somehow, is going to jam you up."

I had stuck it into Bryan Westgate, and now I pushed it up to the hilt. "Johnny, if that bastard's got something on you, for Christ's sake tell me, and I'll cut him off at the knees."

Jonathan's face was now completely white. His silence was louder than any other man's raging. The lips turned down over the buck teeth and I was gazing at a shark.

"Don't you ever, and I mean ever, talk like that again. Bryan is my friend. Don't you dare try any of your tricks on him. Just lay off him, understand?"

I sat tight, looked squarely into his eyes, and steeled down for the fight. It came. Johnny redoubled the verbal challenge.

It clicked in my mind that I had lost. But *really* lost. That lousy little *finocchio* had beaten me again. But that made it doubly important to get into the details of the Bingham-Westgate business.

"Okay, Johnny, let's forget it. If you want me to lay off, from

70

here on in I will. But before we go on, you have to know that I don't now and I never will trust him. Obviously you do, and if that's the case, it's good enough for me."

I put out my hand. We shook on it.

"Back to the *team*," I said. "Who do you want, and will they come?"

"Ballantine and Bryan for Operations and Programming."

"Question. Purely for your own health and peace of mind. Can Bryan handle that big a job?"

This time Jonathan knew that I was being merciless but impersonal. Bryan was just a chattel to be hired or fired.

"I'm sure he can," said Johnny.

"Okay, that's Bryan and Ballantine. Who else?"

"The most important man is Wilson Manning."

"Who the hell is he?"

"He's in the sales department. I'm going to make him V.P. in charge of sales next week, and I want you to know him. Take him to lunch."

"Will do." I took out my black alligator pocket folder with the gold pencil—a Madison Avenue must—and made the entry.

"The only hole is publicity. And we need a powerhouse in that spot."

"I've got the guy," I put in quickly. "He's tailor-made for the spot. You can really go to sleep on this guy."

"Fine," Johnny answered. "You might put him on this immediately. Get some good puff items going. Rumors in *Variety* and the trade papers."

71

"It's as good as done."

There was a moment of silence while both minds ticked. Johnny spoke first. "Why don't you have lunch with your friend Dan Talbot at UBC?"

I pondered a few seconds. "Not yet. He's too smart, and too close to the Old Man and George. And he has a high regard for Louis Lush, their TV division president."

This was my meat. Plotting and scheming goes on every day in big business from the office boy on up, and in this area I stood alone.

"No," I rephrased it, "it's too big for me to tackle Dan Talbot too early. It might be a great shortcut to what we want, but if Dan didn't like the idea or presented it in the wrong way to George, we'd be lost—one shot and no court of appeals."

"That's your department," Johnny answered.

"Now . . . the trick is secrecy. But controlled secrecy. We'll work the *sub rosa* rumor mill. I'll promise to take Chester Plan and Mario Colucci with us. Those two blabbermouths will put it on the street real quick."

Jonathan smiled. It was jelling.

"Nothing gets out," I warned him, "until I'm ready. Okay?"

He nodded, and I continued.

"I must be able to call all bluffs and produce you at a moment's notice. When and where I say—no backups of any kind." I waited.

"You've got it."

"Great! We'll make this work, buddy. Here's to it."

I lifted my glass, we clinked and drank. I spoke again.

"Now that we've got those moves out of the way, there's a problem."

"Shoot."

"Omar is going to appoint Virgil Esty a vice president. Bryan is climbing walls because he isn't getting it first. Virgil told me that he was sitting by the Bel-Air pool talking to Bryan and Bryan got so upset he sounded like a bird whistle. The silly bastard ended up jumping in the pool with his watch and shoes."

The image of Bryan flying into the pool struck Jonathan funny.

"Christ, Joey . . ." He laughed uninhibitedly.

"Here's what I'll do. I'll go to Virgil and give him a guarantee that he gets the V.P. stripes, but for unity he's to go to Omar and take him off the hook by suggesting it would be wise for all if Bryan is appointed first. Now, Omar will be smart enough to see through the maneuver. He'll know I've done it, assume it's what you want and he'll have a built-in face-saving device. All I need is your okay that Virgil gets his next, and soon."

"You're high on Esty, aren't you?"

"Hell, yes," I answered. "He's got balls and he knows his job."

"Omar feels the same way. I think you're both wrong. I think he's nothing."

"Jonathan," I said carefully, "my arm is around him and I need him. He can't do any harm, and I make a bet he does us plenty of good."

"You made your point, Joey. Now, any ideas on the World-Bond Studios situation?"

"Yes. There's a lawyer by the name of Morton Silvern who is chairman of an executive committee looking into the whole setup, because the company is on the verge of bankruptcy. This guy was put in by the banks and the brokerage houses that are loaded with World-Bond stock."

"Do you know Silvern?"

"No—but I will by tomorrow. I know a guy that knows him real good."

"How does all this sit with you?"

"The truth. At first I thought you were nuts, but now I'm excited by it."

"Then let's make it work!"

"We will," I said, and did a quick-change. "How's your sex life?"

"No complaints. I've got a real winner tonight. Met her at a party last week, and she was with some stiff. She moved right into me, so I told her to call. She did, I bought her a drink at Le Valois, and we made plans to meet tonight and swing."

"That easy, huh?"

"Yup. How about you?"

"I think I'm becoming a monk. I hate to admit it, but I think I'm scared of Gina."

"And how *is* the Black Widow?"

"Y'know, you two give me a pain in the ass with your bickering. I'm the one that has to live with her, so stop antagonizing her. She gives me all kinds of hell as it is."

Jonathan chided. "I like her, she doesn't like me."

"Okay, let's drop it."

"Who's Chili Monroe?"

I never heard the question. A wind was puffing all sorts of ideas through my brain: the gigantic moves ahead, the milestones Jonathan and I would pass, the empire to build. All I had worked for, every one of my wild dreams, had a chance to come to fruition now. From the slums to saloons, from nightclubs to motion pictures, and now from television to the top of the world. . . . Not bad for a kid who started without a single betting chance he'd ever break out of poverty and dreams. But here it was, Joey. I pulled out my mental J. Edgar. . . .

JOHN JOSEPH BERTELLI—AKA JOEY BERTELL
Age 37
Black hair, blue eyes
Ruddy complexion
Born: Slutzker, Ohio
Occupation: Actor, producer, dancer, businessman, song-
             writer
Agt. ⓡ Interviewed: LAX, NYC
1043267   NOLNS, MIFA, CHI
Subject is multitalented in entertainment business. Re-

spected both as performer and businessman. Several interviews reveal subject can reach into ⓡ and deliver. Witnesses confirm contact with ⓡ.

Subject spends money in accepted fashion. Frequents nightclubs. Receives treatment reserved for hierarchy in Capo status.

Married to Gina De Castro. Subject's wife further cements ties to ⓡ.

Subject is vulnerable with regard to pride. 1954 walked out of $500,000 contract at L. V. Morano Hotel for $400,-000 at Bon Via because of disagreement with management. Second hotel declared bankruptcy and subject refused to pursue recourse. Explanation supplied by witnesses indicate family and friendship ties which prevented litigation.

Subject has early teen background of bookmaking. Organized ticket-takers at lake resort in Ohio.

Subject wears expensive clothes and jewelry. Subject has apparent weakness for women. Known associate of prostitutes in L.V. Witnesses indicate subject has no physical contact with prostitutes (ACX-51320) but witnesses interviewed show extreme loyalty to subject. Witnesses tend to invent stories to protect subject. With regard to relationship with prostitutes, subject in interview revealed, "Prostitutes are nothing but an extension of show business, and I consider them buddies." Conclusion after interview indicates normal sex life pursuant to accepted practices in ⓡ circles.

Subject has warm personality and is extremely friendly

with middle-class acquaintances. But when aroused, has vicious temper.

Subject once challenged Alex (Bobby Gans) Kossloff ⓡ 312-A-14216 to showdown in Flamingo Hotel, L.V. Witnesses interviewed related incident as being violent with subject at one point exchanging extreme physical contact with Gans and issuing death threats in foreign tongue not further identified.

Further investigation reveals subject won argument and fully backed by influential ⓡ allies.

Investigation reveals subject has unique relationship with ⓡ. Enjoys full membership yet remains autonomously aloof.

Subject commands full respect from ⓡ. Investigation in depth indicates subject is loyal to ⓡ code.

Conclusion: Subject is legitimate, but with ⓡ overtones. Has complete autonomy, and in ⓡ inner thinking (ⓡ-X1032-L1148) is regarded as top-level ⓡ brainpower in entertainment field. Often consulted on top-level policy.

"Who's Chili Monroe?"

My mental J. Edgar dissolved and I woke up on Jonathan's repeated question.

"The most gorgeous broad that ever walked the face of the earth. Why?"

"She called my office looking for you. Barbara gave her your office number. Is it anything I might like?"

"Only the greatest thing in the world—but wrong for you."

"Why?" Jonathan challenged.

"Because she's an all-out hooker. She's no con artist with friends, and she isn't about to jump into bed with you and go through the panting and 'Oh, Baby' lines that put you on. On the other hand, she's liable to get eyes for you one night, jump all over you and eat you alive, toes and all."

"Have you balled her?"

"Never."

"Bullshit."

"I swear." Raising my hand.

"Go on, you're a real shit-heel when it comes to broads."

"I swore, Johnny"

"Don't hand me that crap. You're a cooze-miser and you know it. If I waited for you to get me laid, I'd have gray hair and a snowy white beard."

"Since when did you need me to help you? Besides what you get yourself, you've got those built-in pimps around you, not to mention those orgies on the Coast, which I happen to know about."

The last brought a smile to Jonathan's face. "Anything wrong with a little relaxation?"

"Nothing at all," I answered. "Only from what I hear, you now have the world's record at it."

He looked pleased. He thoroughly enjoyed hearing anything about himself, especially in the broad department. Jonathan went after broads as methodically as he approached any major objective: The little sweethearts were by now a part of his day-to-day routine.

"When am I going to meet her?" he asked.

"You're a persistent sonovabitch, aren't you?"

"I'm in love with her already."

"You're in love with yourself then. I told you Chili won't play tangletoes with friends. With her, you're either a John or a friend. And because of me, you're in the friend category."

"What makes her so special to you?" he asked suspiciously. He watched my eyes and hands for a reaction. I tried to be casual, but I knew he had me plugged in.

"If you want to be Earl Wilson or Ed Sullivan, get yourself a column. What is this interrogation bullshit you've suddenly come up with?"

"Haaaa!" he yelled. He was delighted. He had me nailed in a corner. It was a rare win for him, and he knew it. This made Jonathan's whole day—maybe his entire week. To outsmart me on my side of the fence was like winning a million dollars from me.

"All right, you bastard," I said, "lay off me with regard to Chili. I swear I've never touched her, never kissed her, never did n-o-t-h-i-n-g."

"Yeah," he laughed, "go on."

Now I was really embarrassed. The sadist was not about to let me off the hook. He would stick it in deeper, twist it and turn it until he was tired of playing. In this respect he was the typical twelve-year-old bad little boy.

He looked directly at me, his eyes dancing with laughter. This was his relaxation, and he wasn't going to miss a minute. "Go on, old buddy, I don't want to miss a word."

Now I was between embarrassment and fury. I decided to get out the way I got in.

"How come you're so interested? I never saw you take this much interest before."

"I was kidding you before when I asked you who Chili Monroe was. You've been talking about her on and off for three or four years and it stuck in my craw."

"It's very simple. Every once in a while you meet someone you feel *sympatico* with. I don't know how the hell it happens, but I did with Chili."

He hung on every word.

"Maybe you can help explain the irony of it to me, Johnny. Because you're partly right—I'd love to take her to bed. I'd love to indoctrinate her. My joint comes to life when I just say hello. But what can I do? I'm different from you; I can't ball a hooker. If she ever said, 'Oh, Baby, oh, Daddy, you're the wildest, here it is, here I come,' I'd have to slap her. I'd vomit."

Jonathan was enjoying this no end. I went on.

"Don't get me wrong, I love a nice blow job once in a while. But if you're digging a chick and you want to be uninhibited along with her, how the hell can you really swing if you're wondering whether the last thing in her bread box might have been an eight-inch chocolate eclair . . . with mold."

Jonathan chuckled at that, and I laughed along with him. But it was kidding on the square.

"Johnny, this is where you and I disagree. Hookers are hookers. They fuck for bread, nothing else. They couldn't care less if you had a gold-plated cock, for all the good it would do them. The name of the game is money, m-o-n-e-y. The only time they have an orgasm is when they take your scratch. At no other time do you ever get to them."

"I've gotten to them."

"You poor soul. Do you really believe that?"

"Of course not. Where's your sense of humor?" Jonathan was in great spirits now. The ribbing back and forth was a way to relieve tension. "How did you meet her? Where did this Chili baby come from?"

"Chili is about twenty-four years old now. Her real name is Margaret Monroe, and she's from Denver. I met her in Las Vegas when she was eighteen and not too dry behind the ears. She was absolutely beautiful, but she couldn't hold a job because she could never wake up. Consequently she was always broke and starving. She used to put the bite on me every day for money to buy cans of chili. And that's how she got her name —I used to say, 'Here comes Chili,' and it caught on."

I slopped up the rest of my drink and continued the narrative.

"For some strange goddam reason I liked her. It's impossible to explain. At first she cut into me as if she were my daughter or sister, and I fell into a real protective big-brother bit. Then after a few months she fell ridiculously in love with me. And those are her words, not my ego."

"I understand completely."

"Then, to make matters worse, her roommate was a sneak junkie. They got into a beef and the roommate left town. As she was leaving, she planted half a dozen joints of marijuana in Chili's dresser and called the whiskers. They broke in and nailed Chili with the goods. They silly broad, trying to protect me, doesn't mention my name. They take her downtown and she's booked. In Vegas, if she mentions me, she doesn't even leave the room, but she was concerned about getting me in trouble."

"She was right, pal."

"I don't tell you your business," I snapped. "Don't tell me mine."

"Touché," he answered.

"Anyway, it now comes out that she's a month *short* of being eighteen, and suddenly she's classified as a juvenile."

"Holy Christ!"

"You said it. Suddenly it's Mother and Father time, and the whole ridiculous thing blows way out of proportion."

Jonathan was mesmerized in his chair. I was describing a world that he longed to be in, though he was without any conception of its inner workings.

"By now I'm thankful that nobody has mentioned me. In the beginning my name and 'juice' stops anything, but now I can be dragged in by the balls and crucified. Y'know, it's funny as hell, but I've never been guilty of anything in my life that I've been blamed for. I've gotten away with plenty . . . but I'm as innocent as a newborn babe of the things they blame me for."

"Join the club." Jonathan glanced unobtrusively at his

watch and decided that he wasn't pressed. "For Christ's sake, what happened next?"

"I can assure you that it wasn't easy. I reach all over town for Chili. Believe me, I can fix blackmail, extortion, assault, dope, murder—you name it and I can handle the package. But who do I call that can handle a juvenile case?"

"This would make a great segment in a series."

"Try to sell it to that imbecile Chester Plan, and he'd swear it was a fairy tale. If he *and* Mario Colucci went to a hock shop with a gold nugget, they'd get arrested for loitering."

Jonathan broke up. "Your running gag. Tell the truth, are they a pair of deuces?"

"No gag, they're worse. Remind me the next time we're in a good mood and have some time to tell you how I've got Colucci bullshitted into thinking I'm going to make him president of the network when you move up to the Dentist's job. This poor shit actually believes with all his heart that he *is* going to be president."

Jonathan interrupted. "A coincidence. Vincent Fisk is leaving to go with the Fred Tashley Agency. I'm considering several replacements, but Vincent himself came in to see me and recommended Colucci. I think he's too young, and to be personal, he looks like a pitcher of olive oil. I really can't stand him . . . but if you think he can be a team player, maybe I should go along with it."

This unexpected decision was a dilly. To kingmake this

toilet went against me. I couldn't overlook all his shortcomings. And he was such a spineless ass that even his wife henpecked him. He just looked like a fool at all the worst times.

I had a flashback to a party I once threw at a nightclub I owned, at which "Little Miss Ethnic," as she came to be known, turned to Jonathan and said, "I've been so worried about Mario's career. I feel the name Colucci has an Italian connotation, and I'm trying desperately to have him change it."

Jonathan glanced at the diarrhea mouth and stopped it dead with, "We have no trouble remembering his name." One thing about Jonathan, he had no mercy for a cooze, especially a wife, who demeans her man. Which is exactly what Little Miss Ethnic had done.

Yet as I sized up the Vincent Fisk spot, I felt a malicious temptation to put Colucci into a job that *was* over his head. It would give Jonathan and me many moments of pleasure to put him on. Basically, I must always figure that Colucci is a mental whore and will sell everyone down the river. And yet knowing that he keeps me immune from surprises. A rat-bastard-shit-heel—and that's what Mario Colucci was—could never hurt you if you knew his hole card. And that was always my edge, knowing the hole card.

Meanwhile, I had to answer Jonathan. "Let me think about Mario. I'll take him to lunch, get a reading—and if it works out all right, we'll slip this *skifoso* into the slot. If not, we'll dump him."

But Jonathan probed. "What's your sixth sense feeling at this moment? Forget about after you shape him up—that I know you can do. Right now do you think we can trust him?"

"Let me ask you a question. Could you trust a three-time loser in an open bank vault with five million dollars and nobody around?"

Jonathan didn't answer, so I continued.

"That doesn't make him wrong for us. He knows the company, and he's such a spineless whore that he'll do a competent job if I keep bullshitting him that he can succeed you as president. Finally, and most important, never discount the fact that he's in total fear of you. Believe me, Johnny, when you crap, this guy wipes."

"That sounds worse than I thought. Your characterization of Mario Colucci makes your characterization of Chester Plan sound like a missionary."

I cut in "Wrong, Johnny. Chester is a toilet, a real true rat. The confirmation is that his own wife hates him. She tells everyone who will listen that she despises him. She gets her rocks off by beating him in everything. She whacks him out in cards, tennis, skiing, you name it. I will say, however, that this beady-eyed little *schmuck*, this *vantz*, is a fighter. At least a great infighter. Chester I want on our team. When I was with MGM, Mr. Mayer expressed it this way, and I never forgot it: 'You can't fuck anyone by long distance.'"

Jonathan let that sink in. "Beautiful, really beautiful. He must have been a helluva man, Joey. I wish I could have known him."

"Johnny, he was in a class by himself. He signed me to the movie contract personally. When I met him, he was just fifteen percent of the L. B. Mayer I had heard about, but on his way out the door and ta-ta—and he knew it—he had more talent in his pinkie than all those other studio bastards put together."

Jonathan was listening intently. Of course, I had known that L.B. was one of his idols.

"Johnny, I used to go to his office every day. His secretary, Ida Koverman, and Dick Hanley used to see that I got in. Just sitting with this man was a pleasure. He was everything that you want to be. He had balls, balls, and more balls. A giant, Johnny, a giant. There wasn't one S.O.B. in MGM that he hadn't personally made. When the chips were down and they thought he was weak, they closed in to devour him. Johnny, I only hope to Christ that you don't ever see that day."

Suddenly Jonathan got into a sentimental mood. "That's what I have you for, Joey. I never worry about the rear when you're around."

I took the occasion to be blunt. "As long as you feel that way, I want you to know that they'll have to walk over my dead body to get to you. But . . . I'm only as strong as you make me. If you pull the rug out from under me, you'll not only destroy your best friend and buddy, but you'll also open the floodgates that will eventually drown you. Just so you know. . . . "

"Your biggest problem should be me. Get back to Chili."

"Oh, yeah, I forgot. Anyway, it became apparent that nobody had a connection with the Juvenile Court, so I reached out to find the judge's name. He was practically a city father in Las Vegas. I decided to trap him for myself one evening when he was attending a church social. I'm there about thirty minutes when a man comes right up."

" 'You're Mr. Bertell, aren't you?'

" 'Yes,' I answered.

" 'I'm Judge X. I understand you've been . . . looking for me.'

"I looked him over from top to bottom and and in two seconds realized this was a decent man. This was no time to act like Mickey Spillane's Mike Hammer.

" ' Your Honor,' I started, 'I'm very upset about something and only wish to bring it to your attention. What you do from then on is your own business, but a whole lifetime may be involved, and I won't be able to sleep if I don't do this.'

"He smiled kindly. 'I wouldn't want to see you lose sleep.'

" 'I have a friend, Margaret Monroe, who's coming up before you. They found marijuana in her dresser. It was planted there by a disgruntled roommate, entirely without Margaret's knowledge. Sir, I pledge you my word of honor that this is a nice girl and has never touched, *will* never touch anything like that. Again, sir, I pledge you my word.'

" 'Thank you, Mr. Bertell. It was so nice to meet you.' Again his smile was genuinely warm. Then he walked away."

Jonathan looked puzzled and waited for the development.

"The bottom line, Johnny, is that Margaret had her charges dismissed and received a stern, fatherly warning from the judge."

"Did you ever see him again?"

"No," I answered, "but he made me realize that there are still white knights on white horses roaming the plains. I'm positive, actually, that I had nothing to do with helping Chili, that it would have worked out the same way without me."

"That's not completely correct, Joey. He saw something good in her through the simple action of your going so far out. Judges have a hard job. There's something to the cliché 'Justice tempered with mercy.' "

"How the hell did we ever get on this hearts and flowers kick?"

"Damned if I know," Jonathan laughed. "Are you going to call her?"

"The second I get to the office."

"I've got to meet her. She has to be fabulous to get you this wound up."

I paused a moment. "Fabulous is an understatement. She's out of sight."

"How the hell, if she's what you say, did she become a hooker?"

I shrugged. "Who knows what makes anyone what they are? A bad love affair, wrongo marriage, poverty, career, frustration . . . put them all together and you still don't have the answer. I'm not too sure any of us are happy."

"I don't know about you, pal, but I'm happy," Jonathan replied. "This is just the way I like to live. I've got no complaints, and I sure as hell don't want any changes."

I put the salt shaker in front of his mouth and gravely announced, "Ladies and gentlemen, Mr. Jonathan J. Bingham has kindly agreed to give his views on life to you, our radio audience. Here he is now, Mr. J.J.B. himself. Say something, J.J.B."

"Drop dead!"

"Did you hear those classic words of wisdom? I tell you —"

"All right, all right, enough already." Jonathan was in a good humor. He glanced at his watch again, and this time I knew he was on his way.

"I'll wait to hear from you around five," he said, all business. "You make your moves on UBC and World-Bond. Take care of the Virgil Esty situation and work on your series projects. The network is indebted to you now, and that's known all the way topside. *Don't*," he jabbed, "drop the ball."

"I won't," I answered simply.

"I'm taking a cab and will stop at a place near here." He became abrupt, ready for action. "Okay, buddy." He reached for my hand and we shook. "Charge forward boldly."

He wheeled and strode out into the airport crowd.

Chapter 4

The next few days brought results. I was now ready to make contact with UBC and World-Bond. Just walking through the doors of my office building was an exhilarating experience.

"Hi, Joey," said the doorman.

"Hi, Billy boy, how's business?"

"Just fine. Welcome back. I was off a few days, but they told me you got in. We missed you."

I stepped into the elevator.

"Hi, Frank . . . Dave . . . Bob."

They chorused a greeting. "Joey, we hear you're going to do some new shows. Any truth to the reports?"

"I've got a couple in mind."

"Christ, do them in New York before they turn this place into a funeral parlor."

"I've got one for New York if I can put the pieces together." The elevator door opened, and I gave the fellows a wave as I turned right down the corridor.

The workers and technicians behind the cameras know what's going on. They know, and they care: they either like you or dislike you, and it's contagious. If you're a ball breaker in one studio, when you move on to your next assignment, the real guys in the business will have you marked lousy in spades.

Down the corridor to the corner, I reached for the doorknob and paused to take in the gold nameplate: Cardinal Productions, Inc. As I opened the door to the whole suite and saw all my little bees buzzing in their hive, I couldn't help saying, "Top of the world," under my breath.

Quickening my pace, I approached my private offices. Here I was "Mr. Bertell" to everyone, with two exceptions, during business hours. Only afterward could everyone come in and find "Joey," expect a friendly drink and a few quiet moments.

Vera and Jimmy Craig were in my waiting room.

Vera had come to me from the steno pool, with a lovely face, a *zaftig* figure, and the innocence of a bride. I flashed back to the day when I discussed the facts of life with her.

"Please answer a few questions. Do you know who I am?"

"Yes, sir."

"And what do you know about me?"

"I don't know what you mean."

I really poured it on. "Dearie," I started, "I wrote the book. This is the best job in BCA. You'll make more money than you've ever made, you'll have the best boss you ever had in your life, and you'll be immune from anyone bothering you. So don't turn coy with me. Answer my questions as fast as I ask them, and don't put any con in between. Now what do you know about me?"

She was flustered but picked up the ball. I liked that.

"Well, I do know you're an actor. The fellows in the building all say you're a regular guy. The girls think you're cute but are scared of you . . . and your wife terrifies them. The word is, she's had two secretaries fired."

"They're wrong. It was three."

Vera smiled.

"They were idiots and deserved to be fired. My wife calls up when I'm out of town and asks where I'm staying. One secretary not only declined to tell her, but volunteered the explanation that as a good office 'wife' she had to keep my confidence, and my real wife would understand. I don't have to tell you how that went over. If the little nut had kept her mouth shut, she would have stayed out of trouble. Understand?"

"Yes."

"How much does the network pay you?"

"Ninety-five dollars plus overtime."

"I'll give you an extra hundred a month as a starter, and sign some overtime besides. But from this moment you're loyal to me and no one else. If that's clear and you want the job, it's yours."

"I'd like to try," said Vera.

"There's no room for trying. Just do it." I took her silence for approval of the deal. "Have you a boyfriend?"

She hesitated, then said, "Yes."

"Good. Have him teach you all the four-letter words, so you don't go into shock when you hear 'em around the office. Our business is punctuated with expressive adjectives, but nobody means anything personal by the language."

She smiled."After one year at BCA I can assure you that I've heard the adjectives, and even written them."

I liked what I saw. Vera was going to be loyal, yet not get in my way. It happened that she didn't appeal to me sexually, so that bit wouldn't bother us.

And my confidence that day had been well-placed. I was always pleased when I passed Vera in the waiting room.

On this occasion I simply stretched out my hand for messages as I walked by, gave the two a businesslike, "Follow me," and entered my private inner office.

This had the effect of a lush Park Avenue apartment that had been decorated without regard to cost. Jonathan himself was impressed when he first saw it. Even the Chairman and the Dentist never had it so good.

The desk was five thousand, for low. I immediately had this acquisition lacquered black to go with the color scheme. The painter had tears in his eyes as he sprayed. He kept mumbling, "But it's imported teakwood."

The carpet was three-inch one-hundred-percent wool retailing at forty-four dollars a yard. Cardinal red, naturally.

This office decor was one of the biggest rumor-makers at BCA. Without a known budget, or shows to charge off, furniture, television sets, drapery material, bar fixtures, and artwork kept arriving. Insiders referred to it as "Joey's San Simeon," and suspected that someone must be walking into his own office and discovering a piece missing now and again. How

94

right they were. I always wondered whether the Dentist ever missed that club chair that was taken out for repair. . . . Top of the world. Let his mother worry.

Sitting behind the black desk by now, I became all business. Vera and Jimmy Craig waited.

"Jimmy," I said, handing him a key, "go to my box and get me a thousand. Get back as soon as you can, 'cause I have someplace to go."

"Right, Joey." (Jimmy and my brother-in-law Bill were the two who could call me that.)

Jimmy had access to my safe-deposit box, my cars, and my apartment; he was allowed to bust through my office door unannounced at any time, even when my private-line telephone light was on. He had my complete confidence.

At twenty-one, he was a deceiving picture. Tall and dark, he had sandy hair in a casual comb, and brown eyes that were open and friendly. But he was sharp as a razor, had guts to spare, and he had an insatiable desire to learn. I was grooming him to be either a top producer or head of a talent agency. Odds were that he'd choose the agency end, because he loved to scheme and turn the deal. Once the deal was made, Jimmy somewhat lost interest, and in this respect he was like me.

I had adopted Jimmy as a kid brother. He was the son of a dear friend — from whom I had to save him. Old Man Craig was a helluva a great guy in some ways, but the money miser of all time. He had an old wallet that must have been made to take those oversized Confederate bills . . . and I wouldn't have put it past him to try spending a few. He had a nightly table at the restaurant where he watched the trotters on closed-circuit TV with his guests, and the waiters claimed his favorite three words were "Separate checks, please."

As Jimmy walked out the door, I thumbed through the messages Vera had handed me, and turned to her.

"Call Virgil Esty, Morton Silvern, and Chili Monroe in that order. Forget the rest of them."

"Mr. Colucci called and wanted to know if you could have lunch with him."

"What a presumptuous bastard he is. Call back and say I'm not free for lunch, but I'll meet him at five for a drink at Rose's on Fifty-second Street. Lunch. For Christ's sake, what balls." Vera waited politely. "Okay," I added, "out!"

As Vera left, I went over to the corner and picked up my putter. I had the pile of my rug down pat and could read it like the green of the eighteenth hole. About twenty feet away was a deluxe putting cup from Abercrombie & Fitch: I put three balls right into it.

It was a lesser vice. After six o'clock I couldn't help taking money away from my staff. Between Jimmy and Joel Fryman alone, at a dollar a ball, I was good for an extra fifty a week. They were both better golfers than I was, but they got the "apple" when the money was on the line, and that's what separates the men from the boys in any game. However, after I'd put the collar on my staff for fifty, I'd spend a hundred on food and drinks to make up. As I lined up a fourth ball, the intercom rang.

"Yes?"

"Mr. Virgil Esty on three."

I punched the button. "Hi, Virgil baby."

"Hi, Joey. To what do I owe this early morning call?"

"I have a bee for your bonnet, sweetheart."

"Anything I should worry about?"

"Nuttin,' absolutely nuttin'."

"When you coming over?" he asked anxiously.

"I got a call into a giant and I hope to connect for lunch. I'll drop by at twelve-thirty, and it'll only take three or four minutes. . . "

The private phone rang.

"His nibs is calling, Virgil, I gotta go." I hung up and took Jonathan's call.

"Hi," I said.

"Anything to report?"

"Yeah. I'm seeing Esty at twelve-thirty. He just got back from the Coast, and I'll handle the V.P bit."

"Fine, anything on the other two projects?"

"I have the call in for Silvern now."

"Good. Call me back after you speak to him."

"Okay, buddy."

I hung up and buzzed Vera. "Where's Silvern?"

"I was just going to buzz you. He's on two."

I lit a cigarette quickly and punched the phone button.

"Mr. Silvern, Joey Bertell. How are you?"

"Fine, Mr. Bertell. I understand we have mutual friends. Maybe we should have lunch on that."

"We sure have," I answered, "and I'd love to have lunch at your earliest convenience."

"Well, I'm free today." His voice was a little garbled, and I made myself a bet Silvern was a pipe smoker and had one between his teeth at this moment. "Are you free?" he continued.

"Well, nothing is more important. Name the place and the time."

"Are you familiar with the Attorneys Club on Fifty-first

"Yes."

"All right, Mr. Bertell, I'll meet you there at one o'clock."

"Thank you very much, Mr. Silvern. I'll see you at one."

I hung up, jumped from my chair, grabbed the putter, and clipped a fast one toward the cup. Bull's-eye! I stepped back to the phone and buzzed Vera.

"Where the hell is my dart board?"

"It's been —"

I interrupted. "Don't give me that 'It's been' crap. Get it in here!"

Within three seconds Vera was through the door, at attention . . . empty-handed.

"Now, my darling, it's question-and-answer time. Don't make any mistakes. *Cabeshe?*"

"*Cabeshe.*"

"Who is the most important man in your life?"

"You are."

"Who signs your little check and all your little bullshit over-time cards?"

"You do."

"Excellent, my sweet. Who is the most brilliant, talented, sexiest, richest, most lovable man you've ever worked for?"

"You, Mr. Bertell."

"Then where the hell is my goddam dart board and my two dozen darts?"

She started to speak. I cut her off instantly.

"How the goddam hell am I supposed to support six hundred people, keep a wife, ten mistresses, and a girlfriend, and also control a network if I don't have my dartboard? Answer me that."

"I ordered it, and Gerry was supposed to pick it up two days ago —"

"Don't discuss Gerry, whatever the hell that is, with me. That's your problem. Now you take money out of petty cash when I leave, treat yourself to lunch and *one* drink, then you take an additional hour and hustle your cute little fat butt around town . . . and don't you dare come back without my dart board. *Cabeshe?*"

"*Cabeshe.*"

"Now get out of here before I ship you back to the steno pool."

Vera loved to play the game. "Oh, please, sir, don't do that."

I smiled and waved her out. I went back to the putter.

99

The intercom buzzed, and it was Vera, doubtless in her coat. "Miss Monroe on two."

Adrenalin flushed into my system, and I almost knocked the phone down.

"Darling." I managed a soft, lightly mocking tone. "I love you."

"Jooey!" she cooed. There was a pause, and I could hear her sniff and hold back the tears. If she had been in the same room with me at that moment, she could have turned me inside out. When they use tears for bait, they have me trapped.

"Howya been, honey?"

"Great, Joey, how about you?"

"Just great. Need a stake for chili, or maybe a little pot?"

She laughed. "Same old Joey. No, I've got my own money for chili now, and the other thing never was my cup of tea. Hey, that's a joke!"

I wanted to see this delightful creature in the worst way. I wondered if the mileage was showing, or if she still stopped traffic at all the intersections. "When do I see you?"

"Right now," she answered. "But only if you really want to."

"Really want to? I want to turn on some violin music to answer you by. You've got —"

The private wire interrupted my hearts and flowers, and I asked Chili to hold on.

"Hi," I greeted Jonathan.

"Did you hear yet?"

"Yeah, I'm meeting him at one o'clock at his club."

"Dammit, why didn't you call me right away?"

"This may come as a shock to you, but I got jammed."

He slammed the phone down.

Very calmly I went back to the little chili pepper. Jonathan I had clocked. I could outwait him the best day he ever lived.

"So, my sweet, how about three o'clock at the Forum on Forty-eighth street?"

"You're so exclusive."

"Do you prefer someplace else?"

"No, the Forum will be great."

The private wire rang again, and I smiled. "Hold it a second, Chili." And to Jonathan, "Hello!"

"Sorry, pal. I was just upset over a few things, but I wanted to wish you luck with the luncheon."

"Glad you called. I'm on the regular wire with Chili baby. How 'bout that."

"Give her my best and say I'm looking forward to meeting her."

"Right, pal." The phone clicked, and I indulged in an Oliver Hardy "skull" as I switched back to Chili baby.

"You still there?"

"Aren't I always, dahling?"

"All right, Tallulah, I'll see you at three o'clock at the Forum."

"Do you want to come to my place instead, Joey?"

"No, baby. I'm not up to a rape on a first date. I'll see you at the Forum."

" 'Bye, doll," she said, and hung up.

I went into my black-and-cardinal-red washroom to get ready for my appointments: twelve-thirty with Virgil Esty, one o'clock with Morton Silvern, and three o'clock with Chili. First the comb, then the lime cologne. The day was looking great. Top of the world. Get out of my way!

Jimmy came bouncing through the door, reached into his kick and came out with the loot.

"Count it," he suggested, laying the bills in front of me.

I stashed it in my hip pocket. "Why, when I know where to find you?"

Then I detailed my plans with him so that he could reach me at any point along my itinerary: Esty's office, the Attorneys Club, the Forum — plus our checkpoint, Le Valois. The stakes were getting high. This was the moment to synchronize watches.

I adjusted my tie and started out the door. Vera was waiting with some messages.

"Not now, honey. I don't want any problems or bad news." Then I added, like an easy afterthought, "Call my wife and say I'm busy, tried to get her but her line was busy. And casually — but goddamit, I mean casually — find out if she's leaving the house today. If she is, tell Jimmy and he'll know what to do. *Cabeshe*?"

"*Cabeshe*."

I wheeled back to Jimmy. "Walk with me to the elevator." As we walked down the corridor, I gave him the rest of it.

"If Gina calls and you even sense she's coming downtown, tell her I left money for her with you. Here's a hundred."

Jimmy put it in his wallet.

"Between three and four don't let her get within ten blocks of Forty-eighth Street, Fifth or Sixth Avenue. If she ever sees me with anyone who looks like Chili Monroe, I'm a dead man. But while I'm taking my last breath, I'll shoot you down—that I promise."

Jimmy wasn't too pleased with the mission or the lecture, but he knew I meant it. As I stepped into the elevator, he sniped, "Introduce me to her someday."

The door closed, and I had a laugh. The kid would be a big winner without managing Chili. I'd see Jimmy buy stock from his tightfisted old man yet.

Downstairs, I cursed George for not showing up for work, but managed to jump into a taxi.

"Morris," I said, lamping the driver's nameplate as I shut the door, "BCA Building."

"Okey-dokey, boychik."

I saw I was in for ten minutes of conversation. New York cabbies are a special breed. Once one drove me down a side street, stopped the cab, and auditioned a couple of songs at full lung power. Nutty as he was, I got caught up in the act, sat there and applauded. You figure it out.

Morris's eyes had me in the rear-view mirror. "You're that Joey Bertell guy, ain't cha?"

"My mother always said that."

"My old lady and me watch you all the time. We love those old-time songs, get what I mean? They don't do enough of them anymore, get what I mean? You get so sick of seeing these punk kids with the hair, I'll tell you the truth, you can't tell the girls from the boys, get what I mean? I tell you, if my kid ever came home with a mop of hair like that, I'd break his goddam back, get what I mean?"

He paused to catch his breath.

"I mean, I told my old lady when we saw you on the TV that you looked like a regular guy. I mean, most of them actors and singers are garbage. No offense, get what I mean? There's certain guys that you just know are bedbugs, but you can always spot a 'tom' guy, get what I mean?"

Morris pulled up in front of BCA. I paid the fare and a dollar tip.

"Real nice talkin' to you, Joey, and don't forget to keep up those old-time songs. They're still the greatest, get what I mean?" He threw the flag and roared off. *New York, New York, it's a helluva town . . .*

I tossed a wink at the BCA Building elevator starter and took an express to the fifteenth floor. I walked up to the receptionist, lifted her hand, kissed it, and announced, "I love you, whom do you love?"

"You, Mr. Bertell."

"Excellent, my beauty. Say it loud and with pride."

"I love you, Mr. Bertell."

"Now don't say anything else. I want to remember only those words. I want your beautiful eyes, hair, mouth, and body to be painted in my mind forever. Alas, I must now leave, but remember, princess, it is thee I worship and adore. Nothing can erase the memory of these few fleeting moments. Good-bye, my darling, and good night, Chet."

She was slightly hysterical. "Joey Bertell, you're insane. You really are insane!"

"Be at Room 1205 at the Waldorf in half an hour and bring some rye bread." I turned and skipped through the door. Doll baby was drying her doe eyes with Kleenex.

I walked past Myra, Virgil Esty's secretary, and waved. Virgil was finishing up on the phone. Here was a real down-to-earth good guy who knew his job and handled it in a competent manner. He'd create no waves on the sea or get a monument afterwards. But he'd pass through his career with the respect of his fellow workers. A *hamishe* guy who had the nice wife and family and kept things in good order.

Virgil hung up his phone and greeted me with genuine warmth. "Hi, Joey."

"Hiya, Virgil boy, how's by you?"

"Same old jungle. How was the Coast? Did you see Sweetie Pie?"

"How is it possible to escape Lavender Lips? Dammit, I pleaded with Jonathan not to pack that flea. We could be spending time on important matters instead of trying to get him his cockamamey VP stripes. But all the crapola aside, Virgil, do you know why I'm here?"

"I've got a pretty good idea."

I picked up a cigarette, lit it, inhaled deeply, held it down till it tingled, and began.

"Omar's in trouble. I don't think he can last three months. Head of production on both coasts, and nobody pays any attention to him. He's been so outmaneuvered that he could phone in his job."

"Sad but true," Virgil observed. "How the hell did he let Ballantine and Westgate take him down?"

"Elementary, my dear Watson. They con Omar during the day, then pick up the phone and call Jonathan at night. They make a perfect team, a fag and a thief—although the thief is an artist. Ballantine has the balls and the little gray cells. He brainwashes the fag to call Jonathan for the kill."

"Why in hell does the tall man listen to the fag?"

"I'm sicker than you about it. I've done everything in the world to ace the scumbag out of position. I'd kill him if I thought I could get away with it. The power of the phone . . . how can you stop him from dialing?"

"But it's a shame they can nail Omar to the cross. He's a helluva a great guy, and he'd be a great executive if they gave him half a chance."

I pondered his words—I really liked Omar—then I kicked myself for the fatal flaw of having feelings.

"Virgil, we're in a jungle. These bastards are cannibals. If you don't kick their brains out first, you'll get invited to dinner one night and find out you're the main course. Protect yourself first, pal, then help others."

Virgil sighed. "Why can't I stick to the job, do what I'm supposed to do, and stay out of the intrigue?"

"You can, pal. Get a pair of overalls, a pick and shovel, and I'll have you placed for around sixty-five take-home. Can you be ready this afternoon?"

"You don't mince words, do you?"

"Listen, jerko, you know you're special to me. I think you're a great guy with something to offer, and if it's the last thing I do, I'll shove you down J.J.B.'s throat."

"You've already done that."

We both laughed. "Y'know, Virgil boy, you're right."

I looked at my watch. It was 12:50 already. I could make the Attorneys Club in five minutes. No time to fence anymore, however. Charge forward boldly!

"Virgil, go to Omar and tell him that for the unity of the company, and in fairness to Bryan, who has seniority, you think he should appoint Bryan a VP first and you next." I waited for it to penetrate.

"I knew that was why you came over here."

I gave Virgil ice. "If you knew it, then you know damn well I'm right." I had him thinking now. Bright he wasn't, but he wasn't stupid, either.

"Do you really think it might help Omar?"

"Hell, no, it won't help him. But if you see someone you care for dying, will you just let him die, or will you reach him a straw? Don't put me on the defensive."

"Joey, I wish I were as tough as you—it would make things so much easier."

"Don't let the front fool you, pal. Underneath this three-hundred-dollar suit, twenty-five dollar shirt, and hundred-dollar alligator shoes is a pair of torn shorts."

What could Virgil say? He was a decent guy in a snake pit.

"Okay, Joey, you call the shot and I'll go along."

I reached out and shook his hand. Damn, I liked the guy. I promised myself in that instant to protect Virgil Esty in the clinches. With his luck he'd need protecting.

I had a little game of nicknaming people with double initials. Bryan Westgate was Farley Fag, Jonathan was Paul Power, Omar was Tom Tailor, Chester Plan was Larry Liar, Mario Colucci was Percy President . . . and good old decent Virgil Esty was now Tom Tact. My own *nom de guerre* was Pete Pressure.

I got up to leave, Staring straight into his eyes, I said, "I give you J.J.B.'s word that this favor will not be forgotten. You will get your stripes and your raise within a month. And I give you my word."

"That's the one I'm relying on, Joey," he said. I was touched by Virgil . . . and I now hated Lavender Lips more than ever.

I glanced at my watch: 12:55, and I couldn't be late for

Morton Silvern. "See you, pal." I waved to Virgil, and I was in the corridor.

I headed for the red light at the elevators. As the door opened and I walked in, Wilson Manning brushed past, stepping out.

"Hi, Joey."

"Hi, Will. I'll check your office Wednesday morning for lunch, okay?"

"Either that or I'll call you," he shot back as the door clinked shut. Once more I whipped out the black alligator book and entered Manning's name.

From the bustle of Fifty-first Street, I stepped into the Attorneys Club. It was like stepping from Miami into Iceland.

Men were sitting in dark leather chairs, against a backdrop of dark brown hand-tooled solid walnut. These men were on the other side of fifty, obviously successful, and members of a clan that rebuffed outsiders. The clan uniform was old-fashioned suit with vest, and shoes never brighter than charcoal. I even spotted, across some vests, the thick gold chain, for the gold Hamilton railroad watch in the snug pocket.

I gave my name to the desk man and hesitated to find the right approach. Morton Silvern was not going to be a Chester Plan type. My heart was pumping the rhythm I knew from every opening night. Which was the clue. I told myself, "Play the *part* Joey. You're vice-president of AT&T. You've got a commodity to sell. This guy is no mooch. Six times six is thirty-six to him. He knows what you're here for. If he weren't interested, he'd have put you on a slow boat that first time. Come on, nail this guy!"

The bellman was talking to someone and pointing my way. Either I was about to be arrested or the man coming my way was Morton Silvern.

Hand outstretched, he said, "Mr. Bertell, I'm Morton Silvern. Let's go right in and sit down."

I followed him into a large high-ceilinged dining room, and we sat at a deuce table near a window.

"What's your first name, Mr. Bertell?"

"Joey."

The waiter was there. "All right, Joey, let's have a drink. I'll have a Cutty Sark on the rocks—how about you?"

"I'll have a vodka martini."

The waiter left, and Silvern reached into his side pocket, fishing out pipe and pouch. I remembered my deduction during his phone conversation and waited to see if he clenched it between his teeth.

"Joey, you call me Morton," he began—the pipe was between the molars, and I'd won the daily double—"and since you'd wanted to talk to me, suppose you start." He paused ever so slightly. "You can talk to me about anything except the World-Bond situation."

I smiled. "Then I hope they serve nice Cutty Sarks and martinis, because that's about all we'll be enjoying."

Morton didn't exactly smile, but he remained amiable. Like all the men at the other tables, he was an experienced prober.

He puffed calmly and looked me over. He didn't parry my thrust, he simply ignored it. However, he invited me to make one more thrust.

"What makes you feel you have more to offer than anyone else?"

"I have the one thing you lack and can't buy," I said quickly. "Management. Manpower. You can sell World-Bond, you can run it, or you can liquidate. If you don't sell off the assets and bankrupt the corporation, you'll have to get someone to run it. You only have the lock. I have the key."

"Joey, you sound rather confident. But we've had every big name in the business after the job."

"Big names won't help, Morton. And we're not talking about a job. You need the right man. I've got the right man."

"Who is it, Joey?"

"Jonathan Bingham," I announced with no small pride, and I sat back to enjoy a moment of triumph.

There was absolutely no reaction—and then I realized he had known! But I was playing my role to nail this guy, and pure instinct gave me the line.

"But of course you knew the answer, like any good attorney, before you asked the question, Morton. The real question is, what's your feeling about it?"

"In the first place, I don't think he'll undertake it, and in the second place, he'd be risking too much if he did."

No lines now. Fish die by their mouths, and I wasn't about to die. And now Morton had to come to me.

"Why in the world *would* he want to leave BCA and come to

111

World-Bond? We don't even know whether we can keep it open or not."

"I say he'll go with the right deal. And if he goes, World-Bond stays open."

"I'd like to talk to him at least," offered Morton easily.

"You're talking to him now. . . ." I looked him squarely in the eye. The next second was all-important: I had thrown down the money, he was faded, and let's see what he'd throw.

"All right, Joey, what do you have in mind?"

Now it was my ball. Charge forward boldly.

"Morton, he wants stock, not money. You have a chance because J.J. considers the Chairman an ungrateful old man. J.J. knows where your stock is now. He knows that the announcement of his taking over World-Bond sends that stock up ten points and gives Wall Street some stability to reinvest fresh capital."

"Go on." Morton puffed on his pipe. He was now hearing some lines he had not predicted.

"This guy couldn't win a popularity contest against Hitler, but he's a world's champion profit-and-loss executive. I say that's the name of your clients' game, Morton, but you tell me how wrong I am."

Morton made an actual pause. "That's pretty hard to do when you're right." He puffed, tamped the tobacco, looked out the window, and actually smiled. "Joey, it just might be one helluva shot."

THE CANNIBALS

Such slang from Mr. Morton Silvern at the Attorneys Club was a twenty-one-gun salute.

"Morton, I said management *and* manpower. Every key man on the BCA team will follow Jonathan." I paused for the hammer. "Morton, you will be responsible for bringing the most successful management team in the history of show business over to your store intact."

He smiled again. "But that would have to include you."

"Be careful what you offer," I said, now up to my *crazmere* with confidence. "I went through law school, too, and specialized in contracts."

He got a chuckle out of that. By now I was a Morton Silvern fan. I had him scored as seven percent bullshit, twenty-two-and-a-half percent ego, and the rest pure talent. And most important, one hundred percent gentleman. I knew I could learn things from Morton Silvern and I intended to make this negotiation a private seminar.

"But if the team included you, Joey, where would you stand? Do you want to run production?"

"Absolutely not. I am and will remain the number two man to Jonathan. I have my own little limbo. Whatever has to be done, I do from that limbo." I rephrased the metaphor: "He will call the shots, and you will be goddam sure I'll make it happen."

"That I believe, Joey."

And now came the final fencing.

"I want you to believe it, Morton." I stared at his pupils—not just at his eyes, but at his pupils. I'd made two passes. C'mon dice, charge forward boldly, top of the world *mom*.

"All right, Joey, you've got me convinced. How do we work it out from here?"

Battle stations.

"First, Morton, we must protect Jonathan's position at all costs. We can never put him in the postion of being turned down. Second, you have to shape up your side and put the blocks in order, of that I am aware. Third, I want you to meet Johnny. If we're going into all this together, let's sit down to a TOT party."

"Where did you learn that?"

"What?" I asked.

"Tuchas offen tish."

"Just show business Yiddish. In my language, 'Put it on the table.' "

"Joey, you're expressive in any language."

I felt like a member of the club, and drove on.

"Okay now, Morton. Do you have any problems at your end? I know you're the kingpin, but do you have some dissidents?"

One thing about Morton Silvern. He didn't take the Fifth. He answered, and he talked fact.

"I'm Chairman of the Executive Committee, and I either represent or have been given the power to speak for all the brokerage houses involved. However, you have to understand that the banking community sticks together, and right now they are most concerned with the disposition of that Greek thief. The old man will not get out of the company gracefully. The powers don't want him, but they don't want to put him in jail."

"Do you mean that Nicholas Sidaris, philanthropist, is a common thief? You have to be kidding!"

"No, don't misunderstand. He is not a common thief. He is a great big important thief. He made thieves out of his aunt, uncle, nephews, and I'm not too sure he didn't corrupt his chauffeur. We don't have time enough, Joey, to reckon the amount of money that Sidaris has literally stolen. The only thing I can't fathom is why he wasn't smarter about it."

"He sounds like an out-and-out desperado."

"It's almost inconceivable, but true."

The captain came to the table. "Excuse me, Mr. Bertell, there's a Mr. Bingham on the phone. He says it's important."

I excused myself and stepped out to the desk. "Hello."

"In case there's anyone standing by your phone, we're talking about casting the variety show. How's it going?"

"I can talk, and it's bingo."

"Was he amazed to think I could be even remotely interested?"

I played it straight for the egotistical bastard.

"He certainly was. Believe me, this can be lined up. I didn't miss."

"It never occurred to me that you would. I just thought this little call might give you extra help, that's why I gave the captain my name."

"The next step can be a meeting. I want to get back to the table."

"Excellent. Call the shot, and I'll reserve the private dining room at *my* club. Just call me the second you get finished. So long, buddy."

I set the phone back in its cradle and walked briskly back to Silvern.

"Everything all right?" he asked.

I used it as a throwaway. "Oh, Jonathan is beautiful. He figured he'd add strength to me."

"When I meet him," Morton smiled, "I'll tell him it wasn't necessary. You're pretty darn good on your own."

I accepted this graciously. "Thanks."

"Now, I know what I can do," said Morton, "but let me feel out my key people. I want as many boosters on the team as possible. Let them all think it was their idea. These men are giants —and their egos are giants. But I think the idea is sound."

"All right, Morton," I said, "we'll be in touch on this and meet at Jonathan's club one evening soon around six o'clock. And now I think we can enjoy our Cutty Sarks and martinis without discussing the World-Bond situation, as you first suggested."

We did just that, and enjoyed a pleasant luncheon as well. Morton was no gourmet—the low-calorie special of the Attorneys Club suited him fine—but he was an excellent host, and I turned the conversation this way and that so he could help polish up my knowledge of a few matters.

At. 2:45 he mentioned another appointment and politely offered to show me out.

"No, thanks," I replied, "I left chalk marks on the way in." And so we closed with a smile.

I spotted a pay phone and pushed a dime in the slot. My office rang twice.

"You'd better have my dart board," I told Vera, "but I'm too rushed to hear about it now. What's new?"

"Three inches of phone calls, nothing urgent. I pulled out Marty Cartright of QMA returning your call, Chester Plan about the development board, Bryan Westgate from the Coast, and Mario Colucci—three times—confirming his drink with you later."

"When Colucci calls back next time, tell him four-fifteen at Valois. I'll be in touch."

I pushed in another dime and dialed Jonathan's private line. He answered immediately.

"It's me," I announced.

"How'd it end?"

"Just great. He's checking his people to line everyone up. We'll probably meet again, and then I'll sit you down. But no meets until he declares himself in a position to make the offer."

"Very good. I've got our research guy here breaking down World-Bond. By the time we meet, I'll be able to tell Silvern just what to do."

"I'll be in touch," I said. "I'm off to see Chili baby."

"Have fun." He hung up.

Chapter 5

Walking into the Forum at three made me feel like visiting royalty. When they first opened, I'd been there with parties, and I'd been loyal ever since. It was one of my favorite restaurants, right around the corner from NBC, another network, and a few short blocks from CBS and ABC. Two streets over were the key ad agencies. Also, since it was not marked as a show business spot, you could discuss private business without bumping into colleagues or competitors.

Right through the door, the maitre d' hit me with "Phone call, Mr. Bertell."

"Man or woman?" I asked softly.

"Man."

"I'll take it at my table."

They were most attentive as I walked over, the captain, two waiters, and a busboy all trying to keep pace. The busboy had six hands and couldn't get the phone plug into the jack. The captain and the waiters would have things to say to him later, I could see.

I snatched the stuff out of his hands and said, "I used to be an installer for the phone company"—recalling a certain bookie company—"and let me show you how they go to great expense so that even blind people can fit the jack.

"See this dent?" I pointed to the female socket. "Match the jack to this with your fingers, close your eyes, and put the two together." I gave him the stuff back, and he executed one, two, three.

"Okay now, everybody, *good*-bye." They left, but now. I lifted the receiver, and greeted Jonathan.

"Joey, I wanted your day to be complete. Omar just walked out of here. He told me, 'Jonathan, I've decided to make Bryan Westgate a VP before Virgil Esty, because I think he deserves it and has been with the company longer—if it's all right with you.' I told him to run the department the way he felt best."

"Gee, that was a nice gesture on his part," I observed.

"Yes, Omar does get those subtle thoughts once in a while," Johnny laughed. "He also said he called Bryan."

"Which explains my call from Bryan baby."

"Right, he wants to thank you. I told him you were handling it. Will you please do me a favor and be a little humble when you call back?"

"Call back? Don't be insulting."

"Joey, you're impossible when you're flying. Maybe if Chili knocks you on your can we can get back to work."

"We'll see in a few seconds, buddy, because here she comes— and spare me the repartee."

"Do you want me to say hello?"

"Johnny, I need you at this table like I need Frankie Laine's toupee. Get out of my life."

"You're all heart," he said. "'Bye."

120

And as easily as that, Chili entered my life again. Twenty-four years old, if she had changed at all, it was for the better. Five-four, honey blonde, blue eyes, and all the accessories. A touch of maturity, or a suggestion of cash in the purse—which her clothes bore out. At ten paces you could see that purse was not under a hundred, nor were those blue kid shoes under fifty.

I stood up to greet Chili. I squeezed her arm and gave her a welcoming peck on the check. The skin was like a baby's—except there was just the right amount of Joy behind the ear.

It drove everything else out of my mind. And I was not the only one affected. This chick had frozen every human being from the door to my table. After a beat I managed to rouse the waiter. "Bring the young lady a Cutty Sark on the rocks."

Chili sat down with a smile. "That's it, hon, I never change." She added the latter pointedly and with feeling.

Well, there she was opposite me, a little girl with a devilish look in her eye. "Do I stack up, Joey baby?"

"Strong, sweetheart, strong."

The waiter was already putting down the Cutty Sark plus a vodka martini for me. Either he remembered me, or he was a mind reader, or I was losing my mind and had forgotten ordering it myself.

Chili and I raised our glasses. "You make the toast," I suggested.

She looked right into my pupils and said, "Top of the world."

I echoed it practically in a trance. We clicked and drank.

"Beauty," I began, struggling for a lighter tone, "where have you been?"

"Europe, Joey, and it was a ball."

"How long?"

"Three months in Cannes, a couple of weeks in Rome, Paris and London."

"Did you wind up with anything?"

"It was first-class." She giggled. "I'm up to my *tushie* in clothes, there's a diamond bracelet and ruby watch . . ." She hesitated.

"Really, I commented, playing it straight.

"And five thousand," she concluded.

"So your purse is lined with gold. I'd love to examine it sometime," I said, kicking myself mentally for the crude double entendre.

She helped me by going along. "Baby doll. I thought you didn't like fancy things."

I couldn't resist. "Like it? If it was ventilated, I'd *live* in it!"

She laughed. This classy chick was the sexiest thing in my life, and I'd kept it platonic.

My eyes were now alternating between Chili and the door. Jimmy had his orders, but Gina was one of the great private detectives of our time. I forced myself to forget everything but Chili.

"Was the trip love or business?"

"Business, baby doll. A John is a John. But this one was a nice guy and treated me great."

"Why shouldn't he?" I said, the envy showing. "You're the most class he ever wrapped around his arm, and I guarantee it grew him four inches when you stood next to him."

"Why, Joey, you sound like a boyfriend."

"Now, Chili, I wrote the book. . . ."

"Joey . . ." She looked at me. "You know, of course, that I'm in love with you, and it will always stay that way."

It was a moment infinitely tender, yet powerful beyond reply.

Her hand appeared from under the table, pressed something into my hand, and closed over it.

I regained the power of speech and affected a gentle humor.

"How can you use the word 'love,' Chili, when we haven't even made the scene together? Remember me, the cynic?"

"Joey, I can feel your love the same way I feel *no* love balling a John." Chili could borrow my vocabulary without becoming crude. "You think a woman is just something you roll onto her back and plug into? A woman has more feelings than any man. The Johns that have made every inch of my body don't have one point of what you have. The idiots—they could get more running home and giving their wives a wristwatch.

"Forget it," she concluded. "Who'd want to make it with you anyhow? With my luck, you'd mistake it for a TV camera and do ten minutes of your own songs."

As I broke up, the captain came over and announced a long-distance call. I asked him to bring two more drinks and something to nibble on.

"How 'bout me?" Chili pouted.

"I knew you wouldn't miss that cue," I said, as I blew her

a kiss and picked up the phone. The martinis were getting to me. Gina baby, don't walk in now!

"Joey? Bryan!" limped the phone voice." I just *had* to find you and let you know that Omar is making me a vice-president on Monday."

I signaled Chili that I was talking to a fag, and camped a little.

"Bryan! Just getting this call from you is—I can't tell you—so *important*! Really, so important."

Chili was entranced.

"Joey, I just know your fine hand was in this someplace, and I want you to know that I'll be eternally grateful."

"Why, I don't know if I was helpful or not. But when things come out the right way, that's all that counts."

"Thanks again, Joey. And come out soon, we all miss you."

"Thanks, Bryan, and so long." I hung up.

"Thweetie," Chili lisped, "if you're finished with the big strong man, why don't you open your other hand?"

I had forgotten that I was still holding a fist. Opening it, I found an ultra-thin gold lighter, with my initials small and classic.

"Beauty, it's perfect. Where did you find it?" I leaned over and kissed her, on both cheeks this time.

"In Rome. You see, my mind was on you all the time."

I lit a cigarette instantly. It tasted marvelous.

"How did you know to reach me through Johnny's office?" I asked her after another puff.

"Through Chester Plan."

I thought smoke would come out of my ears. Instinctively, I continued, now the professional investigator.

"Oh, you know Chester?"

"He's one of my clients," she said simply.

My professional poise vanished, for once. "Your *what?*"

"One of my clients, Joey. One of my Johns."

"That weasel!"

"They can't all be gems, you know. Chester visits his psychiatrist Monday, Wednesday, and Friday. After each session he comes over to my place for a change of pace. Lovemaking lessons."

"*Whaat?*" We both looked around self-consciously, and both gave a small prop laugh to take the edge off my break.

"Yes, baby doll. Chester explained how browbeaten he is. His old lady has challenged him so that he can't even Do It."

I sensed there was more. "Tell on." Already I had the germ of an idea. Christ, these girls were the world's best undercover agents. I'd known of fortunes spent so they could steal patterns, patents, governmental secrets. Mata Hari. Hell, why couldn't Joey Bertell organize a coozie network from coast to coast? With a mental short cut I visualized it as a network television series: "BCA is proud to present *The Hookers*, brought to you by Sparta Pharmaceuticals."

I switched back to my first idea and probed. "Tell me what he says to you. Anything—jokes, hot air, business."

"Business! You can't keep him quiet, Joey. Chester runs his

office two hours at a time from my bed. Not bedroom, but bed."

"Business?" With a casual shift of my eyes, I signaled the waiter for two more.

"Yes, Joey. He likes to make business calls while . . . I . . . play with him."

"Ah."

"It's his big flip. Giving reporters secrets about shows and people. Is he all there?"

"Chili," I cautioned, "he's all there. People have risen and fallen from his phone calls."

"I don't mean mentally, I mean sexually. Specifically, he has an inferiority complex."

"Maybe he's just inferior."

"Joey, I know you're pumping me."

"Chili—"

"Don't 'Chili' Chili, Joey. I know you're an even bigger wheel. I know you control this and that. But did you know that you control Chester Plan to the point that he's so busy trying to figure you out he can't have an erection?"

"Good," I blurted. "May the bird of paradise wee-wee all over his balls."

"Ahem," Chili replied. "He likes that, too."

"My God, don't tell me he's a 'golden shower' boy!"

"Chester likes kinky bits, Joey. You should see him strut up and down. I've got my walls mirrored, you know, and a wall-to-wall white bearskin rug. Well, when I do manage to excite him a little, between his telephone calls, he preens himself and demands to know if I think it's the best."

"What do you tell him?"

"Joey, for fifty dollars a visit—guaranteed one hundred fifty a week—I tell him it's gorgeous. What else?"

I laughed quietly. "Tell him the truth! Tell him it's tiny and ugly . . . and we'll take a piece of the psychiatrist's action."

"I think they need their headshrinkers . . . your other buddy included."

I was sipping my drink as Chili said that, and I guarantee it suddenly tasted bitter. "Oh, Johnny. He's a swinging great guy, Chili. You might end up digging him."

"I pass, baby. . . ."

I put down the martini carefully. I didn't want Chili to clam up.

"Tell Daddy what you have been able to find out that I don't know."

"I didn't say anything, Joey. I just pass."

I had to press.

"Chili, you didn't walk by a charming bachelor, the president of a television network, a man who makes a couple of hundred thousand a year plus an expense account that's classical music, just to say, 'I pass.' "

"Joey, I'm sure he's a great guy, or you wouldn't go around with him even for a million a year, but I'm not about to go around with him. I'm no punching bag—can we let it go at that?"

I bristled. "Whoever sold you that story, tell them Joey Bertell said they were full of it." I forgot it was Chili, I was really hot.

"Joey, honey, I haven't seen you in four years. I'm a fifteen-year-old virgin on her first date. I can't argue with you."

"We're not arguing. But this is about a friend. I'm a certain way, and I'll die that way. Nobody can talk to you about my friends but me. Why do they keep rapping this guy?" I rapped the table with my knuckles for emphasis.

I fought for control, my middle name. I leaned over and pecked Chili again. "Apologies," I pleaded. "Let's change the subject. Tell me one thing about my Rome lighter."

"What's that?"

"Where do I hide it?"

I gave her a wink and she smiled. Which was as close as I had ever come with anyone to discussing my wife.

What an edge it is not to cheat! No lies to the wife (or the broad), no wear and tear on the mind. A drink, an out-of-town trip, a broad who puts it in front of a guy, he has to go. But ask a guy if he ever cheated on his wife? You might as well ask him if he ever masturbated. I have to believe the late Dr. Kinsey . . . though why some husband who got jammed up with that book never took a shot at Kinsey I'll never know.

"So Chester Plan mentioned Johnny and me," I picked up, the investigator again.

"Yes. Chester mentioned some series you're developing for BCA. He was talking with somebody on his staff, or at least someone who works for him. This person reads a script and digests the story line for Chester so that when Chester goes to meetings, he's *au courant*."

THE CANNIBALS

I fumed. Chester Plan, a gnome who breaks writers' hearts with his comments—killing scripts before they can get to someone with the brains to visualize them! But here was the chance to test Chili's spy power and win a few laughs for Jonathan.

It began to take shape. I'd set up a phony script meeting in Jonathan's office and see that everyone on staff got the right script. But Chester Plan's stooge would get a script with key changes.

"Chili," I said briskly, "you're going to help me on my way to that top of the world."

"Can I?"

"You bet! I'm not in this ball game to lose, and with you, we're going to win large. We're going to have some fun winning, too."

"You mean you and me?" Chili was still kidding on the square.

Careful, Joey! Chili was dear to me. This was not the rah-rah boy promising a chick a part in the movie if she will accept a few drinks and Be Grateful. Any real guy considers a pimp the lowest form of life.

"Chili," I said, taking her hand in mind, "in my own mixed-up way I really care for you. That's the closest I can come to what you said before, but I mean what you said before, too. You can bank on my word. My word is more important than my life."

She sat silent.

I broke a rule.

"Chili, I married my wife in church and I love her. I'm not some yuk telling you I'm unhappy at home and she doesn't understand me. The bottom line . . . I don't intend ever to be married to anyone else."

Chili's eyes were clear. "You don't soften the blow, do you, Joey? I can hear your voice concluding a business deal . . . or cutting someone's throat."

"Chili, my voice and my words are trying to tell you how I feel. Haven't you been lied to enough in your young life? Do you think for one minute I don't know the lies you hear? Little doll, if I have to lose your friendship, if I never see you again, if the world has to come to an end, I'm not going to lie to my own people."

I hated to lecture, but I was purging myself of something.

"Chili, I grew up on the streets. Poor people were rich next to us. We had to steal to eat, steal to exist. Forget jobs—there were none."

I looked at her. "The first trick you ever turned was because you didn't have the rent money and were going to be kicked out on your little butt, right?"

"Right. Oh, right. Because it wasn't with a John, it was with the landlord." She winced. "I'd rather hear about Joey, not Chili."

"The story of *San Francisco*, Chili, with Joey playing the Clark Gable role. Then the Army.

"The last dishonest thing I ever did was gypsy the dice in a crap game the day before I was mustered out. I won six thou-

130

sand dollars with that and the pool hustling. I lived like a king. And I got my jollies cheating the cheaters."

I took four sugar cubes from the elegant little bowl, removed the Forum wraps, and inked in the dice spots. Then I showed her two cubes.

"This is the square set. The others are ace-deuce flats. They're beveled and scored to throw craps, low points and tens, craps or seven out."

Chili examined the two sets, amazed.

"I worked with three sets—straights, seven-elevens, and bust-outs. So help me, I never threw them in a straight game. But a cheater must take the beating without hollering. I'd make a quick score, get the dice in and out, and that would be it. The creeps would look at their partners! You see, one penny-ante thief never trusts another. He'll blame his partner before he'll suspect you."

"Joey, let me give you a toast."

I lifted my glass, touched it to hers, and waited.

"Joey, here's to whatever you want, whenever you want it, wherever you want it. No strings. But if anything ever fails"— here Chili's voice gave a slight tremor—"you can bet that damn crooked smile of yours that I'll be there to keep you warm. Now drink!"

One word more would have been too much. I drank.

I tried to be offhand afterwards. "Chili, find out the name of this guy who reads Chester's scripts."

"Okay."

"*Importanto*. He must not ever know that you know me."

"Right."

"Ask him who I am because you heard him mention my name and a girl you know likes me. But he's cagey—the girl isn't a good friend of yours, got it?"

"Right."

"Now in 'confidence,' Chili, for his benefit. Jonathan Bingham is going to take over World-Bond Studios. Your girl friend heard me talking to Jonathan in a restaurant and saying that the deal must include Chester Plan."

Chili actually giggled.

"Chili, we'll freak up his mind so that he won't even be able to hold up his golf club, much less anything else. . . ."

"I'll let you know, Joey . . ."

"Here's fifty dollars. Buy the little man a set of cufflinks, and tell him it's the first time you've ever bought a man anything in your life, and you can't understand it. *That'll* get his golf club up."

"All over the mirror," she said, and then blushed.

"Chili, don't misunderstand. Don't ever ball the pigmy free."

"That ball game I know," she assured me. "But now it won't be boring to listen to him, because I'll be listening for your name."

"Also," I said carefully, "you might reach out to your trusted friends on the Coast. I'll compare lists with you, and we may be able to organize the pipeline."

"Ready."

"All we want is information they volunteer—we're not suckering them in."

Chili looked at her watch. "The four o'clock lesson is due," she said.

"By the way, I'm having drinks with Mario Colucci of BCA. . . ."

"Bingo, Joey! He dates a friend of mine on the Coast. I'll fill you in next time."

I motioned for the captain, signed the check, and passed out money all the way to the doorman. "Grab me a cab."

He whistled to the line, the taxi eased up, and I helped Chili into a seat. "Call you later, or first thing in the morning."

She blew me a kiss. I took off toward Fifth Avenue.

Jimmy Craig was already at the bar of Le Valois.

"Nothing urgent," he assured me fast. "Gina didn't come in, after all. So I covered for Vera."

"Mr. Bertell, the usual?" It was Jean Pierre, my favorite bartender.

"Yeah, the full treatment."

This was the real vodka martini. He picked up the chilled glass, poured a teaspoon of Pernod in, swished it, then poured it out. Now the martini went in, and he lit a match. With one hand, he squeezed the lemon rind; with the other, he lit the lemon oil. The twist shot into the martini enveloped in flame.

I took a sip.

"Is it all right?"

"Superb."

And Jean Pierre, master mixologist, walked away happy.

"Okay, Jimmy, shoot. If you see Percy President, dummy up and take a walk after a gracious few minutes."

"Joey, the princess phone has been ringing itself off the hook."

"Jonathan has been reaching me, so it was Gina. How about the other phones?"

"Morton Silvern called, and I took a message carefully. 'The reaction was just what he anticipated and he is sure there's a deal.' " Jimmy was going through his book, a recent present from me.

"Chester Plan called. He had an important five o'clock meeting with Len Rich, the ad executive, and will call you in the morning."

I enjoyed pure contentment. Len Rich wouldn't be caught dead with Chester Plan. Chester was taking a submarine lesson. The plan was starting to work. In fifteen minutes I had his hole card—from now on I'd know if he was lying or not—and he'd be mine.

Jimmy saw me smile. "You swallowed the pussycat?"

"Someone else is doing that right now, Jimmy. Have a drink on me, I'm in a great mood." I motioned Jean Pierre to make two.

"To what do I owe this rare opportunity?" Jimmy asked.

"Just hang on for the ride. Did George call in?"

"He said he'd be in tomorrow, but he really sounded sick."

"Get him back and tell him to keep his germs home. I don't want to get sick when I'm flying."

The martinis came, and I gave Jimmy my toast: "Top of the world."

He tipped his glass, drank, and also nudged my knee. I lit a cigarette, glanced into the bar mirror, and saw Mario Colucci talking to the captain. That's what the captain was paid for. I concentrated on my drink.

A light slap on the back. "Hi, Joey."

I turned around. "Hiya, Mario. You know Jimmy Craig?"

"Sure, I know Jimmy."

"Hi, Mario," said Jimmy, rising. "Please take my stool because I've got to get home. Joey, I'll be in touch with George, and I'll be home all night if you need anything. Nice seeing you, Mario." He left.

"Mario, how about a great vodka martini?"

"I'll have a Cutty Sark on the rocks, Joey."

I ordered the drinks—but slid my own aside still half full. This was no time for a glow.

The drinks arrived.

"Salute."

"Salute."

Social amenities were not called for in this situation.

"Mario, what's on your mind?"

He went through a quick little shock and got into his pitch. "Do I have a chance at Vincent Fisk's job?"

I gave him a mark for directness.

"Can you do his job?"

"I've been doing it for the last eight months. Covering for him on many occasions, Joey."

I took away the mark. Still, that was Mario Colucci, rapping the poor sonovabitch who comes in to recommend him for the job. Class and breeding. Bless his back-stabbing heart.

"But are you big enough for it? The youth goes against you; you're loaded with that eager beaver bullshit."

Mario was stunned. "What do you mean?"

"Let me tell you about Vincent Fisk. I met him head-on in the *Sandstorm* settlement. He was one tough S.O.B. to deal with, and he had a hammerlock on me. Although I had BCA in a vise, Vincent knew I'd never use it . . . and that I knew he knew I'd never use it. We sat across from each other trading punches and developing a healthy respect for each other."

"I know," said Mario sheepishly.

I poured it on, wondering if I could stomach Mario Colucci as the extent of his weakness was exposed. "I negotiated with you first, and you gave me a ridiculous offer. It was an offer you could run up to your boss with to boast how clever you were and how much money you saved BCA. But actually, that offer made you look like a goddam fool because it wasn't ever going to be accepted by me. I just went right over your head—where I was going in the first place. So who lost, Mario, you or me?"

Mario could only nod.

"This job you're asking for now is super-important, because

whoever has it will bounce right into the presidency when the Chairman retires and J.J.B. moves into the Dentist's job."

Flags started to wave in Mario's head. He was buying a Cadillac and a town house, joining the better golf club, and entertaining lavishly. What a big man he would be on Feast Days down in the ghetto.

"I'd like that," he said.

He'd like that! Percy President—I couldn't even compare Mario Colucci and Jonathan J. Bingham without revulsion. Mario had already confided this dream to anyone who would listen.

"What can I do to get the job, Joey?"

Christ, he had tenacity, at any rate.

"One thing you can do is prove you're a Bingham man and a team player."

"I am a Bingham man. I think he's a genius. He knows more about TV than anyone in the business. But I can't get close to him."

"Don't try." I stared right into his kisser and repeated the line, "Don't try."

At that moment the captain came over. "Mr. Bingham is on the phone for you."

I thanked him and told Mario I'd try to make it short.

"Oh, no, Joey, take your time. I've got lots of time." Bless his considerate heart!

But I was in a good mood for Johnny. "Be careful what you say to me and how you say it, pal, because I'm so flush with power I don't know if I need you anymore. One wrong word, and I'll boil you in olive oil."

To my surprise, Jonathan's soft voice sounded a little tipsy.

"This can't be the fabulous Joey Bertell, can it? Is it possible I'm lucky enough to be talking to the most influential man in television?"

"All right, wise ass, you're crabbing my meeting with Percy President; I'm just getting to the good part."

"I'm sitting home in my club chair with a triple martini, just relaxing before my little sparrow arrives, and I thought I'd track you down. Have you given the Boy Scout the facts of life?"

"Yeah," I said bluntly. "This guy can be all right, but I warn you now, if you ever really need him, he'll be a tower of Jello. If he felt you had the upper hand, the two-faced rat would double-cross the Chairman and the Dentist. But, Jonathan, you won't be able to stomach his nearness."

"Well, if he can just take his orders, do his job, and promise not to use his brain, I don't care. What's your final opinion?"

"What time is the sparrow due?"

"Nine."

"I'll be there in a half-hour. I'll call him, you listen in, and we'll make the decision, okay?"

"Okay, old buddy, it'll fall into place."

"That's just the time to be cautious, Jonathan."

"Don't you ever stop playing cops and robbers?"

"I'll stop right this goddam minute if that's what you want."

"Relax, Joey. You don't have to go-go-go with me every minute."

I popped him like a clay pipe in a shooting gallery.

"The only reason you're sitting there with your triple martini is that I'm sitting here looking after the store. All right, make another drink for me. It *has* been a fabulous day. And Morton did call back."

"That's the way it's supposed to be." He got in the smug last word, as usual, and hung up.

By now Mario was really fidgeting at the bar. I walked over and sat down, all smiles.

"Let me level with you, Mario. The decision will be made tonight. It's between two other guys and you."

Mario stopped fidgeting.

"Also, everything else in the world is up."

"You mean at BCA?"

"Omar is out," I replied matter-of-factly.

"Who's taking his place—Chester?"

"Chester is out."

Mario was in a barrage. Within seconds I had authoritatively discussed the hiring and firing of the three top department heads.

"Let's take you first, Mario. I can swing you into the spot"—his eyes lit up—"however, let me make it clear that if I didn't believe you could handle it, I wouldn't make a move for you—got that?"

139

He nodded jerkily. "Thanks."

"Second, stop trying to be a general. You don't have to score *Sandstorm* points with J.J.B. Make a deal that a producer will go with, and let sales okay it. You don't have to saw a producer in half. Otherwise, if he gets lucky with a hit, he won't be back, or else he'll come back with an impossible deal and blame you for not taking it."

"You're right," Mario said.

"I'm more than right, Mario, I'm too late to save you. Wait until the government starts after you guys and looks at your deals. At the ranches, studios, homes, and businesses that are worth zero, which you've been buying from talent at fifty times cost, for their capital gains capers. I've been with these guys, and I know what they have in mind. They'll collar the producers you've sawed in half and make them holler on the others. You're not only on the FCC target, but the SEC target . . . the *center*."

"Joey, you have to understand it isn't so easy if you're not a department head. If you're in, you know what the boss wants and you can carry it through. If you're out, you have to use judgment, and all you get is a protection memo."

"Right, Mario. But everyone knows the rules of this game and has the same amount of protection relatively."

"Joey, who will take Omar's place?"

"I can't tell you yet, Mario—that's the rules of the game too. But it's nothing special—a washed-up guy with a big name. Take my word for it, he'll come in on a wave of publicity—the prodigal son returns—and in six or eight months he'll be cut down, drawn and quartered, and hung out to dry."

I lit a cigarette and went on. "The new guy despises Chester. Still, if Chester had been anything but a weasel, I could have saved him."

"Joey, should I say anything to Chester?"

"Are you going home from here?"

"Yes."

"Well, stay there until I phone you from J.J.B's apartment. If I give you the good news, then you can drop a hint to Chester. But do it right—as a favor to him and to make the team better. Because that's all we're working for, the best for the network and the best for J.J.B. Check?"

"Check."

"Okay, drink up, and we'll take off."

"I want you to know how I appreciate what you're doing for me, and I'll never forget it."

"I haven't done it yet, Mario, so save that old story. Besides, if I do decide to serve you up, how do you know I can deliver?"

Mario smiled. "I'm betting on you."

I studied him for one last moment, got up, and said, "See ya."

On the way out, I called to Jean Pierre. "Sign for me, and throw a deuce on for yourself."

The door closed on his "Thank you, Mr. Bertell."

I staked the doorgirl to a Washington, stepped into a cab that had just let out a passenger, and sped away to J.J.B.'s apartment.

While rolling, I analyzed Mario. Infallible instinct for people was my stock in trade with Jonathan. But now I was straining this instinct . . . and when the stuff hits the fan, even your guardian angel can develop amnesia about how great you were the other ninety-nine times.

Mario was a sneak, a definite stool pigeon in the case of Vincent Fisk, whom he'd faulted for excessive drinking and negligence of duty, and he had no class, which was the biggest flaw of all to me. And yet all that was repairable if he could do something for the team.

What might not be repairable was his reputation on the street. He was a joke. At a bar no guy would invite him to sit down. He just wasn't a man's man. Goddamit, the three lemons clicked into place, Mario was O-U-T.

The cabbie was looking at me in the rear-view mirror, so I returned the compliment and made his I.D. card. William S. DeMarco.

"*Como esta, paisan?*" he opened.

"*Molto bene, gratia,*" I answered.

He switched to English. "Your mind has been going faster than my cab."

"Don't tell me you saw the wheels turning."

He laughed. "I've been hacking twenty-three years, and when a guy is really concentrating, I can practically read his mind."

"Okay, *paisan,* be my adviser."

He didn't waste time. "Whatever—*who*ever you were judging

142

back there lost at the finish wire, I'll tell you dat. Until the last block and a half it was an open race."

"You're so right," I played along. "A guy finished out of the money, and you can tear up the tickets. Too bad, because it was one of our guys."

"Then he must be a real *gagagootz* for you to turn on him."

"Why do you say that? What do you know about me?" I asked.

"Whaddaya, kidding? I hacked in Vegas for five years, off and on in L.A. and Chicago, and now I'm back of the stick in New York. You think you're a secret? *We're* proud you're making it. There have been conversations in this cab, and you're one right Dago, Joey . . . you don't mind if I call you Joey, do you?"

"Not if you let me call you Willie."

"Yeah, yeah. Wait'll I tell my old lady I met you!"

"She'll throw rocks at you?"

"She does, and I'll give her a nine-and-a-half D right in the can, ya know?"

"Right, Willie, keep 'em in line!" And I let it go at that.

Willie fell silent also. He had plenty of smarts. In fact, I had a strange feeling "William S. DeMarco" might be a moon-lighter. The star sapphire on his pinkie hadn't come from cab fares. More likely from money as the business agent of a drivers' union organization. Definitely, he knew that I had him spotted as wise.

"So how come you shut the guy out?" he picked up.

143

"Because he's a whore and I can't trust him."

"Can't you slap him?"

I smiled. "No, wrong situation." I had an impulse to let him make with the advice. "But what bugs me is that the boss figures I can control him so he can use him."

"What more do you need than that?" cracks Willie.

"What?"

"You said the boss can use him. Isn't that enough? You're earning."

He was right in that respect. Who in hell was Mario Colucci to fear? If Jonathan played the game, I could kick a roomful of Mario Coluccis into line.

"Second brownstone from the light," I said, as Willie turned into the block.

He pulled up. I threw him a five. "Keep it, buddy, and good luck." He shot his flag and drove away with a wave.

I was already in the self-service elevator, hitting the button for Jonathan's apartment.

The elevator door slid open, and I stepped out and over to Jonathan's door, used my key, turned the knob, walked right in and whistled. No answer. I could hear Ella Fitzgerald on the hi-fi.

"Where are you?" I yelled.

"I'm just finishing showering, Joey. Make us a drink."

Jonathan had a bar second to none, so I began attempting a Jean Pierre special. This was a man's environment, British club style with plenty of books. Everything was in its place, a

144

J.J.B. touch, and in the far corner of the room was a putter. Next to broads, J.J.B. loved golf.

I took the two vodka martinis into the bathroom. The tall man smiled through shaving lather. "Hi, buddy, how goes it?"

"Great, pal."

He rinsed the lather, patted on the after-shave lotion, and said, "Joey, let us sit down and get up-to-date. I have some things to tell you."

He walked into the front room. Jonathan took Ella off the hi-fi, substituted Jackie Gleason mood music, and dialed the volume down.

"All right," he began easily, "how was your day?"

"Take a good gulp of martini, you'll need it."

He smiled and sipped.

Then I gave him a complete playback of the Chili Monroe meeting. Each little development delighted him more. Chili's repartee had him slouched in the chair, holding his sides.

"My God," he said, "I'd give a hundred dollars to see Chester Plan on the bearskin rug in front of the mirror!"

This, from J.J.B., was like the mint giving samples. He was known to be oblivious to checks. One of his girlfriends, after paying her own carfare, bringing food, and eventually even cooking it, had dubbed Jonathan "Zircon John." A business colleague suggested "J. Beresford Tipton," referring to the philanthropic millionaire. Yes, to say that J.J.B. was cautious with a dollar would be the proverbial understatement of the month.

"How'd she look?" Jonathan was asking. "Still as beautiful?"

"Yes to both questions, old buddy. This is a real stand-up chick, and I'm nutty about her."

"Easy to understand. Did you happen to mention your old buddy?"

"Oh, yes."

"Well?"

"She said she was dying to meet you," I lied.

"Spare me the olive oil. Did she mention any girlfriends?"

"Jonathan, you've got to be kidding. From what I understand you already have a few."

The obvious flattery reached him. His fame—or infamy—with hookers was just another kind of publicity to Jonathan.

"I do get around, don't I?"

"So did that guy on the Coast, and he now has one ball," I cautioned. "The husband used the other one for target practice."

"Joey, why must you always preach? Don't you believe in fun? I remember when you seemed to, and you don't appear to have suffered from it."

I tried to slow down and quiet down the situation. He knew that when I got cool, it meant that the business was hot. After a moment or so I had him paying rapt attention.

"In the first place," I said in a matter-of-fact way, "whatever you do is known. You are talked about from coast to coast, truth plus lies. And that goes for your . . . shall we say adventures in funland." Perhaps I should not have reopened the topic, but I completed my train of thought. "You always told me, pal, that

146

no broad would ever put a ring in your nose, or lead you around by the hickey."

"What in the hell is wrong," Jonathan roared, "with dating a few broads?"

"Nothing, you silly bastard . . . except when they're all in the same night, the same room, the same *bed*!"

Then I had to laugh at myself. "At least, let me know about it next time. I think I'll join your side. It sounds great."

Recovering his poise, Johnny observed, "Those hypocritical bigmouths—at least I'm single."

"What bugs them is this, Johnny. When you're so high on the flagpole and still going up, some jealous S.O.B. must try to chop you down, any way he can. And when he does, it'll be no holds barred."

"When that happens," he shrugged, "there'll be time enough to think."

I said softly, "No, there won't."

At this moment we were just two guys talking straight and trying to help each other in a variety of everyday problems. Usually in our society, business creeps into every conversational crack, and there is no room for sincerity. You can't even trust a dinner invitation from your Aunt Tillie. She probably wants to float a small loan or to discuss how to divide with thirteen grandchildren her estate which consists of a twenty-dollar due bill from Klein's, a 1923 Essex, and, oh, yes, in the safe (just so "It shouldn't get stolen") one hundred thousand shares of Kaiser-Frazer stock. Plus four hundred Dewey buttons, in case he decides to run again. (I wish he would, Aunt Tillie, he'd probably make a great president.)

"It's a goddam lonely thing," Jonathan was saying, "being near the ceiling. What do I do, stay in the house like a hermit? How long can you curl up to a book? I've got to be with somebody."

I shrugged. Now that I had brought up the subject, he had to get a few thoughts out of his system.

"I wish it were in me to have a home, punch a clock, have someone I give a damn about bring me the pipe and slippers and a good chilled martini. That's what it's all about. It's great for good down-to-earth people. It's the *right* way. I'm the wrong one, I know. But that's me. I like to be alone, really alone. And I actually think better alone."

I nodded. He was so right—for himself, and for me, too. My own Gina, whom I loved more than life, was the damnedest nag who ever existed. I was a veritable Jiggs married to Maggie, except that Gina didn't carry a rolling pin.

Even goodies like furs and diamonds didn't close her mouth. "But I don't want material things, I just want you, Joey," she'd say—and I'd upchuck. Because she'd deliver the line walking out the door with four or five C notes in her kick, on the way to Saks Fifth Avenue or Bergdorf's.

De Gaulle could run Paris on what I laid on Gina by accident. What she stole out of my pockets could send a Care package to every kid in Sicily.

There was only one person who was a bigger crook than Gina

—her mother. Mama could take your shoes off while you were running. She was a professional Italian crier who, when she was down to her last five hundred dollars, would threaten to go on relief or take a job in a bag factory rather than live on the charity of a rich son-in-law. It was intolerable for Mama to live without an air conditioner, a fine TV set, and other bare necessities. *And* five dollars for bingo. Mama was one of the bingo addicts of our time. Naturally, she got anything she wanted from me, but it was when I laid that bingo money on her that she'd throw her arms around me and exclaim, "There's nobody like my blue-eyes."

Truly she missed her calling. She'd have been a great fund raiser or charity collector. The only catch was, she'd have been a six-to-five shot to swing with the money she collected. Beneath the two-bit larceny was a woman, and what a woman!

Mama raised her kids when her husband passed away. When times were tough and going on relief was no idle threat, she walked through the snow and brought back the meat on a sled. She lives for those daughters and the son Billy, and for all her swinging never looked at or thought of another man.

I was madly in love with her myself, and she cared for me in a special way. She patched up many an argument—of course reserving the right to star in a few herself. The guy who came up with the title *I Remember Mama* probably had her figured—I don't know—I never saw the show.

And that is what Jonathan was getting at, while I dreamed a little. That was the way to live, for God-fearing people, with the wife, children, home, and all that went with it. Jonathan simply didn't fit the mold, but at least he was honest enough with himself to admit this and dedicate himself totally to another way to live, which, since he was conditioned to it, was completely honest.

The code. That was always the bottom line for Jonathan J. Bingham. And if he made up his mind, in loyalty to his code, to destroy you, he was a rattlesnake with a coat of arms. Somehow you would get a warning before he struck.

Women, always women. My thoughts roamed further. "How do you feel about Bea?" I asked him.

He stretched his long arms sideways, clasped them behind his head, and thought a moment.

I was referring, of course, to Beatrice Halleck, world-famous model, a beauty *très chic* and socially acceptable from a former marriage to a famously untalented motion picture director-producer. Bea's best friend Eve, even more beautiful, was married to a famous, rich, senile comedian known as the great ad lib artist.

If only this artist could have ad-libbed a hard-on, it would have been different. He had that reputation, too. Chili once told me that having sex with this noodle was like getting warm farina poured into her little jewel box.

I had warm memories of Eve. *She* was a woman!

I first dated Eve when she was a beautiful starlet living in Hollywood at the Studio Club, a haven for single girls in show business. Strictly on the up-and-up and efficiently supervised, the Studio Club was one of the true credits to *the* town, which has so often been maligned, but which was—and is—the show business world's heartbeat. Even the egocentrics who gave you many a pain in the *tushie* were always ready for one of our worthy causes. They'd share a buck with you and never let on it was the "case ace." Bless their phony, lovable hearts.

Eve was on hand when I was playing Las Vegas at the Strip's biggest hotel, as the headliner in my own show. A group of famous names came in to catch me, knowing that I had not only the best show in town but also a "piece" of the hotel.

Among the names was the fabulous Mr. Ad Lib, friend and contemporary of that other has-been, Jackie Benson. In addition to the show people, there was a mixture of "Hard Guys," the Baptist belt, and of course the tourists, who are the world's greatest belly laughters. They were all with me all the way.

I could do no wrong that evening. Everything worked, and clicked big. The big laugh jokes ballooned to "boffs," solid applause followed every number, and at the end of the act there was an ovation.

What spoiled my happiness, however, was that all during the act Mr. Ad Lib was talking. He had become obnoxious to his own party. It killed me to introduce him, but being show biz, I gave him the obligatory flowery introduction—whereupon he popped up and took his bows, but without looking at me once in the appropriate thank-you style. At that moment sheer hate crept into my heart.

He sat down, this fugitive from Forest Lawn, next to Eve. She looked great, but what a bad roll to the dice it had been for her. The *momser* had sold her the bill of goods that he was so fond of her that he was going to leave her his money. She booked the bet. At seventy-odd years, this hairpin was still walking around—with a beautiful wife and a couple of stale books he wrote.

Later that night, while returning to the hotel, I decided to walk through the casino, just to hear how they were rolling. When you're a pro gambler or know the business, you can walk into a room and tell by sound which way the money is going. You can't pick the exact roll of the dice, but you can hear which way it's leaning.

Sitting at the blackjack table was Eve. Even at 4:00 A.M. she looked like the prize filly.

I sat down beside her and waved a finger at the pit boss.

"Carl, give me a two-hundred-dollar marker. I'm going over the hump."

Carl okayed the move with the dealer, almost imperceptibly, and eight twenty-five-dollar black chips went into my square.

I looked at Eve. "Where's Moustache?"

"Where else? Sleeping."

"If I go over the hump, you're going with me," I said, shielding my mouth with a drink just set down by the bar girl.

"Oh, really?" she said with a look that could have gone either way.

I had made my play. This was not the time to show weakness.

"That's correct, little doll. If I make that hump, the three passes, you're with me." And I gave her the look, the little sexy stare, back in spades.

"In that case, I may as well bet the same way for luck." And she pushed two five-dollar chips into her betting square.

I got my two cards. They totaled fourteen. I looked into her hand. She had twelve. The dealer had a five showing.

He was a friend of mine, and I kidded him, looking for an edge. "Just tell me if you've got ten under there."

"I'd tell you but I'd lose my job, Joey." There was an infinitesimal pause. The dealer is permitted to chat with the players and even to discuss the rules and techniques of play, to "educate" newcomers. "But if I know you," he added after the pause, "I don't think you'll tap against a five show card. . . ."

That's all I needed. I placed my chips on top of the cards and stood pat. Eve, when I nudged her with my knee, did the same. I didn't want her to draw off a face card or a ten.

With everyone pat, the dealer turned over. Fifteen—he had to draw. He dealt a king—bust. I had started over the hump, two more to go.

When I let the four hundred ride, the other players dropped out to watch.

Cards dealt: Eve fifteen, me twenty, dealer nine up.

I stood.

Eve had to play the averages and draw against the nine. She drew an eight and went bust.

The dealer turned over. Nineteen—it would have beaten Eve, all right, but it wasn't enough to beat me. I now had two to the hump, on top and ready to fall over.

I pushed in the eight hundred, looked at both of them. "This is for all the marbles."

The dealer flipped out the cards, head-on between himself and me. I had fourteen, he had a queen up.

I was tempted to stand and avoid busting out, but that queen looked mighty powerful, and so did the one next to me. I fingered the cards and paused. The dealer pushed his deck hand toward me.

"Hit, Joey?"

I looked into his eyes for maybe one ten-thousandth of a second, and saw what I had to see. I had to take a whack at it now—I knew he had twenty.

I brushed the cards toward me. "Hit."

He snapped it over. It was the most beautiful seven of hearts you ever saw, and I had won the works. Since he didn't have blackjack in the first place, he had either twenty, under sixteen —a compulsory draw—or seventeen—compulsory stand. I held my breath for the last.

He kicked over. Two queens—top of the world!

I called the pit boss over. "Cash me in and take off my marker."

He counted the chips. "Sixteen hundred, Joey, less the two hundred. You've got fourteen hundred coming."

"Thanks, Carl. Take off four blacks for the golden arm, and put the balance in the cage."

He raked off a hundred dollars and put it in the dealer's shirt pocket.

I got up from the table and Eve followed.

"Would you like a drink at the bar?" I asked her.

"Not necessarily," she answered, and now there was no doubt which way it had gone.

"Great, little doll, follow me."

We walked out the door past the pool and in a few short jumps were at my suite. Eve held my hand tightly.

I hope Mr. Ad Lib had lovely dreams that night, because I was about to even the score. Bless his little moustache!

Jonathan unclasped his long arms from behind his head. "What's there in dreamland, Joey? You're smiling like a hyena. Let me in on it."

I sipped my drink, set it down on the marble table, and came back to earth. "When I asked you about Bea, it reminded me of the Vegas bit with Eve and Irving Impotent."

He laughed heartily. "Bill Blackman still talks about that every time we have a drink. Why did I have to miss that night? Or the topper, when she walked in at eight A.M.

" 'Where have you been?' he says.

" 'Out having an orgy, where else?' And he thought that was so funny."

155

"Well, Jonathan, he always was noted for the sense of humor."

I lifted the martini, took a long swig, which seemed extra delicious, and probed: "All right, for the third time, what about Bea?"

"She's great. No question about it, I get along with her beautifully, prize package that I am. But it's not for me, and I've told her so. She just says she's in love with me and always will be and will wait as long as it takes for me to want to marry her. Or even if that time never comes."

"What's your answer to that?"

"I've got someone coming over here in an hour, haven't I?"

"Jonathan, that's not an answer."

"I told Bea to go out and find a guy who'll treat her like a million bucks, and marry him. In the set where she swings, she can have the million figuratively and literally."

"That kind of advice is like trying to kick ants away from honey."

"What else do I do? Pitch her out a window?"

"No," I answered, "but cut her loose, don't talk to her and don't see her anymore if you have any compassion for her at all. You're a professional louse, and a bit of sadist in you enjoys seeing her writhe this way."

He said nothing.

"Either that or you're just hooked on her action in the kip and don't want to lose it."

"She's special in that department, all right. She's been around the block almost as often as I have, and a couple of jades like us appreciate the far-out bits."

"I don't knock it, Johnny, but eventually you'll run out of all bits except screwing in a Ferris wheel."

"Sounds great!" He was warning me off the sermon and getting a laugh at the same time. I could take a hint.

"Do what you want, pal. I've got my own troubles with Gina."

"She still giving you hell?" The change of subject was to his liking.

"Yup."

"Good Lord, doesn't she appreciate that your efforts and work-hours will benefit her?

"She can't understand that at all. And when you and I have a meeting, she gets bugged every time."

"I must be candid," he said. "Gina is most aggravating when she answers the phone. I'm not accustomed to her type of patronizing. Maybe she'd like to see you playing nightclubs again . . . or selling cars."

I couldn't let that one go by. "That day will never come— with or without Gina or anyone else, including you."

"Don't get touchy, Joey. Here, I'll make us both another shooter."

He strode to the bar and mixed the martinis. I walked over, sat on a bar stool, and helped with the extra touch of rinsing the glasses with Pernod. He poured, and we picked up the glasses. He was conscious of my still-hot temper and made the effort to be charming.

"Salute, champ."

"Salute," I smiled.

"Joey, why don't you have Gina meet you at Le Valois one evening and take her to dinner at '21.' We'll have a couple of your Jean Pierre specials, and I'll be special, too. Then you two can go on from there. Would it help?"

I considered. "Yeah, let's give it a whirl." Maybe it would help. "All our arguments," I confirmed, "are really on you. How do you figure her? Can't she see you and I are scheming against a mutual enemy and trying to pull off a few miracles? That's what a win is in this business—a miracle."

"Joey, they are all alike. They are *all* alike. Those lines about not wanting material things. Those lines about love. Just stop giving it to them — both ways — and they walk away so fast it scares you."

"I hate to admit it, Johnny, but there's some truth to that."

"I'm speaking from experience, Joey. Our business demands time for openers. As the stakes mount, it demands more sacrifices. Fun, home life . . . I'll give you my catalogue of jewelry, furs, cars, apartments, town houses . . ."

I was intent on this comparison of Jonathan's situation with mine. He continued.

"For your miracle, you've got to get up earlier, work harder, go home later than the other guy. If you can scheme him down, you have to make damn sure he doesn't get up and start throwing lucky punches. He'll put all he has into it, and they'll be knockout punches. To use your own favorite expression, you can make book on it."

"Are you trying to tell me that the final sacrifice has to come?"

"Joey, I'm just saying I couldn't make it work both ways. Maybe you have a secret, or an angle I didn't have, but I guarantee that you can't let your brain be abused at home and then go out and beat the jungle."

"I know you're right," I said, "but I do want the home and the jungle both. As for abuse, you *can* make book that I let nothing destroy me."

"Now you're talking, and let's get back to business. What's with Mario?"

I glanced at my watch. Mario was probably staring at his phone right now.

"Johnny, on the line. He's a toadstool. I don't like him, and I don't trust him. But as long as you remain strong, I can make the toadstool taste good. Therefore, if you are in control and back me, we'll crown Mario, put Chester in our camp, and get rid of this returning son. In fact, they'll bury him for you."

"Better and better. How do you want to do it?"

"You're set to give him the job in the morning, Johnny?"

"Right, I'll call him at exactly ten A.M."

"Okay, you get on the extension in the other room and listen to me kingmake Percy President."

Jonathan moved, and I was operating again. I grabbed the

phone and dialed like a monarch. It buzzed twice, then came Mario's whimpering salutation. He sounded just about like a Tijuana streetwalker greeting a two-dollar John.

"Mario, this is Joey. Listen carefully. I have only a second, because J.J.B. is in the room shaving. You're getting a call tomorrow at ten A.M. The job is yours."

"God, that's wonderful."

"I've convinced J.J.B. that you're a Bingham man and he can count on you all the way."

"He can, Joey, he can." Would the toadstool never stop?

"All right, get a good night's sleep. In the morning hear it for the first time and play it straight, got it? Good luck."

"Right, Joey, and thanks for all you've done."

"Okay, pal." I felt a touch of my own sadism coming on. "And, Mario . . ."

"Yes."

"Get a haircut."

"I *will*."

I hung up, and Jonathan walked out of the other room with a malicious smile.

"And *awaaaaay* we go," I greeted him with a Jackie Gleason take.

"Do you think he got the message?"

"Johnny, he was receiving. If you'd have wanted a garlic and oil salad, he'd have brought it over in his pushcart."

"Make us a quick shooter and we'll go over the rest of the stuff."

THE CANNIBALS

I looked at my watch: already a couple of hours past my deadline. This was what Gina could never understand, the cameraderie of buddies and business, especially in the case of Jonathan J. Bingham. If I had to go to Canal Street at 4:00 A.M. she'd understand, but with the president of BCA it meant trouble.

Try to figure the cutie-pies. They do the same thing all day with their girlfriends shopping on Fifth Avenue or sitting under the hair dryer. You don't exist, until that ticker hits six o'clock—then every minute is holy war against all men, husbands' buddies in particular. Oh well, they are delicious, and they do smell pretty. Bless their little white panties.

While philosophizing, I was pouring the two martinis. Jonathan and I clinked and this time no toast was necessary. Things were falling into place.

Grudgingly, I admitted, "Now that it's over, I'm pleased with the Mario move."

"I think so. In the first place, he should be adequate in the job that Vincent Fisk taught him so well. In the second place, he can make only a deal that I approve, and then the deal will be executed by his staff. He's in line."

"And if he gets out of line," I growled, "I'll just pull him up short."

"How do you figure Chester and Mario?"

In a way, Jonathan had lived a sheltered life. I had to spell out these little things for him, Machiavelli that he was. "Easy, oh, great white father, because they're like hookers. In Vegas

I knew fifty like them who sat at a bar waiting for a John to buy them a drink so they could 'negotiate' a package. Each hooker was in her own little business. Each John who walked in was a prospective customer for each hooker. So consider the competition. They would knock, lie, cheat, and frame each other in order to make the score. Nothing mattered but the score. They hated each other, but here's the point. These fifty hookers sat on the same stools in the same bar every night. Are you ready? If the chips were down, they'd even do a 'double trick' for you."

Machiavelli was fascinated by the analogy. I think he would have traded in his presidency of BCA for the chance to do business with the Syndicate if he only knew how. As always, what he didn't know, he made it his business to find out. However, heel that he was, he'd always be a gentleman heel and remain hypnotized by my familiarity with such matters.

"Mario and Chester are professional whores." I continued. "Each one has told me privately how much he hates the other. Which now works to our advantage. Mario, who is Percy President all the way, will now try to make his own team. He will tell Chester about his huge new position and try to enlist Chester on that team. He'll have to expose Chester to part of the story, and that's when I have him nailed to the cross. Meanwhile Chester, greedy little whore that he is, won't be satisfied to play it straight with Mario, and he'll find a way to cut into me. When he does, I'll own him, too, and scare the shit out of Mario for disloyalty. *Cabeshe?*"

162

THE CANNIBALS

Jonathan tossed his hands into the air. "I give up! Joey, in eight million years I couldn't think that one through. You are something."

"The grass always looks greener on the other side of the fence, Johnny, but you couldn't live there for one day. You know, I've only admired two guys in my whole life — one who taught me all I know, and one who's making it work. You. But one genius at a time is enough. You keep your cool and play it straight down the line, and I'll deliver the empire you've always wanted to create."

"I know you will." He was dead serious.

At that particular moment and at every other such moment that had gone before, I not only believed in this guy, but had total faith. I knew him better than anyone else and could clock his emotions as well as his thoughts. He knew that I had this total faith, and I knew that he knew. I didn't have to care whether he was right or wrong, as long as we had a wall behind us, two guns, and the strength to fire them. My only concern was the strength — whether he could last.

On this score, my two closest friends in TV (excluding J.J.B., of course) had made it a point to take me to dinner and say their pieces.

Irving Mendelson was a top producer, a stand-up guy, and a guy who cared about Joey Bertell. His wife Junie was a writer-actress from Philadelphia's Main Line, a raving beauty and a veritable female Joey Bertell. June and Irving were a strong combo.

Junie was a special case with me. Somewhere in every man's life is a girl *friend*. This is a relationship based on love and respect, not the pagan sex drive. To begin with, Junie loved her own man, Irving. And why not—he knocked his brains out for her. After Irving, she loved me.

Once over a lunch drink, when Junie loaned me two hundred dollars for my rent, I kidded that if I could ever fill one of Irving's shoes, I'd make a play for her. She got a kick out of that line coming from her "brother." Yes, she loved me, but Irving had it all — plus an extra helping of class. He lived by his word. Just being the Mendelsons' buddy gave me a feeling of security.

Well, one night the Mendelsons took me to dinner at our special hangout, Danny's Hide-a-way on East Forty-fifth Street, and Irving got me into a corner.

"Do you know what you're doing?"

I knew what he meant.

"Joey, you're putting all your eggs in one basket. With the talent you've got, why don't you spread it around?"

"Irv, I know what you're trying to say, but I only know how to go one way. With these cards, that's the way I play the hand."

Irving wouldn't have touched on this delicate matter unless he had it thought out. "Right," he said, "you're doing what you think is best. But let me bring the long-range into focus for a moment. They'll shoot at him through you. You could be destroyed on the way."

I made no attempt to interrupt.

"The other angle is this. If he does make it big and decides to dump you, you'll have no place to go. I don't say he will, but I also don't say he won't. This guy is made out of ice; if he gives even two thoughts to you, then you hold a famous first."

Thus Irving Mendelson, back at Danny's Hide-a-way. As I relived the scene, in Jonathan's apartment, I felt a slight chill, and it wasn't my umpteenth martini. The guy *was* made of ice.

I took a mental inventory of his qualities. Hadn't I seen him do some decent things? No, Irving was wrong in this instance. Dump someone else, maybe, but not me. He wouldn't dump Joey. That was it. J.J.B. was acquitted, and court was adjourned.

"The boys seem pleased about the *Mr. Trouble* show," said the acquitted suspect, taking me back to business.

Weeks before, J.J.B. had tipped me that the Chairman, in his never-ceasing search for respectability, wanted shows on the air created by world-famous novelists, the caliber of O'Hara, Capote, Weidman, Marquand, Winant, or Caldwell. I latched onto that instantly: Terry Winant was an earthy writer who could be of tremendous value to TV. He had been approached by everyone, but turned down all offers. My production company, which was handling my own variety show, was a cinch to bring in a package if it included Winant, and he happened to be a dear friend.

After one meeting with me and then a threesome with Jonathan, Terry agreed to create a new rough-and-tough series.

The lead would be patterned after the late John Garfield, and the shooting would be in New York. No writer could touch Terry Winant on the New York scene. He was the dean.

I knew better, however, than to rave about *Mr. Trouble*. "Yeah, the script is coming along good."

"Well, goddamit, somebody better show it to me. I don't want it to miss, and I haven't seen it." He was mentally in the office now.

"You'll have a copy tonight." I picked up the phone and dialed. It rang for a few seconds.

"Hello."

"Jimmy, Joey. Go to the office and get a copy of the blue script and put it in a plain manila envelope with that fellow's name on it," I ordered, lapsing unnecessarily into bugged-phone jargon. "Drop it off with his doorman, got it?"

"Right."

I hung up. "You'll have it in an hour."

"Good. I'll read it tonight and talk to you in the morning."

I rose, and Jonathan walked to the door with me. He slapped me once on the back and said, in a quiet but warm tone, "Keep it up, buddy, you're doing great."

"Thanks. G'night, pal." We shook hands, and I stepped into the elevator.

Downstairs, out through the lobby into the night, I grabbed a cab and headed home to Gina.

Chapter 6

The world looked great next morning as I headed for my office.

Gina had given me a warm exit line — a happy kiss on the cheek and a lovable "S' long, darling." This was just after I had pushed five C notes on her to go out and amuse herself for the afternoon. It was all right, I loved to see what she could possibly think of to buy.

In Gina's closet, I swear, were a hundred and fifty pairs of shoes *plus* fifty pairs of boots — nothing under a hundred and twenty-five dollars. The dresses filled two closets of their own. Bags lined other shelves, and there were coats for every social occasion and any time of the day. Name the fur coat or stole that Gina didn't have, and I'll run the mile against Kelso— and win. No, there was one exception. Pasted on her mirror was my business card, and on it was written: "I.O.U. one full-length Russian sable coat. I love you. Joey."

Forget the jewel box, which she rearranged every evening. There was everything there that you could think of: watches, rings, brooches, pins, and charms for her bracelets that were made for her by my personal jeweler.

This bum, and I use the word kindly, I had a problem with.

Murray Glasser was a helluva guy. He was a man's man, one of my best friends, and I always got a great deal from him. However, when it came to the bottom line, Murray never forgot that he had been Gina's friend first.

In the early days, when she worked with her sisters in clubs throughout the country, Murray had been her road manager. So now, between these two plotters, it was something else. Gina would go to his booth at the Jewelry Trades Building, and a couple of days later he'd lay the soft con on me.

Well, another check would go to 36 West 47th Street, for whatever sum the little wopalina wanted. What I respected was that he knew I was hip to the procedure, and on the other hand, when I couldn't come up with the money, I always had a tab. This kind of game I didn't mind playing — in fact, it was fun.

It wasn't long from Gina's good-bye to Vera's hello as I walked into my office. She had on a new dress, but was all efficiency, hand outstretched with messages. I grabbed them like a relay racer and headed into the sanctum.

Sitting behind the black teakwood, I then buzzed once for her to follow me in. Twice would have meant on the double and stand at strict attention.

I had arranged with the phone company to rig up a Hollywood premiere light outside my office. When I was on the private line, it lit up, and to my entire staff that meant J.J.B. — God help the poor S.O.B. who walked in on that light.

THE CANNIBALS

The atmosphere in my office crackled with intrigue, but there were some humorous moments. Sometimes these featured my trusted comptroller, Edward Krauthoffer. This diminutive bookworm type had gray hair that stuck out like Harpo Marx, only Krautie was the butt of jokes, not the perpetrator of them.

He was a good guy, the forty-year-old bachelor with the mother in the Bronx, but his naïveté was just too tempting for ribbers. Strictly speaking, this naïveté came from being, fortunately or unfortunately, a "wonderful guy," just one of the millions walking the streets, the salt of the earth.

He had joined the team like this. A company of mine had gone into bankruptcy, and Krautie was working with the CPA who was auditing my books. Things were hectic — with bill collectors at the door, I wasn't seeing visitors or taking phone calls.

But finally this guy buttonholed me — it turned out that he'd been waiting for three days — and gave me a routine about how much he'd always wanted to get into the television business, and how much he had to offer, with his knowledge of the books, and so forth.

He then cracked, "Until you really get started with a new company, I'll work for free," which was the naïveté of him, but at that moment most useful. I hired him on the spot. And from that day on, Krautie was always there when it counted, and his loyalty was absolute.

I frequently joined the Krautie ribbers myself. Once, we were holding a staff meeting on scripts. There must have been about twenty people there, each with a progress report. Suddenly the door burst open and Krautie burst through, all excitement.

"The check came in, J.B.," he yelled. "A messenger just delivered it."

"How much?" I asked.

"Eighty-five thousand."

"Does the notation show what they charged it off to?"

"Program development."

I was relieved. Once you get somebody to put his money down, he's got one foot in the grave. Krautie's happy excitement buzzed through the room. But I fixed him with the cold stare.

"Was that door closed when you came in here?"

The room hushed right down.

"Yes."

"Don't you ever dare walk into my office again without knocking. You get your ass right outside, close the door, and knock."

As he left obediently, I winked around the room and put a finger to my lips.

Three knocks.

"Who is it?" I yelled.

"Edward Krauthoffer!"

"Go away, I'm very busy." I almost broke up, but I got it out.

Well, the screams could have been heard over on Madison

Avenue. All the rest of my guys came in to see what the hell was going on, and we did the bit over again about three times. It seemed to get funnier each time.

Krautie could take these ribs. And he was a buffoon only on the outside. He was razor-sharp inside. Actually, he had everyone's respect.

This was not a morning for ribbing Krautie or anyone else, however. Vera was now standing by with her notebook while I looked through the messages and mail.

"What the hell does Leonard Morris want with me?"

"He said something about a play he's producing."

"Keep it for a record." I handed her the message. "I'll run into him when I'm with Mr. Bingham. I'll look under J.J.B.'s ass and ask him what he wants, the pimp sonovabitch."

"There was a personal call from a man who said he was Louis from New Orleans and that he was a close friend of Paddy from L.A. He wanted to pick something up and said you'd know. He'll call back at one o'clock."

I buzzed Jimmy. As he came in, I waved Vera out.

"Take two hundred and put it in an envelope. A fellow by the name of Louie will call at one. Have Vera give you the call. Make a meet and hand him the envelope. Don't get involved with him for drinks and bullshit. Louis's got the 'shorts,' and a friend of mine wants me to give him the two hundred for WAM."

Jimmy had picked up all my jargon and knew that WAM was short for walking-around money.

"He's a right guy, but I don't want you to be a party to spending the two C's — and believe me, he'll spend it in an afternoon. Send Vera in."

Jimmy walked out, and Vera came back.

"Get me Silvern, Chili, and Chester Plan. Chester first. Send Terry Winant in if he's free — never mind, he's coming now."

Vera walked out, and Terry Winant strode through the door.

He was a vigorous man in his late forties — balding head, big smile, and bigger reputation. Talking him into television was now a huge feather in the cap of Joey Bertell.

He had done it not just because we were dear friends. It was a new challenge, I'd had J.J.B. give Terry his personal word to back the project to the hilt, and last and most important was "Yankee bean soup." That was Winantese for moola, coin, chips, loot, gold, or whatever different people call money.

Terry never used profanity except to put across a rare point. It had been that way at lunch one day when he told me, "Joey, only Yankee bean soup is important. Sleep eight hours, play eight hours, work six hours, and the other two devote to dreaming. But *while* you're doing it all, be sure you keep making the Yankee bean soup. Fuck everything else."

He was now in my sanctum. "Hi, chief, what's up?"

"I gave the script to J.J.B. last night, and we'll know soon."

Terry reflected a moment. "I say he won't like it. I further say we'll then be able to get rid of our *très chic* producer, that study in pure mediocrity. Joey, I can't stomach the conceited ass."

172

I winced. "I sure as hell hope you're wrong. We're doing every goddam thing this network wants us to do. Virgil Esty is working hand in hand with us, Jack Klaver is their choice of line producer, and you're writing according to plan. What else can we do?"

"You're the expert," he said, "but it isn't the show we talked about anymore, and I can't work with that fraud Klaver. You deal with him, I won't."

Vera entered with a note on red paper, which was her way of telling me "urgent" in case I wasn't in the mood to answer her regular intercom. I could tell by her face that we were about to be evicted even before I looked at her note.

I must have turned white, because Terry said, "Tell me quick, if I have to be sick with you."

I took a deep breath and reported, "We're to report at J.J.B.'s office in thirty minutes, and without Klaver." I just let it lie there.

Terry took it in high spirits. "Great, that means he's through!"

"Maybe we are, too. . . ."

"Not a chance, or we wouldn't be called over. This may be a big break."

"Terry, give me a puff on whatever you're smoking."

"Relax, my boy." He was positively exultant. "This will work out for us, you'll see."

I picked up the private line and dialed. He answered.

"Hi, what's up, pal?" I opened.

"I can't speak now." He hung up.

Immediately I could have kicked myself from New York to Texas for a jackass blunder. First of all, I should have read it like Terry. Second, I should have realized that Jonathan wanted a conference, not a private conversation. Subconsciously I knew we were safe, but pressures had been undermining my sense of security a bit.

Vera buzzed. "Chester Plan on two."

"Forget it. Invent something, I've got to duck the call."

I looked at Terry. "I need Chester Plan at this moment like I need malaria."

Another buzz. "Virgil Esty on one."

I snapped up the phone. "Hi."

"Did you get your invitation?"

"Yeah." I spoke solemnly, no emotion.

"How do you read it?"

"Hell, how do *you* read it?"

"We're not going there for tea. Has he read the script?"

"Last night."

"Have you heard whether he likes it or not?"

I let him wait a bit, then, "No, but he just hung up on me, if that'll help your ulcers."

Virgil's silence was deafening.

"Are you still there?"

"Wait a minute," he said, "I'm busy cutting my wrists."

The laugh wouldn't come. I knew only too well that in this kind of business J.J.B. was one cold sonovabitch. He'd slash his own mother's wrists in order to win, and take pleasure doing it.

Terry broke the ice. "I hate to mention it, but you have three cigarettes going." He had caught me lighting one between my lips, and sure enough, two others were in the ashtray.

The private phone rang. I tore it off the hook.

"Hi, honey." It was Gina.

"I'm busy, I'm up to my ass in problems, and I'm in trouble. I'll talk to you later. 'Bye."

Again I kicked myself. This was precisely how to get into trouble with the little woman. How could I expect Gina to understand this kind of pressure? How could she comprehend that the roof might blow at any moment? Women need love steadily. Here I was with more love in me than any ten men, but no time to express it. How could I win this way?

Terry rose. "I'm going to make myself presentable. I'll pick you up in five minutes and we can go together."

I substituted a pencil for the cigarette in my mouth and nodded. Then I buzzed Vera. "Send Jimmy in."

He closed the door behind him. "I heard."

"The trouble with the goddam joint," I snapped, "is that everyone has great big ears, a great big mouth, and doesn't know when to keep it shut."

I was now pacing aimlessly, like a horse in the paddock, but probably more of a nervous wreck than any horse waiting to go onto the track.

"Make me a drink," I said to Jimmy tersely.

"*Now?*"

I wheeled around and glared at him. Without a word, the message reached him.

When I returned a few minutes later, there was a vodka and tonic, with a half lime, on my desk. I gulped most of it, finally smiled, and said to Jimmy, "You're my favorite bartender."

He gave me the smile back, boyish, but wise enough to accept my tacit apology. Strange how you tend to let off steam at a person you like. In the case of love . . . I just wished Gina would take it that way, too.

Vera was buzzing again. "Morton Silvern on one."

I pressed the lighted button. "Hi, counselor."

"Joey," he said firmly, "we're in good shape, and I'm ready to sit down with your man."

"Great, Morton. Now, aside from the deal and the money, we have agreed that it would be his ship to run, correct? Because without that, Morton, we have twelve for a point."

"Joey, it is agreed. This is a company that's in trouble. A ship, as you put it. We want him to right it, not sink it, and he'll have a free hand as captain."

"Fine. What's your best time then?"

"Tonight at six-thirty. Would he still like to have it at his club?"

"Morton," I said coolly, "he'll be at his club at six-thirty with or without chains."

Morton was stingy with real laughs, but he gave a chuckle at that. "Okay, cardinal, I'll see you there."

"Right."

I replaced the receiver with a sense of accomplishment, winked at Jimmy Craig, and commented, "All is not black."

176

"I never thought it was." Again the boyish grin counterbalancing the mature words.

The intercom buzzed. Terry walked in ready to attend D Day. I took the last call from Vera. "Miss Monroe on two."

"Hello, little doll, how's by you?"

"C'mon over, sexy, I want your hot little body."

It broke the tension perfectly. "I'm still dangling in mid-air, strung up by the goodies. Wait until I'm winning, and maybe I'll accept those invitations yet."

"Does it hurt good?"

"Only when I laugh. Seriously, what's up, I'm going to a funeral."

"I did what you asked me to do with Chester."

"Did Mighty Mouse take hold of the bit?"

"And how! He wanted to know if I knew you, if you liked him . . . an hour ago he called again to say you just got someone a big job at BCA and for me to tell my girlfriend that he's a great guy and also that he thinks you're one of the most brilliant and creative men in TV."

"He's right on all counts."

"I see you've taken your confidence pills today." She teased a little. "I thought things were chaotic."

"They are, my little slot machine, I simply couldn't lower myself to false modesty." I winked at Winant, who by now was on to my *kibitzes*.

"Will I see you later?" she asked.

"I don't know. I have the big one at six-thirty, and I'm playing it by ear. It could be a big win."

"Okay, doll. Call me later if you can, 'cause I have some juicy morsels about your friend, and his friends, including a rundown on the gayboy from the coast. He's divorcing his husband Bruce for a clarinet player."

That rated a final smile. "You little vampire, you're enjoying this more than I am. Save it for later, okay?"

"All right, Joey doll, but throw me a kiss through the phone."

I glanced embarrassedly at Terry. "Drop dead, doll. 'Bye." And to Terry, "Let's go." Now it was all business.

We walked out of the office. My staff was trying to be inconspicuous, with about as much success as the proverbial crepe hangers at the wake.

As we got downstairs, George had the car in front of the building, stood erect in his uniform, and held the rear door open. Terry and I jumped in. George closed the door, took the wheel, and headed us crosstown.

We were off to see the wizard, not kindly Frank Morgan in the emerald city of Oz, but the living legend at the levers of power in the land of make-believe called BCA.

For ten blocks nobody broke the ice. Finally Terry spoke. "I wish my mother were here. She would have enjoyed this."

The line hit my funny bone. Terry hooked his mother into all his books, and now he was doing the same thing in real life. Maybe that was his secret. His words had been read by millions, in many languages, and the rapier wit was somehow appreciated by the average Joe. Maybe life's truisms had to be illustrated by personal observations and even experiences. I had always wanted to write a novel, and made a mental note to think about one on Chili.

By a strange thought association, I grabbed the car phone.

"Mobile operator," came the voice.

"This is W3687 New York."

"Go ahead, W3687."

"I want to call Trafalgar 7-7689."

I waited for the connection. Yes, in this moment of crisis I was reaching out for Gina. In my heart, I knew the crisis would pass, but there could be damage, and there could be delay. And I was thinking of Gina.

One ring. Two rings. Three rings.

"Hello."

"*Hi*, honey, whatcha doing?"

"Oh, now the busy man wants to talk. You must be in real trouble."

The epitome of tact . . . I forced myself to be patient.

"I just thought you might want to have lunch today. I could meet you at '21' around one o'clock."

"It's too late now, I couldn't be ready in time. I wouldn't walk in there looking like a hag."

"C'mon, you look better in blue jeans than most of those types with the painted-up faces do in their best imports. C'mon, little star, make the lunch."

"What time, one o'clock?"

"Right."

Gina shifted ground smoothly. "Well, then, please be on time. I don't want to be alone."

"Depend on it. By the way, Terry Winant is with me here in the car and says hello."

"Tell him for me. Where are you going?"

"His nibs called a meeting. I'm in the dark, but it could be rough, and I'm sweating it out."

"Don't worry. Someday we'll meet him in the desert, and I'll have the water."

"You're all heart, Gina."

"Maybe not, but remember, when you see Paul Power, *no* regards."

"Okay, good-bye." I hung up with a faint smile.

"Something amusing?" asked Terry. "Let me in on it—I enjoy an invigorating laugh while I bleed."

Between Gina and Terry, I just might get good-mooded onto a funny farm. . . .

George pulled up. We jumped out of the car before he could open the door and walked into the BCA building. I gave mechanical hellos to several people in the lobby, en route to the elevator.

Inside, Tom, the operator, had some dialogue for me.

"Hi, Joey, I saw you on TV last night in an old movie."

Another mechanical smile.

"Boy, was that old. And it was a real stiff. Why'd you ever do that turkey?"

I looked around at the people in the elevator and decided to stay polite. "I did it just so you'd be able to knock my brains out in front of everybody. I wouldn't want you ever to get bored."

It got the laugh, but the silly S.O.B. was oblivious to the situation.

"You were really young in that movie. When was that, about ten or fifteen years ago?"

Still polite, but icy: "I don't know, Lincoln had just been shot and he was dying in my arms. So y'see, I was busy at the time. Tom, let's change the subject and talk about nuclear fission. I'm sure it's on all our minds at this very moment." I did a skull look at Terry Winant and did a take. He caught it.

"My mother liked you in that movie," he came in. "She told me that when she was a little girl, you were one of her favorites."

I played it straight. "Who, me or Lincoln?"

Terry pretended to scratch his bald head. "Come to think of it, it was Lincoln. I don't think she did like you."

This got the biggest laugh, even from Tom. But I made a note that if the meeting went bad, I'd wait for his down elevator and boot him in the rump for his lousy manners.

At that moment we arrived at the twenty-fifth floor and immediately stepped into an atmosphere subtly different from the production department suite, or even my Cardinal offices. This had the smell of overwhelmingly big-time business.

The main waiting room had marble tables from Italy, not from a New York City shop. The leather chairs were Herman Miller, but you knew they were one of a kind. As a touch, various magazines were cased in matching leather covers. The obligatory photographs of stars had ultra-expensive frames.

That was the feel . . . money. And of course it was hospital clean and tidy, a J.J.B. mania.

Appropriate to the decor was a receptionist who must have been chosen for her smile, voice, and clothes. Strictly the *Vogue* or *Harper's* chic.

"Hello, Mr. Bertell," she said. "Won't you have a seat?"

"Thank you."

"Mr. Bingham will be with you in a moment. He's waiting for all his people to arrive."

Terry found his voice. "My mother should definitely have been *here*."

"I wish she were," I twisted it, "instead of me!"

Seated now, I watched Omar walk by to J.J.B.'s office, accompanied by Arthur Stuart, J.J.B.'s assistant and another presidential aspirant. (How many losers there were going to be in that race.)

The elevator door opened, and now joining the parade were Chester and Virgil, snowlike faces betraying their fear. Virgil was concerned about actual survival.

I was now about to attend one of J.J.B.'s legendary performances. He had, of course, told me of such meetings himself; in fact, he got a vicarious thrill out of going into detail. I would soak up every word and study the significant points later, as if I were at a Harvard seminar being taught by Niccolo Machiavelli.

The side of Jonathan that I understated to the world, his

ruthless, hateful side, I would now have the opportunity to see and judge for myself.

Meanwhile, I toted up the percentage points going for me. Jonathan would never dare humiliate me unless he had warned me in advance. I knew J.J.B. . . . and he knew Joey Bertell. Over the years he had seen that I could stand for a lot and turn my cheek. Indeed, I'd take an actual beating, if I had it coming, and never yell cop or even whimper. But I would never let anyone humiliate me in public—or private. Not Pete Pressure.

My self-reassurances were cut short when J.J.B.'s secretary came down the hallway.

"Mr. Bertell, would you and Mr. Winant come in now, please?"

As we walked back up the hallway with her, I gave her arm a little pinch. "How formal can you get, little doll? Come on, now, any tips?"

Just a quick whisper. "Stop worrying, you're safe."

At that precise moment I damned myself for having gotten tense. I had aces back to back in five-card stud, and instead of playing like my old buddy Nick the Greek, I'd been playing like Dickie the Dunce. There was too much at stake for me to be bluffed.

It was one of those rare slips that even a genius can make, and after all I was entitled to one, especially since I never claimed to be a genius. "I'm no genius," I had often lectured my staff at my own high-powered meetings, "I don't want to be a genius, and I probably can't even win an award for brilliance, but I'll tell you this—no sonovabitch can outmaneuver me the best day he ever lived." I had just my share of brains. My specialty was using the muscle, when I had the hole card.

In good shape now, I landed in J.J.B.'s outer office, with Terry. Sitting there like schoolboys awaiting the class bell were Omar Cone, head of production for both coasts; Arthur Stuart; Mario Colucci, our new and "respected" vice-president in charge of business affairs; Alan Werner, from Chester's department; and, bringing up the rear and now standing next to Terry and me, Chester Plan himself, Omar's vice president for programming, East Coast; and Virgil Esty, the program developer.

Omar spoke first. "Hi, Joey, I'd just as soon leave, if it's all right with you."

He was a nice guy. He had about a day and a half left before his head was chopped off. I was going to miss him.

What irony! Here was my dear friend, the Pulitzer Prize winning novelist-playwright whom the networks couldn't get. Here was Omar, the chief who couldn't be saved from doom. Here was his second in command, Chester, already ordered fired by Omar's successor, himself doomed and unsavable unless little Joey decided to intercede. And neither Omar *nor* Chester could contribute one helpful suggestion to the meeting about Terry Winant's script.

Mamma mia! In a rare flash of lightning I caught onto J.J.B.'s move. This was a meeting that he was going to *use for* the firing of Omar and the reorganization of the team. Friend or no friend, this guy really didn't have a soul. Maybe Irving Mendelson was right.

Yes, I repeated my own verdict on J.J.B., Irving was right, but not with me. Joey Bertell was the one exception. I was with Jonathan J. Bingham, and *let* the rest of the world drop dead. Top of the world!

The buzzer was like a roar to the schoolboys. "Would you go in, please," said the chic secretary.

It was the Bataan death march. It was somber, it was mysterious. But after my slip into the fear bowl, I was now well out. I had drawn the last card to an inside straight. The little receptionist had been right. I was safe—safer than she was.

As we filed into the papal chambers, J.J.B. was still on his private line—by design. In fact, if I knew this Marquis de Sade, there was nobody on the other end. He was setting the play.

I glanced at him, but he gave no sign of recognition. As he had it figured, all eyes were on *me*. Oh, man, would this be a dilly.

Even with the preparation of J.J.B.'s waiting room, his private office was amazing. It was really huge, really magnificent. And a third of it was dominated by his desk. It was a giant free-form with him at the focus of the major curve. Not even a paper clip marred its surface. Only the phone and the internetwork intercom. On that, each executive had a number that could be direct-dialed, bypassing secretaries and switchboards. And with the exception of J.J.B. himself, men who got calls on that became afflicted with slight cases of palsy.

At the left, J.J.B.'s "good" side, were three television sets. With a knee switch, he controlled all channels of the major competition. He could also cut off the audio on any two stations, and follow the third on a master monitor.

Just beyond was another complex of monitors that showed what his own channel had on the air, plus rehearsals of shows and taping sessions at all the BCA studios. J. Edgar never had a better spy system.

Only I knew that he had an identical installation in his apartment. J.J.B. missed no bet.

Still farther down was a complete living room: couch, coffee tables, informal chairs, and the works. "Only when I'm impressing someone or electrocuting someone does a man ever sit in that living room." I had the move clocked: We would now sit in that living room.

I stood around with the sheep, waiting to be led.

J.J.B. now hung up and said with a seething smile, "Suppose we all get comfortable over *here*." Sure enough, he walked to the living room end and casually touched a chair. I would have given a thousand to see the fireworks if anyone other than Jonathan J. Bingham had sat down in that chair.

I walked over to the couch and sat down. It was apparent

this was curtain time. Terry Winant raced over. "I think I'll sit by you. It's safer. . . ."

And now the curtain was actually rising. In the background was soft music. But it was so soft that if I had not known J.J.B., I would not have heard it. He had it on twenty-four hours a day.

J.J.B. fooled me right off: He walked over to a switch panel and turned the music off. Then he buzzed the secretary and instructed her to take messages on *all* calls. Strolling back to *the* chair, he sat, cupped his hands, thought for a moment, and then started to speak in a genteel whisper that obliged every-one to strain to catch the words.

"Well, let's talk a little. . . ."

I took a puff on a cigarette and crossed my legs. Terry fold-ed his arms across his chest. The rest of the staff appeared paralyzed.

"Terry, I read your script last night." He looked straight at Winant.

"I'm sure you disliked it as much as I did," Terry said hur-riedly, attempting a kind of humor that could go either way.

Jonathan was relentless. "I couldn't believe what I was read-ing. It didn't have the slightest evidence of being close to the show I wanted."

Nobody else was going to say a word at this point. I was going to be absolutely dumb unless spoken to—and I hope Terry's mother would have approved.

"I have always felt that there was a place in television for a hard-hitting newspaperman series based in New York, and I've gone into this with my staff over and over again. Yet in the two scripts you've written, the newspaperman is in a small town helping someone with a mortgage. That's not the show I asked for."

J.J.B. looked down at his shoes a moment, then continued.

"Terry Winant, I have always been your fan. I've read all of your books. They prove that if anyone can capture New York, it's you."

"Thank you."

"When Joey got us together over lunch, I was extremely happy to announce to the Chairman that you had made the decision to enter television and do so in our shop."

He looked at his people with a contemptuous expression, then turned to Terry and continued. "Somewhere we've gotten off the track. I can only assume that my people don't understand what I want, so I certainly can't expect you to know. But I want this show!

"Once again, I want a newspaperman, of Considine stature, and I want it patterned like a John Garfield role, and I want it shot in New York, which means Terry Winant. Would you like to take a crack at that show?"

Terry was excited. "Yes, I would, and I'll have in your office today ten pages of treatment of just exactly what you want, and I assure you that you'll like it."

"I know I will."

"One thing you can do for Joey and me."

I held my breath. What the hell was Terry coming up with now?

"Name it," said J.J.B.

"Get rid of our producer Klaver, I can't stand him. He's wasted my time, he's arrogant, but most of all he's untalented. Do this for my mother."

J.J.B. smiled at the last line, looked at his staff. "Where did he come from? Who hired him?"

There were mixed mumblings of amoebas trying to protect each other. J.J.B. did not wait for an answer.

"Get rid of him right after this meeting. Then press some buttons and get this thing rolling. We're already late for the pilot. But we're going to make it—and this is firm!"

They nodded sheepishly.

J.J.B. stuck the knife in deeper. "Terry, I'm sorry for all this. I apologize for my staff. If you need anything on this project, you or Joey call me personally."

Terry jumped from his chair and shook Jonathan's hand warmly. "Jonathan, it *will* be done."

Then he looked at me and said, "Let's go to work."

Everyone stood up and the meeting was over.

However, there came a terse sequel. "I'd like my people to stay a minute."

Terry Winant and Joey Bertell almost ran out of the office, with fleeting looks back at Jonathan's stricken staff. At the elevator I pressed a finger to my lips, but we pumped each other's hand silently. We went down, out the lobby, and into the car.

"Drop me at '21,' " I told George, "take Mr. Winant where-ever he wants to go, then come back and wait." George nodded.

I turned to Terry. "Well, are you happy?"

"I thank you, my wife thanks you, and my children thank you."

"What happened to your mother?"

"She never thanks anybody."

I didn't mind being topped by a talent, and was in a sunny mood when I hopped out at "21" and walked through the iron doors. As far as I was concerned, this was the best restaurant in the world, and the owners were friends when I was broke, rich, and in between. This was New York. Take "21" off Fifty-second Street and you have Elyria, Ohio.

"Hi, Joey," said Chuck at the door.

A right guy. I shook his hand, whisked off my coat, and handed it to a new coat-check boy. He handed me a claim check.

"Don't be insulting," I kidded.

Chuck, Gary, and Shel walked over to him and administered the bloodbath in loud terms. "Put Mr. Bertell's coat on his hook!"

The boy was frightened, and I decided to give him a five on the way out instead of the usual ace. He'd take the education more kindly then.

The byplay took me back years to Hollywood's Brown Derby, where I had just been given a charge account.

THE CANNIBALS

When I paid that tab, I marked a ten-dollar tip for the waiter and signed. He came running after me a few minutes later and asked me to print my name. I accommodated him—but also erased a zero and moved the decimal point one place to the left, making it a one-dollar tip.

"Next time I come in, if you remember me, you've got nine dollars coming." Which taught him all he needed to know about Mr. Bertell.

Meanwhile I was walking to the downstairs stand-up bar, the only place for VIP's to eat, and heading to my table. It was reserved every day, and used likewise. My phone was plugged into its jack, my Gina was on the phone, and I could tell from her expression that the call was for me.

"Jonathan J. Bingham on six," she announced sarcastically as I sat down. She had the sense to cover the phone, but the sarcasm irritated me. I grabbed the call.

"Hello."

"Hiya, baby," came the answer. "Was it beautiful?"

"Yeah." I paused briefly. "It was just great."

"You didn't think it would go any other way, did you?"

I had a problem carrying on in front of Gina, but what the hell. "Seriously, Johnny, you were beautiful. It was something to watch."

"Was Winant impressed?"

"I think he called his mother."

"Okay, pal, that's one down and two to go. How are you coming on the other projects?"

"Fine. I'm in daily contact with Bryan, since those two will be done out there, and for your info, I'm making no waves."

"Good. Let Bryan handle everything. That's his town."

I couldn't reply as I wanted, with Gina there, but I'd grab J.J.B. later. To end it, I said, "Six-thirty tonight, Silvern."

"Will do." The phone clicked.

Gina's opening line was, "Do you shower with him, too? Can't I have one lousy lunch without hearing his name?"

I shrugged. Gina looked around the room. I tried again.

"Come on, honey, let's enjoy a drink. I'm celebrating."

"You're always celebrating something. What did you do today, buy Chicago?"

Even though she was in a mood, I could look at her warmly. She was beautiful. She had the point made in two spots: inside and outside. Gina symbolized everything I ever wanted, and here I was wondering if I could hold onto her.

That meant nothing less than applying myself fully. But if I did that, everything else I'd ever dreamed of might go down the drain.

I was centered, like any man. Maybe I was a little more masochistic than most, because I seemed to get a little security out of the browbeatings. It proved that she cared about me.

I never got outsmarted in a deal where I had even an underdog's forty-sixty chance, but women could do it every time. You can muff it even if you know their combination.

Theoretically, to hold these special creatures is a cinch. For openers, love. I mean make them feel needed. Convince them

192

that you need their help, that you're depending on them, and the broads will go through walls to watch you rob banks.

Second, let your hair down once or twice. Put your head in that fabulous nook between the shoulder, elbow and breast, and you'll get the security to keep you from taking the gas pipe.

In return, they'll give you love, stability, and children. But be sure to return that love continually. If they have a man who belongs to them that way, they don't worry about the food, clothing, and shelter bit. Their man will work it out. But miss for a few weeks and their security goes. You might blow your chickadee forever.

Joey the philosopher looked adoringly at Gina and wondered why he was such a stupid bastard when it was so easy. When would the fatal moment of neglect come? With all that was going on, I felt like a prisoner under death sentence, living on one pardon after another.

I was running fast so the fatal moment wouldn't catch up. I'd make it and quit. The famous last words that Joey the philosopher shared with millions of other guys . . .

Gina turned back toward me and must have read my thoughts. She thawed. It was that warm heart, if you could wait her out.

"I ordered you a drink," she said. "Relax and try to unwind, or you'll end up in the cemetery a little earlier."

Those were the moments that proved to me that she cared. That's why I loved her.

"With all this crap going on," I said, "thank God my variety

193

show is taped. How could I rehearse the songs and dance routines?"

"After you have your drink, I'll tell you something about your show."

"Tell me now, you know I'm the curious type."

The vodka martini arrived anyway, so I clinked it against Gina's whiskey sour. "Here's to you, doll baby. *Now* what about my show?"

She looked into my eyes, and I began to see that she wanted to help about something.

"Jerry Kent took off on your again last night. Did anyone else tell you yet?"

"No, they all leave it to you," I quipped, a bit snappishly.

"Joey, I'm as pro as you are. Do you think I like to see my husband rapped? Do you think I don't want everyone to respect you and continue to realize you're a big talent?"

I went ice. Jerry Kent, an extremely minor talent, had a late night show for one of the major networks. He was important—that I give him—but he was a louse. A drunken louse, to boot —but he was coast to coast, and being a panel show with name guests entertaining, he commanded a big audience.

When he'd blasted me once before, I'd had Irving call his brown-nose announcer and warn him. I also collared Dan Talbot of UBC about Kent's remarks on the air and warned him as my friend to stop the lush, or I would. Dan promised to take care of it. But everything seemed to have bounced.

Well, no living S.O.B. was going to make a jocko out of me.

THE CANNIBALS

Say things, hit me, indict me, kill me, but don't make a jocko out of me. I held a three-second trial for Jerry Kent, and the verdict was in. He had to learn respect—not the way he was accustomed to, but my way. He had to get slapped.

I had already dropped him a note and sent emissaries. He just couldn't be stupid enough to forget Joey Bertell from the old days! Or he thought he was backed. Or . . . I was being used as a stalking horse.

UBC had found out I was moving in, on Jonathan's behalf. Irving had tipped me that their "Louis Lush" network president had assigned a public relations man to destroy Jonathan. Well, to get J.J.B., he'd have to go through me, in the end destroy me, too.

Dan Talbot was too great a guy to suspect. The Old Man of UBC, or son George, would never stoop to it. But Louis Lush would. And it was also possible, my contact at QMA pointed out, that Louis Lush had the Old Man's son George in his hip pocket.

Okay, Jerry Kent, you bucked the wrong guy.

Gina was reading my mind again. "God only knows what's going on in back of those evil eyes. Do you realize that hate is leaking out?"

I smiled and took her hand. "When you love, honey, love—and when you hate, give it all you've got."

Gina knew that the word "hate" was just a code identification for the enemy. And the enemy had to be eaten alive before they gathered, put on their tribal war dance, caught you, and made you their soup course for dinner. When you deal with cannibals, you have to turn cannibal yourself.

"You're not going to let him get away with it, are you?" Gina asked.

"What do you think?" I was really interested in her opinion.

"Joey, you have to stop him so you don't become a topical laugh in a comic's monologue."

Gina knew show biz. She grew up in it. Her judgments of it were never wrong. I began to rethink the problem, from a cold calculation standpoint.

"You're right." From me, this was an ovation.

"You wouldn't do anything really bad, would you?"

I never lied to Gina . . . but on certain occasions I had to shade the truth.

I looked at her with adoration and said, "A man must do what he must do."

Gina squeezed my hand and dropped the subject. She knew me and my emotions like a book. She was a great girl.

The food arrived. Gina had ordered just what I was now in the mood for.

"How's Mama and the family?" I asked, thus letting her know how happy I was with her.

"Jimmy and Doris are playing a club date on Saturday. Mama's going to bingo with Ann. How's Billy doing with you?"

"Great. I put him in production, and he has charge of agency relations, too. He had two strikes on him, being my brother-in-law, but everybody likes him, and I'm proud of the job he's doing."

"Joey, he wants to take an apartment in New York to be close to work. But he shouldn't do that. He'll get in with all the wrong people."

"Honey, why don't all of you just leave the kid alone? If you keep your skirts off him, he can make it—and big. He's a helluva guy and deserves a chance. I'm harder on him than anyone else, but it's for a purpose. He's ready to spread his wings. Let him fly a little."

"I shouldn't have expected any help from you. You won't be happy until he goes out and robs a few trains."

"I'd be very proud of that," I kidded, "but only if he doesn't get caught."

Gina never knew I was kidding on the square. In this instance, there had been a midnight call from Mama and some hysterical sisters. Their seventeen-year-old Billy had been pinched robbing the door off a car in a parking lot in Jersey.

It turned out to be the best thing that could have happened. Instead of bailing him out, I let him stay in the can overnight, using some excuse about unavailability of the right bondsman.

Next morning I went over to the small-town jail and sat down with the captain, who recognized me immediately.

"What's his gig?" I asked.

"Theft."

I held my breath. "Not armed?"

"No."

"Has he got a story?"

"He sure has," the captain laughed. "His buddy's car needed a door, and they had no money. Billy wouldn't take part in the actual robbery, but agreed to be a lookout."

"You mean he played 'chickie'?"

"That's right. He was to whistle if the owners or the police appeared."

"And . . ."

"He got nervous and couldn't whistle."

"Christ, now I've heard them all."

"Well, strangely enough, it seems to be true."

"How about the others?"

"They got away."

"Did he give them up?"

"No. He said he wouldn't say anything until you got here, and he wouldn't even tell us *your* name."

I was proud, and hid a smile. "That's a redeeming quality, in a way."

The captain puffed on his pipe. "He seems like a good kid."

I took that as a cue.

"Captain, let me lay it on the line with you. I'll bail him out, make restitution to the parties concerned, and give you my word that you'll never see him in here again. I can assure you Billy listens to me. Don't hurt him, he's a good kid. Just give me that break."

"That I'll do, but he's booked, you know."

"Don't worry, I got him a fine lawyer, and we'll work it out. Captain, thanks a million!"

"All right, I guess the release is in order. I'll take you to him."

We walked into the back room, and there was Billy, behind a chicken wire cage, the picture of remorse.

I tried to bring him some warmth. "Hi, knuckles."

"Hi, pal," he answered, but with eyes down.

Billy stayed depressed throughout the whole release procedure and remained silent in the car as I drove him back toward New York City. Now was my time.

"Okay pal, let me do some talking. Don't interrupt, just listen. This whole thing we forget now. I've made the family promise not to lecture also, so it's a closed issue. Besides, you don't know how to rob, so goddamit don't try. I'd even be embarrassed to tell my friends that you were behind chicken wire, not even real bars."

Billy laughed nervously.

"And the chickie story," I ended relentlessly, "takes the cake. Now give me your word: Never again, Willie Sutton, never again."

He finally looked into my face, stuck out his hand, and we shook in the car. Five years later that shake was still good, bless the little whistler. . . .

So that was my kidding on the square with Gina—who was now bringing me back to the present with a new subject.

"How're the shows coming?"

"Great, honey. Jonathan confirmed *Mr. Trouble* to Terry and me this morning. And we're a cinch with *The Karen Wallace Show* and also *The Barnabys of Bermuda*."

"That's great."

"I put Leroy Schultz on the Karen script, and Bryan Westgate put on two additional writers from the Coast. Not to mention Leroy's brothers, who will help him secretly. I'm sure we have a winner there."

Gina's frankness came into play. "*They're* great, but she stinks. She's a phony carbon copy of Trudy Small. Why in the world are you going with her?"

"Farley Fag likes her, that's why. As for Trudy, if I could deliver a huge star like that, it would be something else."

"But, Joey, it's your production. That no-talent can spoil a big chance." This time Gina was talking like a pro, I had to admit.

"Gina, I never lie to you. I have no choice. I can't figure out why, but Farley Fag can maneuver Jonathan around his panty girdle. I'm more frustrated than you."

"Really," she said knowingly, one eyebrow slightly raised.

"Yes, really," I replied, "and let's get off it because I'm not in a mood to argue."

"That's the only argument you run from, isn't it?"

Gina was good at baiting me, but we both had other things on our mind, so I took the backward step. "Where are you going from here, Wopalina?"

"With Jody, to look in the stores. She's meeting me here." (Pause) "Okay?"

"Of course." I got the hint. "You busted?"

Gina gave her disarming laugh. "Well, I never turn anything down."

I reached into my pocket, and she added a barb. "I know you'll be generous. You always are. . . ."

For that, I had to make her ask pretty please. "Have fun, sweetheart," and handed her a folded twenty.

Gina took it and gave it the quick eagle. "That'll be great—for cabs. How about an extra present for your wife, Joey, since you've had such a successful day?" Touché. Mama would have been proud of her.

"Do you love your blue-eyes?" I insisted, to save face.

"Hell, yes," she laughed.

The laughter was contagious. I broke up, ended by throwing two C's on the table, and pecked her on the cheek. "I've got to run. See you tonight, but it'll probably be late. I love you."

"Whatever you have in mind, be sure you protect yourself." I understood her cryptic remark, but did not acknowledge it.

"See you," I said, and walked to the door.

The new kid had my coat in his hand. "Have a nice day, Mr. Bertell."

"Thanks, buddy, you too." I whacked him with Mr. Lincoln and walked out. Nice kid. Sharp.

George was waiting, and I got into the car. "Drive to Chili's."

I grabbed the phone and gave the mobile operator Chili's number. This was the private number, so after three rings I guessed she wasn't home, but finally I heard the familiar "Hello."

"It's me, can I drop by?"

"Sweetie," she cooed, "of course."

"Are you free?"

"Yes, you bad little boy. Chester had to cancel his lesson. He got reamed out by your buddy, and he's in hysterics wondering whether you're mad at him."

"We're on the airwaves, little doll, be careful what you say. I'll be there in ten minutes."

"Yes, master." She hung up.

I turned my attention to George. After all these years he could tell when something was up. He had that guinea instinct, too.

"When you drop me, go to Jimmy Craig and pick up a thousand. Then reach out and find Bobby D. Put him on the first plane for Vegas and tell him that shit-heel is playing there. He'll know what to do."

"Joey, let me go," George pleaded.

"No, goddamit, and don't bug me. If he yells, this could leak back. Besides, you're too emotional where I'm concerned. I don't want the sonovabitch really hurt. I want him slapped and scared, that's all."

"Joey, I give you my word on my mother, I wouldn't hurt him. Please let me take it."

"I'll call the shots," I blew, "not you. If you dare, if you frigging *dare* to do anything on your own, I'll knock your stupid head off your shoulders. *Cabeshe*?"

George knew I was gone. "*Cabeshe*," he said soothingly. "Okay."

"But I *don't* like it, and you *could* have let me handle it safely. How I'd have liked just one piece of the bastard. . . ."

I ended the subject with a little love slap on George's cap. "If it doesn't work, we'll handle it together, like the old times. But for now tell Bobby D. no rough stuff in the face, get it? Whale him in the gut, give him a little kick in the balls, but don't touch the face. That's important. And if there's any yell, he's to contact the guy we spoke about, and it'll be handled. Now, have you got it straight?"

"Straight, pal."

"Thanks, George."

We were now at Chili's, and I gave George his final instructions. "Make it clear to Bobby D. Also, he calls me tomorrow night at the pay phone number, the time we agreed on."

I felt better as I jumped out and headed for the Park Avenue lobby.

Chili's doorman called upstairs, got the okay, and I was up rapping on her door without delay.

"Get your cute little keister *in* here," she greeted me. "I want to show you this layout!"

She pulled me by the hand, and there was the bedroom, with the white bearskin rug and the heart-shaped bed surrounded by mirrors. It really stopped me, and then while I took my eyes off her, she surprised me with a shove, toppled me off balance onto the bed, and jumped right on top of me.

With a passionate welcome, she pressed her lips to mine. Overdue guest that I was, I returned Chili's kiss. A few uninhibited minutes went by. On the bed and all, I commenced warming up. With great restraint I pushed her body aside.

"You little bunny, I'm not a robot. I've got a few other things to do."

Reluctantly she let me up. "I'll get you yet," she teased.

I made for the phone and dialed Vera. "What's up? Who called?"

"Everyone. Mario, Chester, assorted agents you can call later. Also Leonard Morris about some show and said he'll take a few points on it. Krautie received another check and is in seventh heaven. And Joel Fryman wants to talk to you."

"Switch me to him."

Vera buzzed Joel and he picked up.

"Tell me, Joey, I'm dying."

"We're in."

"Congratulations!"

I knew Joel really meant it. I said, "We go right to pilot, and we'll be on the air. Call around town and line up the key guys. Steal 'em, pay 'em more, I don't care how, but get only the best cameramen, gaffers, props, wardrobe, and whole team in the business. Let's go."

"Right, Joey."

"Take hold, Joel, it's your ball game."

"I will, buddy." He hung up.

"Sounds like great news, baby doll," said Chili.

I turned to her and smiled. "Stick with me, Chili. We'll own the woild, and Brooklyn, too."

I picked up again and dialed Mario on his private line.

He answered promptly: "Mario Colucci."

"What the hell are you doing still in that old office, big shot?"

"Hey, *paisan*, how are you?"

The presumptuous ass had the temerity to address me as his *paisan*! If he was that drunk with power, I felt it my duty to give him a slightly cold shower.

Dropping my voice, I solemnly said, "How about that meeting for those poor souls? Aren't you glad you're not in the production department?"

"You said it." He waited a second. "Omar was told he was out."

I gave him the ice. "Is this supposed to be a shock to you or me? Besides, Omar will stay on in another capacity."

He giggled, the jackass. "You really know, don't you?"

It had been simple deduction. Omar started as a slide rule boy and worked closely, at one time, with the Dentist. Thus, J.J.B. would consider it a wise move to be somewhat benevolent to dear Omar, and would make big points explaining to that gray-haired Hitler that he couldn't just cast Omar aside, Johnny baby was shrewd.

"Good luck on the job, Mario. I offer you my formal congratulations."

"Thanks a lot, Joey." At that second I believe he was being sincere. He continued, "I talked to Chester, and he desperately wants to speak with you."

"I know, he's called several times. What do you think, since you're now a team player?"

"I think he can be trusted."

"Mario baby, he can never be trusted . . . but he can be *valuable*. For our own protection, we've got to have balance against Bryan and his returning prodigal son who, with his tired *Studio 6* show, is replacing Omar. He's a sure bet to bring in his own number two man."

Chili beckoned and whispered, "Do you want a nice drink?" I nodded and threw her a kiss.

Back to Mario. "You heard the firm pilot deal. I'll have Harold, my attorney, request pre-production money. Expedite it for me."

"Right."

"And say something nice downstairs to your replacement, so I don't have headaches there. I just don't have the time for social amenities."

"Right."

"Okay, Mario baby. Charge forward boldly." I clicked the phone down and picked up my drink.

"We're on our way, Chili. Here's to the combine."

"To you, Joey baby, and whatever you want."

I was relaxed with Chili, but the atmosphere scarcely desexed me. In this little pad, with the colored lights on dimmers that could tone down to candlepower, a charwoman would have looked like Theda Bara. Chili, in the elastic toreadors that clung to her *tushie* like kid gloves, was really something else.

"Joey, how do you think I'd look as a redhead?"

"Now how the hell would I know?"

"Here, I'll show you." She ran to a walk-in closet, opened folding doors that exposed every kind of outfit imaginable, and brought down a wig box. She took out a full soft red hair-do. "Well, say something."

"Great," I said. "Really, really great."

She came back, put her arms around me, and we rubbed noses. "Always tell me what you like, and I'll change, just for you."

I kissed Chili baby tentatively, more in charge this time and experimenting to see if she'd really grown up. With my arms around her now, I met her halfway, as she stood on tiptoes. Her lips were warm and moist, fresh and delicious. The tip of her tongue made contact. Her firm young body pressed tighter and rubbed encouragingly. Yes, oh, yes, really, really yes, Chili had grown up. . . . I had gotten the message from my little barometer, which had come to life and was seeking more room.

Chili broke away teasingly. "That's only a sample. Now make your phone calls, big man, and when you finally decide

207

to 'place your bet,' as you put it, I'll show you that I really do love you. And then, Joey baby, you'll be hooked, and I don't mean on junk, I mean on Chili."

She stuck out the tip of her tongue, this time in kid fashion, and went to refill the drinks.

Perhaps if Bryan had been there, she might have converted him, at least to a half-queen. More than that not even Chili could accomplish.

I was dialing the private line. He answered.

"It's me, pal. Can you talk?"

"Well, well, well. How are you? Yes, I can talk."

He was in one of those moods. Thank the Lord for small favors.

"Are you prepared for the Silvern meeting?"

He replied with our favorite expression. "Don't be insulting."

"Pardon me, oh, great white father. What else is new?"

"I've reserved the private dining room for drinks and the meeting."

"Good. Let me set the stage, recap everything, and then I'll throw the ball to you two. After about fifteen or twenty minutes I'll take a powder, so you two giants can discuss super business. How does that fit?"

"Fine. Have you talked to Chester yet?"

"I wanted to be sure to check in with you first."

"You can be sure he got the message this morning. I reamed them out as they have never been reamed out before."

"Tell me all," I prodded.

208

"I told them all that they wouldn't be around if they didn't follow through on exactly what I said, when I said it."

"Sounds clear enough."

"It better be," he answered. "As for your boy Virgil Esty, I don't care what you say, he has absolutely nothing on the ball. You've never been wrong yet, but you have a loser in this guy and I'll bet on it. He doesn't have it."

"Just give him a chance, Johnny. He plays ball and deserves it."

"All right, all right, but get him going. I can tell he's fumbling the ball."

That was J.J.B. Only results counted. In this he was best—make no mistake about it, the best—and that's what kept everybody shook up. Studying him, I could learn in seconds what other men took years to absorb.

"I'll see Chester now. He stays on, right?"

"Right, Joey, and make it crystal clear that the new guy despises him, in fact his first official act was to fire him, only I then told him Chester could not be fired. By the way, what is that nickname you gave the new guy? It's been eluding me all morning."

"Calvin Clothes."

He laughed. "That fits him to a T. All right, let's get him and get him out. I think the Chairman's losing his marbles."

"I know how to get him out in quick order."

"How?"

"Simple. Promise the job to Chester."

209

"Beautiful. Do it."

"Will do. By the way, how'd you like to be Calvin Clothes with Chester cutting your neck?"

"Not for twenty million dollars. I wouldn't put it past the sonovabitch to use an actual knife."

I laughed. "I might just arrange it."

"Next, how are we doing on UBC?"

That was a question I hadn't wanted. All my meetings and my pipelines had convinced me that it wasn't possible at this time. UBC generally took three years to fire someone of stature. Usually they booted him upstairs first. There was no room at the top in this instance, however, because of the family situation.

It was important to keep Jonathan high, yet not lie to him. UBC was his goal—and he would make it, to be sure, if he could wait it out. He had to realize that the Old Man and son George at UBC had heart and class, something unknown to the Chairman and the Dentist.

"Buddy, the reaction from the line was fantastic," I encouraged him, "but the timing's wrong. They have a warm feeling for the drunk and aren't ready to cut him loose. Be patient and that'll work, too."

"Fine, but keep looking into it!" Jonathan was emphatic.

"Will do. Anything else?"

"Not at the moment. Where are you?"

"Having a bowl of Chili." I winked at the little doll.

"You've got your nerve . . . while I slave here . . . shall I come over?"

"Don't be insulting!"

He hung up.

I had to laugh. Johnny still had a sense of humor.

"What's up?" Chili asked, seeing my smile.

"He hung up when I didn't invite him over."

"Was he kidding?" she asked, setting down the fresh drinks.

"Let's light a candle that he was," I teased. "All rightie, and now we'll make Chester Plan's day. Wanta listen?"

She nodded. I dialed his private and heard the shrill voice.

I answered somberly. "Chester, Joey."

"*Hi!*" I thought he'd crash through the phone. "I've tried to get you."

I cut him off quick. "I have to see you right away. Can you make it?" What a ridiculous question!

"Yes, yes. Anywhere you say."

"Richelieu Restaurant in ten minutes."

"It's so close—do you think it's wise?"

The impertinence. "I don't care how close it is. I'm proud to be seen with you." Chili swallowed an ice cube on that one. I had to get off the phone. "Ten minutes—Richelieu!" And I hung up just as Miss Utopia reached her limit.

"Good grief, Joey, he actually trembled. You get him more excited than I do."

"No, baby, he's all 'urine.' " She dug the bit and laughed.

Next thing I knew, she was snuggled up to me on the bed. Businesslike, yet coy, she said, "I have some reports for you." A devilish smile. "From my West Coast offices . . ."

"I'm waiting with bated breath." I sipped my martini. What

a doll. What a life. Who needed a TV series? On second thought, why not have it all?

"First, Omar Cone. He's supposed to be a square guy; there's no rundown on him." She was going right down the list I had given her. "Same with Virgil Esty."

I put in sincerely, "Glad to hear it."

"Leonard Morris is a weirdo who digs seeing girls make it together. In fact, the chick he goes steady with in New York is an out-and-out dyke. Some of the kids he's put her with see her on the outside."

The report was improving rapidly.

"Joe Ballantine swings. Bryan is a fag, and as I told you, he is now married to a clarinet player named John."

"How groovy."

This reminded me it was urgent to call Bryan. I snapped up the phone, called BCA, and had me put through to the Coast. He came on the wire.

"I was just about to call you again," he gushed. "How *arrre* you?"

"Just great, Bryan baby, how's by you?"

"I'm in seventh heaven," he gooed. (I made a bet he'd never get into first heaven.) "Your script on the Karen show arrived, and it was great. We're going to incorporate most of it into the one that was done out here by the other writers. We like their premise better. We'll let your friend Leroy Schultz do six or eight scripts on the show, but we're going with the other team as writers and story editors."

212

I seethed. "You're wrong, Bryan, the Schultz script is fifteen times funnier. It was written by better people—you know who helped on it?"

"I know, Joey, but even Karen likes the other one better."

Sonovabitch, he had me collared. With that no-talent douche bag as the star, he'd always have the veto. I fought to stay agreeable. "What else?"

I couldn't afford to tip this S.O.B. off. Hadn't Jonathan said to me, "Let Bryan run it, it's his town."

Bryan continued. "I have a surprise for you. I want your day to be complete."

Only if he had a stroke would it be complete. . . .

"In the other script we wrote a big part for 'the guy next door,' who's no love threat but it's a place to drop in and it opens up the way for comic relief."

"What's his character?"

"He's a way-out musician."

I dropped the phone, walked over to the wall, punched it, and goddam near broke my right hand. I looked at Chili and raised the fist again.

"I'll kill him, I swear it."

I was close to tears, in that dangerous frenzy that even a wise man runs from. You can get annihilated by a guy in an argument if he suddenly gets "crying mad."

Meanwhile, the phone was dangling, and Bryan's voice came "Hello . . . hello . . . hello."

With a physical effort I recovered, picked up the receiver, and said, "Can you hear me?"

"Yes, I can now. We must have been cut off."

"What's the name of the guy next door, and where did you find him?"

"John Feldman. He has a fantastic sense of humor."

"Has he done anything before?"

"No, but that's not important. He has talent."

My life, my show, and he tells me experience is not important! "How does Karen feel about it . . . as if I didn't know?"

"She's *wiiild* about him. I had them both over for dinner the other night. They hit it off at once. And, Joey," he confided, "we have to humor her because, frankly, she's furious that you own the production company."

"Who the hell created the show?" I screamed over the phone. "If she can write her name two different ways, I'll give her a medal. The nerve of that bitch."

"I'll handle everything," he hastened to placate me. "Just leave it to me."

I had to say something, I had to get it in. "Don't make him any kind of a musician—at least make him different. A clarinet player, maybe."

"That's what he is. It'll be divine, just wait and see, sweetie."

I gave up. This was more than I could take without being thoroughly drunk.

"Okay, Bryan baby, Johnny says it's all in your hands. How about my other show?"

"I'm progressing rapidly on that one, too."

How nice. The little faggot had really climbed in. I wasn't

using him, he was using me. And to top it off, he had Jonathan's backing. Suddenly I was getting out front, where I could be attacked, instead of guarding the number two position, where I was in control.

"Okay, Bryan baby, I'll see you."

"Are you coming out next week with Johnny?"

"No, I don't think so." He could bet his goddam ass and clarinet that I'd be there now. "I'll call you on the horn in a few days. So long." I slammed down the receiver.

I wheeled on Chili. "What about Chester?"

"Me in New York for love lessons, and on the Coast a little starlet about twenty-five years younger than him. Her name is Doris O'Brian."

"That I know. The silly ass told Bryan on the plane that he was going to divorce his wife for her. Can you imagine asking Bryan's advice?"

"Knowing Chester, I can imagine it. But I have the cutest thing of all."

"What?"

"They walk in the hills and he reads her poetry."

"Poetry?" I laughed. "He should go on tour, he'd make a fortune."

"He's madly in love with her. He's told me so, too."

"Yeah, while you gave him a lesson. Forget that kind of love. He's a twenty-four-carat sickee, believe me."

"Your appointment is now," she said, looking at her watch.

"He'll wait. Continue with your list."

"Mario. He's a hooker boy. By the way he's a lousy lay. All the girls grab at him, 'cause it's one, two, three. Then they have to make excuses because he loves to go to dinner."

"Anything kinky about him?"

"No. As I told you, he can barely make the scene as it is."

"That figured."

"Don't you want to know how the girls are paid?"

"That's easy. They pad their expenses accounts and pay off with the overage."

"Uh-uh," Chili teased.

My ears pricked up.

"BCA pays for screwing *directly*."

"How? And quickly!"

"Your guy, Farley Fag, has a guy in casting that recruits whores for all your big shots."

"The Chairman and the Dentist included?"

"Oh, yes, baby." She laid it in.

"How about Johnny?"

"He gets them by the dozen, in assorted packages."

I filed all this in my little mind.

"He's a real bad scene, and there's a big problem getting chicks to go with him. On the square, Joey, this guy is bad news."

I decided to pass that until I had lots of time. Somewhere here was a key to the lock, and I just had to find it.

"Back to casting. What's the payoff?"

"You're going to laugh, it's so easy."

"Fine, I need a few hysterical moments."

"They're paid as actresses on one-day checks. They sign the chit, pick up the hundred or whatever it is, and that's it."

"You mean they don't even have to report for work?"

"I've made at least three thousand as an actress for BCA, using different names, and I haven't the slightest idea where the studio is even located."

"Doll, you've made my day." I was back in gear again, especially with the knowledge that Farley Fag was the chief pimp. Bless his little clarinet. "And now, my appointment."

I kissed her on the cheek and shot out the door on my way to meet the poet.

I walked briskly down Madison Avenue, turned, and entered the Richelieu. It was after the rush traffic. I spotted Chester in back at a table in the almost empty room. He waved to me, and I started on my way back to the table, sizing him up as I approached.

Here was Chester Plan. Five feet seven and one-half inches of tapioca. Gray, kinky hair, blue eyes that stared back at you out of two sneaky slits. A gnarled body to match. And, pound for pound, the most dangerous opponent you would ever have to encounter.

Lying with Chester came easy. It's always easy when you're pathological and you actually believe what you're saying.

Chester's great value, to himself and any allies of the moment, was the bank account of contacts in the working press that he had carefully built up. That they despised him was irrelevant; he was their source of secret information.

He was a born press agent, with all the good and bad connotations of that term. He could select and demand precise favors, in return for the dirt that he shoveled out free, and at a given moment would practically specify the copy he wanted in the article. Without admitting any lack of real talent, Chester Plan never lusted to succeed; he only wanted to *survive*. I had made the decision to give him that chance.

He put his hand out. "Hi, Joey."

"I got tied up, Chester. Hope I didn't hold you up."

"Hell, no. Two appointments I could cancel. I didn't want to meet Leonard Morris, anyway."

"How is pimp number one?"

"Who knows? What the hell does our boy see in him?"

J.J.B. had suddenly become "his" boy also. I must remember that.

"Chester, no need for you and me to bullshit each other. Calvin Clothes can't fire you. I had J.J.B. tell him he can run the department any way he wants, and he can hire and fire, but you stay. For that, you are a Bingham man, and no screwing around."

"Are you kidding?"

"Chester, I never kid on anything as important as that."

"How the hell did you do it? He's always hated me. I cut his throat a few times. I figured to be the first one fired if he came back."

"You were," I said pointedly.

Chester was not a buffoon like Mario Colucci, but a guy who went right to the hammer and the bottom line. Thus, he had no need of Amy Vanderbilt's book of etiquette to answer me.

"What can I do to help *you*?"

I told him. "One—*Mr. Trouble* goes in New York—that you found out. Don't fight it—join! Two, be a booster for the two West Coast shows. They're going to go on without pilots. It's a new concept of J.J.B.'s: If the ideas are good, and the proper casting is made, pilots are just a waste of money."

"I've always said that," he echoed. He shifted his Toulouse-Lautrec body from side to side and finally spewed out the question that had been churning in his mind. "Is J.J.B. going to take over World-Bond? It's all over the street and in *Variety*."

And in Chili Monroe's de luxe bed, I felt like adding. "I'll know more tonight, Chester. We're going to a meeting with them. Now, if we do make that move, can we count on you to go along?"

"You sure as hell can."

"Then again," I mused out loud, "if we don't make that move, I know J.J.B., he'll parlay it into increased power right at BCA."

"Do you think the Chairman will ever retire?"

"My personal opinion is no—unless he can buy something like *The New York Times*, which he certainly can't. Now that he's an old man, he loves to sit in an ivory tower. Without some balcony to speak from, he might as well take a Brody."

"It sounds reasonable."

I now made my real move. "Chester, how'd you like to have Calvin Clothes' job?"

He laughed nervously.

"I mean it."

He became serious instantly. "You mean he's not coming back, after all?"

"He's coming back, after all . . . but we're going to get him out again as fast as possible. Do you read me?"

"Loud and clear."

"Don't help him one bit. Play the con with him, but don't help."

"You can depend on it." He paused for a moment, little slits blinking furiously, then got it out: "Does J.J.B. like me?"

"What's the difference—I do!"

I let him sink into that one until the sand was up to his knees. He couldn't look up to face my stare.

"Chester, understand something. Don't look to win popularity contests; do your job with him—that's all that counts. Nothing else. This guy is ice, but if I were you, that's the way I'd prefer it. I remind you of one thing. You're now on the team. We're together on this."

"Great."

"Did Mario mention our maneuver to you?"

Like any good courtroom cross-examiner, I knew the answer before I asked the question. To Chester's credit, he leveled: "Yes, he did. I never thought he'd get the job."

"Why?"

"It didn't figure. Nowhere did it figure. He's not that sharp."

"Is he loyal?"

"Not in my book." Again he leveled—I liked him for that. He came right out with it, no nonsense.

My opinion confirmed, I changed the subject.

"If you ever want a shoulder on anything personal, let me know," I said ambiguously.

"What do you mean?"

"I mean . . . you've got to be nuts to sit in a public airliner and discuss with Bryan Westgate the notion of leaving your wife for Doris O'Brian."

He looked up and frowned.

"That, and the pretty picture of Chester Plan reading a starlet's poetry, is now a public secret from coast to coast. First thing you know, your confidences will hit that scandal sheet out there. When that guy starts on you, you'll know it."

"That guy is a miserable sonovabitch."

"He can write, though. I've read his sheet a few times."

"Too bad someone doesn't shoot him."

"Someone probably will, one time he goes too far."

"I hope that time comes soon."

"Meanwhile, we have our own problems." I had slipped in the harpoon, given a half-twist, and removed it. Chester was eager to change the subject.

"How are you making out with Bryan, that bastard?"

"I'm staying even. No better, no worse."

"How the hell can—"

I raised my hand. "Please. Don't you ask me that same stupid question. Between Farley Fag and Leonard Morris, I have insomnia.

"At least Morris you can figure," I continued. "He's just a high-class procurer. He's also a high-class voyeur. He deserves one of my copyrighted nicknames. How about Wally Watch?"

"It fits. Do I have one?"

"Not a real one. J.J.B. and I have a private code on you, but let's make up one for the trade. I've got it—Sidney Shrewd."

"Great." Chester beamed. He was delighted to become a full member of the club.

He was now becoming intimate.

"Listen, you were at UBC, right?"

"What have you heard?"

"Nothing."

"Keep your ears open," I ordered. "That's what J.J.B. really wants."

"He'd be great for that company. They've been losing because they operate by committee. What they need is a leader."

Chester was saying the right things, but I felt his intimacy had gone far enough. Besides, my feet were reminding my brain that it was time to move along.

"Okay, Sidney Shrewd, I'll talk to you later. You're in great shape. By the way, here are my private numbers at the office and at home." I jotted him a note, snatched the check, signed it, and left.

Good meeting.

THE CANNIBALS

I had some time to kill before the six-thirty between Jonathan and Silvern. I decided to skip a trip back to the office and duck the inevitable phone calls. It was excitement that kept me on my feet, but sometimes now the pace was getting almost too great.

To relieve the tension, I slowed down on Sixth Avenue (which is what I still call the Avenue of the Americas). A lot of "in" shops are there, and I'd begun to miss some of the old New Yorky feeling.

By the time I reached Seventh Avenue, I was enjoying the window shopping. I was now across the street from a familiar building. It occurred to me that I had a music publishing office there.

For five years I hadn't been inside it. But it was standard procedure to maintain an office, it gave me a place for writers to work in, and of course I was always hoping they'd come up with a good tune for me.

I took out the old key ring and searched for the right one. I was in the mood to slum a little. Besides, this was a perfect place to shave. It was one of many medicine cabinets around town that I kept stocked with a razor, my own cologne, and hair lube.

Entering the building, I was taken aback by a rancid dining-car smell. I stepped into the elevator quickly and pressed my button.

As we reached my floor, I decided it wasn't a dining-car smell, but "pot." Somebody was enjoying himself. Ah, writers. Good luck Charlie!

223

I slipped in the old key, opened the door, and the pot—but about six tons of it—hit me in the kisser. This was a *convention* of Charlies.

On the floor (on my nice red rug) were four bodies—nude, writhing, and evidently competing madly to invent new ways. And I don't mean new ways to rhyme Moon with June.

"Hey, daddy-o," laughed Charlie number one in all his ecstasy, "you got the wrong office, baby."

"He's groovy," said the little Chinese chick.

"Hey, honey, join us," put in the darker one.

The other guy smiled with his eyes. His mouth was a bit too occupied to talk.

"Swing, babies," I improvised quickly, stepping over the bare asses, "the owner of this office laid a key on me and told me I could duck in for a shave. I got a gig to play later. Don't worry, I won't bother you."

"Hey, man, what do you blow?" the guy with the busy mouth paused long enough to ask.

"Trumpet, baby, and some half-assed sax. Nothing great, mother."

"I'll bet you do something great," the Chink broad invited.

"Do you wanna get straight?" one bare ass said, offering me a joint of pot.

"No, baby," I said, never stopping, "I gotta stay groovy for the gig. See you in a minute."

Shaving in the little bathroom was wild amid the murmurs and exclamations of love. Thank God, they didn't recognize me, or I'd have had to run out of the place.

THE CANNIBALS

At one point I stepped out with lather on my face to get a towel. The bare asses had now changed places: It was now the girls against the boys for the big prize.

I stepped back, finished shaving, put on my coat, and stepped my way carefully over the bodies. According to the heaves and sighs it was just about time for the prize.

As I reached the door, that Chink keister looked as cute as a bug, so I gave it a cute little slap in passing.

"Once more," she pleaded, "and harder!"

I wound up and gave her a shot she'd long remember.

"Yeah!" she screamed. "That did it, baby, that did it!"

As I closed the door behind me, I heard the dark chick say, "He's a groove."

New York, New York . . .

6:29 P.M. Walking into J.J.B.'s club, I walked right into Morton Silvern, pipe already in his mouth, and attaché case at the ready.

"Hi, counselor, how do you feel?"

"Good, young man. How about you?"

"Fine." I turned to the attendant. "Is Mr. Arthur here?"

"Yes," he answered austerely. "Are you Mr. Bertell and Mr. Silvern?"

"I'm Mr. Bertell, and I'll vouch that this is Mr. Silvern."

The clod didn't smile. Oh, well, not every audience is a jewel.

He led us up the antique staircase and into the private dining room where Romeo was awaiting our arrival.

He had on a brand-new dark gray suit, a blue shirt with the BCA cufflinks, a deep red and black striped tie . . . and new shoes of a heavy, conservative style that must have been designed for privates in World War I. He was cleanly shaven, and had plainly been to the barber's.

I looked him over from the haircut back down to the brogans. He looked like the friggin' money. He could always spot anyone cards and spades and still wind up with the game. He had it all.

"Johnny, say hello to Morton Silvern."

They shook hands, and we slipped easily into about five minutes of pleasantries, from the law to club life, ranging over many cities and touching on mutual friends.

Then, at what I felt was the auspicious moment, I began.

"Fellows, let me sort of set the stage and make the air clear. If I say anything that's not correct, or is a misinterpretation of the facts, speak up." I felt like I was back in the law school classroom.

Johnny gave me his full attention. Morton shifted in his seat to listen better.

It scared the hell out of me. I had two giants here, who now had the respect to catch my every word. How far they were above the level of Farley Fag, Percy President, and Sidney Shrewd!

I directed my next words to Jonathan. "Johnny, when we first discussed the World-Bond situation, with all its pros and cons, the conclusion was that it would be a perfect platform from which to launch what could possibly be, from the financial standpoint, an entertainment bonanza."

The listening was intense.

"I then reached out for Morton through friends of mine in the SEC. I explained what I thought could be done with the stock, just on the announcement of your becoming president, and the extra bonus of your bringing over your own successful team completely intact."

I puffed my cigarette. Morton drew on his pipe. Jonathan sat calmly, fingers clasped. He was Citation heading for the wire. He had class and breeding and would finish first, that you could sleep on. Onward.

"At first Morton thought the idea ludicrous—strictly from your standpoint. But after developing it further with me, he felt, by instinct, that we all had a real shot, his clients, the stockholders, and the partners included.

"One thing I made very clear, and Morton wholeheartedly agreed, was that in your position, under no circumstances can you be even remotely 'considered' for a new position. The new position must be offered to you outright. If you accept it, you're the kingpin. You have autonomy.

"The rest would be strictly business, stock and all the things that need not concern us at the moment.

"That's both sides, fellows, and I assume we're all here to make it work. That's all I have to say."

Jonathan gave a warm smile. I knew he was proud of me.

Morton spoke. "I can't fault that report in any manner. First let me say, John, that this young man has a belief in you that is contagious. I don't mean to imply that you needed his help, but I would be remiss if I didn't praise it. Thus I feel it incumbent on me to state that great as my respect already was for you and your impressive record, it has been augmented by your friend."

That was damn nice of him. I had felt when we met that he was that type.

Jonathan finally spoke. "We've been close friends for a long time," he said. "Joey is quite out of the ordinary."

Both of them now looked at me warmly. For one of the few times in my life, I felt humble and proud.

"One more thing," I added, "and then I'm going to say good-bye and let you two guys go to business head to head."

They were all attention.

"I want to say that it is not beyond the realm of possibility that when we leave BCA, World-Bond will have several deals with our alma mater."

They smiled, and no further comment seemed necessary.

I shook hands and walked out. Fish die by their mouths, I reflected again; I wasn't about to make that mistake.

I grabbed a cab and gave my address, mentally adding, "Take me home to Gina!"

Chapter 7

I slapped a single into the waiting hand of the doorman as he opened the door of my convertible for me. It was twelve o'clock high, and the sun was overhead. When it came to weather, California had it made.

I had on one of my brand-new business suits (the other twenty-four were on fresh hangers in my closet), and I sported a new haircut. The actor-sharpie long had been replaced by the Madison Avenue neat close-crop. Only the long sideburns I retained—a sort of Joey Bertell protest against the Establishment, or a badge of honor. It was all right to be a producer and look the part, but you didn't have to be a Marty Kissoff, bless his fat belly. I never dug T-shirts, anyway. . . .

I had the top down so I could absorb the golden rays. As I drove down Sunset Boulevard, I realized what a frantic pace it had become.

BCA had literally flipped over the revised Winant script. The popularity of Jonathan's concept, now that it had been correctly carried out, was sensational. But we were to start shooting in two days, and the pressure was on.

As for the cast, leading men had virtually lined up for the role of "Mr. Trouble," the reporter. I was now rushing to a meeting in the executive dining room of BCA to close the deal with Perry Bennett. He had been my choice all along, and Terry and J.J.B. both agreed he was the best guy.

There were wardrobe, location, and key personnel.

The technical end Joel Fryman had pretty well locked up.

The producer, however, was already a special headache. I had stolen a line producer from one of my competitors, partly because he had the additional reputation of being a fine writer. He had asked me to hire his wife as an assistant, which I did because she had a very special talent and was a lovely person besides.

During the last two weeks of preparation, however, the producer had begun trying to inflict his literary taste on Winant, and the wife had become an irritant as well.

So here we were at the starting gate with a sweet personality problem. I had given the guy a good deal, and the bell was about to ring. But by now Winant would talk only to me. Why couldn't those other peabrains realize that Winant was the indispensable man? This was not sentiment, it was the big leagues, and only results counted. Winant knew I didn't divide my loyalties. The others would have to be dumped.

Turning into the BCA parking lot, therefore, I was ready for action. The Perry Bennett deal was one that I damn well was not going to blow.

He had insisted on assurance that I would sit down with him on the west coast before he got on the plane for the New York shooting, even though Bryan and Ballantine could have handled the business with him and his agent, Morty Salk. I was only too glad to fly out, and as a special coup I had arranged for J.J.B., who was on the coast anyhow, to attend the meeting.

Terry's script had made everything possible. It was ten minutes early when I walked through the doors of the dining room, but Perry and Morty were already there, along with another agent from the same company, Bill Ferber. Bill was a friend, he had been influential in setting up aspects of the whole deal, and I wanted him to take a bow. Besides, he was a bright, classy guy who would bear watching, and I wanted to cut him into J.J.B.

I came in with a "Hi" to the fellows, and stuck out my hand to Perry.

"*Como esta, paisan,*" he greeted me.

"*Molte bene, gratia,*" I answered. "At long last we meet. I swear you're my favorite actor."

"Wha'cha doing stealing my lines? I was going to say that I always watch your variety show and I think you're the greatest."

Perry was dark-haired, with a face that was interesting without being pretty-boy. He came over warm and full of fun, with a devilish quality that was certain to please the broads without antagonizing the men. As we stood there, I liked him instantly and sensed he felt the same way about me. Pros have a chemistry about that, it doesn't take a long-drawn-out evaluation.

"Perry, I want you to know there was no second choice with me on this role. You were always it."

"That's nice of you to say, Joey."

The doors at the end of the room opened. In walked J.J.B., Joe Ballantine . . . and Lavender Lips.

"Suppose we all sit down at the table," he said, tippytoeing around the room and leaving a wake of cologne. He pulled out a chair and indicated that it was for J.J.B., who accepted it as a matter of form.

"Johnny, would you care to take over?" he purred. He'd have made a cute pet.

I spotted that J.J.B. was going to make this quick and to the point, bless everyone quickly, and then take off for the golf course. On Coast trips it was golf and broads for him, in that order.

"Perry," he started softly, "we want you to know that we're delighted to have you with us. We know the show's going to be a big success. Do you like the script?"

Morty Salk answered. "John"—everyone was now on a first name basis—"Perry and all of us just loved it."

J.J.B. cut him dead with a look of contemptuous annoyance. "What did you think, Perry?"

"I thought it was the best script I ever read. I had never wanted to do a series at all, but this convinced me."

"We feel the same way," said J.J.B.

"Joey told me earlier that he's going to look out for me, and that meant more than anything. I'm really sick of these phony producers who don't care about what an actor thinks or does. I tell you it's damn frustrating to work with them."

The table nodded accord, suddenly all sympathy for actors.

"But I know I can get along with this guy," continued Perry, pointing to me, "because an actor understands actors."

"Joey will take care of you," Jonathan confirmed.

Morty Salk spoke up again. "I think he's going to be a great producer."

"We want you to know, Joey, that we're *all* behind you," Bryan interjected.

I'd like to be behind you, Bryan baby, and give you a good kick in the ass, for blowing your one chance to say something nice.

"Perry, after we get under way," I kidded, "I'll even guest-star on your show."

J.J.B. cut right in. "The day you do that is the day you won't be a producer anymore."

"Hey, I can still act," I laughed, trying to keep it light.

J.J.B. glared back. "I mean it, Joey."

There was a moment of unrest at the table, which I figured I'd better end fast.

"I hereby formally retire from the screen."

Smiles returned to scared faces. J.J.B. turned back to Perry.

"I have to run with Joey from here to another meeting, but I want you to know that I'm in back of this show, and I now have every expectation that we're all going to have a big hit on our hands."

"Thanks, John," said Perry.

J.J.B. rose, and that was the cricket match. Everyone else rose also.

I went up to Perry, grabbed his hand, shook it tightly, and looked straight into his eyes.

"I'm with you all the way. I don't change—we'll win or lose together. I give you my word on it," I ended quietly. The conviction came from my heart. My word meant that I was now bound to Perry, to stand by him, protect him, and see him through, whatever the cost. It was total commitment.

"Me too, Joey." He had picked up the feeling.

J.J.B. and I now made our perfunctory good-byes and left for his upstairs office. As we walked into the suite, he motioned me to the inner room, while he glanced over the messages with his secretary.

I took the moment to use his phone and call my hotel for any panic messages from my office or the little wopalina. Through everything, she had remained in the back of my mind.

Jonathan then walked in. As he closed the door and I tried to predict his mood, it occurred to me that I had pigeonholed the three sides of his complex character under three different names. Talking about him to business associates, I referred to him as J.J.B. To our team, I called him Jonathan. Talking to him, or for personal effect to an outsider on an equal basis, like Morton Silvern, it was Johnny. As for Gina, she had invented his *nom de guerre* in my code, "Paul Power," just as she had invented my own "Pete Pressure." Even in business, there was a little part of Gina in me. Thank God for it!

Jonathan turned to me, and I now saw that he was totally relaxed.

"Want to play golf?"

"I can't."

"Why not? We're in good shape."

"This, coming from my teacher!" I kidded him. "We start shooting in two days, and I'm not going to drop the ball. Everything is at stake. I can play golf twenty years from now. Also, I want to get back to Gina . . . because she needs me at this particular time."

Cunning bastard that he was, he'd pick up your words but react only to his own thoughts. He smiled like a fox and said, "I'm proud of you—you're using your goddam head. You get back and whip the hell out of them. Get the job done."

I didn't feel like bragging at this moment. I had weight on me that even Kelso would have found hard to pack.

"I will."

"When are you leaving?"

"I've got the nine P.M. flight, and that'll give me Sunday morning home. Then I'll go to the office."

"Tuesday morning is D day."

"Fire and cannon, buddy."

"Don't worry," he said warmly. "It's all going to fall into place."

"Johnny, do you think anyone realizes how hard we work? Do you think anyone appreciates it or even gives a shit? Does the Chairman or the Dentist know what goes into a deal? Do they care, do they feel, do they have any emotions at all? I'm looking for an answer, I mean it. Is it all worth it, or are we both nuts?"

"Joey, I know just how you feel." He reflected a moment, then went on.

"I'm not going to kid you. They don't give a good holler in hell whether you live or die. They only worry about keeping the stockholders in line and tossing them a few pennies to keep them happy so that they themselves can continue to skim the millions and live in luxury. You ask me if they care? The Chairman is an old man who cares that nobody should print his middle name is Julius. The Dentist hasn't got a friend— not even a single friend—who cares even about his middle name."

"What an emptiness. Aren't they lonely?"

"What do *you* care? Would you like to be with them on a daily basis?"

I thought that one over. "No."

"There's your answer. That's why I can't stand the sight of either one of them."

"The Chairman's still the boss. He can still cut you off at the knees."

"After I've made him forty million dollars? The stockholders would lynch him!"

"Johnny, even Bryan told me you're making a mistake in

that regard, that you should try to be friendly with the Chairman, or at least accept his dinner invitations."

Jonathan flared up. "Bryan talks like a woman, thinks like a woman—"

"*Is* a woman." I got it in!

"That's beside the point. I don't like the old sonovabitch or his wife, and the Dentist is as dull as"—he searched for a word—"backgammon. I will *not* be friendly with them. 'Bryan said!' Now let's get off that," he snorted.

"All right, Johnny. Now I'm going to take off, go see my mother, and then get the hell out of make-believe town. Tuesday I put Terry to work in New York. How about you?"

"I'm going to keep my golf date, then pick up Bea and go to the Springs or Vegas."

"Go to Vegas and I'll see that you enjoy yourself. But go, don't say you will and then fail to show up."

"Great idea. I'll leave tonight at nine P.M. I need that relaxation."

"Good. Stay at the India Hotel. You'll have two presidential suites and be at every show in town. I'll handle it—just show up."

"Definitely."

Suddenly a light came on behind his cunning eyes. "Lord, tell me about the windup of the Jerry Kent incident. You wouldn't talk on the phone, and I'm dying to hear."

I relaxed and told him the tale in "fly-on-the-wall narrative," my own fly on the wall having been the faithful Bobby D.

3:00 A.M. Walking into the casino was like walking into a beehive. (The buzz of talk, the click of chips and money, and the clink of glassware was a sound that Bobby D. was used to.)

He walked aimlessly around, scanning faces to locate the prey. It was to be dog against dog.

Past the milling crowds, into the coffee shop, out again and down through the arcade, his eyes were looking, shifting, searching. Then back up through the casino, past the bingo parlor, up and down the slot machine aisles.

3:30 A.M. Feet dragging a little, but still alert, Bobby D. took a turn around the hotel, two or three chips in his hand, flicking them occasionally as he stalked.

3:45 A.M. Bingo! Jerry Kent came weaving into the lounge with two or three leeches and a chick.

Bobby D's heart started pounding, but he walked casually to the bar and ordered a drink. "Give me a Scotch on the rocks," he said, watching his quarry carefully in the mirror.

Kent and his little group were standing nearby, breaking up their evening with small talk. They finally finished their drinks, exchanged loud farewells, and walked separate ways, Kent heading for the hotel room section.

3:59 A.M. Bobby D. slid off his stool and followed. The quarry had been found, flushed, and was within point-blank range.

4:00 A.M. Bobby D. caught up with Jerry Kent in the deserted corridor. Bobby D. spun him around and snapped eight inches of arm into his gut. Kent went back against the corridor wall, paralyzed.

Kent gasped for breath and agonizingly managed, "What are you doing?"

Bobby D. slapped him back and forth, left cheek, right cheek, left cheek, a machine-gun pace on the punching bag. "Shut up, rabbit. I talk, you listen."

"Okay," Kent said.

Left cheek, right cheek, left cheek. "I talk, you *listen*."

Kent froze.

"Lay off that actor. If you so much as mention his name again, you'll be a grease spot on a garage floor."

He gave Kent one more in the gut and let him sag to the corridor floor.

"Listen to my voice. It's from New York. *I'm* from where *you're* from. Remember, don't mention that actor's name again."

Tears were now streaming down Kent's face. He broke silence through sheer terror. "For God's sake, which actor? I know hundreds of them."

4:02 A.M. Bobby D. had to make a quick decision. Should he give the name?

"Joey Bertell," he said.

Kent cowered on the floor. "I won't. I won't."

4:03 A.M. Bobby D. walked down the corridor alone and slipped out into the night.

Jonathan was in ecstasy. "He should have made a highway out of him," he said.

Tough, naïve Johnny. He'd been reading too many mystery novels. I let him come up for air.

"What'ya going to shoot today?"

"I'm now in such a good mood I think I'll come in with a seventy-three."

"I'll put the *mojo* on you. A double sawbuck says you don't break seventy-six."

"It's like stealing."

"I apologize. It isn't fair to take your money. . . ."

"Joey, you asked for it. You've got a bet."

"All I ask is that you pay. Even if it's with those Confederate bills you've been hoarding all these years."

"Now listen, relax. I've got something to tell you. I want you to realize it's for the best."

It was instinct. Suddenly he didn't have to tell me, *I knew.* The whole conversation had been rigged by Jonathan to go just this way.

"Joey, I talked to Morton Silvern today and turned down World-Bond."

He was looking at me for a reaction. He got absolutely none.

"Top management offered me a deal I couldn't pass up to stay at BCA. I had to accept it."

"I don't blame you." And I just let it lie there.

"Joey, it'll be bigger and better than ever for both of us."

"You're calling the shot, Johnny. If you say that's the way it is, then that's the way we go."

"Well, it's the only way to go at this moment. But it'll make the UBC move stronger when the timing is right."

Machiavelli! *Did he know* UBC had turned me down? I still gave absolutely no reaction.

"How did Morton take it?"

"He was disappointed, Joey, but he understood. Lawyers have this happen thousands of times. Through it, we all became friends, and in the future who knows what it can lead to?"

I sat for a moment, looked out the window, lit a cigarette, swallowed the smoke, and held it in until I almost exploded. Turning back to Jonathan, I spoke evenly. "I hope it's taken right when I say that it's a shame, with all that time and effort involved. I worked like a sonovabitch on that deal, and never let up for a moment."

"Joey, you delivered. I never doubted that you would deliver. But how bad off are you? You're off and running with three shows on the air."

"Maybe," I said simply and with a touch of melancholy, "I just wanted to be an executive vice-president. It could have been fun."

"Forget that crap," he said easily. "You and I can't afford to have feelings."

He walked over and put out his hand. "Charge forward boldly!"

I looked momentarily at the hand and then up into Jonathan's eyes. I had to be honest with myself in evaluating the situation. I couldn't push the subtle warnings from friends out of my mind. This time Jonathan J. Bingham could not be acquitted. He was guilty. He had given me his word that he would take the World-Bond deal if offered. Instead, he had used it as a lever for a new contract at BCA, in his own private feud with the Chairman and the Dentist. This unspoken fact I knew, because I knew Jonathan J. Bingham.

However, "how bad off" was I, really? Jonathan's finesse had logic. I had the three shows on the air. The point was, I *had* to go along, whether I wanted to or not.

The bottom line added up to one fact, which could, on logic, be forgiven. Jonathan had only used me; he had not double-crossed me.

I grabbed his hand and shook firmly. "Charge forward boldly, pal."

"Okay, buddy, now let's get the hell out of here."

We left the building, got into our cars, and rolled in opposite directions.

For me it was my mother, then home and Gina, then D day.

Sunday back in New York was beautiful. The sky was blue, the air brisk and chilly, and the sun poured over the skyscrapers with a feeling of warmth.

Sitting inside St. Catherine of Siena Church, holding Gina's hand, gave me a good feeling.

THE CANNIBALS

We knelt. I stole a glance at her. I felt proud that Gina would shortly be giving me a son. . . .

We had waited almost nine years and had finally planned on adopting a child from Italy next summer. There'd be no need to decide on a girl's name because it definitely would be a boy. He'd inherit the best of us, hopefully, and carry on the name. This was normal thinking. Every man dreams of it. A son—a son to take to ball games, teach, and make into a pal.

The mass at St. Catherine of Siena was particularly beautiful this Sunday. Everything was beautiful. Gina was healthy. We had money. The future was great. God had smiled on Joey Bertell. I was grateful—I was humble in His presence.

As the celebration ended and the people filed out, I asked Gina to stay seated.

"I want to stop and see St. Jude."

She nodded, with a madonnalike smile. You can understand the traditional joke that men should marry only pregnant women. All pregnant women are beautiful. They have the glow that radiates love.

Finally the church was empty. Gina and I walked over to the shrine of St. Jude. He was my favorite . . . the saint of impossible things.

Once, while angry, I had dropped a statue of him, and I vowed to make it up to him if it was the last thing I ever did.

Gina and I lit candles. My thoughts were on the son. With Gina's candle were thoughts sacred to her.

I crossed myself.

Saint Jude, please look upon me who is not worthy of your help. Our first child is arriving: My heart cries out for a son. I ask only that you give him to me strong and healthy. I want this more than life itself. And if you do smile on me, I will be your servant for life. If God chooses to give me a girl, I will take this, too, as a divine plan and will love her also with all my heart. Please smile on her then and give her health and wisdom, since it will be harder for me to speak to a girl. I pledge you my love forever. In the name of the Father, the Son, and the Holy Ghost. Amen.

I stood up. I reached in my pocket and took out my money. There was five or six hundred dollars.

I handed Gina a five-dollar bill and whispered, "Hold this for the cab fare."

The rest was something more than money. I stuffed it hurriedly into an envelope and dropped it into the locked iron box. I took my Gina's arm, and we left.

Hopping out of the cab in front of my office, I gave Gina a peck on the cheek.

"When will you be home?"

"I don't know, honey. I'm up at bat. I'm meeting Bill Blackman now, then I have to goose my people and make eight thousand phone calls. I'll be here if you need me. Do you want me to have George drive you to New Jersey for a visit?"

"I don't feel up to that trip. Anyway, say hello to Bill."

"Why don't you call the 'other sister' in New York? You can talk about all those intellectual things, discuss the underdogs of the world." This was a subconscious dig. All families have a black sheep, and Gina's was no exception.

"Oh, Joey, don't you ever stop?"

"Gina baby, forgive the slip. But as for your sister, nobody turns down my offer of friendship twice. Don't ever match that one up with the rest of the kids. She has no heart, none at all. To have heart," I couldn't restrain myself from adding, "you have to have talent. See you later, beautiful."

The cab sped down the street. I walked into the building and prepared for an entrance to the Cardinal production offices.

As the door opened, it was obvious that my little bees were buzzing. I announced myself melodiously. "Come in, Vera."

She followed me into the sanctum. "You're in high spirits today."

"Why not? My business is flourishng, and my son is on his way. Life is great."

"I'm happy for you."

"Thanks." I was now in a fabulous mood, really one to remember.

I stared at Vera, in all her *hamishe* splendor; the *zaftig* figure . . . the boots, yet.

"Vera, I've held this back long enough. I love you. Every night when I go to bed, I wish I had your warm body next to mine."

She blushed. That made me go on.

"I don't give a damn about your boyfriend, it's you and me. Vera, I can't take it anymore, I've got to have you."

"Mr. Ber—"

"Please don't interrupt. These inner feelings must come out. Do you think I can stand to have pimples spoil this face, the face that millions have come to know and love? Vera, in the name of compassion and all human emotion, decency demands that you grant me one small boon. Is that too much for a mortal man to expect? Don't I deserve some small token of gratitude for all I've done for you? Just do me this one thing so that I know a teeny portion of my love is returned. Will you?"

"What do you want?"

"My dart board, angel—bring it in!"

She scurried out, returned with the new dart board, hung it on the old hook, and gave a ceremonious flourish.

"These two dozen extra darts are presented by Jimmy Craig and myself to our leader."

I took the bag and examined them. "Your leader thanks you and accepts in all humility." I put one hand over my heart. "Now I ask only that you leave my office at once. There is one weakness that I cannot permit myself to display, even to you. Tears are always, to say the least, embarrassing. *Out!*"

She left with a smile. On cue, the private rang. I picked up. "Hello."

"Will you please stop the goddam champagne!" the soft voice kidded.

"Hi, buddy, how's it going?"

"Great, we're having a ball, but everywhere I sit down, somebody trots up with a bottle of champagne, 'compliments of Joey.' "

"How are the suites?"

"Farouk never had it so good. It's like being in two palaces. They just can't do enough."

"Good. Are you enjoying the fun and games?"

"Unbelievable!"

"I must hear the hoary details when you get back."

"Just a minute, Bea wants to say hello." I heard the extension click.

"Hi, big shot."

"Hi, beautiful, how goes it?"

"Maddening, dahling, absolutely and positively maddening."

"Christ, don't wear him out. Save a piece of him that I can talk to. I need all the help I can get."

"From what I hear, dahling, you don't need anything."

"How's Eve baby?"

"Still sweating it out. She sends regards."

"How's Irving Impotent?"

"He is, you know." Bea laughed. "Why don't you come out? We'll send for her . . ."

"Great idea, maybe it'll give him a stroke, and we'll all cash in."

Johnny broke in. "Save your hopes, Joey. If he can't take it with him, he's just not going." All three of us laughed.

"Bea, since Johnny's been with you, he's become a comedian. What are you doing to make him laugh?"

"Why don't you come to Vegas and find out? There's enough for all," she teased.

She was some gal. Always the sense of humor. She had

breeding, class—and she really cared for Jonathan. Poor kid, she was just another J.J.B. chattel and would be discarded when he tired of her. I hoped that somehow I was wrong.

"See you later," she said, and hung up.

"Sounds wild," I commented to Jonathan.

"Maybe I'll never come back."

"Don't spend any cash out there. It's all on the arm, understand? Don't pay for nuttin'."

"Don't be insulting," he toppered. "I was just checking to see that you were on the ball."

"Don't worry, while you're playing I'm slaving. Big Irish is due in a few minutes. I let him read the script."

"Attaboy. He's with the new agency now, and they're going to take a position in your show."

"I wonder how that happened."

"I told you everything was going to work. What are you doing now?"

"If I told you, you wouldn't believe me."

"Try me."

"I'm playing darts with myself."

" 'Byyye." He hung up.

Vera buzzed. "Bill Blackman to see you."

"Send him in."

Bill made an entrance; Six-three, about two hundred pounds, and all the Celtic handsomeness. He was a member of the original clique, one who had stuck. He'd never make the top, because he was just too lovable. There wasn't a curve in

248

him—except for the curves of his weight, which he worried about, but he was still losing out to himself, because he ate like he was going to the chair.

Bill's big "fence" was a failure to make up his mind just what he wanted to do. It was deep. He had a fabulous talent as a writer, had the stuff to be an important playwright. Like many talented guys, however, he didn't have a money cushion and had to work to live. Up against that grind for ten or twelve hours a day, Bill wasn't quite up to pounding the keys at night. I considered it a failure for which Bill could not really be faulted.

I got up and met him halfway. "Hiya, buddy. Let's sit down and cut up some touches." I adapted one of J.J.B.'s tricks and installed him on the sofa.

"Halfback," he said, "you're looking good."

"Plowing around end, pal, but I've had good blocking. How's your new job?"

"It looks like it could be something."

"Blacker-than-most," I smiled, using an old nickname for him, "how about a drink?"

"What day is it, and what time?"

"Sunday, and one o'clock."

"I accept."

"*Vera!*"

At my yell, she scrambled in.

"A little libation for myself and friend."

"We're out of keys to the liquor cabinet. You hid them all."

I always hid keys to liquor cabinets. Before I became a boss, I used to furnish my home bar with the finest stock that could be obtained from the offices of my own employers. They would never do that to me.

"Break the lock," I commanded. "*Out!*"

Back to Bill. "C'mon, buddy; am I nuts, or is the script good?"

"Pure Winant, which has always been good enough for me."

I was pleased by the sincerity. "This is my day."

"Your only problem," he added, "is whether this guy can keep writing at this level, with all the eggheads who are trying to interfere."

I thought this one over, while Vera appeared with bottles and ice, set everything on the coffee table, and disappeared. I poured the belts.

"He can do it, Bill. He has talent *and* integrity. They won't push him around like some hack."

"Well, he did get rid of Klaver."

"Oh, you know about that?"

"Joey, you are the master of all secrets, but don't begrudge us poor plebeians a few spare morsels of information."

"Drink your drink and save your 'lefties' for someone else, you rascal."

"You look happy, buddy."

I looked at Bill and knew he meant it. "Yeah, Blackie, really happy."

"We had fun at the Masters Golf Tournament, didn't we?"

"You said it. That was a great time."

"Joey, what the hell was that salad that you made for all of us?"

"The *ensalada pomidoro*."

"I tried to make one when I came back, but it was awful. Later I walked into Broadway Joe's and described it—they're calling it the Joey Bertell salad."

I beamed. "Want the recipe? Just take six tomatoes, eighth them, and cut in one large onion. Next pour in enough olive oil to cover the bottom."

"What kind?"

"Pure olive oil. Mama Mia or Bertolli is good. Then you take four generous pinches of oregano, about fifteen dashes of salt and pepper. And finally . . . the secret."

"What, what?"

"Use your hands to mix it. All the time you're squeezing the good juice out of the tomatoes."

"Then what?"

"Eat it, you stupid bastard!"

We both had a good laugh and belted down a shot or two.

"Bill, how do we look on the show?"

"We're in. And I hear that Gottfried is putting the Tobacco Company in. You're home free."

"Do you really like the package?"

"Joey, I think it's great. With the exception of the usual protection memos to take our balls out of the vise in case of a squeeze, we're in line, and you're on the air."

"I haven't written a protection memo in some time, probably because I haven't had a job to protect, being my own boss. But let's have some fun, Billy boy: I'll write your protection memo for you.

"In my opinion, I feel that the Mr. Trouble *series has great merit. It shows possibilities of becoming a long-range popular television story. However, much of the aforementioned depends upon the writing of the scripts, the casting of the players, and lush production—combined with technical skill and labor. Sincerely yours, William Blackman."*

"Beautiful, Joey, beautiful. However, you left out the clincher."

"What was that?"

"I find the entire project interesting."

"Touché."

"The show can't miss, honestly."

"Terry Winant deserves the credit."

"With an assist from Jonathan. But don't kid yourself, you earned it. Nobody doubts that. And how are the other two shows coming? Maybe we'll be in all three."

There was no sense in lying to one of my "originals." "On the other two shows, it's strictly a sham. That queen has control of them."

If you can't let down your hair to a trusted friend, you'd better take a small flat in Plainfield and rot away. The truth over drinks sometimes has a way of letting the bitterness flush down, besides.

In this case, Bill was holding his sides from laughing.

"What the hell is so funny?"

"You won't believe it—" He collapsed into laughter again, and I finally joined him, entirely ignorant of what was breaking him up.

"Tell me, for God's sake!"

He finally got it out. "Clete told me this one. His wife Nickie called him at the office one day and said there was a strange guy on their front lawn.

" 'Does he look like a troublemaker?' Clete asked.

" 'He looks like a fucking butterfly,' replied Nickie—you know her reputation for the sporting language.

" 'Go out and ask him what he wants, and I'll hold on.'

"Nickie walked outside and said to Forrest Fruit, 'What the hell are you doing in my fucking yard?'

" 'I'm so sorry,' he minced, 'but I've lost our chimpanzee, and I've looked all over for him.'

" 'There's no gorillas around here, you goddam fag. Now screw out of here!'

" 'I'm sorry, ma'am,' he lisped, 'but if my boyfriend finds out that I lost Gertrude, he'll never speak to me again.'

" 'Oh, shit!' said the Emily Post of Hollywood Hills, and went back to the house.

"She picked up the phone and told an anxious Clete not to worry, it was only a fag looking for a chimpanzee. They hung up.

"Nickie was walking around the house twenty minutes later, cleaning, when the phone rang.

" 'Nickie, Clete. I'm coming home. Break out a bottle. We're going to get blind. Do you hear me, goddam blind!'

" 'What's up, lover?'

" 'I've waited two weeks for a meeting with that asshole Bryan Westgate, and he just ran in here in tears. Do you hear what I'm saying? Goddam tears, the slimy sonovabitch!'

" 'What the hell is wrong with him, lover?''

" 'I'll tell you what's wrong with him—he lost his goddam monkey!'

" 'Oh, shit,' said Queen Nickie. End of story."

Bill was on the floor by the end of the retelling, and I was right with him.

"Bill, that's Nickie all over. She must have been a sailor in some previous incarnation."

"Either that," suggested Bill, "or her schoolteacher was the parrot that belonged to Captain Kidd."

I poured another shooter. "You know, Willie, this is like old times. I really miss the gang and the football games, when you and I and Clete and Jonathan were the Four Horsemen."

Bill nodded, we drank, and I continued.

"It's not like that anymore. Even this meeting, for all its fun, is business. It has to end in a few minutes, and then it'll be a couple of months before we see each other again."

"You're right, Joey." The sentimental Irishman had a tear in the corner of his eye, and I knew it wasn't just the drinks. "I miss it, too. Who says guys can't be soft once in a while? Sometimes I wonder if we all shouldn't set aside one day regularly to get together, eat, drink, and have a general good time. It would do everyone a world of good."

I smiled, but I knew realistically the jungle wouldn't permit it. The jungle keeps growing, the bushes and strangling vines get higher and higher. You have to keep chopping away before you're slowed down and swallowed up.

"Well, anyway, Blackie, you can have a good time seeing the pilot with Johnny and me if you want."

"Wonderful, I'd like that. What time slot do you think you'll get?"

"Probably the ten P.M. anthology. It's had its run and tapered off sharply."

"That's what Manning guessed."

"He should know, he's on top of everything and also real tight with J.J.B."

"Joey, do you think you'll miss performing?"

I thought it over and had to confess. "More than you'll ever know. But how about you and the great American novel?"

"At the rate I'm going, I ought to bring it in by the turn of 1984—or *Brave New World*."

"Speaking of new worlds . . . did you know that Johnny signed a new deal at BCA instead of taking over World-Bond?"

"It hasn't been up in lights in Times Square, but that's the only place. The whole universe knows it, Joey. And the word is that you got shafted."

I tried to smile, but I guess it was a sickly one. Bill's report was a bitter pill to swallow. "I delivered, Bill . . ."

"Nobody's taking that away from you. But they say that Joey boy must have been dreaming to imagine Johnny would go."

"The only answer I have is that he said he'd go. His word has always been good enough for me."

"I'd have bet my life that he'd only use the deal for leverage against the Chairman."

"You would have won your bet. Also," I threw the needle back, "there are some great races in yesterday's *Form*. Would you like to pick a few winners there also?"

Bill had to smile. "On that warm and friendly note, I take my leave."

"Where are you going?"

"To take in the rest of the Giants game over a few shooters. Want to join me?"

"I have to pass, Bill. Something to do."

"Okay, tycoon." He threw out that big paw. I grabbed it.

"So long, Blacker-than-most."

He ambled out the door. A good guy. I turned, picked up my darts, and started throwing . . . and thinking.

Monday, 8:00 A.M. I walked briskly into our offices. This was a pre-production day, and that meant nine hundred people on the set in one hour.

Vera looked at me as if I were a ghost. "I don't believe it. Eight o'clock! Are you all *right*?"

"You're a real smart ass, aren't you? But I'm still your boss, and I command you to give me respect. Do you understand?"

"Yes, sire."

"I keep telling you, stupid, it's 'your worship.' "

"Yes, your worship."

"Excellent, my dear. Have the cashier give you an extra double sawbuck as a small good luck token and a measure of appreciation from your grateful emperor."

"Thank you, your worship."

"Please, no groveling." I walked into my office, then added over my shoulder, "Send in noble James."

I picked up the putter and lined two balls solidly into the cup. Grabbing two darts, I flung them at the target, with somewhat less success. Stupid game—it would require a little more of my time.

Jimmy stood on the threshold with a huge grin on his face.

"Enter, sir knight. But why do you smile?"

"They want to know if you've lost your marbles."

"Give me 'their' names, you little stool pigeon, and I'll have twenty lashes striped across their naked backs."

"I can't do that, sire."

"*Your worship*, you stupid jackass."

"I forgot. Your worship."

"Okay, what's new?"

"Joel has taken everyone out to look at tomorrow's locations."

I buzzed Vera.

"Send everyone opening-day wires. Make it rah-rah. Sign my name. I'll write the notes to Winant and Perry personally."

I looked at my notebook. "Jimmy, follow through with Joel

and see if Perry's got a haircut. J.J.B.'s driving me out of my mind on it."

"Will do."

"Vera, have Krautie cash a check for a couple hundred and bring it to me."

"Yes, your worship."

"All right, already. Later, later." I waved off the games.

"We shoot at the newspaper tomorrow. Get me my brother-in-law on the phone."

Vera used my phone and interdialed to the studio, spoke for a moment, and handed it to me. "Billy's on now."

"Willie, call Bill Blackman and invite him to the studio for a look-around. Take money, buy him and his people lunch. Make points—they'll be the sponsors for half of the hour."

"Anything you want me to lay in?"

"No, buddy. Just use your judgment, I know it'll be good. But be smart and tell your boss what I've just asked you to do. Is he there?"

"No, he stepped out."

"Good. Tell him I called him and *then* spoke to you. I couldn't care less, but it'll be better for you that way. Okay?"

"Right, Joey, and thanks." That was it.

I'd started to give Vera more instructions when the private rang. Vera and Jimmy heard it and filed out. That was the rule.

"Hello," I said.

"Did you give Bill Blackman a script of *Mr. Trouble*?" The voice was soft but annoyed.

"Yeah—and he loved it."

"I don't care if he went to bed with it"—the voice took on a slightly rough edge—"the stupid sonovabitch had a couple of drinks at '21,' and, trying to be helpful, told Gottfried von Klung how great it was."

"So?"

"*So*? Don't you understand these two-year-olds? They're jealous of each other—who gets this first, who gets that. It's their whole pathetic life . . . and you play right into their hands."

I started to get hot. "Hold it. Are you trying to say that Bill's not our buddy and that I was wrong to give him a script?"

"I'm saying that you can't give a script to *anyone* who has a few drinks and a big flannel mouth." As I got hot, Jonathan's voice got cold. "We've got this show sold out, and you're making waves."

"Goddamit, he's your friend, too." I blew sky-high. "What the hell are you getting salty with me for? Save that shit for Chester or Mario or Farley Fag."

"I didn't give him the script, you did. Straighten it out!" He hung up.

Vera started back in.

"Come in when I call you!" I yelled.

I was now doing the Danny Thomas "automobile jack" story. The ungrateful bastard, talking to me like that. I'd go over there and knock him on his ass, then kick him where the jewels were.

The private rang.

I answered with no emotion. "Yes."

"Have you done anything yet?"

"No ..."

He hung up again.

I dialed his private number ...

"John Bingham."

"Fuck you." And I hung up.

I walked out the door, coat in hand, found Vera and Jimmy gaping in amazement. They had heard—there was little doubt of that.

"Let that private ring, and when Bingham's secretary calls on the other line, say I'm out for the day."

I'll freak his mind out. By God, he'll go berserk when he can't find me. Let his mother worry. He'll never see the day he'll control Joey Bertell.

I hustled to the elevator, jumped in, and rode downstairs.

George was waiting with the car. I jumped into the front seat. He knew by that move alone that I was hot. .

"Where to, pal?" He purposely dropped the Mr.

"Drive to Brooklyn."

"Why?" he asked cautiously, trying to hold me back if I was loose.

"Because I'm going to whip your ass in pool that's why! I've listened to your bragging long enough."

"You're faded." And that ended that.

THE CANNIBALS

Today was the day. It was a cold, brisk morning as I waited downstairs for George to pick me up. The lobby clock was straight up: 6:00 A.M.

Here it was at long last, back in the film business again. Live-and-tape is fun, but only to an entertainer. Actors like that stop-and-go protection. The close-ups, over-the-shoulder shots, and cuts to the other actors can be used if they look wrong or act badly.

But for me, it would be the other side of the camera: approving cast, scripts, and viewing "rushes," or "dailies"—trade term for film shot the day before and needing approval before it went to the cutter.

Rushes are usually shown at noontime, for the director, producer, cameraman, and key personnel. As a courtesy, the leads in the series are invited, but only if they won't "shake up" from what they see. They're apt to react in one of two ways—falling in love with themselves or dismayed that they look awful. Either way, you book a loser.

After a while I glanced at my watch and was surprised to find that it was six-twenty. George must have gotten tied up at crosstown lights picking up Terry Winant. But then, at the corner, I spotted the black limo waiting for a green. I walked over to the curb and waited.

"Hi, writer."

"Hi, producer." Terry was beaming. "This is it—the start of the Bertell-Winant saga."

I slapped him on the knee and smiled warmly. For a man never before exposed to the jungle, he had stand-up strength. Still, I had to keep him close to me, so that those lesser talents not even fit to sharpen his pencil couldn't chip away at him. Already, Mr. and Mrs. Underdog were making their moves. But I hadn't let it materialize, and I meant to keep things that way.

"What are you thinking?" he asked.

"We've got the big edge, Terry: a fine script, great leading man, good solid actor for the second banana, and name guest stars lined up."

"Tell me more." That infectious grin broke out all over his face.

"One thing I know for sure, we've got the best damn director in the business, for this type of series." I was being emphatic for a purpose. "I don't know anyone better than Tim Rice."

"I'll tell my mother not to sell her bonds."

"Does she have money?" I asked courteously.

"Yes, but it's all tied up in Yankee bean soup." As an afterthought, "You'd make a great straight man."

"If you can afford it, I'd like the role."

These parries were my true joy and broke the tension. And that went double for Terry, the professional worrier.

By now we had reached location, an actual newspaper building. It had recently folded and was shuttered up. My discovery and rental of it had been important. One thing the critics wouldn't ever say was that *Mr. Trouble* lacked authenticity.

Terry and I walked up two flights of broad stairs and into the old city room, which was now a maze of lights, cameras, and sound equipment. A hundred or more extras were already there in proper wardrobe. The dead newspaper was beginning to stir with life again: It was pure motion picture magic.

And as for Allie and Sniffles, they were talented people, and conscientious—not that that would be a substitute for judgment under pressure, and results.

Terry and I walked over and shook their hands.

"Good luck, kids," I said.

"Me, too," said Terry in a perfunctory manner.

"How's it going, Allie?"

"Our big star hasn't arrived yet," he said, just a bit formally.

"Oh? Where is he?"

"All I know is he isn't on the set. He was twenty-five minutes late for makeup, I believe."

"Are you ready for him?"

"No, but he could be rehearsing. Gerry Morell is here and would like to go over lines."

Terry's face dropped several inches. Come on! Not panic in the first hour. I stepped in fast.

"Relax, it's a first-day shakedown. Where is the new John Garfield's makeup?"

"One flight up," Marge answered, wiping her nose daintily with a hankie.

As we headed for the stairs, Terry said, "Now you know why I call her 'Sniffles.' "

Not a bad nickname. But I sensed the feud was still simmering. What price success?

We found Perry in a makeup room full of lead sinks. It had been the newspaper's roto department. He jumped out of his chair and greeted us warmly.

"There's my producer. Hey, *paisan*, how are you? Hi, Terry."

One thing about Perry Bennett, he had enthusiasm. Also, he was honest. He was artistic. He was a spoiled baby. In fact, he was nuts. But he wouldn't lie. In the last day and a half I had picked that up. With the exception of the usual personal shadings of any star, what Perry said would be the truth.

Meanwhile, I saw that we still had the hair problem.

"Trim his locks a little. Make it neat," I said to the makeup man.

He looked at me, realizing that I knew this could be a union problem. After all, my dear mother had been a hairdresser for thirty years at the top Hollywood studios. For that very reason, I could usually come up with these little tricks.

"This is a *character* part," I said, thereby reclassifying the haircut from one union jurisdiction to another. "I see a little off here"—pointing to the spots I wanted clipped—"and a little off there."

"Excuse me, chief," said the makeup man, going along smoothly, "I didn't realize this was a costume picture."

"Right. The swords and horses don't arrive until this afternoon." I winked, and he smiled back. Good guy!

"Don't I have anything to say about this?" Perry put in.

"Of course you do, star. It's just that we won't listen. Good luck, pal!" I whacked him on the back and made a quick exit, Terry bustling along.

Heading for the stairs, I explained, "Let's get out of here before we make a big blunder and get blamed for something."

"We can always put it on Sniffles," he said.

"One way to get rid of her, eh?"

Chapter 8

Back at the office, I walked past a beaming Vera, all decked out in a new dress.

I kissed her on the cheek and for once made no jokes. "Thanks for your help." Her look told me she appreciated the thought.

"I put some wires on your desk."

I walked in, closed the door, and sat behind the black teakwood. The telegrams told the story.

```
MR. JOEY BERTELL
BCA PRODUCERS CENTER
NEW YORK, N.Y.
THIS IS A BIG MOMENT FOR YOU AND I WANT YOU
TO KNOW HOW PROUD I AM. IT'S ONLY THE BEGINNING.
                                        JOHNNY
```

The other wires were similarly addressed.

```
YOU'RE GOING FOR YOUR FIRST BULL'S-EYE. THE
OTHER TWO WILL HIT NEXT WEEK. FONDLY.
                                        BRYAN

GOOD LUCK, BUDDY, I HOPE IT'S A HIT. MAMA
NEEDS BINGO MONEY. BEST.
                                        BILLY
```

267

THE BEST, JOEY. YOU HAVE A WINNER ON YOUR
HANDS, I KNOW. GRATEFULLY.

CHESTER

DON'T WORRY, DOLL. YOU CAN ALWAYS HAVE CHILI ON A
BEARSKIN RUG. WITH FINGERS CROSSED,
MY LOVE TO YOU!

CHILI

GOOD LUCK.
MARIO COLUCCI, V.P. FINANCIAL AFFAIRS

I paused to look at that one again. The simple ass. He might as well have added "Candidate for President." God save me from immigrants!

IF THIS IS A HIT, MY MOTHER WANTS YOU OVER FOR
STUFFED CABBAGE AND STRUDEL. GOOD LUCK, PARTNER.

TERRY

WE'RE ROOTING FOR YOU ALL THE WAY. YOU CAN'T MISS.
VERA AND JIMMY

YOU'RE GOING TO WIN, PAL. JUST LIKE YOU'VE ALWAYS
DONE. YOUR BUDDY.

GEORGE

I WISH YOU ALL THE LUCK IN THE WORLD DARLING.
I KNOW YOU'LL MAKE IT. ALL MY LOVE.

MOTHER

OVER THE FALLS, PAL. THIS IS THE ONE YOU'VE
DREAMED OF.

BILL BLACKMAN

GOOD LUCK, JOEY. WE'RE BEHIND YOU.
                    GOTTFRIED VON KLUNG

Vera had saved the good one for last.

KNOCK EM DEAD, HONEY. YOU HAVE THREE REASONS.
LITTLE CHRISTOPHER, ME, AND MY I.O.U. I LOOK
GREAT IN SABLE. I LOVE YOU.
                              GINA

I looked at the calendar. Yes, two more months and Christopher would be here. I'd give him a christening party that New York would never forget!

I buzzed Vera. "Get me Billy."

She rang back in a few seconds. "He's on two."

"Thanks for the wire, pal."

"You know I mean it, and without any lack of faith when I wish you good luck."

"Thanks again. *Now* . . . Call Gottfried von Klung. Give him the same invite you gave Bill Blackman—the same treatment. Ask him if he liked the script. Of course he'll say he didn't get any script, at which point you have a stroke. Fumble around your desk and find it. Apologize all over the joint and tell him if I hear about this I'll blow my top. Got it?"

He hesitated.

"You're playing the outside for me, understand? I didn't send him the script, and he blew the whistle over at BCA. Now have you got it?"

"Even Mama could understand that."

269

"Okay, Willie Sutton. Keep it up and I'll squeal on you. Chickie, indeed!" I hung up. Good kid.

Now I could pick up the private. After talking to Billy, I knew it was as good as done. I dialed.

"Busy?"

"No, I was just wondering how you were doing."

"It's going well, so far. By the way, thanks for the wire. I appreciated it."

"You deserve it, buddy. Don't ever think I'm unaware of how hard you've worked."

"Put that other situation, with Von Klung, out of your mind. It's handled."

"I knew it would be." The silky soft voice again.

"How's Calvin Clothes doing the last week or so?"

"I don't know. Holding meetings, I guess. What difference does it make? He's running up and down and getting nowhere."

"I'm sure Chester is a help to him. . . ."

"I'll bet he is. Calvin should be starting to bleed from the ears about now."

I laughed. "Alas, poor Calvin. I knew him well . . ."

"Why don't you promise Chester the Chairman's job while you're at it?"

I topped him. "I'm sure we can get the Dentist's okay."

And so yesterday's blowup was over. Neither one of us had to refer to it. To your friends, you never have to explain; your enemies won't believe you, anyway.

"A quickie later?" he suggested.

"Sure, I'll meet you at Le Valois. I'll have Gina meet me. You meeting anyone?"

"Len Weston, the boy doctor."

"How boring. Gina will be happy, though. She thinks he's the greatest thing since ice cubes."

"Go figure it, I can't."

"I can't either, Johnny. This guy couldn't get laid in a whorehouse, and Gina told me the other day that the only one I ever had to worry about was him."

"Maybe your wopalina should have married a good Jewish doctor."

"I'll sell her if he'll pay me alimony."

"Would you really?"

"Of course. One night with that yo-yo would drive her to the funny farm. Maybe that would be a good way to kick her into line."

"No, it would be unconstitutional. 'Strange and unusual punishment.'"

Jonathan was in rare form. But it was a relief. The cat-and-mouse mood could get tiring.

"Okay, pal, see you later." I replaced the receiver.

As soon as the light went out, Vera buzzed.

"Joel on three."

"Hi, tiger. How's it going?"

"Good but slow. This guy Perry is a real prima donna. He's got the big head and the star complex a mile high. It's driving everyone nuts."

"Humor him. Let's look at the rushes. Don't rock any boats."

"Okay, but Tim Rice really hates him now. Joey, the guy is a screwball."

"Unscrew him . . . but be nice."

"Okay, boss."

I buzzed Vera. "Send in Jimmy Craig."

He was prompt. "You want me?"

"No, I'm testing the electronic system for Conelrad. Pick up the yellow darts. I'm going to give you a lesson you'll never forget."

"I can't afford it."

"What do you make now?"

"You've given me three raises, I'm up to a hundred seventy-five."

I buzzed Krautie.

"Kraut! As of now, Jimmy Craig gets two hundred dollars a week."

"It's not in the budget."

"Cut down on coffee!" I slammed the phone down.

"Okay, pigeon, a deuce a game. Double if either one doesn't make two hundred."

I picked up the phone and buzzed Vera. "No calls, I'm in conference."

When I walked into Le Valois, it was 7:00 P.M. by the clock above the bar.

It had been a great day. The crew had broken for dinner and were working one hour overtime in order to get rid of the hundred extras. Carrying them over into the next day would be not only costly but confusing. It's harder to shoot with people moving about.

While I was daydreaming. Jean Pierre made the martini. He now set it down in front of me.

As I took a sip, Len Weston slipped onto the stool next to me.

"Hi, Joey."

"Hi, doc, how's your stethoscope?"

"Great. Jonathan get here yet?"

"No. Do you want a bet on who walks in first, Gina or him?"

"Are they *both* coming?"

"Correct."

"I should have brought my crash helmet."

His Cutty Sark on the rocks now arrived, and he toasted me. "Here's to your shows." We clinked glasses.

"Gina said she and her sister were up to see you the other day. She's concerned about her sister's weight."

"It's no problem at all, Joey, she'll be fine in a month or so. I did warn her about those crash diets; an extra few weeks won't hurt."

"You're so right. By the way, Lochinvar, my little wopalina is quite taken by you."

"She's a great gal."

"She's been ribbing me that the only other man for her would be you and that she wished I were more like you."

"God forbid," he said.

"I felt the same way," I said pointedly.

And now coming through the door like the 20th Century Limited was Jonathan. He was a professional walker and had probably made the twelve blocks in record time. Shedding the coat, he advanced with a wide grin.

"What are you two hatching up?" And to Jean Pierre, "A special."

"We're awaiting the arrival of the mother-to-be, Gina Bertell," reported the good doctor.

"Yeah," I said slyly, "they've decided to bring their romance out into the open."

Doc blushed as if he'd been caught with his Eagle Scout pin tarnished.

Jonathan asked, "What's on the fire tonight, doc? Have we some little sparrows joining us?"

"There's a party in about thirty minutes that we can go to, and I know there'll be some cute chicks."

"Whose pad?" Jonathan asked.

"Nick Cutter's. He's a well-known model."

I did a triple skull and gave Jonathan the eyebrows. He realized I'd speak to him later about it. Suddenly he turned and burst into song: "*Here* she comes, *Miss America* . . ." Len and I joined in on the last few notes.

Gina was walking in. She had on a beige cashmere suit, gold charm bracelet, high doeskin boots—and the coal-black hair and flashing eyes topped it off.

"Hi, Joey." She smiled and gave me a peck on the cheek.

"Hi, Lenny." She giggled, then devilishly threw her arms around him, also giving him the kiss.

"Hello, beautiful," he replied with a smile.

"Hi, Paul Power." She walked over and gave him a conspicuously formal "Hollywood" kiss.

Jonathan broke out in a buck-toothed laugh. "You're all heart, Gina."

"I'm a star, will you please discover me?"

Excellent, I thought. And now, so that we'd have a chance for one good get-together, I jockeyed Gina onto my stool, where she could talk to the good doctor.

I looked him over again: tall, black-haired, young, and good-looking. But no competition, I told myself. I had this twinge of dislike for Lenny, and it seemed unwarranted. I didn't usually dwell on trivia.

Moving over to Jonathan and turning my back on Bill and Coo, I said, "Let me tell you about this guy whose pad you're going to tonight."

"Go ahead," he smiled, knowing it would be a juicy tidbit.

"This guy is low on brains, and everybody acts on it accordingly. About five years ago, when he was really busted, he concocted a robbery on himself to get some insurance money."

Jonathan was all ears.

"He banged his head against the door a few times, called the police, then handcuffed one arm to the radiator. When they ran in, he told them a wild tale of guns and robbers.

275

That his diamond ring, watches, jockstrap, everything was stolen."

Jonathan was already laughing quietly, and I started building to the finish.

"The police asked him exactly when he had called the station, and he gave them the time. Then they took the cuff off him . . . and said, 'You're under arrest.' "

I was now laughing along with Jonathan. After a moment he demanded, "For Christ's sake, what happened?"

"The silly bastard forgot the phone was thirty feet away from the radiator. How could he have used it if the robbers handcuffed him?"

Jonathan was always a great audience. He held his sides and roared at that. "Did he confess?"

"Did day follow night?"

Gina broke in. "Only God knows what your two evil minds have hatched. It could only be broads." And you'd never be able to convince her that it wasn't. We were off and running to our hundred and sixty-third divorce.

"Okay, happy girl, it's your night. Let's go to dinner and leave the Rover Boys to their drinks. Where do you want to eat?"

"La Scala," she answered quickly. And to Jonathan, "You ought to try it some night, it's the best Italian food in New York. Take one of your little swingers there, she'll enjoy it."

Jonathan's lips smiled over slightly clenched teeth.

276

THE CANNIBALS

Gina turned away. "Lenny, you're adorable. One of these days . . . va-va-va-voom!"

Then she surprised Jonathan again with a peck on the cheek. "So long, Paul Power. See you on the desert."

He dug the punch-line and scowled.

I gave Johnny the wink bit, said good-bye to Len, grabbed Gina's hand, and went happily out into the night.

I sat anxiously in the projection room with the BCA boys— Virgil Esty, Chester, two or three fellows in the production department, Arthur Stuart, and Mario Colucci, whom I had invited so he could see where the money was going.

Projection rooms are nothing less than miniature movie houses. They have the same seats, the same screen except smaller, and the characteristic projection windows upper rear.

The back row of seats has a long table in front of it with lights for notes, and a master control panel for volume, etc.

In this case, though I was keyed up, the results were a foregone conclusion. No first-day rushes in the history of the business ever receive less than brilliant accolades. This is the time for the intelligentsia of every department to throw in the promiscuous adjectives—*marvelous, fabulous, great,* and *tremendous* are good enough for openers.

Tim Rice walked in along with Allie and Sniffles. Terry Winant came over and sat next to me.

The technicians were scattered through the room.

Perry Bennett walked in with a very uninvited guest, a buddy who was his New York alter ego. I let it pass for the moment.

"Okay, Tim," I said, "go when ready."

Tim looked at Joel Fryman. "Are they threaded up yet?"

Joel nodded.

Tim picked up the phone to the booth. "Let 'em roll."

The lights dimmed, and on the other side of the wall the projection machine hummed, flashing the magic of motion picture film out to the screen. I relaxed a little bit. It took form on the screen, and the operator adjusted it to bring it into sharp focus.

It came alive. People were milling, swarming, hustling around in a real newspaper office. The city desk, typewriters, chairs, maps, and phones *were* the real McCoy. Great writers had really filed hot copy from the scene that was being flashed in front of my eyes. I was thrilled.

The camera started moving. I knew from experience it was now rolling on its dolly—a rubber-tired truck. As it went around a corner, following a copy boy, I was subconsciously directing stagehands to move chairs and props so the path would be clear for the camera's silent progress.

Above the stewing crowd, on a high-platform dolly, the long arm of the boom was racing to keep up with the action, the mike anchored at the end of a mechanical fishpole that could be pointed in any direction to pick up a quick sound or snatches of background dialogue.

278

THE CANNIBALS

Extras were weaving in and out of camera, stopping to chat, sharpening pencils, typing, and doing their chores with well-rehearsed casualness. It was make-believe. It was exciting. It was television.

"Beautiful shot!" Tim yelled to the cameraman.

Perry applauded his first entrance. It went over like a lead balloon. I glanced at his face in the dim light and saw that he was hurt by this.

An argument scene came on between Perry and his editor. It was true Winantese—long and good.

"That's a scene, Terry," I commented, omitting the adjectives.

Along with all this, the makeup man was telling himself how good everyone *looked*; the gaffers loved the lights; wardrobe went crazy about the clothes; Tim Rice admired his directing; and the BCA boys sighed their first sigh of relief in days.

The lights came on. I turned to Tim Rice. "Real good."

Tim turned to the crew. "Thirty minutes, fellows."

Perry got up to leave, then turned to me. Actors are helpless in these moments. They need a confirmation. These are easier to give when you don't have to lie. In Perry's case, I could give happily.

"Just great, buddy," I whispered to him. "I'll be over with you later. Honestly, you looked wonderful. Have a good lunch and keep it up." I hit him a mock jab in the belly. "No spaghetti."

He laughed and walked happily to the door with his entourage of one.

Great happiness was general. The BCA boys made their appropriate remarks and left.

Technicians out, the projection room became a quick meeting place for my staff.

"I think it's excellent," I opened. "Any problems?"

They converged on me fast with raps on Perry.

"He's a pain in the ass." (Allie)

"He doesn't know his lines." (Tim)

"He's cost us two hours already. He's never on time, and he's playing the big star bit." (Joel)

I stood up and put my hand on my head.

"He's trouble, Joey." (Sniffles)

Terry Winant gave her a look of disdain, and I decided it was time to get one thing straight.

"Is anyone in this room trying to tell me that Perry Bennett is not coming through on the screen?"

Silence.

"Would someone like to venture the opinion that we've miscast the role and should stop, get a new leading man, and then start over?"

More silence.

"I saw film today. He looked great to me. I don't know about problems like being late, not knowing lines, or any of that other crap. I saw no billboards on the screen that told me that. I do know the guy has *got it*. So put up with him. How bad is a few more days?"

Terry jumped in. "I agree with Joey. He comes through. The mere fact that he's a shit is unimportant."

Everyone laughed at Terry's succinct appraisal, and I hopped on it.

"Okay, kids, go to work and we'll talk about it later."

Amid grumbling, face-saving ad libs, everyone filed out.

Chapter 9

George was driving me uptown from the Hall of Records, where he had been finishing a location shot with Perry. I sat silently in the back seat of the car, staring out into space as if in a hypnotic trance.

Even George was quiet. We were all bushed and showing the signs of strain and temperament. We had three more days to go to complete the pilot. Our results so far had been achieved at a premium price in human emotions.

By now Perry Bennett had everyone hating him. He was using my protection to flaunt the power that he wouldn't otherwise have had. Allie and Sniffles were annoying Terry Winant to the point where he couldn't stand to be in the same room with them. Joel Fryman, in doing his job, cracking the whip continuously to meet the deadline, had been nicknamed —warmly, if not lovingly—"Bill Bar Mitzvah." Tim Rice, knowing that this pilot would be screened for the top echelon, was working as if for a personal audition, which brought results, but at another premium price. Making films is a team effort: The "showboat" individual brews his own poison.

George pulled up in front of my apartment. I said good-bye and dispatched him back downtown. Terry hadn't made his usual ride home with me. He wanted to see the rest of the scene and be sure it was finished.

I was increasingly apprehensive about the bickering, but generally happy with the results. And that was the bottom line —results.

It was only 8:00 P.M. by my watch as I walked into the elevator, but I could have fallen asleep from fatigue as I leaned against the button.

As I walked into the apartment, there was Gina sitting on the couch, with the long face.

"Your cold veal cutlets are on the stove. Don't ever ask me to cook dinner for you again."

I ignored her, took off my coat, made it to the bar, and mixed myself a martini. I brought it back to the chair, put it down, flipped myself into the seat, kicked off my loafers, and drank half at one gulp.

"Is that your new bit?"

I looked at her. "What's that?"

"The martini routine. Next thing you know, you'll be putting it on Corn Flakes."

"Do me a great favor and take a walk." I put my head back on the chair and closed my eyes.

"True to form—now comes the sleep act. You'll fall asleep in the chair for three or four hours, then get up and watch television till there's only a dot left in the tube."

I ignored her again. It was a hard choice: She couldn't

284

stand silence, but if I joined the argument, it meant a battle. I had ace-deuce for a point either way. I couldn't win.

But I couldn't care less. There just wasn't any strength in me. A bowl of *schvat* spaghetti had more strength in it than I did at this particular moment.

"I was over to my sister's today."

Cautiously: "Which one?"

"Bobbi."

"How thrilling." (Less cautiously) "What new gems did she and her brilliant husband come up with?"

"You really hate them, don't you?"

"In order for Joey Bertell to hate anyone, he has to respect him. I neither hate nor respect either one of them. I consider both of them mental welfare patients in the clinic of human life. Please leave me alone."

I gulped the other half of my drink, got up, made another one, plunked down in the chair again, and took another generous swig of the joy juice.

"Keep on drinking and you'll be an AA before you know it."

"If I thought it would make me deaf to your nagging voice I'd hook myself on heroin."

"You really are a bastard, aren't you?"

"If you say so."

Silence in the room for another minute or two, while Gina wheeled up the big guns. She *was* going to argue, come hell or high water.

"You hate my family."

"I don't."

"Yes, you do."

"Okay, I do."

"I knew it!"

If I'd had the strength, I would have thrown a chair at her. She sounded like the wife in *The Bickersons*. Frances Langford couldn't have played the part better.

"I don't hate your family. I love them. Mama is like my own mother. Billy I adore—he's like my kid brother. With the exception of that phony Bobbi, I love your sisters, and forgetting that fraud husband of hers, I like my brothers-in-law. What the hell more do you want?"

"You wouldn't understand."

"Just tell me, I haven't heard it in the last twenty-four hours."

She picked up the challenge and knocked the chip off my shoulder.

"You really think *you're* something, don't you?"

"Yes." I knew that would annoy her.

"Maybe it would interest you to know that Bobbi and Horace don't like you. In fact, they hate your guts."

"That, my darling, is only a confirmation of my greatness."

"You're disgusting."

"Agreed. But at least I'm not a phony. I don't fly under false colors like those two frauds you profess to be so fond of. Nickel and dime con artists . . ."

THE CANNIBALS

I gulped more of my martini and went on. "They're one hundred percent bullshit. If I hear any more of their crappy dialogue on the Negro problem, so help me, I'll vomit on both of them."

I caught my breath and blurted out more wrath.

"Bobbi and her gnat-sized mind is the pseudo-intellectual of our generation. She is Mrs. Malaprop. She can't understand or even pronounce the English language . . . and she has the gall, the intense gall, to put *you* down every chance she has. And you, who have more brains in your ass than she has in her whole body, take it like some dropout waif in slumtown."

"What's wrong with her trying to improve her mind?"

"She *has* no goddam mind," I flared up. "And she's under the spell of an imbecile whose answer to being out of a job is to grow a beard."

"Are you putting him down because he can't get a job?"

"You know me better than that. I don't put anyone down on career, ambition, or anything else, so don't try to put me on the defensive. They're goddam phonies, and the thing that infuriates me is that you know it but won't admit it."

"You're just mad because you can't win the whole family over. You want everyone to belong to you—to be under the Joey Bertell spell."

That did it. I was now furious—not really at Gina, at everything: Perry, the pilot, the pressure . . . and now these two synthetic human beings.

"They couldn't be with me if they had gold-plated wallets stuffed with thousand-dollar bills. They're full of shit."

I was on my feet now. "You believe in family, right? In ten years how many Christmases, how many Easters, how many Thanksgivings have those two warts spent with Mama? I'll tell you how many: none, n-o-n-e, none."

"Horace wants it that way."

"Screw Horace. Would you let me do that to you?"

"No."

"You're goddam right you wouldn't let me, and I wouldn't try. Do you know why? Because I care. Neither one of those freaks cares. If the truth were known, they don't even care for each other."

Gina remained silent.

"I'll bet my life that they secretly hate every good thing that's happened for you."

"That's the only thing you have. She's still my sister, though."

"Great. Keep her, keep Horace. Take two strikes and hit to right field. But don't bring their embarrassing names up to me again."

She was defiant. "They are sincere in what they believe. On that I won't give in."

Now I was really upset. Damn her, why won't a woman give in when she's wrong—why? Must her pride come into everything? Gina was no dummy. She had faithfully repeated every conversation these two zircons had with her in my absence. Knowing I had fit the pieces of my picture of them together from their own words, she still fought me.

288

"Sincere my ass," I screamed. "I've got their 'I'm for the Negro' speech coming out of my ears."

"Since when have you been prejudiced?"

"Never. Only I'm not the rotten white trash that gives lip service to the problem. In my world, actions still speak louder than words."

She knew me, and she knew she was whipped.

"Take a thousand dollars and give it to those bullshit artists for expenses. Let them go to Jackson, Mississippi, and march. Let them stand up and be counted. Sammy Davis did it, Marlon Brando did it."

"Why don't you?"

"Because I accomplish more in my own way than if I marched in all the cities in America."

She waited, but she knew. I pounded my chest. I was really unhooked.

"Who broke the color line in Las Vegas? I'll tell you who— Joey Bertell. Ask Sammy who went to Las Vegas Harlem to visit him in his room? Ask the Golden Gate Quartet who went to the bosses and got permission to have them at my closing-night party—in the lobby, right out in front of everyone."

She sat back on the couch staring at me.

"Who hired Della, Hamp, and a hundred others on my shows? Who's fought for equal rights more than me? Answer me!"

She remained mute.

"I do it with actions, not words. I don't sit around intellec-

289

tuals' apartments drinking coffee, trying to impress everyone with how liberal I am. *I do it, baby*."

The angry outburst had stunned her.

"They're phony sons-of-bitches, and I'll bet you my life they won't even be there when you die and get lowered into the grave."

She jumped up and ran out of the room in tears. I'd gone too far. Now that it was over I was sorry for my outburst. But only for the effect of it on my Gina—I was right, I told myself. She asked for it and she got it. Still, there's no kidding yourself, an argument isn't a lecture. I could have handled it in a much different manner. What the hell had she really done to deserve such lousy treatment? Would the arguing be one more price that would have to be paid in this nerve-racking business?

I put on my coat. I'd go to the Athletic Club and let Gina cool off. Then maybe I'd call her—or better yet, maybe she'd call me. If she did that, I'd come home and shower her with love. If not, I'd have to ride out the storm.

As I opened the door to leave, the phone rang. After a moment's hesitation I stepped back to answer it. It was Joel Fryman—in a panic.

"Joey, all hell has broken loose."

"What happened?"

"Perry Bennett walked off the set."

I was instantly alert. "Why?"

"He and Tim Rice had words, and one thing led to another.

They began yelling and screaming at each other, and Tim threatened to punch him in the nose."

"That's all I need." I was too stunned to go on.

"Joey, Terry Winant is next to me and wants to talk to you."

"Put him on."

"Joey," Terry began, "it's just dreadful. It's the biggest display of amateurism I've seen in all my years. They were like schoolboys."

I listened, while Terry went on in high excitement, so rare for him.

"Perry is a total ass. Really, Joey, I'm not at all sure that he isn't insane. I hate to tell you, but everything that everyone has been saying about him is true. I'm sure if you had stayed, it wouldn't have happened."

"Thanks, you've made my night."

"I know it's tough to hear, but it's true."

"Did you get into it?"

"No, I stayed clear so I could talk to you."

"Thank God for a smart partner."

"We've got to have a meeting right away. I don't think Perry's coming back. He said he was going home to pack."

"When did he leave?"

"George took him back to his hotel about five minutes ago."

I smiled to myself. When all was chaos, good old George had the insight to put a collar on him. One thing I knew: Perry Bennett would be on no planes. I was now back in command.

"Terry . . . bring everybody here to my apartment. Tell them I'm seething. I'll do the rest. Play it straight and just side with me."

"Excellent. They need a good scare. But I warn you, we're in for nothing but trouble with this Bennett fellow."

"We'll handle it. Get over here fast, okay?"

"We'll be there."

"And, Terry . . ." I added quickly.

"Yes?"

"Don't bring your mother." I hung up.

Gina, who had silently walked into the room, asked, "Do you think he'll stay?"

"Sure," I said lightly.

"Whose side are you on?"

"The winning side, of course."

"Perry?"

"Naturally."

"Naturally."

"It's really easy for you, isn't it? I mean, nothing seems to unnerve you. Everyone else is shaking, and you seem to love it."

"I love a fight," I answered with a faint smile.

"God bless you, if you can take it."

I got up, walked over, and put my arms around her. She snuggled into them, and I said my usual line to her, which always got a smile and ended our arguments.

"I forgive you."

THE CANNIBALS

"You're nuts," she said playfully, pushing me away.

"You're right," I answered, "—about you."

I went over and turned on the tapes of *The Dukes of Dixieland* and waited for the fight crowd to arrive. I had made a decision not to make a move till I talked to my people.

Gina walked over with a martini and handed it to me. "Here's to the winner."

I pulled her down on the couch and put my arms around her again. I needed Perry Bennett and my staff like I needed smallpox.

The doorbell rang. I slowly released Gina, gave her a wink, walked over and opened the door.

"Come on in and sit down."

They walked in with long faces, showing the strain of overwork.

I had previously set bottles of Cutty Sark, bourbon, and vodka on the coffee table, along with mixers and ice.

"Grab a drink and then let's talk."

They rushed to the table like a herd of buffalo and returned to their chairs slowly.

I lifted my own glass. "Here's to the most stupidly created mess of all time." They drank sheepishly.

Now I turned calmly to Tim Rice. "All right, fighter, let's have it."

"Joey, it *was* stupid. But one thing led to another, and he made a fool of me in front of my crew."

"Did you hit him?"

"No. I think there was a push . . ."

I turned to Allie. "Where were you?"

"Right there."

"What did you do?"

"There was nothing anyone could do, it happened so fast."

Back to Tim Rice. "Did you finish the set?"

"I wanted one more shot, but we don't really need it. We have a protection shot of the clerk as Perry walks out of the scene."

"That's a relief."

I picked up the phone and called Saul Cahn, Perry's agent in New York. He wasn't home.

The moment I hung up the phone rang.

"Joey. George."

"Just give it to me. Don't mince words, and don't throw color into it."

"He won't come back if Tim Rice is on the set. He wants to leave. He doesn't like anyone, but he hates Rice. He can't stand Allie, his wife, or Joel."

"What else?"

"Saul Cahn is with him."

"Go back upstairs, get him on the side, and tell him I said to help but don't call me. This has to be handled between Perry and myself."

"What do I do?"

"You stay with him and don't let him out of the room until I call. Or wait, better yet, get him to call me, then take him to Canal Street and buy him some food. Soften him up."

"Right."

I put the phone down, looked at Tim Rice, and announced, "His price for coming back is simple. He wants you fired."

"That I figured on," Tim answered.

"Allie, he's also unhappy with you."

"How about me?" chimed in Terry Winant.

"You he loves."

"Dammit, I wanted to be one of the boys." The Winant wit flourished at all times.

Sniffles came alive. It was time for one of her profound comments. "What do we do now?"

"You hang yourselves." It was Gina who broke the tension. Everybody laughed, and I looked over at her approvingly.

The phone rang, and instantly the laughs hushed.

"Joey, Perry."

The voice was loaded with emotion. I didn't give a damn what anyone else thought, I liked him. He figured to be around after everyone else had stuck a knife in my back. At least, that was my snap judgment.

I had pledged him my word on loyalty, but I couldn't let him get away with running my ship. Being for him was one thing, but that was another. I prepared to play him like a violin.

"Well, well," I started out on a kidding note, "how is the Rocky Marciano of TV?"

"Joey, I can't take that S.O.B. any longer. Am I the star in this series, or am I nothing?"

"Go on, you talk."

"He humiliated me. I want him fired. I won't be on the set if he's there."

I remained silent.

"Well, say something!"

"Tell me what to say that you'd like to hear, and I'll be glad to say it."

"I'm serious. I want this guy fired."

"You've made that clear to me—you want him fired." I wanted that heard in the room.

Perry was really at his wit's end. His voice was trembling. "For God's sake, Joey, back me up."

I rose and carried the phone on its fifty-foot extension cord around the room, now becoming oblivious to my people.

"Did I give you my word I'd back you?"

"Yes."

"I keep my word. Tim Rice is fired. You also are a goddam fool. When Jonathan hears about this, Tim Rice will never see the day he'll work at BCA again. You're giving him a lovely Christmas present, and you're inheriting six hundred enemies every time you walk on the set."

Silence.

"He's going to go, buddy, and I'm doing it at your request. It's your shot to call. But remember, I warned you. You're dead ass wrong. He's a good man, and you look like eight million bucks on the screen. How bad can he be? You're a real *gagagootz* if you do this, *cabeshe*?"

"He has to apologize to me. He humiliated me, and he has to apologize."

I had him now. Perry was whipped. I had to finish him for his own good. I didn't want him to be hated. He didn't deserve that. Those peons I was hooked up with just didn't understand actors.

"He's not going to apologize . . . and neither are you. You're both going to forget it."

"No, he *has* to apologize."

I stopped pacing and flared into a rage. "No goddamit, you listen to me. Don't you fucking dare to call me on my word unless you're prepared to keep your own. What is this, a one-way street? I've done everything I said I'd do. I've watched over you like you were my own brother, because I have a *sympatico* for you. But I'm the guy with the sack. I'm the one who'll be letting *him* down. Do you want to do this to me? *Do you?*"

"No."

"Then you be on that set promptly tomorrow. I'll be there, too. We'll go next door to the bar, since it's a one o'clock call, and I'll send for Tim Rice, and we'll have a drink. We won't say one word about this jackass argument. You'll just shake, and I bet you my life that you come out of it looking like a big man. That's it. Now, are you with me or against me?"

"I'm with you."

I lowered my voice, remembered my audience, and relaxed

my grip on the phone. "Thanks, *paisan*, I was never in doubt. Why don't you go out with George and have some *scungili*, and I'll see you tomorrow, okay?"

"Okay, Joey." The phone clicked.

Terry Winant jumped up from his chair, dashed over, and started pumping my hand. "Wonderful, absolutely wonderful. I'm proud to be your partner."

Tim Rice could only say, "Thanks, Joey, I appreciate that."

I looked around the room and grabbed everyone's attention. "Go home and get some sleep. We're done in two days, and that's it. We've got a good show. We're all just tired."

They filed out with appropriate good-byes.

Then I took Gina's hand and walked into the bedroom for my first good night's sleep. Tonight's crisis had insured finishing the pilot without further incident.

Which we did.

Terry Winant walked into my office on pink clouds.

"He really liked it."

I beamed. "Yep, old buddy, we're off to the races."

"Jonathan called me at home this morning and said pretty much what you told me a few days ago."

"It's still nice to hear it from the boss, isn't it?"

Terry grinned. "It's the difference between pencil and ink."

The buzzer rang. Vera's voice came on sharp and clear. "Chester Plan on two."

"Hi, Chester."

"Hi, producer. How do you feel?"

"Great. And you?"

"I'm in high gear. You're all set—the sponsors are in, and we announce the schedule Monday. We firm it tomorrow."

"Sidney Shrewd, you are a champion."

"By the way, have your cutter bring the film over to the BCA projection room. I'm screening two shows for the Chairman tonight."

"Are you kidding? The opticals aren't in, the credits aren't on. We'll get killed."

"He has to see the show."

"Does he see every show?"

"Of course."

"What happens," I asked, "if he doesn't like it?"

"How the hell would he know what's good or bad?" This was a secure Chester Plan talking.

"He's still the Chairman. I found that out with *Sandstorm*. . . ."

"Forget it. He wouldn't know how to make a decision on anything except banana brands."

He rolled on. "Did you get the final on Jackie Benson?"

"I knew it was going to a vote."

"I'm sure your boy will tell you, anyway. We didn't even vote, we just took him out of the schedule. He can bore people somewhere else now."

I knew J.J.B. would nail him. Not taking a vote was a further sign of contempt.

"How are we doing on the Calvin Clothes project?" he asked.

"You'll have the job after the schedule is set and probably just before production starts."

"I can hardly wait."

"You'll be interviewing a guy from the Coast for your job. His name is Tom Brady, he's an account man for an advertising agency."

Chester was quick to be suspicious. "He's a Bryan Westgate man, isn't he?"

"Chester, old buddy, we'll make him our man. Good enough?"

"Great by me."

"What time are you running?"

"Eight P.M. sharp. I'm putting yours on first, while he's still fresh."

"Thank you, Sidney. Talk to you later." Click.

I buzzed Joel Fryman's office. He lost no time walking in.

"We're home free. Have the film at the executive projection room at BCA by seven-forty-five P.M. Take Marty, our cutter, with you."

"The Chairman?" he asked.

"Right, but no problem. However, don't leave that room. I want to know his exact reaction—and Chester's. Call me at nine-thirty promptly at '21.' I'll go there and wait you out."

Terry, who had stood by and sized this all up, now said, "Call me at nine-thirty-two, Joey, I have insomnia."

"Okay, will do. Come on, Terry, I'll buy you lunch and then I'm going to do some Christmas shopping. Joel, see you later. Nine-thirty call me. '21.' "

There is no clock at the bar at "21" that you can read without a microscope, so I consulted my watch. Nine-thirty sharp —and the page boy was heading my way.

"Call for Mr. Bertell."

I went to the booth. It was Joel.

"He loved it."

I must have grinned from ear to ear.

"He got up at the end and said, 'That's a good one. Don't let that one get away.' He also wanted to know how we got the newspaper, and Chester said the producer arranged it."

"Great work, Joel."

"Oh, one other thing. He said he thought it would be the best hour show on the network."

"Excellent. Have Marty remember that. All these bastards develop amnesia when you need them."

"Will do."

"Thanks again."

I gave the telephone operator Terry's number, and she dialed it.

"Relax, partner, he loved it." I went through Joel's dialogue, and Terry was genuinely pleased.

"What do we do now?" he quipped. "I'm lost with no pressure."

301

"I'll tell you what we do, Terry, my buddy. We have Christmas and New Year's and a few week's rest. Then we start on the *real* grind. By that time my son will be here, and he'll help out."

"When is the future President due?"

"February, just like his old man."

"Good luck!"

"So long, pal."

That was it. In the bag. Merry Christmas. Top of the world!

Chapter 10

Walking into the hospital maternity wing was bad enough, but by the time we'd gone through the admission formalities, and finally when I saw Gina being wheeled by, stretched out underneath a sheet, I was, to say the least, frightened.

I approached Dr. Davids and asked, "Is she all right?"

"We're going to deliver the baby right now. You just go to the waiting room on the ninth floor." He turned and walked away, adding over his shoulder, "I'll call you there."

I tried to keep active upstairs, like the traditional father-to-be. I leafed through several magazines, lit another cigarette. I glared at the phone, wondering why it didn't ring. Then I glanced at my watch. I had been there all of five minutes. . . .

At long last the day had arrived. The past two months had been great fun. Late in January we had started preparing scripts for production. The *Mr. Trouble* series looked like a big winner. Terry was just as happy as I.

The two Coast shows were now sold out and also ready for production. We had obtained Pete Carr from TV and Broadway to star in *Barnabys*, and we had Karen—and Bryan's clarinet player—for the other.

For business and political reasons I had opened West Coast

offices in Beverly Hills and placed Sol Mack in charge. He had a vast background as producer of fine motion pictures and had the plus value to me of being a fine story editor.

The announcement of Sol Mack's appointment as West Coast head of Cardinal Productions brought great prestige to my organization. Also, it gave me personal pleasure, since he was a close friend. And although he was my senior by fifteen or twenty years, we worked together perfectly.

On the other hand, I didn't envy him his position on the West Coast. In a way, he'd be a castrated bull out there. His strength was knowing what to do creatively. Already he was bombarding me with memos on the scripts for the *Karen* and *Barnabys* shows, with regard to story construction, characterizations, and comedy relief. But I knew that any day would bring the panic call, after the significance of being ignored by Farley Fag set in.

After weeks of procrastination by Allie and Sniffles, who presided as if the scripts were coming along well, and weeks of rejection memos from the network which was systematically disapproving the scripts, and weeks of daily pressure from Terry, I tied the can on Allie and Sniffles.

My next move was to make the network responsible for choosing a new line producer. In the game of musical chairs at BCA, Tom Brady, Bryan's man, was now vice-president of East Coast programming.

Calvin Clothes had been unceremoniously fired by J.J.B. Of course it came in the accepted Madison Avenue fashion—

the letter of resignation from Calvin baby and the "regretful" acceptance by Jonathan J. Bingham. The "street," however, knew the story.

Jonathan had allowed Calvin to come in on a Saturday morning to make a thirty-minute presentation of future projects. The presentation was detailed, yet to the point, and actually had more than a little merit.

At the conclusion Calvin said, "Well, John, what do you think?"

"I'm letting you go. . . ."

Another chapter in the legend of Jonathan Bingham. That quick, that cold, and that true.

By Saturday noon the facts, with the usual embellishments, had penetrated all the way down to the BCA mailroom.

Thirty minutes after the event I took a call at my home.

"Joey, Chester. Calvin Clothes isn't with us anymore."

I cut him in half at once. "I expected your call fifteen minutes ago. What kept you?"

"You rascal," he laughed.

"Well, Sidney Shrewd, is our word good or not? I told you how and when it would happen."

"You're too much, Joey."

"My birthday is tomorrow, and this is a great present. I'm very happy for you."

Next day a gift box arrived with three expensive ties and a card: "To Joey, who makes every day my birthday. Chester."

I took the card and carefully placed it in Jimmy Craig's

hands. "Put this in my box—along with the payola reports on Chester's driveway and home furnishings that Leonard Morris bought him through his company."

Jimmy looked at the card and grinned.

"Were the ties nice?"

"Only if you don't have taste." Squelch.

So there it was. Chester Plan, infighter extraordinary, had now managed to elevate himself to vice-president, head of production, East and West Coasts.

My satisfaction was that I had allowed it to happen, and even arranged it over the tears and tantrums of good old Lavender Lips Bryan Westgate.

The only reason it didn't send him into premature menopause was that he was able to put Tom Brady into Chester's old job and thus had a pipeline into the home base.

Upon Tom's recommendation, and with Chester's approval, Tim Rice was made producer of *Mr. Trouble*. But the hell with business. My son was on his way. I'd give him a party that New York wouldn't forget.

I'd already made plans to take over Danny's Hide-a-way for an evening. All floors would have music, food, and liquor, and champagne would flow like the Thames.

At six years, I start my son on pony rides and see that he gets swimming lessons. Nothing can stop him in those fun and formative years.

At ten or twelve, the Mets and the Giants every weekend. He'd also get a proper introduction to hockey and basketball.

Fourteen would be the time for camping trips and hunting.

At fifteen, I'd give him trips to the office. More than casual trips—I'd break him in slowly but surely to the jungle. He'd learn fast, and it would be good background.

Occasionally I'd take him to the other side of the street and teach him honor and code. He'd pick it up quickly because it'd be born in him. He'd find out that he must live by his word, that his handshake was final, that there was no turning around in an argument.

Sixteen and seventeen, he'd earn his own money. That's what counts. It gives confidence.

Seventeen, I'd knock him on his ass the first time he dared show disrespect to his mother or me. And he would. All boys do.

Eighteen would be girl time, and after the "facts of life" talk, he'd be on his own. There would be nothing more I could do, and nothing he would let me. He'd be that headstrong.

The phone was ringing, bringing me out of fantasy land. It was Dr. Davids.

"Come downstairs, you're the father of a gorgeous baby girl."

Jauntily I walked past Vera and Jimmy. "Follow me."

I picked up the private in a particularly happy mood. He answered.

"Buddy, I want you to be the first to know that my *son* has arrived."

Vera and Jimmy beamed.

"Congratulations, pal!"

"Thanks," I answered. "His name is Maria."

He broke up. "You silly bastard."

Vera and Jimmy muffled their laughs.

"Are you disappointed?"

"I can't answer now, I'm busy cutting my wrists."

He hung up.

"Vera, send that wire to Gina's family, my family, and the key BCA guys. Leave out the 'wrist' line."

She giggled and left.

"Jimmy, take care of the cigars at Nat Sherman's. Cancel the 'It's a boy' and bring me a thousand of the other. Do it now, so I can hit the street with them."

He started to leave, but I stopped him.

"Have George drive you, and tell him the good news."

He hesitated. "I'm happy for you, Joey."

He said it so sincerely that I was touched. I went over and poured two shots of vodka, giving him one. I lifted my glass to his and slapped him on the shoulder.

"Thanks, pal."

He drank and left.

I buzzed Vera.

"Send two dozen roses to my wife at the hospital. Be sure they're yellow. Put on the card, 'To my two dolls.' "

"Should I sign it 'Joey?' "

"No, sign it 'Morris Lipshitz.' Of *course* sign it 'Joey.' One of these days, Vera . . ."

"Would you mind if I sent flowers to Mrs. Bertell?"

"No, it would be very sweet. But put it on my bill, I don't want you going for any cash. Don't double-X me, I don't want you to spend money. Now, say you love me."

"I love you."

"Good. Get me Tom Brady."

In a few seconds he was on the line. "Hi, Daddy."

"News spreads fast."

"Take me off your wire list. I've already heard the Maria line."

I broke up. "Who told you?"

"J.J.B. told Chester—how much further than that do you have to go?"

"I see you're already acclimatized to New York. How about lunch?"

"Great. One o'clock—where?"

"Let's not hide—'21.' "

"See you there." *Click.*

Terry Winant came bursting into the room, smile wide and bald head shining.

"Please pay me my ten dollars for your son who didn't arrive."

"Winant, I've always known there was a sadistic streak in you, but I never realized it went so deep."

"Never mind your feeble attempt at a Freudian lecture, I'll be happy to accept my money and leave quietly. I understand Italians pay off."

"We always do—if we can borrow from you at six-for-five. You Jews have kept my people in poverty for years."

"You're right, Joey. Why don't we form a team and gang up on the Polacks?"

How could you top Winant? He had that ethnic humor that was razor sharp, but never offensive. He should have been in a cabinet post called Human Relations. Maybe there wouldn't be any bigotry then, and we could discuss things on a business basis.

"What's up, Terry?"

"Right on the line, Joey. I sense that the network is floundering again with all the change of personnel. We have to get through readers, sub-junior executives, and junior executives. It's awful—we interview writers, get story ideas, and end up with rejection memos from underling women."

"Tim Rice complained about the same thing, so I'm meeting Tom Brady for lunch. I'll get into it."

"Joey, it's insane, this business. How can we be a hit with a pilot one minute, have everyone kissing us on both cheeks, and then submit to changes in concept? This show has changed eight times since the Jonathan meeting."

"Terry, it's good and it's bad. There's a great Yiddish show business line that says, 'Little *tsauris*, little picture, big *tsauris*, big picture.' "

"I'll have to discuss it with my mother, but if it means what I think, then we've got the biggest picture since *Birth of a Nation*."

Without Terry to break the ice, certain days would have been unbearable.

Vera buzzed me. "Bryan Westgate on line three."

"Bryan baby, how's by you?"

"Congratulations, how's Gina?"

"Fine, thanks. Both girls doing fine. How're the shows coming?"

"They're in good shape. I had your Sol Mack in here for a meeting."

"That's great, Bryan. One of the reasons I hired him," I reminded him, "was because you recommended him."

"Oh, he'll be just fine. He's a little eager, and I asked him to give any suggestions he has to Sid Kup, who is our creative supervisor on comedy shows."

So poor Sol was castrated already, and there was nothing I could do. Since I'd been warned by J.J.B. to let Farley Fag take care of everything, my company on the West Coast was a sham. I had gone for the money to open offices and hire Sol so we didn't look like fools.

I kicked myself in the ass for not taking a royalty for creating the shows, and ducking this production company phoniness. Who needed Farley Fag as a captain?

Still, if Bryan could pick good people, which was becoming more dubious, it could catapult Cardinal into real prominence.

On balance, it was now the biggest producing company of the year. *Variety* had parlayed the three shows into a headline story. Trade columnists were perpetuating the legend. Overnight I had become a power in the business.

In theory, Cardinal was the biggest buyer of talent, writers, and directors in TV, and Joey Bertell the most sought-after packager on the "must-see" list.

This also made me vulnerable. The Leonard Morrises became jealous; agents resented deals being made without them.

Jonathan's new theory was to bypass agents. He hated them with a passion. One major agency he absolutely refused to do business with because they had double-crossed him on reruns of a hook-nosed comedian who was money in the bank. The comedian was a big talent and loved St. Jude as much as I did. In my personal encounters with him he had proved to be a warm human being. We had been under contract to the same studio, and I had an instinct to go to him, explain the rerun double-cross, and save the deal—but Johnny wouldn't hear of it. He was riding so high that his reaction was to blackball the agency and snub the unfortunate star. The fallout on my friend the star had, in fact, given me a little tickle of apprehension that with Jonathan riding so high and me being so vulnerable there could be waves.

"Joey"—Bryan broke into my thoughts—"when are you coming out here again?"

"When the two shows are done, or before that if you need me. Why?"

"I'm upset about Johnny. There's so-o-o much talk about him. He just seems to be running wild, and I must talk to you about it."

"Anything really bad?" I pressed.

"Not at the moment, but it's all building up. The rumors are just awful, and maybe you can talk some sense into him. Even Hitler fell, you know!"

Bryan was obviously in a frightened state. Fags are vicious when they're sniping at you, but when they run scared, they just pull their little dresses over their heads and hide.

"Have you heard of *Face?*" he went on. "It's a weekly trade paper."

"The one that Morry Weinstein runs?"

"Yes."

"I know the sheet. I don't know him, though."

"He's just awful, Joey. He's not allowed anywhere. He's a parasite in the trade."

"I read him a few times. He's a goddam good writer. As a matter of fact, he writes funny—I used to get a kick out of it."

"He's now starting on Jonathan."

"For what?"

"Well, you, Joey, and a number of other things."

"What the hell have I got to do with it?"

"He has begun implying that you and Jonathan are partners."

"Let him imply."

"Joey, we must protect Jonathan."

313

"From what?" ("From Farley Fag" would have been the best answer. Shirley Temple aged six had more spunk than this bedpan.)

He was now a bit hysterical. "Joey, we really *must* talk!"

I had to calm him before he lost his Tampax. "Okay, Bryan, I'll come out. I'll talk to you later." I hung up.

Staring at the top of my desk, I reviewed the conversation. It was now apparent that Bryan baby knew more than he was saying.

He had trapped himself with me by duking me into the fact that the articles in *Face* would be getting worse and would include me.

I was a natural patsy for anyone who was aiming at Jonathan, yet Farley Fag seemed to know more about all this than he should. Either he was planting Morry Weinstein's dirt himself or was having someone do it for him. It could also be UBC, or the talent agency. Or Chester—this was Chester's forte.

I had to get copies of the sheet, and more information fast, before it got out of hand. The rumors of J.J.B. being my partner, even though unfounded, could not be allowed to continue.

"Trouble?" asked Terry, who had been standing by silently through all this.

"No, partner, just more of the same crap from Bryan. He's in a trauma; I think he lost his douche bag."

"No girl should be without one," Terry quipped. "I'm going back to work. See you, Daddy."

THE CANNIBALS

"Regards to your mother."

He left. I picked my darts and threw six that didn't even come close to the money circle.

It was a particularly crowded day at the "21" bar. Every day there is like New Year's, but a television season makes it even more so. With the schedules set and production ready to roll, all the account executives for the advertising agencies and all the network brainpowers-that-be seemed to have gathered. It was like a roomful of Cardinal Productions representing all the different time slots there are on the air.

In "my" little group were Bill Blackman, Gottfried von Klung, Tom Brady, and Mario Colucci.

We said our hellos and kept the conversation completely away from business.

"How's Gina?" Bill asked.

"Fine, Blackie."

I turned to Gottfried. "I know where you can pick up a thousand used swastikas."

"We have plenty of those. It's Lugers that we need . . . guns and ammunition to rise again."

We gave him a mock Nazi salute and drank our shooters. Gottfried always took the kidding in good fashion, which is why he was welcomed in any group.

Mario caught my eye and maneuvered himself next to me.

"Did you hear anything about my raise?"

"No."

"I've got to have it," he whimpered.

"Do you want me to find out about it?"

"Will you?"

"Of course. I'll let you know late this afternoon or in the morning."

I turned my attention to Tom Brady.

"Let's get our lunch and talk."

Bill commented, "I'd like to be in on that crisis."

"I have a feeling that you were," I shot back.

Now the Nazi put in his quip: "Is Bill interfering in *our* series?"

Tom answered in a lordly manner: "Bill has proved to be of invaluable assistance with his profound suggestions from time to time."

"You're only saying that because it's true," Bill threw away.

"It's up to my knees already," I snorted. "I can't take this any longer."

Tom and I walked over to our table, sat down, ordered another shooter, and got the lunch order out of the way.

Tom Brady was in his early or at most his middle forties— black hair, soft eyes, and the typical Irish kisser. He was a good family man, with two well-adjusted children and a wife who had more than her share of intestinal fortitude. I liked the Bradys, and Gina got along fine with the wife.

Tom was an exceptionally good handshaker. He knew how to play politics and figured to hold any job as long as he wanted it. He had a quick wit—could trade lines with the best of them and come out on top. In appearance, he was the personification of Madison Avenue, from the crew cut to the alligator pocket wallet.

And he was a guy I liked. He pulled no punches, didn't veer from side to side . . . and could definitely be trusted.

As I looked him over, I realized it was becoming decision time on Tom Brady. I knew Chester Plan would ultimately try to nail him, so a side had to be picked. I couldn't straddle the fence much longer.

Chester knew that Tom was getting close to me and was already close to Bryan Westgate. In recent meetings I had seen the distrust start to form in Chester's eyes at the mention of Tom Brady's name, and I reminded myself that a look in Chester's eyes was always something to watch for.

It wasn't that Chester Plan was a complete rat—he had only enough guts to be a mouse. But he was cunning. He had refined to a highly personal skill the art of stealing the cheese without letting the trap spring down to destroy him.

If Chester had had even a sparse portion of ability and talent, he could have shot to the top echelon. And he would have stayed there, through his peculiar ability to be continually involved in double-crosses, yet dance away at the proper moment, and, from a safe distance, watch the destruction hit everyone else.

It was time to open the conversation with Tom.

"I heard from Bryan today."

"Anything up?"

"Not particularly. He's in a tizzy about some writer out there who's starting on Jonathan."

"Not Morry Weinstein?"

"Yeah."

"Holy Christ," said the smiling Irishman.

I felt for the first time that it might be worth looking into, after all, but I stayed casual with Tom.

"What's so terrifying about Weinstein?"

"He's not terrifying. In fact, he's laughable."

"Still, nobody is laughable if he has a typewriter and can get into print."

"That's my point, Joey. Why is he on Jonathan?"

"I would guess he's been steered on him."

"But why?"

"Dale Carnegie, Jonathan ain't."

"That is an understatement." Tom thought for a second or two, then added, "So let him write. What the hell can he say? Let him write."

I wanted no panic and showed no alarm. "You're no doubt right." I raised my glass. "Over the falls, buddy."

"Here's to *Mr. Trouble*," Tom added with a warm and believable smile.

We drank away and set down our glasses—the limit. (If you ordered more than two in a known "business" restaurant constantly, you were open to drunk lines when the enemy took potshots at you.)

"About *Mr. Trouble*," I picked up, "what the hell is the static on scripts?"

"It's par for the course, Joey."

"What kind of an answer is that?"

"From here on, we have sponsor interference, program practices, network thinking."

"The network!" I flared. "Name me one brain there that thinks!"

He gave me a pained look.

I dug the bit. "Except you, of course."

"Thank you."

"Seriously. How the hell can you make a pilot that everyone likes, including the Chairman, that was immediately sold out to sponsors—and now suddenly we're changing characters and rejecting scripts?"

"For the very reason that it's a hot show: All the guys want to feel they've contributed."

"Contributed! You can screw up Wheaties if you put kerosene and salt on it."

"Have you tried it?"

"Oh, you are funny. You ought to do a spot on Sullivan."

"Relax, Joey. *Mr. Trouble*'s going to be all right, you'll see."

"I didn't get on the air by staying in bed and relaxing."

I lifted the empty martini glass, slipped a piece of ice into my mouth and cracked it. Then I continued. "Besides, I've got Terry Winant to contend with. He is my partner, and I do have to give him answers. He likes answers that are facts, not inside jargon lines."

"One fact is that Terry Winant writes long and tedious dialogue scenes."

"That's Winant. That's what you bought."

"That doesn't make it good TV fare."

"Tom, if you use those clichés with me, I'll pee in your soup."

"It isn't just a cliché, it's the general opinion."

"Whose opinion? Chester never read a script in his life, and you know it."

Tom laughed. "Yes, I heard about your practical joke on the big script meeting where you altered the key pages."

"Did Chester know it was me?"

"Who else doesn't have to worry about losing a job?"

"Touché. But who else had that opinion about Winant?"

"Bryan, for one."

"Oh, is *she* sticking *her* thing in this, too?"

"You can do a lot of damage with a phone call. . . ."

That was it. Little Joey baby now had to tighten up and start checking out positions.

By a turn of events I was now a big shot, a living, walking target . . . *vulnerable to my own game.*

Well, they had another guess coming. This was Joey Bertell they were up against, not some punk on the street in Harlem hustling numbers for the bank. I'd show them moves that would turn the tentacles around and throttle their own throats.

The first move was to spread love and joy into all my conversations. I had now been alerted, poor souls, and would not spoil the trick by letting them know. Nothing is better than holding a kicker in draw poker—especially if you make the fill.

"You may be right, Tom old buddy," I said in good humor.

320

"Let's ride it out together. Nobody is looking to make a flop."

"I think that's wise, Joey."

After family talk and the usual good fun remarks about my new daughter Maria, we finished lunch.

"I hope we have all twelve scripts done *before* we go into production, Tom."

"It would be a great coup. When do you shoot?"

"Six weeks. We've got to get the jump so that we don't catch up with ourselves. We're doing a one-hour show in eight or nine days, plus cutting and editing, so it wouldn't take long once they play one a week to fall behind."

"Don't remind me."

"Don't *delay* me," I twisted it. But the tension was over, and we were back in good spirits.

"How's Perry?" he asked.

"Down to about ten complaints a day and a hundred long-distance calls a week."

"I don't envy you having to nurse him day and night."

"All I want him to do is keep coming through on film and I'll be happy. He's a good guy and a big talent."

"You like him, don't you?"

"It's funny, but I do. He's loaded with charm. He's like a little boy."

"My own little boy can be tiring sometimes. . . ."

"Maybe I'll bring Perry over someday so they can play blocks together."

"Perry would get mad. My son would be too smart for him."

"Good day, Tom Brady." I snatched the check and left.

Chapter 11

Echoes of "Hi, Daddy," were sounding throughout the office as I walked past Vera. She handed me wires of congratulations and three inches of messages.

On top of the pile was an internetwork manila envelope from Jonathan's office. I opened it, and out popped the latest edition of *Face* magazine. Bold cover lines predicted J.J.B.'s early demise at BCA. Attached to the magazine was a handwritten note:

```
File under B and burn.

                        J.J.B.
```

As I perused *Face*, I spotted my name planted insignificantly; also the ominous postscript—*more to come.*

Weinstein was taking on almost the whole network. Chester Plan was missing. Not so Bryan: He was excoriated as a fag, a limp wrist, and sundry other unflattering nouns and descriptive adjectives.

I became engrossed. The guy could write. He had a ballsiness that grabbed your attention, a command of the language, and

323

he was cute. I remembered he had written a book that impressed me at the time, and now I knew that Morry Weinstein was not the kind of guy to fool with.

He was onto a Big Key: Public companies were vulnerable to ridicule and unfavorable publicity on their top executives. Corporate machinations are easily explained, but personal peccadilloes are not.

If anyone ever lived in glass houses it was J.J.B. and Bryan, not to mention Chester Plan. Chester reading poetry to his adolescent starlet mistress, or his sex lessons with Chili, would be good for eight issues with black headlines.

And if Weinstein ever got on to the whore setup, the "actresses" who collected their hundred-dollar fees from BCA for balling the executives, it would be sheer hell. And Weinstein would, sooner or later.

All the wise asses were underestimating this guy, but I wasn't about to go along with their fatal error.

Already I could spot his particular *schtick*. He'd build a story on pure fantasy. Then the dirt planters and the rumor mongers would fill him in. He'd then cross-match the stories and come up with something closer to the truth.

Close enough, in the case of BCA, to make the biggies run for cover.

The laugh was that everyone professed not to read Weinstein, predicted that he'd be out of business and fade away. What fools! This guy had it made, and in their stupidity, instead of placating him and taking the self-praising ads, they decided to ignore him and even boot him off their lots!

THE CANNIBALS

All my life in show business I had proved the success of a policy to take my lumps as they came. If a newspaper guy praised me, I thanked him. If I got the rap, I gave him the benefit of his opinion and his right to comment.

But that was lumps as a performer. I had never run across the reporter who hurt me at home or in any way harmed my family. That would be another complaint.

On impulse I grabbed the private and dialed J.J.B. He was there.

"Johnny, Joey. I got that sheet."

"Isn't it a joke?"

"No, and Bryan doesn't think so, either."

"That's because he's in it."

"It's stronger than that. This guy has to be spoken to, he can't be ignored."

"Forget it, let him rant and rave."

"He'll do more."

Jonathan laughed. "The silly bastard mails his paper to the Chairman and the Dentist every week, plus a copy to the board of directors."

I was stunned. "And that strikes you as funny?"

"Of course. They think he's a mental case."

"They're wrong."

"Joey, don't bother me anymore with that lunatic. What else?"

"I had lunch with Tom Brady at '21.' "

"Is he in the camp?"

"Yes."

"Does he know who's the boss?"

I threw in the zinger. "He's not sure whether it's you or Bryan."

"Did you call to heckle me?"

"Only in part."

"Well, drop it. Things are going too well to waste time on numbskulls."

"I'm on record—unless you want me to 'yes' you like your brown-nose brigade."

"Call me when you're in a good mood," he snapped, and hung up.

One thing I knew, I had made the right move. I had planted it in his mind. Now he'd start thinking about it.

I'd go to the hospital now and see him later for a farewell drink. His trip to London would take a few weeks during which I could delve further into the *Face* matter.

I'd reach out and find out about this guy Weinstein and then go to the Coast. As they say, forewarned is forearmed.

I buzzed Vera. She appeared promptly.

"Make reservations for me on the morning flight to the Coast three weeks from today. I'll be gone two weeks, and then back to start shooting."

"Yes, your worship."

"Not your worship, stupid. Daddy."

I patted her on her generous *tushie* as I left. "California, Here I Come. . . ."

THE CANNIBALS

The doorbell rang and the room service waiter wheeled in the table. With great care he arranged the bottles of Cutty Sark, bourbon, and vodka on the bar, then the various mixes, the glasses, and the ice buckets.

"Anything else, Mr. Bertell?"

"No, thanks." I signed the check.

He never glanced at the signature or tip. "We're all happy to have you back. Enjoy your stay."

"Thanks. Where are the broads?"

He laughed. "If they have any brains, they'll all be up here."

"Good answer." I watched him leave.

I mixed a vodka and tonic and waited for Sol Mack to arrive. He would fill me in on the two shows out here, and California gossip in general, before I went over to BCA-West and Farley Fag.

The doorbell rang, on the dot, and in he lumbered, a big bear with untamed hair topping a large but soft and gentle face. Sol Mack in a brand-new three-hundred-dollar suit and thirty-dollar shirt was no more impressive than Sol Mack in a fifty-dollar suit and two-ninety-five shirt would have been. But either way he was well-liked and respected in the movie community. Sincerity was his strong point, and that's what I needed at the moment. I could count on it: He was absolutely loyal to whomever he worked for.

He entered with a warm grin. "Welcome to Cardinal Productions West Coast."

"Thanks, Sol. It's really good to see you."

I made him a quick drink and sat him down with it.

"Joey, how's it going in New York?"

I handed him a reverse. "You've read the scripts we're doing —what do you think?"

"They're all right, but Winant is missing in them. It's not the pilot."

Candid Sol Mack had hit it on the nose. Tactful he couldn't be, but right he was.

"You're psychic," I said.

"Not really. If you're aiming for the pilot and the original idea, then you don't have it. But if you've changed format and conception, then you may have what you want."

"What's your opinion?"

"I don't like it as well."

"Neither do I."

"How does Terry Winant feel?"

"He and his mother don't like it, either."

"Why don't you mention it to Jonathan?"

"I will, at the right time. He's in London now."

I pondered Sol's comment a moment, however. That was one aspect of the jigsaw puzzle. The changes in format and conception had indeed been too apparent for J.J.B. *not* to know. And if he did, why, I wondered, had he not tipped or consulted with me?

A furtive thought tingled my mind. Maybe he was coppering his bet and had decided not to pioneer with a brilliant writer like Terry Winant, even though it had been the Chairman's wish. Or perhaps he was just compromising with Winant plus the usual pedestrian but tried and true television formula. Columbus J.J.B. wasn't.

Don't panic, Joey, that's reserved for the latrine cleaners.

"Sol, how's it really going out here?"

"Awful."

"What does that mean?"

"It means that any help we might give is not wanted."

I waited.

"I was invited over to the network and treated royally. Bryan and Joe Ballantine couldn't have been more gracious. But they let me know that outside of having our name on the films, we were not controlling or even producing either one."

"Just that flat out?"

"Exactly."

"Both of them?"

"Bryan talked. Ballantine nodded in accord."

Another part of the jigsaw puzzle. I wondered where it would fit.

"What else? Did they mention me?"

"Yes, they praised your talent and said that you had agreed to the hands-off situation."

"Any lefties?"

"Bryan in his catty way said that he'd be making you a millionaire."

"I'll sell now for a thousand dollars."

"I'll buy for that price."

"You'd better wait, Sol. On the one show, the only sure thing is that Karen and the fruit will find a way to screw it up. And if they need help, the clarinet player will be there to join in."

"Is he a fag, too?"

"Well, I wouldn't say that moving Bryan's husband out and taking his place proves you're a fag, but when you move in your clothes and play leapfrog, something is sure as hell going on. . . ."

"How does he get away with it with Jonathan?"

"If I knew that, I could retire to a life of luxury."

"Have you any ideas?"

"Sol, if I really did, do you think I'd let it out?"

"No."

"That's your answer. Now, let's have one more, and then I'm going to take it easy. Tonight I'm having dinner with my mother."

"I'll have one more, too, but light."

I walked to the bar and made him his light one. Mine I made a heavy. I needed it. I brought them back, handed him his, and lifted mine in a toast. "Don't worry, we'll win."

"I have no doubt of that." Sol then changed the subject. "What's with that trade weekly that's on J.J.B.?"

"It's a six-page dirt sheet in trade size, like the *Reporter* or *Daily Variety*. But there the comparison ends."

"Do you know the guy?"

"No."

"Do you want to meet him?"

"Can you arrange it?"

"He's called here for a meeting with you."

"What did you say?"

"I said you weren't in town."

"Keep it that way."

"Have you read the last few issues? It's disgusting."

"He's a good writer."

"Do you really think so?"

"Don't you? You're the pro."

"He has style," Sol grudgingly admitted.

"Then he's a writer."

"You could be right."

"On that I am right. I'm also right that his information about me is pure bullshit. He has me actually carrying money all over the world."

"At least he has imagination."

"Now you're agreeing with me."

"Joey, what are you going to do? Do these open letters mean anything?"

"The answer to that depends on if he's smart enough to analyze whether they mean anything."

"Then they do?"

"A drop of water every ten seconds can erode a cliff in time."

Sol smiled in appreciation of the analogy.

I quickly switched the subject. "How's *The Barnabys* coming?"

"It's a different situation on that one. Bill Riley is producing and will direct a few, so it's in good shape. If the actors make it live, it will be a fine show."

"I had two meetings with Riley, and he was a regular guy."

"Joey, the man is a pro. The other silly show is now ridiculous. They don't know what the hell they're doing. But Riley has things in working order."

"That's good."

"There's one peril, which you can appreciate from being in the comedy field all your life. Nothing is more dangerous than six comedy writers sitting around the office hysterically laughing at their own jokes."

"Amen."

"These guys can sway whoever listens to them, but it takes an off-distance mind—or audience—to prove if material is really funny."

"Right, Sol"—it was something I did indeed have firsthand knowledge of—"and a laugh track won't help."

"God save us from laugh tracks."

"As long as you're talking to God, have Him send us a couple of real ones."

Wanting to conclude the meeting, I now went to our company's future business. "Sol"—this was now an order—"forget how you feel about these production slights. We have other work."

"Shoot."

"I completed the development deal with BCA on the pilot for next season, or the midseason fallouts."

"Are we staying with the name, *The Bridge?*"

"Yes, J.J.B. likes it, and it has good acceptance from Chester and Tom."

"How are *they* getting along?"

"A matter of time."

"Who are you backing?"

"Tom Brady."

"Bryan is in his corner."

"That's good. They say that a woman makes the man. . . ."

"She fills that bill."

I smiled at Sol, pleased he was so fast. His humor, which he had in abundance, was usually dry.

"Anyway, on this show I want you on top of everything. You'll be the executive producer."

"Did you set the three writers?"

"Yes, two from the Coast, and I'll work with the one in New York. We'll pick the best script, and that's the one we'll shoot."

"How are you coming on the half-hour comedy pilot for the soap company?"

"Bill Blackman, who's the agency man, says it's firm. They love the idea, and I'm going to make a deal with Nate Forman to write it—for half the action."

"Isn't he a little old-hat?"

"Yeah, but he still has that bullshit name."

"I thought he retired."

"He's had more retirements than Harry Lauder, but he's still half-ass salable."

Sol laughed at that. The phone rang, and I picked it up.

"Hello."

333

"Joey, how are you?"

"Who's this?"

"The world's greatest actor!"

"It can't be that I'm talking to myself."

"You egomaniac—it's Perry!"

"Perry who?"

He picked up on the rib. "Hiya, sweetheart."

For an instant I forgot we were back in Hollywood, where such terms are commonplace.

"Great. Have you been receiving the scripts I've been sending?"

"Yeah, I've read them all."

"Am I taking care of my favorite star?"

"You sure are. I have a few suggestions I'll go over with you. . . ."

"I also have a suggestion for you."

"Name it, pal."

"Stick *your* suggestions up your ass."

He took a three-second pause, but recovered beautifully.

"Tell the truth—you love me."

"Perry, is there anyone who doesn't?"

Sol figured out the straight line, and pointed eagerly to himself.

"Joey baby, are we having dinner before you leave?" He sounded like Chili.

"How's tomorrow night?"

"Perfect, name it."

"Pick me up here at eight P.M. and we'll play it by skyhook."

"Okay, see you tomorrow." *Click.*

"How do you keep all these things in your mind?" Sol asked.

"Don't make me explain or I'll lose the formula. Easy it ain't."

"Okay. Now, I keep on top of the two shows here. We get *The Bridge* scripts out fast, pick the best one and go. You'll keep me advised on the half-hour comedy pilot. And that's it, right?"

"Wrong. Make a deal yourself. Keep getting business."

"Will do."

We shook hands and he left. Good meeting.

Chapter 12

I had now enjoyed five days of golf, six thousand phone calls, dinner with Perry, and more meetings with Sol.

I had insisted that all meetings be made around the pool. The sun obliged, in its well-publicized splendor, as if the Chamber of Commerce had been burning candles. So it was a golden-brown producer who finally strode into the executive offices of BCA.

It was obvious they were set to greet me like visiting royalty. There was even a cute receptionist who called me Jo-Jo, and I wondered if she was compliments of BCA.

Royalty was a game I played naturally. When the secretary asked me to wait, I just walked past her to the open door of Bryan Westgate's office. He was startled, but waved me in.

Bryan was on the phone laughing hysterically and hardly able to catch his breath. "Wonderful . . . beautiful . . . gorgeous . . . delightful . . . lovely," he would manage. And after each laugh he would flick a lock of hair back from his eye. (A plucked eyebrow should never, never be covered.)

The conversation finally over, he greeted me with, "You've got to hear this, it's the funniest scene of the year."

Still laughing, he skipped over and shut the door, then back to his desk and buzzed the secretary. "Hold the calls."

Back to me. "Joey, you look marvelous. The tan is very becoming. And I do love the haircut—although you have such beautiful hair, anyway, that it wouldn't matter what you did with it."

I felt it appropriate to return the compliment and managed to bring forth a cliché that would appeal to him.

"By the way, Bryan, you've lost some weight." Who knew?

Bingo. "Can you really see it?"

"As soon as I walked in."

"I take three simply marvelous pills that my doctor gave me." He went over to a file cabinet, slid out a drawer, and there were about three hundred bottles. He pulled out one, unscrewed the cap, shook out a capsule, and showed it to me. With pride yet!

As I looked at the multicolored gelatin, I tried to fathom how this unctuous ass had ever become a top executive, or, to be honest with myself, to fathom how Jonathan, the stickler for strength, could bear to have him around. Just how the frig could anyone with even the mentality of a giraffe possibly display a diet pill with such pleasure, as if it were the latest Jonas Salk vaccine.

I restrained my disgust and spoke admiringly. "It looks great."

"I can't tell you how great it *is*. Would you like me to get you some?"

The cooze! "Could you?" I had now practically lost the battle to keep from vomiting, but he'd never realize it.

"Of course. I'll have them sent to your hotel this afternoon."

"Thanks, Bryan. I appreciate it."

I wanted to ask him if he got K-Y at wholesale rates, but with my luck, he'd consider the kibitz an advance. Wouldn't that be a great bit: Lavender Lips going all over town telling his boyfriends, "Joey Bertell made a play for me."

Enough of the ludicrous. "You were going to tell me the funniest scene of the year," I reminded him.

He started laughing again. "You know Delbert Marsh?"

"Yeah."

"I played the greatest rib of all time on him."

"Bryan, stop making a career out of the introduction and tell me the story."

He wheeled around in his chair and crossed his legs primly. Telling his story, he was imagining a pin spot on him as the curtain slowly rose. . . .

"Del is in the hospital for a few days to have some little thing done with his liver. No surgery or anything, he was just bored in general. . . ."

Again the laugh, the silly bitch.

"I got hold of a very beautiful girl who we use from time to time for the New York boys, and sent her down to Western Costume for a fitting. . . ."

"Not the gorilla routine. . . ."

"No!" he screamed. "This one was sheer joy."

"Not an armored knight?"

"No." He pursed his lips and waited happily.

339

"I give up."

"A nun."

I forced myself to stay calm. This nut was really a yo-yo.

"She went over to the hospital with a basket of fruit and some books that we picked up at Martindale's. She took the elevator to his floor and walked down the hall past people who gave her the smiles and the nods. 'Hello, Sister.'

"Now, this is exactly how *she* told it to me," Bryan cooed.

"She walked into the room and smiled sweetly. 'You must be Mr. Marsh.' "

" 'I am. Sister, but I think you've made a mistake, I'm not Catholic.'

" 'That doesn't matter, Mr. Marsh. It's part of our Order's way to try to bring a little cheer to all of those who have been confined.'

"At this point," said Bryan, "she handed him the fruit and books.

" 'This is very sweet of you, Sister,' he said in a truly appreciative manner.

" 'You're most certainly welcome, Mr. Marsh.'

" 'Yes, since I'm not of your faith, this is a very nice gesture.'

" 'Our aim is to spread happiness.'

"She rose from her chair and approached the bed. As she did, Marsh could observe the classic beauty of her face, and automatically noted also that the Sister had generously shaped breasts that even the habit could not conceal. He was instantly ashamed of the degenerate thought and dismissed it from his mind.

" 'I understand,' she said, 'that you are a television producer for some company.'

" 'Yes, I'm with BCA.'

" 'How nice, I always wanted to know more about that field. It must be fascinating.'

" 'It is,' he agreed, 'but it's also hard work.'

"She looked at him with soft eyes and lightly put her hand on his forehead. 'Possibly that's why you look so tense.'

" 'Yes, it tells on you sooner or later.'

"Her thumbs slowly massaged Marsh's temples. 'Just close your eyes and lightly dream good thoughts, and you'll see how quickly you can erase tension,' she said graciously.

"Her fingers started to work in professional feather-like strokes up and down his sideburns, then across his closed eyelashes.

"After dreamy minutes, during which Marsh struggled again with his degenerate thoughts, the hands drifted down to his cheekbones, across his mouth, then lightly to his neck and around to the shoulder blades.

" 'Is it easing you?'

"Marsh answered from a drugged distance. 'Yes.'

" 'That's good. Now relax and let your muscles free themselves.'

"The fingertips moved around to his nipples and hovered

341

just long enough to check the increasing firmness of the tips. Down the road-map of his body the hands slid until they reached the incredible goal.

"With it firmly encased in one hand, the other sought its two suspended partners and started massaging.

"Marsh was now in a riot of confusion and ecstasy, and the doves were ready to take wing.

"At precisely the right moment, the girl knelt by the side of the bed and delivered a long, rhythmic kiss of mercy to the area she had prepared.

"Marsh was now in a director's heaven, starring in a scene of Vesuvius erupting, trembling and erupting again, with hot white lava spurting and pouring down the hill and draining into a cool little pink lake. He came out of it in a complete daze to see the 'Sister' delicately touch her lips with the bed-sheet, rise, walk over to the chair, pick up her bag, and move silently toward the door. There she silently turned and blessed her parishioner with an innocent smile.

" 'Good-bye, I hope you enjoyed yourself.' A slight pause. 'It was brought to you through the courtesy of Bryan Westgate and BCA.'

"She left him as she found him, confused, but happy."

At the conclusion of Bryan's version of the girl's report, I stared at his fairy face, and just objectively, like any normal God-fearing man, I actually despised him.

I had previously rated as the dirtiest two-faced louse in the world a man hated and puked on by everyone—Chester Plan.

THE CANNIBALS

Right under him I had rated another man, laughed at and joked about, treated as an ignorant ass-kissing clown with not one ounce of leadership—Mario Colucci, the mental parasite.

But Bryan Westgate now had the dubious distinction, in my ranking, of making both of them look like saints.

This creep, this toad, this worm, this toilet, this scum. He was beneath contempt. His presence covered me with slime.

Jonathan, you sonovabitch bastard, I said to myself, *why? Just tell me why, and maybe I'll understand. Trust me. Try me. Give me a chance to fathom the reason. Chester, yes. Mario, yes. Ballantine, yes. The Chairman, yes. The Dentist, yes. Bea, yes. Omar, yes. Whores, yes. Morton Silvern, yes. BCA, yes. UBC, yes. World-Bond, yes. Calvin Clothes, yes. Leonard Morris, yes. Fred Tashley, yes.* Sandstorm, *yes. Jackie Benson, yes. Irving Impotent, yes. Your whole jaded life, yes. But this sacrilegious, dirty, filthy, degenerate cocksucker— WHY?*

As I talked to myself, the musical background was Farley Fag laughing, and then talking and further describing the act of indecency of which he was the sole proud architect—although the money, he gaily bragged, was really being paid by the Chairman, his stockholders and stooges.

"And serves him right," he queened in the musical background. "I have to get *him* whores when he comes out here. I'm entitled to a little fun myself. . . ."

What a rodent. I excused myself to leave for the little boys' room, so I could rid myself in safety of the urge to stomp him.

As I returned, the receptionist smiled at me. I had another wave of repugnance and determined to prevent this "Compliments of Bryan Westgate" possibility from ever happening.

The cute little secretary also smiled at me and said, "There's a call from New York. You can take it in that side office if you like." I walked through the door she pointed to, and picked up the phone.

"How's the weather?" It was Mario Colucci.

"Beautiful. What's up?"

"Are you alone, Joey?"

"Yes."

"I just wanted you to know the raise came through."

"That's no surprise. I told you J.J.B. approved it and sent it upstairs for the Dentist's signature."

"Well, it came back down signed all right, and J.J.B.'s office notified me. Just wanted to let you know. Also to thank you."

Somehow it didn't ring true. I decided to play a silent duke.

"Have you heard from him?" he asked.

"He called me from London last night."

"Leonard Morris is over there, too—did you know that?"

"Don't be insulting."

That still wasn't it, that was just Percy President's way of killing time until he got to the point.

"Have you seen Bryan?"

"I'm in a meeting with him now. I just stepped out when this call came through."

344

"Does he know it was me?"

"No, I stepped out originally for the call of nature."

"Good, because I'm a little upset with him."

Aha! I let the silence grow.

"I'd like your advice."

"Shoot. But lay it on the line, Mario—don't bullshit around, I'm up to my eyeballs in bullshit now. And I have to get back to his office."

"Joey, it's this. Bryan and Joe Ballantine are taking the position that the West Coast is autonomous and they can make their own deals."

"So?"

"George Robbins, who reports to me from out there, is now making deals without consulting me."

"Fire him."

"I've gotten scuttlebutt that I can't."

"From whom?"

"Chester."

"What does he have to do with your department?"

"Nothing, but I asked his opinion."

What a jockstrap. The jerk was really beyond help, and I mused on whether I should advise him at all. But the logic of it was too simple to withhold.

"Did you call me when you wanted this job?"

"Yes."

"And when you wanted the raise?"

"Yes."

"Yet now you've switched to Sidney Shrewd to discuss a major problem."

"I guess I was wrong."

"Do you now! Just because you discussed a major problem with someone who sees a psychiatrist three times a week, has a wife who browbeats him, is in love with an adolescent chick he can't hold, and pays a hundred and fifty a week to get laid?"

"Okay, okay."

"And don't give me the 'Okay, okay' con. There's a great racket expression that I learned years ago. 'You didn't invite me to the wedding—don't invite me to the funeral.' "

"What you're saying is you think I'd lose if I tried to fire my own man?"

"In the simplest possible terms, I'm saying that if it were me, I wouldn't take the *chance* of losing."

"Is Bryan that strong?"

"He's a helluva lot stronger than you and Sidney Shrewd put together."

The phone was silent. I tried to elucidate for the poor guy.

"I have him stalemated. He can't hurt me. He doesn't try to, but every so often he pecks away. That's his nature and I put up with it. Now, *why* he's got power I can't tell you, but it's there. J.J.B. backs him to the hilt."

"Then I have no choice, I'll have to go along with him."

"Correct."

"But how can I call myself head of a department if my man on the Coast is independent?"

"Don't switch things around. *You* screwed it up. Vincent Fisk, who broke you in, never had the problem. With you, maybe Chester bugged them into it—how do I know? The point is, this battle is lost—but not the war. When they make one bad deal, you can knock their brains out. So sit tight."

"Okay. Joey, when are you coming back?"

"Tomorrow. We start shooting in a week. I'll see you then."
Click.

A real *stupido*. If he'd just push his pencil and stop trying to think . . .

I left the room, returned to Bryan's office, and sat down.

"Sorry to be so long. I had to take a call . . . from Mario."

"I'm sure I know what he wanted."

"I'm sure you're right."

"What did you say?"

"I told him that if he bucked you he was going to lose."

I studied him for a reaction as I continued: "I told him that I stay out of your kingdom and you stay out of mine, and he should do likewise. And I further told him to try to keep his mouth shut."

"Joey, he's impossible. Can you imagine him trying to negotiate with important stars or their agents? New York's limited market is one thing, but this is a whole different world. Out here we have a private community, and Mario doesn't have the class to be accepted into it."

"Bryan, we've got enough problems. Let's forget Percy President for a while."

"Oh, I think that nickname is divine. We use it all the time."

"It sure as hell fits."

"Jonathan told me the one for Chester, but I can't remember it."

"Sidney Shrewd."

"Oh, precious, truly precious."

Not as precious, I smiled to myself, as Farley Fag.

"Now what the hell, Bryan, has gotten you so upset?"

"I'm worried about Johnny."

"He's not worried . . . and I can tip you off that he resents *your* worrying."

"I know," he sulked, "he told Joe Ballantine and me to stay out of his life."

"So why don't you?"

"Because the rumors about him are getting out of hand. And he certainly isn't helping matters any with his opinions of the Chairman that he voices to anyone who will listen."

"Why tell me? You're as close to him as I am."

"We're not in New York, you are."

"You've got the phone," I parried.

"It's not the same thing. The only person he really listens to is you."

"Well, he knows I don't lie to him, which is one good reason . . ."

"Joey, we need your help. Jim and I are tied to him. *If he goes, we all go. You're the one who's safe. You're not in the company.*"

"Continue."

"Some of the things we've done to cover for him would stand your hair on end."

"Try me."

"For one thing, women."

"He's single, for Christ's sake. Let him swing."

"But his parties at the hotel are starting to become common gossip. Bachelors swing—but girls talk, you know."

"They do?" I asked—staring at the number one example.

"Yes, they do."

He recrossed his legs to the opposite side, opened a pill box, took out a Librium, and washed it down with a gulp of water from a glass that was always near the phone.

"So he screws at the hotel. Let him get it soundproofed if it bothers the other guests. Not that they aren't doing the same thing, anyhow."

"But it's not just . . . screwing. He has six at a time, in all sizes, shapes, and colors. He *directs* them in all sorts of orgy routines."

I laughed.

Bryan stood up. He had a petulant look. He started pacing up and down and was obviously more than upset.

"Bryan baby. Calm down and let me show you how you're making a mountain out of a molehill."

He turned around and struck a pose, model style.

"Do you think I'm a fairly ballsy guy?"

"Yes, Joey."

"A guy you'd like to have on your side in a street fight?"

"Yes."

"Do I have any trouble nailing chicks?"

"No."

"Am I one of the troops, do they dig having me around?"

"Yes."

"Then how in the hell do you expect me to go to Johnny and suggest to him that he stop getting laid? He'd look at me like I was nuts. No, thank you, I pass."

"But, Joey, there's more to it than that. He thinks he's the indispensable man, he doesn't even use caution. We have trouble at this point getting broads to go with him."

"What's that mean?"

"It means he places orders with us, and we have to arrange for the girls."

"Who's 'we'?" I had him going now.

"You know Phil Peck, he used to run the theater in Van Nuys? He's in our program department here. He has all the girl contacts."

"Yeah, I know him."

"He's running out of new broads, and those who have been there won't go back."

"Give them some bread, they'll go back."

"My dear, they get paid a hundred and fifty dollars a shot."

"I know," I said pointedly, wanting him to pick it up now. Which he did.

"What do you mean, you know?"

Bless little Chili baby, she was right on everything.

"Just what I said, Bryan. I know your whores, who gets them, the amount they're paid ... *how* they're paid ..."

"Jonathan doesn't even know that!"

"I'm not Jonathan. He wouldn't know how to get laid in a whorehouse, with thousand-dollar bills."

Lavender Lips turned ice-white. Fear sweat started to pop along his brow. He went back to his chair, sat down again, crossed his legs, and tried hard to appear calm. Unfortunately, he sevened out.

"Did you tell Johnny?" he asked.

"I don't *tell*, as you put it, anybody, anything."

"I didn't mean it like that, Joey, forgive me."

I gave him a wave to forget it.

He looked all around the room as if bedeviled by secret agents or bugging devices, then in an unnerved yet campy way blurted it out.

"Do you know about the secretary and the Cadillac?"

Now I'd pump his little ass and show him how to bluff. This poor neophyte. He was Mickey Mouse taking on King Kong.

"My information was, two girls and two Cadillacs."

Tears shone in his eyes. "Good Lord," he nanced, "is nothing safe? We can be ruined with all of this." By now he was running up and down like a Las Vegas chorus girl doing her limbering up exercises.

"How'd you like *Face* magazine to print this?"

"She" brought out a sadistic urge in me, and I pushed to the brink of terror.

"He'll get it, Bryan baby. A secret is not a secret when more than one person knows it. He'll find out—do you realize why?"

"Tell me," he screamed.

"Because *he's looking*."

"Oh, dear, oh, dear"—more prancing—"well, what have you got to say?"

"I think 'Oh, dear' sums it up pretty well."

"Stop it, Joey, it's not funny."

"I never thought it was. However, Johnny thinks it is. He thinks Morry Weinstein is an imbecile."

"Doesn't it bother *you*? He's got you in headlines every week. He says you're Jonathan's partner, that you're a bagman for Las Vegas, that you saved Jonathan from being killed."

"You seem to have memorized my publicity clips."

"Dammit," he shrieked, "doesn't it frighten you?"

"Hell, no."

"*Why?*"

"Because I'm the only one who knows he's bluffing. I'm merely a name headline."

He hung on every word.

"What scares me is what I *don't* know. On this stuff I'm clean, I'll escape easily. He might as well write that I'm Billy Graham in disguise. In fact, that might be nearer the truth."

"A joke like that, at a time like this—"

"If it'll make you feel any better, open the window and I'll jump with you."

"I can't take this teasing—stop it!"

For Jonathan to see this foldup of his great friend Bryan Westgate I would have given five thousand, minimum. Bryan, to have gotten the backing from Jonathan and enjoyed it for so long, must have a photo of him in bed with a goat, two chickens, an Arabian horse, and a parakeet, at the very least— and a second negative tucked away in his bank vault, too.

"Calm down and listen to me," I snapped. "You carry on as you've been doing only for your own sake."

"All right," he whimpered.

"Let me call it for you. One, J.J.B. won't let you stop. Two, you simpleton, think of all the other people in it now. Three, if you change your pattern, you'll scare one of your own people and he'll stool on you."

"Oh, dear me."

"Four and final, the next time—and I hope there never is a next time—he gets jammed up to the point where you have to give away Cadillacs to square the beef, just remember Cadillacs have to be bought, registered, and a million more details that would take ten years to explain to you. . . . *Call me first!*"

I thought he was going to cry, but I had to give him the final.

"If you don't, Mr. Vice-President of a Public Corporation, you'll have ten years to read books in the library as a guest of the government."

Bryan ran to the file cabinet, slid out the drawer, took two more Libriums, slid back the drawer, locked the cabinet, and looked at me with ashen face.

"I'm ill, I've got to go home."

He then *fled* out the door.

Business finished, I headed for New York—and production.

Chapter 13

I rushed past Vera, snatching the wire she held out, opened the door to my office with the other hand, and grabbed the private phone that was ringing.

"Hello."

"Just wanted to say good luck," came the quiet voice. "I sent you a wire also."

What coordination—I managed to open it with one hand as we talked.

```
THIS IS THE BEGINNING OF EVERYTHING YOU'VE
WORKED FOR. CHARGE FORWARD BOLDLY.
                                    JOHNNY
```

"Thanks, and I won't let you down."

"I'm sure of that," he answered. "Did you cut his hair?"

"Personally."

"I liked the first script. It's going to be a good one."

"Well, they caused me enough trouble on it. Thank God I finally got it to you, or we'd be in our tenth rewrite. Your guys are a pain in the ass."

"You should know what they've done to Leonard Morris. He's ready for a breakdown, and I still won't approve the script."

"That touches me deeply."

"You're all heart."

"By the way, how is the Sammy Glick of TV? I hear he's got a great show for next week—interviewing De Gaulle, Mao Tse-tung, Castro, and Bert O'Brien."

"Bert O'Brien? He did a column on Morris that was brutal."

"See what a liar you are," I kidded him. "You told me you never read him."

"I only read him when he raps you," he countered.

"He was crazy about me until I met you. How much will you take so I can buy my introduction back?"

"No chance, I love to see you get belted in print. Maybe he'll take a real punch at you—he's supposed to be tough. He once knocked a sixteen-year-old girl down in the Stork Club, and I heard the other night he hit a cripple in a restaurant."

"I don't know about the girl, but I do know from some friends of mine that he sucker-punched the guy in the restaurant."

"That's always been your strategy."

"Damn right. Hit first—that's the big one."

"What do you do if the guy gets up?"

"Growl at him. Then if he still keeps coming—run!"

"Get over on that set and watch the store."

"I was planning on taking the day off."

"Good-bye." *Click*.

I buzzed twice for Vera. In she popped with a nice new first-day-of-shooting dress.

"You look very nice."

"Thank you, your worship."

"What time did they get the first shot?"

"Joel Fryman called and said ten-thirty."

"Good. Any problems?"

"Perry Bennett was twenty minutes late."

I mouthed a small oath under my breath.

"Get George on the car phone now, and Sol Mack on the Coast while I'm talking. Send Krautie in so he can listen."

Picking up my darts, I zipped in four bull's-eyes. Six months of practice makes the difference. I would soon turn this proficiency into ready cash—I had to get a new gaff, since no one would putt with me anymore.

Vera buzzed.

"George?"

"Yeah, boss."

"Didn't I tell you to stay with that meatball and get him to work?"

"I got him there on time."

"Bullshit, he was twenty minutes late."

"*After* I got him there, he went next door for coffee and got involved impressing the natives."

"You know what you can do with that excuse."

"It won't fit—I've got too much up there already."

Krautie walked through the door. I motioned for him to sit down.

357

"Okay, George, watch him!" *Click*.

"Perry was late—" Krautie started.

"Not you, too."

"It's costing money."

"Another county heard from."

"We're also way over on scripts."

That I penciled down. "That's BCA's fault, not ours. Get it from them."

Vera buzzed again. I turned to Krautie. "This is on the two Coast shows. Listen good, so I don't have to write you a memo."

"Hello, Sol."

"Hi, Joey, good luck today."

"Thanks. Did you see the rough cuts on the two *Karen* shows and the two *Barnabys*?"

"Yes. They were good."

"Which is better?"

"*Barnabys* is slicker and better produced, but Karen's isn't bad."

Not bad news at all. "Is she behaving herself?"

"Yes. She's busy acting, writing, directing, *and* producing."

"Does she ever go to the can?"

"No, I think she pipes it out."

"Funny, funny." Nodding at Krautie, I changed the subject. "Let me explain how these pilotless shows work."

"Shoot."

"Don't say that, because I have a couple of people in mind."

"I'm building my own list. May I ask you a favor?"

"Go ahead."

"Can I put Bryan on mine?"

"Only if you don't miss."

"Seriously, Joey, he is actually devoid of talent. Some of his ideas border on the childish."

"Did you get your check this week?"

"Yes."

"Then don't bother me with your little *kvetches*. He's all yours, sweetheart."

"I feel there's a message there. . . ."

I now brought him back to business. "We've got *firm* twenty-six-week deals on both shows. The first two films on both of them will be looked at by the sponsors and the Chairman. If they stand up as indicated, we're on the air. If not, they can get out. It's a handshake deal."

"How about us?"

"We get paid, but they can cancel production."

"They'll never cancel."

"You have a tidbit?"

"Sure. They were at the screening already—and loved both shows."

"Beautiful. You've made my year."

"I wish we had creative control of those shows, Joey. On the *Karen* show, there's no captain. Her latest is that she wants to work with the cutter because she feels she knows comedy better than anyone."

"That's Farley Fag's problem, so keep out of the firing line. Meanwhile, are the writers busy developing *The Bridge?*"

"Yes, and it's going to be a big one. How's your writer doing?"

"Okay, and Virgil Esty is on top of it for the networks. Also Tom Brady is the champion for the project."

"How does Chester feel about it?"

"Openly he's for it, but I'm getting a little static from him. I wish he'd take an extra day with the headshrinker. He's got the top job, and he distrusts everybody around him."

"Tom Brady," he said pointedly, "is a Bryan Westgate man."

"He's an acquaintance, not 'his man.' Chester is wrong. This guy is good—and that's what's scaring him."

"He'll get him then."

"Like hell he will. I already put him together with J.J.B., and he's got his backing to run the way he sees fit."

"You love jigsaw puzzles."

"Only when the pieces fit."

"I'll be in touch daily."

"Okay, Sol baby." *Click.*

Krautie got up to leave.

"All filled in?"

"Right."

"Keep on top of that account out there. It's cost-plus, so we don't have to worry, but I want those books and records perfect."

"They will be." He left, hair flying.

THE CANNIBALS

I buzzed the intercom.

"Vera baby, get me Tom Brady, then Virgil Esty."

In a few seconds she buzzed back: "Tom Brady on two."

"Is this the Tom Brady who's Vice-President in charge of Production, East Coast?"

"No," he answered, "this is the Tom Brady who's the patsy, who's in the middle, who's being fired upon from all sides— and who's the Vice-President in charge of Production, East Coast."

"Where the hell are we getting all this static from, Tom? You guys are driving us nuts. I've got fifteen okays for script starts, another okay for ten—eight days later I get stops on them. We're going out hiring writers, what are you doing to us?"

"Perry Como gets letters, I get memos, every day."

"From who, for Christ's sake?"

"The little destroyer upstairs."

"That little sonovabitch, is he starting again?"

"I didn't know he ever stopped."

"By God, Sidney Shrewd better stop. I'm getting sick of him. What is he doing, still sulking because I put that talent show on the air over his head? All I did was hand him a hit in the Top Ten."

"He's also mad at me because I recommended it."

"You had the backing of the President of the Network, didn't you? You heard it from his own lips—he wanted it on. We had the other votes come in from the Coast: Bryan okayed it, Joe Ballantine okayed it, Wilson Manning okayed it. What the hell does this guy want?"

"Joey, he doesn't trust me."

"Screw him, I don't care who he trusts. He's the one who made the stupid statement that the show would get on only over his dead body."

"That's true."

"Well, it was over his dead body—but it wound up in the Top Ten. Just because he hates the producer, why should he keep a good show off the air? Is he working for BCA, or is he working for Chester Plan?"

"You've got to be kidding, with that question."

"I scared the shit out of him when I took the show over to UBC and sold an option on it. Only because that guy was so scared of Jonathan J. Bingham did he renege."

"You scared him, I'll admit that."

"Wouldn't you be scared if a top summer show in the Top Ten went over to a rival network, and you were the big man who said it would get on only over his dead body, and you didn't like it in the first place? And *then* the dirty bastard switched around and took all the credit. What the hell more does he want?"

"One of the things he wants is to get rid of me."

"Not the best day he ever lived. *He'll* do *that* over *my* dead body."

"You know he and Mario have become very close."

"I know how close they've become, and I don't like it.

Something's up, something smells. I don't like the smell of things at all. They better pray to God these three shows aren't hits, they just better pray."

"They aren't only going to pray, Joey, they're going to do everything in the world they can to hurt those shows."

"Please, do me a favor, Tom, don't give me lessons. I don't mean to be ungrateful, but I'm well aware of what they're doing—all their potshots."

Tom hesitated briefly and then asked a question. "Is Jonathan leaving BCA?"

"Tom, not you, too. . . ."

"I merely asked a question."

"The answer is no," I barked. "The answer a second time is no, and the answer a third time is no. Forget it!" I changed the subject. "We're having dinner with the wives tonight, correct?"

"Right."

"What time?"

"How about eight-thirty?" he answered.

"Great, where do you want to eat?"

"You pick it, Joey."

"If I pick it, it's La Scala on Fifty-fourth Street. Gina is crazy about Roberto and Alberto, and that's how I keep fighting these pounds. The damn food is delicious. Incidentally, I think you really will enjoy it—we'll take you there. Eight-thirty at La Scala, Fifty-fourth Street across from City Center." *Click.*

I spoke curtly. "Hi, Virgil."

The intercom buzzed immediately: "Virgil Esty on one."

"What's wrong? You sound mad as hell."

"Just stupid little things. That little *vonce* upstairs is driving me nuts."

"Why don't you stop worrying about him?"

"Because he's fighting the whole goddam network and every production on the network. I don't know what the hell's going on. But something is, and I've got to find out what."

"Very simple, he's insecure."

"The silly bastard has the top job—what in the world will make him secure?"

"How the hell do I know? He's up to four days a week with the psychiatrist, trying to find out the answer to that question."

"I'd like to smack him in the mouth with his wife's tennis racket, that's what I'd like to do."

"I don't think she needs any help."

I went quickly to a different subject. "Do we leave next week for Chicago?"

"That's the way the plans are now. Tuesday we go. We'll get some great locations. We're supposed to be there on Thursday, and as you know, I have to take a train 'cause I don't fly."

"Oh, little boy doesn't fly. . . ."

"A man's entitled to his eccentricities," he answered laughingly.

"Let's stay midtown so we can move around."

THE CANNIBALS

"Good idea, I'd rather not go into the chi-chi hotels any-way."

"I agree with you. I'm taking three men from here: Joel Fryman, the unit manager, and one of the writers. I want them to get the feel and the flavor of Chicago. Incidentally, I think *The Bridge* is going to be one of the best shows we've ever done. It's really exciting."

"Sounds great. I probably won't be talking to you until then, so I'll have my secretary phone your office to confirm the res-ervations, and we'll meet there on Thursday, okay?"

"Fine," I answered, "see you in Chicago." *Click.*

I picked up a dart, threw it at the bull's-eye, and missed the whole goddam target. Lousy Chester Plan!

Vera came charging through the door. I looked at her in amazement.

"Pick up two, it's Joel Fryman."

I grabbed the phone, pressed the button. "Yeah, Joel."

"Joey, get over here to the studio right away—the sonova-bitch has walked off again! He's in his dressing room with the door locked. I think he's nuts—I really think he's insane."

"Calm down, I'll be right there."

I hung up the phone, walked to the middle of the room, raised my hands above my head, looked at the ceiling as if I were talking to God and said, "But why *me*?"

I walked out the door, brushing past Vera. "I'll be at the studio. The Clark Gable of TV has walked off again."

At the elevators, the doors of an up car opened and out

stepped Terry Winant. He was not smiling. He was not the usual Terry Winant at all.

"Joey, he's insane. Do you hear what I'm telling you? He's not funny, he's not eccentric, he's not temperamental. He's totally, unequivocally insane."

"I'm going over there right now. Do you want to come back with me?"

"I don't want to be in the vicinity of this lunatic—I'd throttle him."

"Okay, buddy," I said without smiling, "I'll check with you later."

I caught a down car, hurried out through the lobby, and just kept walking to the studios, a few blocks away.

I walked onto the crowded set. The buzz of voices abruptly hushed.

There was no friendly look on my face, and everybody knew I had had it.

I headed over to Tim Rice.

"What is it?" I said.

"I'll tell you what it is," said Tim Rice, who usually took things in stride. "I don't care how you size it up, Joey, this guy is a baby—a total baby. He really is a dirty sonovabitch. And he's not worth the trouble. This no-good bastard is costing us two to three hours a day, and, boy, that's money!"

I didn't even bother to answer Tim Rice. I turned on my heel, loped for the stairs, and shot up to Perry Bennett's dressing room.

The doorknob wouldn't turn. Making a fist, I beat three good raps on the mahogany door. I was allowing fifteen seconds before I kicked it in on him.

No answer. However, I knew somebody was inside because I could hear the record player. At about fourteen seconds, footsteps. The door slowly opened two inches, and Perry Bennett peeked out.

"Do I come in," I demanded, "or do I stand out here and stare at you?"

"Joey," he said effusively, "I'm so glad to see you. Come in —I've been waiting for you."

I walked in, took off my coat, threw it on a chair impatiently, strode over to the record player and clicked it off, sat down and began.

"I can tell by your breath you've been drinking. Is there any more left?"

"Yes," he said childishly, "would you like a drink?"

"Yeah, I'd like a drink, Perry. Pour two for us, and make 'em goddam stiff."

This was the fade. I wasn't going to screw around with him any longer.

He went over to the little bar that cost me five thousand to build for him, picked up two cocktail glasses, dropped ice cubes in to the rim, and poured Cutty Sark all the way to the top. He handed me one.

I took it and stared at him.

"Now, let's see what kind of a drinker you are. Here's to whatever you and I have between us."

I clinked the glass with him and drained it.

"Finish it," I said. "Let's see what you've got going for you."

"I don't drink that much."

"Oh stop your pretending."

With great effort, he chug-a-lugged the Scotch.

"Okay, Perry baby. We premiere next week. We go on the air. You got a shot at being the biggest star on television, with backing like you never had in your life. Now, give me your story, and make it quick. And don't bullshit me, because let me tell you, I've had it right up to my neck."

"What are you getting mad at me for? You know I love you."

"Don't give me that I-love-you shit. My head's on the block here. What's this walking off the set? What's bothering you? Are you nuts?"

Perry was terribly Italian—terribly emotional. Tears welled up in his eyes.

"Joey, you don't understand. They're all against me, they're all against me, I tell you. The only friend I have is you, and you never come around, you're always so goddam busy. Don't you understand? They hate me!"

"Nobody hates you, you silly sonovabitch. Everybody's rooting you in. Why do you act like this?"

The tears now streamed down his face. He was upset—and also mad. Crying mad. I didn't know if I could stop him.

I knew how he felt, and I had compassion. There was just

368

one thing—he was destroying me. And I was the best friend he had. Scratch that, I was his *only* friend.

"Perry, you're making a damn fool out of yourself."

"Joey, I've got problems, I'm not happy. Do you know they're keeping track of what time I come on the set and what time I leave. They're telling me I'm costing the company money. . . ."

"Do you think you're not?" I snapped.

No answer.

"You don't know your lines, you're drinking too much, you're never on time. . . . *Will you get ahold of yourself?*"

More tears. "You know the problems I have."

"Have you still got troubles at home?"

"Yes, Shirley's driving me crazy."

"Then let me bring her in here. I'll put her up at a hotel, I'll pay for it. Let her be near you if it'll make you feel better."

"No, she'll only upset me more. I don't want her around me when I work."

"Perry," I cut in coldly, "listen to me. I love you like a brother. But you are absolutely, totally nuts. And more important, you're costing me thousands and thousands of dollars. I'm the best friend you ever had in your life. I'm paying you seventy-five hundred dollars a week, I bought you ten thousand dollars' worth of furniture, I've flown you back and forth so many times you've become a commuter. What is this bullshit of walking on and off the set? Are you nuts?"

"Maybe I am," he sobbed.

"Do you know that with the show one week away from being reviewed, stories have leaked all over town about you being a prima donna, causing us to go over budget, and you stand a good chance of being dumped?"

"Yes, I've heard rumors."

"The rumors are true. Terry Winant doesn't even want you in the show anymore."

"I know he's against me. I told you everyone's against me."

"I'm with you. I'll stick with you, I gave you my word. Here I am. What do you think I'm doing here, mooching your liquor? I have my own bottles. I don't even drink Scotch!"

"Joey, tell me what to do. I'm so upset. Shirley's got me crazy, everybody's watching me. Just tell me what to do."

I turned cold as ice. "I'll tell you what you do, Perry. You repay my friendship. Goddamit, I mean repay it. You get your goddam Italian ass down there onto that set, and you say not one word to anybody. You walk on that set and you do your job—because if you don't do your job, you're not only through in this series, but you're through in this business, and you've lost me and everybody connected with you, and that includes Shirley."

He was stunned.

"Do you know what the program is right at this moment? Terry Winant is so pissed off at you that he wants to write a new show. What do you think of this: *The Cub Reporter*—a spinoff. Because in a segment of this one, he has you dying in

370

a plane crash, and there's no more Perry Bennett. Is that what you want?"

"He wouldn't do that, would he?"

"Yes, he would do. Not only would he do it, but I have authorized the script."

"Joey! How could you do that to me? You're supposed to be my friend—my brother."

"I didn't say we'd shoot the goddam script, did I? I said I *authorized* the script. Do you think I can keep on bucking Terry Winant? He's a Pulitzer Prize winner. He's my partner. Do you think I can fight the whole world? Between you and Jonathan Bingham, you're driving *me* nuts."

Another childlike response. "Why don't you ever come to see me?"

"I don't come to see you because I'm too fucking busy!" I screamed.

The obscenity and the screaming, from one wopo to another, helped calm things. He knew at least that he was with one of his own, and there was some comfort in that. One thing I had going for me, at least.

Perry Bennett walked across the room and threw his arms around me, a masculine Italian embrace.

"Joey, I'm sorry. Forgive me. Tell me what to do again. I'll listen."

"I want you to go downstairs like a man, like nothing happened. Finish this scene, and it'll all be over by tomorrow. Did I steer you wrong in that other fight? Who is actually your booster and close friend—Tim Rice. Am I correct?"

"Yes."

"Keep this up, and he'll hate you again. Now I want you to go downstairs now and get us out of this thing. You're the one who put us into this—get us out."

"Okay, Joey. And . . . I'm sorry."

"Don't be sorry about anything other than temperament, because I'm sure you're coming through. I'll tell you—and it's God's truth, Perry—you can go right through the roof in this series."

He was smiling again. "You really believe that, Joey?"

"With all my heart." I moved to the door, opened it, and said over my shoulder, "I'm going downstairs to get them ready to crank up. You come down in exactly five minutes, walk on the set, and do the scene as if nothing had happened. I can assure you nobody will say anything, and it'll all be over. Okay?"

"Okay, Joey."

I left.

I walked downstairs and made an entrance amid anxious looks. I went straight to Tim Rice.

"Get ready to roll—he'll be down in exacty five minutes. He'll say nothing, go in and do the scene. It's all forgotten. I don't want to hear any more of it."

Tim laughed. "I don't know how you do it, but you do. You're the only one who seems to understand him."

"Maybe it's because he understands me."

THE CANNIBALS

That was enough pressure for me, for the time being, so out I went.

Early in the morning I was packing my suitcase when Gina walked into the room.

"I certainly wish the Joey Bertell who was host at La Scala was my Joey Bertell."

"What do you mean?"

"You were so charming to the Bradys, and to me."

"I'm always charming when the pressure is off for an hour or so."

"Are you trying to say that I put any pressure on you?"

"Gina my sweet, if only the kind of pressure you put on me were on me twenty-four hours a day, I'd be a totally happy man."

"Ignoring the double entendre, thank you. My only question is, why do you insist on keeping business out of these rare moments?"

"And my only question is, why do you insist on bringing it in?"

"Well, after all, Joey, when men are getting ready to go on a business trip, wives might like to know some of the details."

"You know that I'm one man who doesn't discuss business details with his wife—especially in public."

"How about now? You haven't even said how long you'll be gone. Can't you even tell me that?"

"Probably three or four days, but possibly a week. We want to pick locations and meet with the police commissioner."

"Who's going to be there?"

"I'm taking Joel Fryman, a writer, and the unit manager, Sid Raymond. Virgil Esty is going by train, and I'll fly in Sol Mack from the coast. He's going to produce it."

"Are you taking any secretaries, little boy?"

"No, I'm not, little girl."

"You better not let me hear about it if you do. Remember, I used to play Chicago. I have a lot of friends there. I wouldn't want you to embarrass me."

"I promise you," I teased, "I'll never do that. Whatever I do will be discreet—no one will ever know."

She threw one of her bedroom slippers and hit me right on the head.

"You're all heart, darling."

"By the way," I asked, "what are you going to be doing?"

"I'll be doing what you'll be doing."

"If that's the case, I'm not going to go."

She threw the other slipper and hit me again.

"Gina, you are totally sadistic. However, you're nice."

"Thank you, your worship."

I turned around, looked at her, then laughed.

"Where the hell did you hear that?"

"I know everything that goes on in your office."

"That's taking in a lot."

"If you don't start coming home a little more often," she

said, kidding on the square, "the only thing you're going to find in bed with you is your dart board."

I looked up at the ceiling, raised my hands, and talked to Him. "She even knows about my dart board. Is *nothing* sacred?"

The silence was broken by Maria's little cry, and Gina rushed out of the room. One thing about Gina, she was a great mother. We had a cook, a maid, and a nurse, but Gina had a standing rule: When the baby woke up and cried, Mother had to be the one who went in. Gina wanted it that way and was convinced that Maria did, too. I liked the idea.

Back came Gina now, with Maria in her arms.

"Kiss your little doll good-bye," she said to me.

I walked over to them, put my arm around Gina, bent down, and gave Maria a little nip on the cheek.

"Why do you always bite her on the cheek? You're going to hurt her."

"Do I bite you on the cheek?"

"Yes."

"Do I love you?"

"Yes."

"Then I love her. Why should she be left out? A man has to have somebody to bite."

"You're insane."

"Insanity is a form of brilliance," I boasted.

"Just keep the furs and jewels coming, and you can say anything you want about yourself."

"I can't stand a woman who can be bought."

"That's where you're misjudging me. Material things mean nothing to me."

"Please, Gina, never lie when you have Maria in your arms."

"Come on, darling," she cooed to Maria, "let's leave the genius to himself, his favorite person."

With that, Gina carried her out of the room.

I finished packing, Gina walked me to the door, I kissed her good-bye, and down in the elevator I went.

George was waiting with the limousine to take me to the airport.

Next stop, Chicago.

The car was rolling along the Van Wyck Expressway on the way to Kennedy International. I was up next to George, just sitting, looking out the window at the new high-rise apartments, and thinking.

Suddenly the buzzer rang on the telephone. I picked it up, and it was Vera.

"What's up?"

"Tom Brady wants you to call him at his office at BCA."

"Anything urgent?"

"He said to tell you it's important but not urgent. It's about premiere week and the first segment they've scheduled for the *Mr. Trouble* series."

"Okay, I'll call him right now. Anything else while I've got you on the phone?"

"Tim Rice said to tell you that everything's going smoothly. Perry is still late, still playing the prima donna bit, but at least he's not walking off any sets."

"Thank God for small favors. What else?"

"Your West Coast office reports that Sol Mack has left on the plane and will meet you at the hotel in Chicago."

"Go ahead, anything else?"

"Another issue of *Face* magazine came in today."

"Better or worse?"

"This one is really terrible."

Disgustedly, I wisecracked to myself, "File it under B and burn it."

"Also," said Vera, "Chili Monroe called to say that she'll be out of town for six or seven days and will be in touch when she gets back."

"Thank you, where's she going?"

"To Chicago," said Vera, without comment.

"Did you tip to her where I was staying, or even that I was going to Chicago?"

"No."

"If she calls back, *don't* indicate that's where I'm going. I've got enough on my mind as it is."

"Right."

"By the way, take the expensive cologne out of my desk and lock it in the file cabinet. Jimmy Craig is a born thief."

"Does he use that?"

"He's either using it or drinking it—one of the two."

Vera laughed. She was in one of her infrequent gay moods.

"Don't call me unless it's urgent," I reminded her. "I'll check with you twice a day, noontime and six."

"Yes, your worship."

"Are you the bigmouth who told Gina about the 'your worship' bit?"

"And get beheaded? Of course not."

"Then we have a spy in the office."

"Mrs. Bertell has talked to Krautie a number of times . . . when she needs money."

"Problem solved, now I know. Talking to him is like advertising in the *Times* and *News*."

Vera defended Krautie. "He's really very nice."

"I didn't say he isn't nice, I said he's a blabbermouth."

Vera laughed again.

"All right," I concluded, "let me get off the phone. I'll call Tom Brady right away. Tell me you love me."

"I love you."

"Excellent. Take the rest of the day off." *Click.*

I switched to another channel, got the mobile operator, and gave her the BCA number. When they made the connection, I asked for Tom Brady's office.

"Put him on," I said to the secretary. "This is Joey Bertell, I'm calling him from the car on my way to the airport. He's looking to reach me."

378

He came on. "Do you have a bar in the car also?"

"They're installing it while I'm away. What's up?"

"I just wanted you to know that we had a meeting this morning, and we're leading off with segment number three for the *Mr. Trouble* premiere."

"It's nice of you to report a *fait accompli*. And what the hell are we going with that one for?"

"All of us feel it will be better for the New York critics."

"What happened to the other forty-nine states? It's not the best show. That segment takes place on three sets. That's not what Jonathan wants to emphasize. Don't you remember all those memos you've been bombarding me with? 'Get out on the street . . . shoot . . . make it look expensive . . . make it look lush . . . make it look bright?' All of a sudden you're leading off with a dingy segment."

"Jonathan was in the meeting."

"I still tell you it's wrong. We've got three other segments that are much better natural leads. There's the one about the movie star, the one about the kidnapping, or the police procedure one with the maniac killer on the loose. What the hell are we going with the dingy one for? Besides, we don't have big names in that one."

"That was the decision."

"Well, how did you vote?"

"I sincerely felt it was the show to go with."

"Why?"

"Because it has the element that will appeal to the New York critics. It's sophisticated."

"Can I do anything about this?" I asked. "I don't believe in your decision. It's bad judgment—it's not show business. We should smack them between the eyes with our best and most expensive-looking show. Let them show this dingy segment for number four."

"I don't feel it would be wise. . . ."

"I have a feeling you're trying to tell me something."

"I'm merely telling you it's done—the publicity has already gone out for the newspaper listings."

"My feelings are strong about this. Did anybody agree with my point of view?"

"Yes."

"Well, don't play games with me—who?"

"Wilson Manning."

"So. One brain still operating."

"Thank you, your worship."

"Oh, Christ, not you too!"

"I also have spies."

"Who told you—as if I didn't know."

"I cannot divulge my source . . . but she's Italian, has black hair, flashing eyes, and is married to one of the world's greatest producer-director-actor-writers."

"I love you, and drop dead." *Click.*

We were now at my airline departure building. I got out,

gave my two-suiter to the redcap, and turned back to speak with George.

"You know where to reach me. In case of trouble, give me a buzz."

"Yes, your worship."

"If *you* pull that shit with me, I'm going to kick you right in the ass."

I slammed the door and walked away. Then, over my shoulder, I winked at him. George smiled and drove off.

Chapter 14

Sitting in my Chicago hotel suite, I felt exhilarated.

I had my staff around me on my new show—my exciting new project.

"Joel," I began, "you take the political end. I want you to meet with the police chief, the commissioner, and all the hierarchy of the town. Get us permission to do what we want to do. We're not going to hurt anybody. Whatever we do, a law-and-order image will come out of that television tube. They'll have no problems about that—we'll guarantee it in writing if we have to."

I switched my attention to Sol Mack.

"You're the executive producer. Take our writer with you and just go up and down every street, in and out of every corner. Grab color, get the feel of this city—that's what we have to capture. Chicago is the theme.

"Virgil and I will be the third team. We'll back your two teams, but we'll be looking at it from the network standpoint. We'll all meet and put what we have together."

The phone rang. I picked it up.

It was Jonathan. "Can we talk?" he asked.

"Just a moment, I'll take it in the other room." I put my

hand over the phone and said to Virgil, "Hang up the phone when I pick up in the bedroom."

He took it, I walked briskly through the door, grabbed the extension, and yelled to Virgil to hang up. He did.

"What's up, buddy?" I asked.

"Did you hear about the latest *Face* article?"

"Yes, Vera told me about it on the car phone yesterday, and I had her read it to me this morning."

"Well, what did you think?"

"The same thing I've always thought—it's awful."

"Joey, that bastard has got to be stopped."

"This is a helluva time to change your mind, Johnny. He should have been stopped a long time ago."

"Well, stop him now," he blurted. "It's causing nothing but trouble around here."

"How much trouble?"

"Real trouble. This guy has been writing an open letter every week now either to the Chairman, the Dentist, the FCC . . . the only person he hasn't written one to is Castro."

"Have you heard from upstairs?"

"I've got four memos on my desk right now, including two from Washington."

"Well, what the hell are you suddenly getting so panicky about? Nothing he says is true. Why the worry now?"

"Who says there's any worry? He's just got to be stopped, that's all."

"I bet you a hundred dollars you heard from Bryan West-gate."

"You win the bet. Does that make you feel like a big man?"

"What are you yelling at me for? I was the first guy to tell you Morry Weinstein should be handled. You're the one who sent the memo 'File it under B and burn it.' "

"Goddam you," he shouted, "this is serious."

"What do I do, drop everything and come back?"

"You don't have to come back, but, by God, you give it some thought."

"I'll give it plenty of thought. I haven't sloughed anything off yet, have I?"

There was a slight pause. "At least I'll have to admit that," Jonathan said grudgingly.

"You just listen to me, buddy. I'll handle it. As soon as I get back, I promise you I'll handle it, one way or another. While I'm here, I'll do some talking, and I'll reach out. I'll handle it. Is that good enough for you?"

"That's good enough for me."

A thought suddenly struck me. "While I have you on the phone, why the hell are you going with that segment for the premiere show of *Mr. Trouble*?"

"We all agreed that it was the best show."

"Just for the record, Johnny—everybody agreed but me. It's not the right show. It's a good show, but it's not the one to lead off with."

"Joey, I'm not going to argue with you, I have too much on my mind right now. Just take my word for it, it's the right show to go with."

"Hey, what the hell would I argue for? You're the boss."

"I'm glad somebody remembers that."

I suddenly felt sorry that I was giving him pressure. I softened. "Johnny, let's you and I not argue. There are enough other people for us to fight. Remember what we've always said. If we stand pat, nobody can lick us."

He softened also. "You're so right, buddy, let's keep it that way. If you get lucky and wind up with a wild chick there one night," he added, "give her a shot for me."

I laughed. "If I get lucky, I'll never give you a second thought."

Click.

I walked back into the living room.

"Okay, everybody. Let's take off and give Chicago the once-over."

After five days of walking into every corner of Chicago, from the slums to the Gold Coast, I decided to take a day off. I told Sol Mack he was on his own.

Pre-production work on any television series can be the most boring part of any operation. You never realize, when you see a scene taking place on a street in Chicago or any other city, that the original location—that particular stoop, those double-pane doors—had to be found by someone.

And after the street was found, you had to discuss feasibility. Could traffic be tied up in that section? Then that stoop and the doors—permission from the apartment owners, permission from the individual tenants.

A scene that wouldn't play for more than five minutes would take weeks to set up and two days to shoot.

I was almost ready to go back to New York and fight with Perry Bennett or placate Terry Winant, or even fly to the Coast and have lunch with Lavender Lips. I might include Percy President in that group, but weighing Mario Colucci's presence against the boredom of location-hunting made me dismiss my ironic fancies.

I walked aimlessly around the Loop, over toward Mike Fritzel's, a restaurant well-known to gourmets and sports addicts, as well as lawyers, judges, and city founding fathers. Fritzel's was a kind of Chicago melting pot.

It was 11:00 A.M., still too early to call the Coast and find out how the reviews were on *The Karen Wallace Show*. It had premiered last night, and according to the New York Arbitron overnight ratings, it had made an extremely strong showing against the power—star-studded movies.

The Barnabys, which had premiered the night before, had gotten excellent reviews, generally complementing the slick production work and comedy techniques. However, it got clobbered in its rating against the rival network, which had premiered with a very slick soap opera, and it was apparent the soap opera would become a runaway hit.

I walked into Mike Fritzel's, satisfied myself that the hat-check filly was a thoroughbred, and proceeded directly to the Lounge Bar.

It was now about eleven-fifteen, and I knew some old cronies would be at their usual tables cutting up touches.

Sure enough, I was met with warm smiles and firm hand-shakes and happy greetings.

"What's the matter, Joey," one of them said, "have you been ducking your old friends? We read in Kup's column that you were in town for five days."

"I've been working my tail off," I replied easily. "What's new in Chi town?"

"Same old razzle-dazzle," another guy answered. "Scratching for a buck, that's about it."

"I'm beginning to believe there's no easy way."

"Christ, Joey, you're sitting on top of the world—don't tell me you're complaining."

"I'm greedy, I want it all."

"Hey, there's nothing wrong with that. Just leave a little for us. How about a drink, pal?"

"It's a little early . . . but you've convinced me. I'll take a vodka martini."

He snapped his fingers, called out the order uninhibitedly, and the waiter was over and back within seconds. He set the martini down in front of me.

"Here's the first but not the last of the day," I said. "*Salute*, fellows."

Everybody answered the toast and drank.

The next few minutes were spent catching up on each other's friends. I filled them in on New York, Miami, and Los Angeles; they filled me in on the Middle West.

"By the way," one of them then said to me, "that item that was in the paper—that wasn't your buddy, was it?"

I became alert. "What item are you talking about?"

"There was an item in a New York gossip column that some network president was going to be canned and is being followed by private detectives."

I tried to light another cigarette casually, then took another sip of the martini.

"I'm sure it's not him."

"Boy, I sure hope not, Joey. He's been very good to you, hasn't he?"

"Yeah, he's been jam-up, no question about it. Helluva guy."

"How come I can't fall into a guy like that? All I get is guys who want to borrow money."

I winked at him. "I understand that's pretty good, too."

"You don't begrudge me a little *vig* now and then, do you?" The table laughed at the inside.

The hatcheck filly whom I had noticed on the way in came over. "Are you Mr. Bertell?"

"Yes."

"There's a phone call for you."

"Thank you."

I excused myself from the table and walked over to the phone.

"Hello," I said.

"Joey, this is Virgil."

"Hi, buddy, you coming over for lunch?"

"No, I can't . . . I'm packing."

"What do you mean, you're packing? We've got another few days."

"Tom Brady just got fired."

I couldn't answer for a moment.

"Who's taking his place?"

"Bryan's assistant from the West Coast, Ted Michaels."

"Are you sure?" I asked, still incredulous.

"I'm positive."

"Okay, I'll be right back. Just keep packing and stay calm."

I hung up, went back to the table, told the fellows I had a crisis and would see them later.

Good-bye Loop. I rushed back to the hotel.

While walking back along State Street, I had my usual recapitulation talk with myself. Tom Brady, a Joey Bertell-backed man, further backed up by Jonathan, had now been canned.

The blind item in the paper, brought to my attention by my friends, further indicated to me that Jonathan was in trouble.

What infuriated me was that I couldn't figure out where the concealed siege guns were firing from.

Thanks to *Face*, rumors were flying hot and heavy that Jonathan was on the take, that he was a partner in a favored agency business, and that he had a piece of my action. To spice up the story, there was the legend of his insatiable sex appetite and sundry other improvisations by whoever was trying to nail him.

Trying to analyze it, I considered the conniving of Chester Plan and Mario Colucci in New York, and Bryan Westgate on the coast. (I considered Joe Ballantine a neutral, giving him the benefit of class.) If Jonathan was really weakening, if he was in fact being set up for the guillotine, and any of these bastards caught wind of it, they'd go "into the tank" quicker than the outspoken enemies.

Only one thing was definite. He was not on the take with me. A lunch, an exchange of minor Christmas presents—that was it. Joey Bertell never had a partner.

As I approached the entrance to the lobby, the Edison lamp went on, in my mind. The decision came in that same flash. . . . For the moment screw Chicago. If it was going to be total war, I wanted to be in the front lines.

Sol Mack had twenty years of experience in the business as a top executive. Joel Fryman was the best associate producer in television. Nobody topped Sid Raymond as a unit manager. There was no necessity for my staying. They could do their jobs and orient the writer as well.

I walked into my hotel suite and picked up the phone, giving Jonathan's private number to the long-distance operator. While waiting for the call to go through, I resolved to stick by my judgment that the time for action was now. I was going to get the hell out of here and handle our unique little case personally.

He came on the phone. "Jonathan, Joey. I heard about the Tom Brady situation."

"I can't talk about it now," he said ominously.

"Virgil Esty is shaking in his boots. Where does he stand?"

"I told you, I can't talk now."

"I'm leaving for St. Louis and I'm going to take care of that little situation, one way or the other. If you can't talk, then listen to me, and don't answer. See that Virgil is safe till I get back. I realize now's not the time to discuss it, but you're being maneuvered."

"I understand."

I knew instantly, having played this scene a million times, that someone was in his office.

"Could I possibly get back to you in fifteen minutes?"

"No, I'm on my way. I have a plane to catch."

"Don't you think it's important that we have a chat?"

"For what I'm going to do, I don't need any help."

"You know best on that. Call me the very second you can."
Click.

That was it, the bottom line was exposed. I could now handle Mr. Morry Weinstein any goddam way he wanted to call the turn of the card.

Meet me in St. Louis, Louie. . . .

Chapter 15

As the stewardess made her usual announcement of keep your seats until the plane has come to a complete halt, we slowly but surely taxied into the St. Louis airport.

The adrenalin was running through my body. I quickly snapped up my black attaché case and rose, so that I could be one of the first to depart.

This time on the plane there had been no kidding around with the stewardesses. I gave them their smiles, but it was all business. This was the jungle. I was in it now and ready to meet the best fighters there. Only this time the cannibals were on my side. And these particular cannibals were not from the entertainment business. Nor had they gotten into the fight to lose. They had aces back to back, and all the cards were out.

As the door sprang open, I briskly walked out and into the tunnel toward the flight gate, where friends and relatives were waiting with passengers for another departing flight. I looked around, saw no familiar face, so attaché case in hand, I headed for the airline's main gate. Past banks of pay telephone booths and coin lockers I walked, nonchalant and always looking straight ahead. The first move would be up to someone else, and I was geared to spot it in a matter of seconds.

As I emerged from the airline gate into the modernistic main lobby of the new St. Louis airport and toward the general entrance, I saw a man, heavy-set and in his middle thirties, pick me up. It was easy to spot out of the corner of my eye. I kept walking, but slowed my pace a little.

Within seconds, he was alongside of me.

"Hi, Joey. Did you have a good trip?"

I looked him over casually. "Yes, it was fine."

"We have the car waiting downstairs."

With that, he stuck out his hand and added, "I'm Lou."

I grabbed it, shook it firmly. "Nice to meet you, Lou."

"Have you got any luggage?"

"No, just this case."

"Okay, fine. Follow me and we'll go right to the car."

I walked side by side with Lou out the general entrance of the St. Louis airport down the ramp. The street was filled with cabs.

As we approached the curb, a black Chrysler Le Baron pulled up in front of us, with two men in the front seat. Lou opened the back door for me, and I hopped in. He jumped in beside me and closed the door. We took off.

Driving the car was Steve "Bets," a swarthy, stocky man in his late forties. Steve had gotten his nickname from his many years of being around horses and people who played horses. The inference was fairly obvious. There was no doubt about the fact that Steve was the boss.

THE CANNIBALS

"What do you say, Joey?" he said in his good strong voice. "How do you feel?"

"Pretty good, Steve."

"You know Sammy, don't you?"

I looked over at the other man in the front seat. "Sure, I know Sammy." I put my hand over and we shook.

The big car moved along until it hit the expressway, then it accelerated to about eighty miles an hour and we headed to our destination.

"How's it been going, Steve?" I asked lightly.

"Pretty good, Joey. The town's warm as usual, everybody seems to have . . . measles."

"That's pretty true all over. Anything particular?"

"No, just a new man in town is up to one of the crusades they have every ten or fifteen years. It'll cool off."

"Where are we going?" I asked. "Into the city?"

"No, we're going to a motel that a couple of friends of mine own, out in the suburbs."

"Oh, fine."

"You'll love it, you'll think you're back in Vegas again."

"No kidding."

"It's probably the most beautiful place you've ever seen in your life. Two swimming pools—one with a canopy over it so that when it rains all they have to do is close it in. It's almost like the Houston Astrodome."

"In St. Louis?"

"What do you mean, 'In St. Louis?' What's wrong with St. Louis?"

"Nothing," I kidded him, "only I thought the only thing they had here was beer."

Sammy spoke up for the first time. "Steve, throw him out of the car if he's going to talk like that about St. Louis." Of course, he said it good-naturedly.

The sleek black car ate up the mileage, and we finally reached an exit, turned right, and eased onto another super-highway. In the distance now we could see bright lights that reminded me, in a way, of the Strip in Las Vegas.

Light conversation continued along the superhighway, because all the frivolity would be in this car. Once we hit the meeting room, it would be all business.

I had come for a reason—to discuss a problem. It would be discussed. The only voice in the room would be that of Steve "Bets."

"By the way," he asked, "How'd you make out with that creep Jerry Kent? I haven't heard him mention you anymore."

"I handled it myself, Stevie."

"Personally?"

"No, I sent Bobby D. out there, and . . . just gave him a slap, that's all."

"How is Bobby? I haven't seen him in some time."

"He's earning, Steve, but it's tough right now. There's measles all over."

"Do you still carry that kid with you?"

THE CANNIBALS

"You mean George?"

"Yeah, yeah, that's the guy. He's a nice kid."

"Yeah, George is still with me. I wouldn't know what to do without him, it would be like losing a schoolmate."

"He used to be one rough sonovabitch—can he still go?"

"Hey, don't worry about George, he can still handle himself in any situation. My biggest problem is to try and keep his temper down—he blows it too quick."

"Well, that's no good either."

"I agree with you, but it's better than having a guy who's going to run the other way, isn't it?"

Steve "Bets" laughed at that. "Of course it is, but who the hell's going to be around that kind of a guy anyway?"

"You've got a point."

The black sedan started slowing down. Up ahead I could see the bright neon lights spelling out "Monticello Motel."

It was a beautiful layout and looked like money. Maybe six hundred rooms in a sprawling double-decker that was astonishing to come upon in the suburbs. Everything that Steve "Bets" had said it was.

We pulled into a large circular drive and stopped at the entrance. A doorman was ready for the car.

I took my attaché case and we all went inside.

The lobby was well-appointed, lush. Brass chandeliers were reminiscent of the Vegas Strip. It was obvious I wasn't going to the registration desk; I followed Steve, Lou, and Sammy into the bar.

As we walked past the red-coated bartenders toward the cocktail lounge in the rear, I noticed there were some extremely beautiful young girls sitting there, sipping on what looked to be Coca-Colas. "Fruit salad" was always prevalent in this type of place. I thought to myself, I still can't believe it—St. Louis, yet! Who the hell needs Vegas, with this around?

We walked to the far corner of the lounge where there was a table large enough for six or eight people. Steve automatically went to the seat facing the door. It's a tradition for the top man to see who's coming in: Backs always make good targets.

The waiter came running over like he'd been shot out of a rocket. "What's your pleasure, Mr. B?" he asked, looking only at the one man.

"Three Cutty Sarks on the rocks—how about you, Joey?"

"Make mine a vodka martini."

"You still go that route, huh?"

"I don't know. I just got hooked on martinis, what can I tell you?"

"Keep drinking those fish bowls and you'll wind up with half a stomach."

"You know, you could be right." I looked at the waiter. "Change mine to a vodka and tonic, with a lime."

The waiter smiled and walked away.

Approaching our table now was an extremely sharp-looking man around forty-five years old. He had on a black silk suit with expensive alligator shoes, a large blue star sapphire on his pinkie, and what looked to be a platinum Patek-Philippe watch. He was immaculately groomed.

He arrived, shook hands with Steve, then the rest of the boys, and sat down.

"Joey, say hello to Skip."

I stood up, put out my hand. Skip grabbed it and we shook.

We sat down. Skip looked at my attaché case.

"That yours?"

"Yes."

"Is that all you've got?"

"Yeah."

He gave a quick glance at a waiter, who came running over.

"Take this case, give it to Tommy, and tell him to put it in the room."

The drinks arrived. We all picked them up, said, "*Salute*," and touched glasses.

Mine tasted particularly good to me, because I was on edge.

Steve glanced up at me. "Okay, Joey, just sit back, relax, have a couple of drinks, we'll have a little dinner, and then we'll go to the room and talk. Okay, buddy?"

"Great with me, B., anything you say."

Skip snapped his fingers, and the waiter charged over.

"Keep putting drinks on the table—we'll tell you when to stop."

I looked at Skip. "B. tells me you own the joint."

He gave the semblance of a smile. "Yeah, me and seventeen mortgage companies. The only thing I haven't got up for it is my wife and kids."

"It's one helluva layout, I'll say that. As a matter of fact, it's really out of sight. Those are pretty cute decorations you've got sitting at the bar."

"You looking for decorations tonight?" Skip asked.

"Don't tempt me," I kidded him, "or I'm liable to forget what I came here for."

Steve immediately picked up on that one. "Leave him alone, Skip, he's got a wife who'll cut his heart out."

At this point, four waiters stormed the table, setting down every kind of antipasto you could possibly dream of. It looked absolutely delicious, and everyone ate like they were going to the chair, leaving nothing of the antipasto but the plates. More drinks arrived, followed by food of every description.

We spent the next hour and a half relaxing, drinking, and cutting up touches on personal friends all over the country. It was a great chance for me to have a fill-in on who was doing what and where.

Steve "Bets" looked at his watch. The hands were pointing straight up: twelve o'clock, dead center.

"Okay," he said tersely, "let's go."

We all got up, walked out the door, down a ramp past the pool area, and into a suite.

The meet was about to begin.

Once in the lush suite, we all sat around the oak dining room table. Steve "Bets" sat at the head and chaired. The room grew quiet, tense, and filled with electricity.

Steve looked at me, pointed to Skip, and began.

"Joey, Skip is with me, so feel free to speak in any manner that you want and to say what you want."

"Right, B.," I answered.

"All of us are up-to-date on this guy from the Coast, we've read all the magazines you sent us. So as far as we're concerned, it's pretty much up to you what you want done. Now let me tell you, in the first place, what we've looked into on our own."

This was not the time to miss a word: I listened intently.

"Skip made a connection out on the Coast with someone who could reach this guy. We told him definitely under no circumstances to mention your name or what it was about. All we wanted to do was feel this guy out and find out if he was a take artist."

B. reached into his inside pocket, picked out a cigar, took the cellophane wrapper off, lit it with a match and puffed furiously. The need hit me: I lit a cigarette, took a deep drag, holding it down until it practically exploded in my lungs. Then I exhaled, and it gave me a sense of relaxation.

"Our opinion is very simple. He's a penny-ante shakedown artist. He's connected with nobody. He has no rabbi, no bishop, nobody to go to bat for him. But that's also good, because it means he can't run anywhere. Whether he takes or not is only a guess, but it's certainly too dangerous to try and approach him."

My eyes darted to the other men at the table. Their stares

were fixed on the boss. He was talking—there was no room for anyone else. Staring me straight in the eye, B. continued.

"Joey, one thing I want to ask you. One of the headlines read that you had approached him, or sent someone to him, and tried to bribe him to put the fix in. Is it true or not?"

"Absolutely untrue. B., you know me well enough—if I didn't have a key for the lock, I wouldn't take a chance on an unknown quantity for all the tea in China."

"Good boy. That at least gets that out of the way. What about your buddy, this Jonathan Bingham? How long have you known him?"

This suddenly became vouch time. I couldn't straddle the fence, I had to lay it on the line and call it as I saw it.

"B., I've known the guy for a long, long time. He's kept his word with me, he's helped me; I in turn have practically laid myself on the line for him. If you're asking me to tell you can I trust him, I've got to say yes—but only for ninety percent. I can't throw away the other ten percent with you, because we're different kinds of people. How the hell do I know what this guy will do under pressure? He's liable to get panicky, he's liable to buckle—and the one thing that scares the shit out of me is that another one of his best friends is a goddam fruit and for some unknown reason has some kind of a hold on him."

"Any ideas what that hold is?" B. was methodical now.

"My personal opinion is that it's probably loyalty out of the past. I have a feeling this guy helped Jonathan when he needed help, went to bat for him when he needed a job, or in some way helped him in the chi-chi world. I am personally convinced that's all it is."

B. accentuated his next line by tapping his finger on the table. "Joey, you're too smart for me to sit around and try to lecture you. You're over twenty-one, you know what you're doing. But I don't have to remind you that being close to a fruit is like being close to a junkie. If either one of them starts sweating, you're as good as in the can. Even if you never had a parking ticket in your life, they dream up things about you that only Dick Tracy could understand—"

"One thing I can tell you, B.," I broke in, "you can bet your ass he's got nothing on me."

B. smiled at me. "Joey, do me a favor, bet your ass, don't bet mine."

Everybody broke up. It relieved the tension.

But with the little joke over, we were back to business. B. now spoke crisply and directly.

"Okay, Joey. At the moment that's what we have to tell you. But you're running the game—what do you want to do?"

"B.," I answered, "whatever the cost, I've got to stop this guy."

"How far do you want to go?"

I measured my words, then spoke them with force. "As far as I have to."

"What do you have in mind?"

"B., in the first place, nobody can afford to try to lay money on him because there's no chance to clock him. Who the hell is he? Nobody knows him, nobody can vouch for him, he's nothing. There's no possible way to make a play at him."

"On that you're right." His stare was cold, and the stares of the others expressed assent.

"I will tell you this," I continued. "I've had my own trial, and if he doesn't stop, there's going to be trouble. Big trouble. I ask no help, I don't want to involve anybody. It's my problem, I'll handle it myself."

"Remember one thing," B. cautioned. "He's a newspaper-man—

"Excuse me, B.," I said, carefully observing proper respect in a meeting, "he's not a newspaperman, he's a writer of bullshit. And I don't put up with bullshit."

"He's got that paper. Regardless of what a piece of bullshit it may be, it's still a paper, it's still in print, somebody reads it."

"B., that's my point. Either he or the paper goes out of print. On that I've made up my mind."

"Joey, what has to be done has to be done, and I know you're going to do what's needed. All I want to do is help you think. We're not here for our health, we're not here to drink, we're not here to fool around with broads. The whole purpose of the meeting is to try to be of help."

"Excuse me, B.," I said respectfully, "I understand that. I know how you feel, and if I've offended anyone in the room, I apologize. We wouldn't all be here—I know exactly what you mean."

THE CANNIBALS

There was no need for further discussion in that area. Everyone accepted what I said at face value. There was a vast mutual respect.

Sammy, who until now had not said one word, looked at me with cold eyes. Among those who knew him well his nickname was "The Assassin." It was a matter of conjecture how literally or how frequently he lived up to the nickname.

"Joey, how far are you going to go?"

I met his gaze. "As far as I have to."

"That takes in a lot of territory."

I still didn't flinch. "I've got a lot at stake. There's plenty to lose, Sammy."

B. took over immediately. "If you don't plan it right, Joey, the big loser can only be you."

That didn't stop me for a moment. I looked him square in the eye and with an icy delivery answered him. "B., that's a draw I'll have to take. I live and I die by what I believe in. Which should be very obvious to you—we all have the same code."

Suddenly the temper of the conversation changed. Steve "Bets" was the boss again. "I asked you once before, I'll ask you again—what do you have in mind? Spill it, get it out on the table. Let's not bullshit around."

It would take years to explain a man's emotions when he's in a meeting of this type. You can't explain it to a plumber, a carpenter, a furniture salesman. They might possibly visualize borrowing money on a six-for-five basis, but this was really the bottom line. I now had to answer B., and I calculated my words quickly. They had to be to the point and strong. There was no possibility to hedge the bet.

"B., you gave me the bottom line." I paused, lit a cigarette, inhaled deeply, blew the smoke out, and started again.

"This shake sonovabitch has picked on me, and I don't deserve it. He's lied in everything he's written. There's not one goddam ounce of truth in it. He's picked on my man, which means he's picking on me. When he picks on me, he's affecting the lives of my wife and my family. That also includes my mother and the rest of my family and everyone connected with Gina. If he just goes along the way he's going now, and if he stops me from earning, I don't mind. But if it gets worse—"

As boss of the meeting, B. took the prerogative of interrupting.

"I asked you a question directly, Joey, and you still haven't answered it. How far are you going to go?"

This was the fade. No more fence-straddling. But I was ready. I had the answer rehearsed because I knew the question would come up again, and here it was.

"I'll kill him. . . ."

There was no delay in B.'s answer. "If that's your decision and that's the way you're going to go, you can't kill just him."

"Why?"

Con Edison couldn't supply the power for the electricity that now filled the room.

"He's easy to trap, Joey."

THE CANNIBALS

Each word was drama, intrigue, desperation, and planning. Because of my emotions, I didn't pick up B.'s point.

"What do you mean?" I asked.

"If you take him out, you also have to take out the other two."

I still wasn't thinking straight, and failed to grasp the full import of B.'s statement.

"The other two?"

"Joey, for Christ's sake," he snapped, "do you think for one minute that you can put one guy away, with your friend Jonathan Bingham knowing about it, and also the fruit? You gotta be crazy—what do you want to do, go to the electric chair?"

It hit me like a bolt of lightning—this was like bank night with the free dishes: A cup and a saucer didn't do you any good—you had to have the whole set. All I had to do was shoot this sonovabitch. Jonathan would know about it, because he asked me to handle it in the first place, and God only knew if he'd told the faggot.

I could visualize myself trying to get a night's sleep knowing that Farley Fag knew I'd shot Morry Weinstein. Even though his testimony would be hearsay, the ramifications would be unbelievable.

Coming back from this quick trip of mental calculations, I looked at B.

"Give me an alternative."

It was like sinking into quicksand, with this difference—you're never doomed when you're with friends. Whatever finally came out of this conversation would be designed to help a buddy.

"Skip put a lot of time into this," B. started again, "and I think he came up with a good angle, one that will certainly stop you from going off the deep end unnecessarily. I don't say that you're wrong, but I do say it should be a last resort."

I knew an idea was on its way, and I geared myself to hear it and understand it right.

"Joey, what would you say if we could put this guy out of business?"

"Meaning what?"

"He's got a magazine, right?"

"Right."

"He can only distribute through three houses. We've got the key to that lock."

"You mean you can stop him from putting the magazine on the stands?"

"That's exactly what I'm saying."

"What's the tariff?"

"What's your lid?" he countered.

No sense in bluffing now. I came right to the point. "I talked it over with Jonathan. I got ten thousand to play with."

"It can be done for that. And if it can be done for any less, there's nobody here who's looking to make a quarter from you."

I smiled. "Without going into a lot of crap, I just want you to know that I appreciate it."

B. huffed and puffed on his cigar, completely ignoring the

remark, as did everyone else at the table. My statement had been self-servicing. Deep inside, however, I know that they had a real concern for my declaration.

"You're right about one thing, Joey," B. then said. "Whether it's your way or our way or a combination of the two, he's got to be stopped. This guy is a nut. The only person he hasn't written to in one of his stupid open letters is John Philip Sousa, and that poor sonovabitch I think they buried."

Once again laughter in the room relieved the tension.

B. looked around the room, stopping at Sammy and Lou. "Okay, I think we've put the facts on the table, now let's open it up for discussion. Anyone who's got any ideas, speak up."

Lou opened his mouth for the first time.

"Nobody said anything about breaking his horns. Why don't we just whack him up a bit? That always wakes a few people."

All eyes turned to me.

"I'm against whacking a newspaper guy, even a bullshit one. There's a kind of tradition about not hitting them. It seems to have worked for a few thousand years, so I got to go along with it."

B. went to my side immediately. "I got to agree with that. You just can't whack those guys. You either have to take them out or forget it."

It now was Sammy's turn.

"Joey, if B. gives the okay, I'll give you a birthday present— take them out myself, and it won't cost you a dime. It'll be my pleasure."

I looked at him in silent appreciation.

B. suddenly looked from Sammy to me. An idea had obviously flashed into his mind.

"Joey, have you ever met this guy?"

"No, I haven't."

"Have you tried?"

"The guy who runs my office out on the West Coast tells me he's called three or four times. He wants to meet with me."

"For Christ Almighty's sake, you're not a missionary—meet with the guy, what have you got to lose?"

"Why give him something else to write about?" I answered.

B. reached into the manila envelope that had come through the mail, picked out sixteen copies of *Face* with headlines featuring my name, threw them down in front of me, and said, "You mean to tell me he can do worse than this?"

It didn't take me long to follow his reasoning and appreciate his point. He was no dummy—that's why he was the boss.

It's amazing the astuteness and business acumen that some of these "gentlemen" have. It's sad to realize that if pointed in the right direction, some of them could have become industrial tycoons or even public servants—dollar-a-year men in the finest sense of the word. The cunning of these gentlemen's minds would do credit to a Harvard or Princeton professor— or Yale, if you prefer.

Sammy was now breaking into the conversation again. I liked The Assassin for some reason. His kind of coldness had a tinge of heart. I amused myself, looking at him and imagining him pulling the trigger with a smile. He might even say to himself, softly, "Good-bye."

The supposition on my part had a certain artistic satisfaction. Besides the mental relaxation of this small personal joke was the fairy tale of bringing Sammy into my casting office to apply for the role of a killer. I could just hear Tim Rice or Terry Winant or even Perry Bennett saying, "He's too small, he's too thin, he's too wiry. He doesn't look like he could be a killer." Bless their little imbecile brains.

Sammy was looking at me with those steel brown eyes. "What about Skip's idea of putting the guy out of business? You could do it for the ten grand, and you'd be rid of the sonovabitch."

B. now made sure this possibility was detailed for the record.

"I told Joey," he said, looking at Skip, "that you told me there are only three distributors Weinstein can possibly have in that area. You told me that these guys, because they're friends of ours, will refuse his magazine, and he won't be able to get anyone else. He won't be on the stands with the magazine, and all it'll cost us in ten grand. Is that correct?"

"That's right, B."

B. probed further. "You know these people?"

"Yes," Skip answered.

"I mean, do you really know them? Do you vouch for them, do you put your back up for them?"

"Absolutely," Skip said without a second's hesitation. "And

411

besides, Bobby Sugar has got a piece of all three joints—what more do I have to say?"

B. listened intently, then shifted his gaze to me. "That's good enough for me, Joey."

"And me," I responded.

"I still think we ought to break his horns," Lou unexpectedly put in.

B. stopped him dead with a stare and said, "We've already discussed that, and we all agreed that's not the way to do it. It's over—let's drop it."

Lou didn't even bother to shrug.

I lit another cigarette and decided it was my turn to speak and close the meeting.

"B., you've made great sense to me tonight, and I want you to know I appreciate it. You've also opened my eyes to a couple of other things. I thought I was pretty cute in a lot of areas, but it's obvious I missed the boat."

Without emotion, B. took me off the hook. "Joey, nobody can think straight for himself—that's why there are meetings. That's why you're welcome and will always be welcome. Don't forget, it's a two-way street. We may come to you one day and need your advice, your help. There are no people in the world so brilliant that they can operate alone."

I accepted the compliment silently, then went into my conclusion.

"I'm going to get on that plane and go back to New York. By the time I get there, I'll have made my own decision on which way I'm going to go. The big thing I had overlooked, B., you've brought to my attention. This guy that's knocking my brains out, the guy that I'm sitting down discussing whether I should whack him, put him out of business, or take him out, is the only guy I haven't talked to. By some goddam fluke, he just might be a right guy."

B. smiled paternally. "Now you're using that head of yours, Joey. Now you're really thinking. That's what I like to hear." And he smiled proudly.

"So," I went on, "that's the way I'm going to go, at the moment. I'm going to go out, and I'm going to brace this guy myself, with no help. And I don't give a goddam what Jonathan says or what his fruitcake says. I'm doing what I want to do, and my decision is based on this meeting. I'm not going to whack him, and at the moment I'm not going to go the other route. If it becomes necessary, I'll go that way, but you're also right on another thing, fellows. If I go that way, I've got real problems, because I've got a couple of observers. And you couldn't be more right, they'll absolutely have to go, too. The *finocchio* I don't give a shit about, but the other guy is my friend, and he doesn't deserve to go. As far as I'm concerned, he's got a pass with me for life."

I looked at my watch. Forty-five minutes before plane time.

I rose, walked to the far end of the table. B. stood up. I shook his hand warmly, looking him in the eye.

"You know how much I appreciate this."

"You don't have to say it, buddy," he answered.

413

"I'll tell you this. You've made me think clear again. The trip wasn't wasted, and most importantly, I know again that when I need help, I have it."

B. looked at me kindly. The meeting was now over, and he reverted to tradition.

He raised his right hand, slid it behind my head, and cupped it warmly over my right ear.

"Joey, whatever it is, you got it. And that goes for everybody in this room."

I looked around. I could feel the warmth. It was relaxing, it was redeeming. I shook hands all around. Lou and I walked out, continued to the car, and headed back to the airport, New York, and a meeting with Jonathan.

That meeting would take place forthwith.

Chapter 16

The aroma of freshly brewed coffee awoke me from a half-night's sleep. Gina walked in wearing one of her Saks Fifth Avenue negligees which, out of still sleepy eyes, I pegged to be about a hundred and fifty dollars, carrying a tray with the cup of coffee with cream already in it, and sugar on the side.

"Good morning, gangster," she said lightly. "It's time to get up."

Gina could make me laugh just by reciting the alphabet or reading the telephone book. What the hell could I do—I dug her.

"What time is it?"

"Seven o'clock."

"You must want something," I commented suspiciously. 'You don't usually get up until ten o'clock—and only then to let the maid in the front door."

"What time did you get in last night?" she asked, letting the comment go by.

"Around five."

"Why didn't you call?"

"Do I usually call when I'm away on a meet?"

"Who are we bombing this week?"

"Come here," I ordered.

She set the tray down on the table and sat down on the bed next to me. I sat up, grabbed her in my arms, and put my lips against hers. Even at seven o'clock in the morning they were delicious. She kissed me in response, which is the real answer, put her arms around me, and held me with the firmness that makes you know that your woman cares.

For no particular reason, I put my hand around on her little *tushie*. It was cute, firm, and, most importantly, it fit right into the palm of my hand as if it had been made just for me.

After these preliminaries District Attorney Gina went to work. "Where did you go?"

"Out of town."

Gina loved to play the game of Twenty Questions, and I knew I was in for a session. She couldn't possibly get any answers out of me that I didn't want to give, but it was fun for her to try.

"Did you go south?"

"No."

"West?"

"No."

"North?"

"No."

"Did you stay east?"

"No."

"You're not playing fair," she complained tartly.

"I'm playing fair, you just happen to be a dummy."

416

"If you didn't go south, west, north, or east, then where did you go?"

"Maybe I went in the middle."

"Aha!" she laughed gleefully, "now I know where you went. You think you're going to put anything over on me? All right, tell the truth—how did Steve 'Bets' look?"

"I didn't see Steve 'Bets.'"

"However," I added, "he did send his best."

She smiled triumphantly and walked out of the room.

I proceeded to drink the rest of my coffee, shave, and get dressed.

In New York standing on a street corner waiting for a cab is ridiculous, but I hadn't had time enough to phone George and have him pick me up. By a stroke of luck, however, I grabbed a cabbie. I got in and directed him to BCA Production.

He pumped the foot pedal and we sped away toward midtown Manhattan.

"Good to see you again, Mr. Bertell," he said.

I looked into the mirror at his face, then over to the name plate. It was Morris, who had driven me to BCA several months ago, the day I met Morton Silvern. I realized I was in for another one-way conversation.

For years I've been telling broads who went around with me that if they ever got accosted on the street, for Christ's sake lie back, relax, and enjoy it. Don't fight it because there's nothing

you can do. With Morris, I was now in the same spot, so I just
looked out the window and listened.

"Ya know, Joey—you don't mind if I call you Joey, do you,
Mr. Bertell?"

"No, I'm getting to the point where I feel like I know you."

"Yeah, it's a strange coincidence that I should pick you up
again, ya know what I mean? But I'll tell you, it happens to
me a lot of times. I pick up stars right and left, they just seem
to get into my cab. Ya know, I spend a lot of time around the
BCA production Center, ABC, CBS, NBC. All the time I'm always around stars. Then at night when I work late—ya know,
because sometimes my wife don't let me—well, when I work
late, I'm always around the theater area. So I get nothing but
stars, ya know what I mean?"

He put a cigarette in his mouth and lit a match one-handed,
rubbing it against the folder—a trick I used to do to impress
broads—and while doing so almost hit two cars he was maneu-
vering around.

I didn't flinch—what was the use?

"I sure miss that show. Joey, I'll tell you the truth. Like I
told you last time, my old lady and myself really love those
old-time songs, ya know what I mean? What are ya doing now
that the series is over, what ever happened to you? Aren't you
in show business anymore?"

I started to answer, but it didn't do any good. He cut in
immediately.

"I mean what's wrong with these bastards, don't they appreciate talent? Ya know the only trouble with television, the only trouble with movies, they don't give a damn what people want to see, ya know what I mean? All they care about is what they want to put on. I may not want to see that show. Ya know, my old lady and I, we switch the dial constantly. We go from one program to another, they can't tell us what to see, ya know what I mean?"

At that moment a car jumping the light and pulling out of a side street almost hit us. He swerved around, which cut off his monologue only momentarily.

"Did you see that? Are you going to believe the way they drive in New York City? I tell ya something, you take your life in your hands when you drive a cab, ya know what I mean? I mean, this isn't an easy job. I try and I try to get other jobs, but I tell you the truth, I don't have the time. My wife has me working in the afternoons—ya know, doin' up the house, doin' little chores around, maybe doin' a little shopping, ya know what I mean? I don't have any time. But I don't want to be a cab driver. I'll tell you the truth, ya know what I'd like to be? I'd like to be in show business."

I couldn't resist. "What do you like to do?"

"Do you really want to know?"

"No, I'm testing out my vocal cords. What do you mean, do I really want to know? You tell me you want to do something, I ask you what you want to do. Why don't you answer me, ya know what I mean?"

"You're going to laugh at me," said Morris, "but I do great

419

imitations. I do imitations that nobody does. Did you ever hear anybody do Vincent Price? I do him. I also do the old-timers. I do John Bubbles, I do Eddie Cantor, I do Al Jolson —you want to have a laugh, I even do George DeWitt."

That stopped me. "You're trying to tell me that you really do George DeWitt?"

"I'm telling you it's the truth. I do the best George DeWitt in the country."

"Give me four lines," I said quickly, "but just four lines."

With that, he went into George DeWitt announcing the start of *Name That Tune*. As he finished the quick impression, I applauded.

"Absolutely great. Will you believe me when I tell you it is absolutely great? Now I got one for you, and believe me, if you can do *this*, it can make you a star."

"No kiddin'—" he asked excitedly.

"I'm not kidding. But be prepared, it's a tough one."

"You name it and I'll do it."

"Can you impersonate Jan Murray?"

"Who's he? I never heard of him."

"You don't know who Jan Murray is?"

"I swear to you, I never heard of him. Who the hell is Jan Murray? Tell me, I'll find him, I'll do the impersonation."

"If you can get the impersonation of Jan Murray down pat . . . Listen to me," I put him on, "you know what it can mean to you?"

"No."

"I tell you, if the impersonation is great, it means a Sullivan shot for you."

"But I never heard of this bum. What's he ever done, what's he ever appeared in?"

"That's the point, that's why it's important. *He's never done anything*. He's strictly a Borscht Belt comic. But they're holding him in reserve. The agency that he's with thinks he's one of the greatest comedians of all time. Do you know what it could possibly mean to your career to be able to get an impersonation down of Jan Murray *before* he becomes a star?"

"Yeah, yeah, yeah, I get what ya mean. You couldn't be more right. If I was the first person to do him, it would be like Vaughn Meader when he did the record on the Kennedy family, ya remember that, ya know what I mean? That could be it, it could be a start. I'll look up this bum, where can I find him?"

"Probably the best way to find him is an agent in town who's a real great friend of mine. His name is Charlie Rapp—R-A-P-P—one helluva guy. He does all the bar mitzvahs, all the club dates, books all of the mountain resorts. You gotta try to find somebody in his office. Get close to him and find out where Jan Murray is working. He usually works weekends."

"Yeah, yeah, yeah, you're right; I'll do it, I'll do it. Ya know, that's the answer, you've got to have a gimmick, ya know what I mean?"

By this time we were in front of the BCA production offices.

He swung the meter, I tossed him the money, plus the usual

dollar tip, and said, "For God's sake, don't muff this, it's the chance of a lifetime—absolutely the chance of a lifetime. You must learn how to impersonate Jan Murray!"

"I promise you," Morris said, "the next time I get you in my cab, I'll have him down so pat—nice to talk to you again, Joey, it's a real pleasure seeing you, get what I mean?"

And with that, Morris sped off.

I could hardly wait to see Jan. He had a wild sense of humor. He was a big star and my favorite comedian, and I knew he'd get a kick out of it.

Walking into my offices, I brushed past Vera as if she were a mere painting on the wall. "Get me Sol Mack on the Coast," I snapped, "right away."

She was incredulous. "You mean you want him *now*? The three hour time differential—"

I stopped and glared. "I told you to get Sol Mack on the phone." Then I went into my office and slammed the door behind me.

I walked behind the big desk and shoved all the mail over to the side of the black teakwood, picked up the phone and buzzed the intercom. Vera came on immediately.

"Send Jimmy Craig in here right away."

Within a few minutes Jimmy walked through the door.

"What's up?" he asked.

"I got problems. Get me a bottle of vodka, some ice cubes,

some tonic water, and some limes, and bring them in here right away, and then I've got some things for you to do."

Jimmy looked at me warmly, with the obvious friendship he had always displayed over the last couple of years, and said, "Why don't you forget the vodka?"

"I told you what I wanted," I snapped in reflex action. "Now either do me a favor and go get it or get the hell out of here."

He left silently, on his alcoholic mission.

The intercom rang. "I tried the offices," Vera said, "but there's nobody there at this hour. Do you want me to try him at home?"

"I don't give a goddam if you try him in Tahiti, I said get him on the phone." I hung up abruptly.

The door opened and Jimmy Craig walked in with all the ingredients for my vodka and tonics. I grabbed the new bottle of vodka from him, rimmed the top with my fingernail, and snapped open the cap.

"Bring two glasses over—you and I are going to have one helluva belt."

"You've got to be kidding. I can't drink this early."

"Then congratulations, pal, you're crossing a new frontier by starting right now."

I took the two glasses, dropped in the ice cubes, slipped the little knife off my key ring, cut the lime in half, squeezed each half into a glass, poured at least three shots of vodka into each, and filled with the tonic. I stirred with my finger, then handed him one of the drinks.

"Drink."

"What am I drinking to?"

"To friendship," I answered, lifting my glass, "and to where-ever it leads."

He clinked his glass against mine and took a careful sip. I devoured half of mine in one gulp.

"Can I do anything to help?" he then asked.

"Yes, you can. Just keep your big mouth shut, and keep me company."

Vera knocked and came through the door.

"Well?"

"Sol Mack is on two. I got him at home, he's a little foggy. I told him it was urgent."

I pushed the lighted button and lifted the receiver.

"Sol? Joey."

"It's six o'clock out here," he said groggily.

I ignored that and went right to my point. "Get ahold of Morry Weinstein, I want a meet."

"I thought you told me that wasn't a good idea."

"I've changed my mind. I want to meet him, and I want to meet him as fast as possible."

"Does that mean you're coming out here?"

"That means I'm leaving on the noon plane."

"Is it that important?"

"No, it isn't really that important," I snapped, "but I'm due

424

out there for an Israeli bond drive anyway. . . . Of *course* it's that important."

"When should I set up the meeting?"

"Tomorrow at four o'clock in our offices."

"What if he won't come here?"

I blew a fuse. "Am I nuts, or have you been telling me that he's called the office four, five, six times asking to meet me? Am I nuts, or am I correct?"

"Yes, he's been calling—"

"Then, goddamit, set up the meeting—in my offices, I'm not going to his."

"Joey, I can tell you're upset. I'll do my best."

"Sol, your best won't be good enough—just *do it*, that's all I ask."

"Will do, Joey. Do you want me to pick you up at the airport?"

"No, I'll rent a car and come in myself."

"Where are you going to stay?"

"I'll stay at the Beverly Hills Hotel. Make a reservation for me."

"Shall I call you back to confirm the meeting?"

"No, goddamit. *Make* the meeting—I'll be there. I don't want any excuses on this, it's probably the most important thing I've ever asked you. Just deliver." *Click*.

As I hung up the receiver, I picked up the vodka and tonic, downed the rest of it, and looked at Jimmy.

"Fill me in—what's happening on the production? How's it going? How's that idiot doing?"

"If you mean Perry, he's driving everyone out of their minds."

"What is there about me? I seem to have inherited all the jerks of the world."

"You inherited a real beauty in this guy, Joey. He is something."

"Did the unit manager do what I asked and put a clock on him? I want a daily report on how much money this man is costing us."

"It's been done, and it's up-to-date," Jimmy answered.

I picked up the intercom and buzzed. Vera came on.

"Get me out on the twelve o'clock plane for the Coast," I started to hang up, but had an afterthought. "And by the way, Vera . . ."

"Yes?"

"I love you madly."

"Thank you, your worship," She hung up.

As I put down the regular phone, I picked up the private and dialed his nibs.

"John Bingham," he answered.

"Johnny, Joey."

"Where the hell have you been?" He spoke excitedly and more loudly than usual. "I've been trying to get you for two days now."

"I had my meeting in St. Louis, and I'm leaving for the Coast at twelve o'clock. I have to see you before I go."

"I'll meet you at the place in ten minutes."

"Make it fifteen," I ordered.

"Okay, you got it." *Click.*

Now I was ready for action. I rose.

"Jimmy, go to my box, get me a thousand dollars in cash, get ahold of George, tell him to stand by. Call the set—I don't care what he's doing, I want him with me. Tell him he's going to drive me to the airport."

Jimmy ran out the door, caught up in the excitement of the moment. Over his shoulder he said, "Will do, boss."

I checked my watch: eleven minutes to make Le Valois . . . and Jonathan.

I walked past Vera, then reversed myself, walked over and kissed her lightly on the forehead.

"That's for putting up with a meanie, sweetheart. Now pack my briefcase, give it to George, and see that I have the first-class ticket to California and back. I won't need any clothes, I have them out in the Coast office. Never mind the reservation. Sol Mack is booking me into the Beverly Hills Hotel . . . but check in with him and get my exact timetable for the day."

I wheeled around and left.

As I hit the street in front of the BCA Production Center, some gray flannel suit boys were getting out of a cab, and I quickly commandeered it.

"Le Valois, Fifty-eighth street."

I checked the watch again. I didn't want to be late for this one. "Don't waste any time," I told the driver.

Catching all the lights, we pulled up in front of Le Valois in six minutes. I paid the driver, tipped him, and went right inside.

As I sat down at the bar, Jean Pierre looked up in amazement. "What are you doing here this early?"

"I'm heading for the Coast, old buddy. Make me a special."

With his usual professionalism, he had it whipped up in a matter of seconds. I took a healthy sip and waited. I was pleased the bar was empty. It meant that when Jonathan arrived, we would have a private conversation. Because if there was ever a time for privacy, it was now.

"Make another one," I told Jean Pierre, "Mr. Bingham will be here in a few seconds."

He went about his chore briskly again, and just as he set down the second drink, Jonathan walked in and slid onto the stool beside me.

"Take a drink, buddy," I greeted him tartly. "I've got something to tell you, and let me do the talking."

"Shoot."

"Half an hour ago I got Sol Mack on the phone and told him to set up a meeting for me with Morry Weinstein."

Jonathan just listened.

I looked him square in the eye. "I've got to meet this guy head-on."

Now he spoke. "I don't think it's wise—"

"Johnny, I don't care what you think. I'm going to meet with him."

"It's dangerous, Joey. Nobody's ever been able to handle him." He was definitely perturbed.

"Give me the names of two people who have tried."

He had no answer on that one.

"There's three or four ways to go, and I'm willing to take that draw, but I've got to sit down with this man first."

"Why?"

"Because I and . . . everybody whom I've talked to said that's the way it has to be."

"Bryan and Joe Ballantine think you're wrong."

I looked at him in silent contempt. How had I gotten myself into this impossible spot? I had counted on this man's brilliance, his generalship. Now this czar, this autonomous dictator of the television industry, this man I looked up to as my leader, had suddenly shrunken into a pitiful example of fear. Bryan Westgate . . . I had a flash of The Assassin's face as he offered to take out Morry, Johnny, *and* Bryan as a birthday present.

Holy Christ, Joey, I said to myself, forget Johnny's "Charge forward boldly." Take two steps backward and protect yourself!

"Screw Bryan," I said to him, "and screw Joe Ballantine. I don't see them within three thousand miles of the firing line. I'm the one who's up front right now, and I'm the one who's going to call the shot."

"Well, don't go today," he pleaded. "Think it over, and let's talk about it."

"I've done all the thinking and talking I'm going to do. And don't help me by sending any more of your memos like 'File it under B and burn it.' "

That hit home. He stayed quiet as a little puppy dog for a moment, and when he spoke again he was obviously oriented to my departure come hell or high water.

"When are you leaving?"

"I leave on the twelve o'clock plane."

He looked around him as if the bar were filled with a thousand people and he needed their support.

"Joey, don't go. I tell you, it's wrong—don't go."

"I said I'm going," I snapped fiercely, "and that's *it*. I'll be on that plane, and I'll meet with Morry Weinstein."

"Just remember," he now angled, "I told you it was wrong. You're liable to blow the whole ball game."

I looked him square in the eyeballs. "I heard what you told me, and I tell you that maybe you've been wrong, and maybe you've blown the whole ball game. One of us is wrong, that's for goddam sure."

He paused and sipped his drink, now looking for strength there.

"Johnny, for Christ's sake, don't run scared now. I'm telling you, I know what I'm doing."

"Maybe you do," he said quietly, "but I don't believe in it."

I wheeled around. "Now listen to me, buddy, you've got me out front here, I'm the guy with my neck out. You're the guy who asked me to handle it, and by God you're going to see me

430

do it my way. I don't want any help from you or any of your two-for-a-nickel friends."

He had nothing more to say. The die was cast.

Jean Pierre came over and discreetly interrupted the conversation. "There's a phone call for you, Mr. Bertell. At the captain's desk."

I rose, walked over, picked up the phone, and said, "Hello."

"Joey, this is George."

"Pick me up in five minutes," I said, and hung up.

When I walked back to my seat and looked into Jonathan's eyes, it was obvious to me that some way, somehow, I had to put some starch into his spine.

"What the hell is wrong with you?" I asked him softly but coldly. "Are you losing your grip?"

"Joey, for Christ's sake, this guy is dangerous. You can't count on him. Nobody's been able to handle him. I think you're making the biggest mistake of all time."

"You made the mistake. We should have handled him sooner."

"Did you ever stop to think what the ramifications could be if this thing blew up?"

"You think like a loser if you want to, buddy—I don't. I say I'm going to handle him, and when I say it, that's the bottom line."

Jonathan sat stunned. He had never heard me talk like this before. I looked at his face, his eyes. He was visibly frightened. He was not the czar at this moment. He was not calling the shots.

Once again I looked him right in the eyes. "He isn't going to lick me the best day he ever lived."

"Do you really think you can handle him?" The question had a childish tone.

"How the hell do I know," I flared, "but by God, I'm going to take the draw."

I looked at him and saw the fear again. For the first time he was exposed.

"Johnny, where the hell are your *guts*? This isn't the Jonathan Bingham I know."

"Maybe you're stronger than I am," he said simply.

"Maybe you're right."

I finished my drink, got up, and walked out into the street to wait for George.

California . . . again. Sitting in the Scandia Restaurant, I sipped my martini and checked my watch. Three-forty-five—I had fifteen minutes before meeting the unknown factor in the whole equation, Morry Weinstein.

I chug-a-lugged the last half of the martini, signed the check, and walked out.

In the parking lot I handed the boy my ticket, and within minutes he drove my car up, slid out, and held the door open for me. I slapped a dollar into his hand, slammed the door, and rolled toward the exit.

In a moment I was headed along Sunset Boulevard toward Beverly Drive. There I turned left and in a few minutes was at my office. I parked, walked in the side entrance, and cut through the lobby.

Upstairs I greeted my receptionist cordially, and she lit up.

"Hello, Mr. Bertell, glad to have you back."

"Thank you."

In the mood for business now, I walked past her and proceeded right into Sol Mack's private office. My first glance was Sol Mack at a beautifully appointed desk in a forest of mahogany. The furniture was expensive. The built-in bar was a conversation piece.

My second glance was the man sitting next to him. He was carefully dressed, medium height, athletically trim. This was obviously Morry Weinstein.

Sol did the honors. "Joey, I'd like you to meet Morry Weinstein—Mr. Weinstein, this is Joey Bertell."

I shook his hand firmly. "Nice to meet you. I'm sorry I'm late—I looked at my watch on the way in and see that I lost about five minutes."

Morry was sizing me up. "Don't worry, I was early, anyway."

I felt that remark tended to make me an underdog and maneuvered to get out of that position immediately. Walking casually over to the bar, I prepared a quick vodka and tonic and then asked, "What can I get you, Morry?"

"I'll take a ginger ale if you have it."

"You've got it. How about you, Sol?"

"I'll have a Scotch on the rocks."

I made them their two drinks, then brought all three over to the coffee table. I looked at Sol and Morry and said, "All right, let's sit over here, and maybe we'll have a little chat."

I picked up my drink and toasted with strict cordiality: "Here's to everyone." And I made it a point to wait and watch everyone pick up his drink.

I took a gulp and set down my vodka and tonic.

"At last we meet," I said to Morry Weinstein, giving him a long look.

"It has taken some time," he answered, "but here we are."

As I studied him, I realized that I couldn't have been more completely wrong. Contrary to my mental image, here was a man immaculately groomed. His hair had just been trimmed, and more important, I sensed that his mind was groomed and trim. I silently cursed Jonathan for thinking Weinstein could be a dummy in any sense of the word.

Actually, I hadn't expected to meet a sleazy character. A shake artist, a fraud, a phony, maybe. But his writing had impressed me, for openers, and now I knew more. I was facing a well-educated, well-prepared opponent.

"Morry," I started quietly, "let me say a few words, make a couple of statements to you, then you can answer me and we'll go from there. Is that all right with you?"

"Certainly, go right ahead."

"When Sol first mentioned that you had called suggesting a meeting if I wanted to correct the record, as you put it in your magazine, I told him no, that I wasn't interested and wouldn't sit down. I changed my position on that, called him, and asked him to set up this meeting.

"In the first place, I appreciate your coming and I want you to know that there's no question you can ask me that I won't answer. I want to clear up this mess, because in the first place it's getting out of hand, and in the second place you claimed in one of your articles that if what you were writing was wrong, all I had to do was sit down with you and explain where you were wrong. Is that much correct?"

"That's exactly what I wrote."

I lit a cigarette, puffed easily, and went on.

"I'm sitting down with you now against the recommendation of everyone—with the exception of Sol Mack right here, who wanted us to sit down earlier, I must admit. Anyway," I went on kiddingly, "I was curious to find out just what the hell there was about you that's got everyone else scared to death."

He smiled, but said nothing. This was a real shrewdie.

"Now come on," I said, "let's hear from you. How would you like to proceed?"

"I would like to do an article on you from the point of view of 'Joey Bertell tells his side of the story.' I will do the piece exactly as you say it, and, in addition, act as your counselor as you're telling it and read my version of it before I print it."

I gave Sol Mack a quizzical look.

"What the hell is wrong with that? I fail to see where this guy is any kind of a louse at all."

Morry Weinstein had to laugh at that. "Thank you."

"Morry, I pledge you my word, if you play square with me, I'll play square with you."

"That seems fair enough."

Go fight City Hall! I actually liked this guy—I liked the way he looked. I liked the way he acted. How had all this fuss built up? The guy was educated, he had breeding, he dressed well, he spoke well. I began to wonder if I was losing all my marbles. Here was a guy who had attacked me unmercifully, practically demolished my public image, brought me to the point where I was wasting days trying to figure how to put him out of commission—and all of a sudden Morry Weinstein had Joey Bertell liking him.

"Okay, Morry," I began, "for the record . . . nobody, but absolutely nobody, has a piece of Cardinal Productions. I have no partners. The stockholders are my wife, my little girl, my kid sister—she takes care of the accounting here and is in the other room right now—and my comptroller in New York. My comptroller has exactly one share of the stock, the rest is completely in the family."

Morry just sat, listening intently.

"Aren't you going to write any of this down?"

Then I saw the reporter's inevitable small piece of paper and pencil stub in his hands. He held them up and said, "I'm just going to make spot notes."

I plunged into my narrative and went methodically through the last few years, starting with *Sandstorm* and ending with the three shows now on the air. At the conclusion I looked at him and said, "That's about it. Anything else you'd like to know?"

"No, Joey, that's pretty well rounded out."

"There's just one more thing I want to get into, then," I said. "Whether you believe it or not, Jonathan Bingham is one helluva guy. He probably—"

The door opened, and my kid sister walked in.

I snapped to my feet and walked quickly over to her. At that moment she was the only one in the room as far as I was concerned. Family was always that way with me.

I put my arm around her and took a good long minute before proceeding with office manners. At last I walked her over to the coffee table.

"Nikki, I'd like you to meet Mr. Weinstein."

"Nice to know you, Mr. Weinstein." She put out her hand.

Morry rose, took it gently, and said, "Nice to meet you."

She looked at me warmly and said, "If you need me, I'll be glad to stay."

"No, thanks, sweetheart, you go home and relax"

"Nice to have met you, Mr. Weinstein," she said with a smile.

"Thank you very much," he said.

Nikki went to the door, opened it, and looked around the room once more. I saw that look, and so did everyone else in the room.

"Don't worry," I said to her easily.

She smiled, stepped through the door, and closed it behind her.

As long as I was up, I fixed another vodka and tonic for myself and another Scotch on the rocks for Sol. Morry declined another ginger ale.

Once I was back at the coffee table, I carefully picked up my last remarks to Morry.

"I was talking to you about Jonathan, so let me continue from there. Morry, I've known him for years. He's a stand-up guy, he's got guts, and he's one of the most brilliant men I've ever met in my life.

"The only reason he'd ever get attacked by anybody—and I don't mean you in particular—is because he's at the top of the ladder. This guy has got them all beat. He can outthink anybody in the television business, and they just hate to see a guy who's right all the time. Which is what he's been—right one hundred percent of the time. The only thing he's got going against him is that he's a loner. He's a myth, nobody knows him. And when that happens, a guy is bound to make enemies."

"I hear they're going to fire him at BCA," said Morry without any preliminaries.

"Utterly ridiculous." My words were quick and sharp, but I kept the tone low and friendly, which we had all done since the meeting began.

"I'm telling you, I heard it, and I've heard it from a lot of people . . . including his own people. He doesn't have the same loyalty from them, Joey, that he has from you."

"I tell you, Morry, he's as safe as gold. He has absolutely no chance of getting the can tied to him."

438

Morry pointedly changed the subject. "How are your shows doing?"

"Two are going excellent, the other's playing opposite a runaway hit."

"That you can't help."

"I'm trying like hell to get the show moved to a different time slot so it has a chance. It's a good show. It's a well-produced show."

"How are the ratings?"

"*Mr. Trouble* is doing very well, *Karen* is holding her own, and *The Barnabys*, like I said, is getting slaughtered. Strangely enough, however, the sponsor is very happy with it, so we're only fighting for that time change. I don't care how good your show is, if you're slotted against a runaway hit—and that's what that soap opera is, a runaway hit—there's just not a damn thing you can do about it."

Morry seemed interested. "That makes sense."

"Now I'd like you to do me a favor, Morry."

"If I can, I will."

"I had the guts to sit down and face you, didn't I?"

"Yes."

"And everything I've told you is the truth, I give you my word. Nobody is my partner. I want you to lay off my shows and give them a chance. If you find out at any time that anything I've told you isn't the truth, then you can blast me any way you want. But those shows don't deserve to be crucified—give them a chance."

"Joey, I won't bother the shows at all—you have my word

439

on it. And I'll lay off the Jonathan Bingham story for six to eight weeks. But if there's any part of the story that is true—or if he is going to get fired—then I'm going to delve into it as much as I can and print it. After all, that's what I'm running a magazine for."

"You've got a deal, Morry, and I thank you."

With that, he stood up, shook hands with me and Sol Mack. "I'll call you tomorrow. I'll meet you somewhere and read you the article, as promised."

"More than that," I said, "I can't ask for."

He turned around and walked out the door.

I looked at Sol. "I think it was a helluva good meeting."

He beamed. "I told you it would be the best thing to sit down with him."

"Tell me, Sol, am I nuts? I like the guy."

Sol reflected a moment. "To be honest with you, Joey, I couldn't find anything in him to dislike."

It was a qualified comment, but it served my purpose. I grabbed my car keys from the coffee table.

"I've got a couple of people to meet at the Polo Lounge, so I'll talk to you the first thing in the morning."

"Okay, Joey."

As I started to leave, I added over my shoulder, "Thanks Sol, I think it *was* a good thing that we had this meeting."

He smiled.

Away I went.

Chapter 17

My first week and a half back in New York from the Coast had all but disappeared in a flurry of work and one long splitting headache of production problems.

With Jonathan's return from Canada, however, I was about to steal an hour to reconvene the BCA-Cardinal Mutual Admiration Society.

Resting expectantly in the back seat of a Yellow Cab on my way over to Le Valois, I reminisced about the events that had now taken place. Tucked in my pocket was the latest issue of *Face* magazine, featuring the complete Morry Weinstein interview. That interview wasn't good, it wasn't excellent—it was absolutely and positively fabulous.

I had spoken to Jonathan earlier in the afternoon, and he told me he had sent a copy of it up to the Chairman. This was wasted motion, because Morry Weinstein had made a policy of sending a copy of each issue not only to the Chairman and the Dentist but to the entire board of directors. From Jonathan's standpoint, however, it was still a good move.

We arrived at Le Valois. I got out of the cab, paid the meter, tipped the driver handsomely because of the rare mood I was in, and walked through the door.

As I headed for the bar, I was surprised to see that Jonathan was waiting for me, for a change. On the bar were two Jean Pierre specials. Johnny was beaming.

"I didn't even sip my drink, buddy—I waited for you. Sit down and pick up your glass. Here's to you, you sonovabitch! You're absolutely the greatest—I cannot believe it. The article was magnificent. Or, to put it into your jargon, it was superb."

"Modesty forbids me from gloating, you bastard," I replied, "but here's to you. *Salute*."

We clinked glasses and took healthy gulps to accompany the smiles.

"The article is everything that Morry Weinstein told me it would be, it's everything he read to me the next day—he kept his word."

I had become a Morry Weinstein booster, and I now picked up the business from that point of view.

"You sent it to the Chairman, right?"

"I not only sent it to the Chairman," crowed Jonathan, "I sent it to the Dentist and four or five other key executives. Joey, I have to hand it to you."

"Johnny, he kept his word—that's the story in a nutshell."

"I openly admit I was wrong. I couldn't have been more wrong."

"Johnny, one thing I must confess, I'm not a genius. I had a lot of help in St. Louis—everyone was willing to do anything I wanted. But they told me that I absolutely must sit down first with this man."

"Well, I give them their due as well—they were right. I was wrong."

"That's a big statement, coming from you."

"You have an expression I've always liked, and it applies here. 'They still have erasers on pencils, don't they?' Well, this time I had to use one."

I pressed the compliment. "It takes a big man to admit he's wrong."

"Wrong, buddy: It takes a stupid man to make the mistake in the first place. Now for God's sake tell me—I haven't seen you in ten days—what is Morry Weinstein like?"

"I won't say he's a Jewish John Lindsay—but he's close to it."

"I knew just from our phone call when I was leaving for Toronto that you were taken with him."

"Johnny, I not only respected the guy, but, I'll tell you the truth, I found myself liking him."

"What does he look like?"

"Very clean-cut guy. Dresses great, immaculately groomed, and obviously well-educated."

"About how old?"

"I'd say forty—early forties."

"If he has that kind of talent and presence, why does he run a crap sheet? Why isn't he with a trade paper or a national magazine or a big publishing house instead of doing scum writing?"

"Johnny, he's got to be either a shake artist—or a crusader. Maybe it's a mixture of both."

"Did he try to shake you?"

"Absolutely not. And he could have. . . ."

"Amazing. The whole situation is amazing."

I lit a cigarette, then put it down without smoking it.

"Johnny, it's too bad we didn't go after this guy sooner—I mean it. He's taken a tremendous toll, I want you to know that."

Furrows appeared in Jonathan's brow.

"On that you're right. He's already had his effect. I hadn't mentioned it before, but I had many memos come down from upstairs regarding those articles. As you know, he mailed them every week to the Chairman and the Dentist."

"Johnny, that's exactly why I decided not to go through with the ten-thousand-dollar deal that I spoke to you about from St. Louis."

"What was your reasoning on that?"

"Very simple. You can put a guy out of business, but how are you going to stop him from buying a postage stamp?"

"I never thought of that," he said simply.

"Don't feel bad about it, neither did a lot of people." I was thinking about Steve "Bets" and crew. "What did Bryan baby and Ballantine think about the article?" I now probed.

"They called me last night and read it to me. They thought it was just great. Bryan said he thought you handled yourself beautifully."

I took a little sip of joy juice and probed deeper. Facing Jonathan directly, I asked, "Are you in trouble with your job?"

444

"No," he answered softly. "But I don't think I'll be there a year from now."

I took the small bolt of lightning impassively. "Why do you say that?"

"Joey, I'm tired of the grind. I'm tired of making money for everybody but myself. I'm tired of making producers rich on ideas that are mine and they have nothing to do with. I practically have to tell them how to produce the shows. It's unrewarding, and the thrill is lost."

"Morry Weinstein asked me if you were going to get fired," I rephrased diplomatically, "and I told him it was ridiculous. But are you in trouble?"

"Hell, no. The Chairman wouldn't fire me—he wouldn't dare. The stockholders would lynch him."

"He claims he heard it from a lot of people, including your own. That should give you something to think about."

"Screw them all, Joey. Let them talk, let them talk—they've *been* talking, and it hasn't done them any good."

I left the theme momentarily and shifted to my own problems.

"Are we going to be able to make that time switch on *The Barnabys*?"

"We're trying to work it out now. Wilson Manning is very much for it. He's getting static from the advertisers, who are perfectly happy with the show—except they aren't getting the rating."

"Can you imagine getting time-slotted against that runaway

445

hit? The only one of the year—and I got to get slotted against it."

"Joey, when I gave you that spot for that show, it looked like the softest cushion on TV. Nobody ever figured that show to last eight weeks without getting canceled, that's the kind of trouble they were in. All of a sudden the public ate it up. You can't figure it sometimes. The Chairman said yours was the finest half-hour comedy show that we had on the networks."

"With the ratings the way they are now, he probably has amnesia."

"He's always had a loss of memory on his bad picks. But I'll still say one thing, the show is good. It's a damn good show."

"Johnny, I'll tell you flat out, Bryan's doing a lousy job on the Karen show."

"You're right, I never should have let him handle it."

"Instead of fighting that dizzy broad, he's joining her. It's like real chaos. The set is a total madhouse."

"She's a bitch, all right, but her ratings are good, and they'll pick up. As soon as the movies run out of those first big ones and settle down to normal pictures, she'll pick up and take the time slot, you'll see."

"I hope you're right. Also, your guys are driving us nuts on the *Mr. Trouble* series, I want you to know that. They've changed my format fifteen different times, they've got Terry Winant going out of his head. And all of a sudden in the eighth week Perry's a police reporter, for Christ's sake. They keep bringing in guest stars . . . it's a joke. It started off so damn good, had a great pilot—and, Johnny, I'm no fool, they're not doing it without your backing. You're behind it somewhere."

"That's true. I've . . . tried to stimulate them into thinking creatively. I want the show to have more guts and dynamics. I think the flak about violence shows is over now, and maybe we can go back to what the public used to buy in big quantities."

"Well, it's costing us a goddam fortune, I'll tell you that. You keep asking us for production, you keep asking us to work hours, you keep asking us to go outside. We just don't have it in the budget."

"Find a way to get it, but get it done, because that's what I want."

"Listen, I'm pressuring everyone over there as it is."

"Do it, and do more. The show is slick—it looks expensive."

"It not only looks expensive, it *is* expensive."

"I don't care what it costs. Just get it done and see that it looks it."

"As long as I keep asking for money and they keep sending it over . . ."

"Then what are you complaining about?"

"Come to think of it, I have no complaints."

Now I returned to my earlier theme and went to the clincher.

"Johnny, I promised to deliver something for Morry Weinstein."

"What's that?"

"He's going to lay off you. He's definitely going to lay off my shows. He'll only start picking on you again if he finds out you're going to get fired."

"Well, I'm not going to get fired—don't bring it up again."

"Okay, that's what I said."

"What did you promise?"

"This guy wants to be recognized as a reporter, like the other trade papers. But he's been blackballed and barred from every lot in town. Believe me what I tell you, they're making the biggest mistake of their lives. Now, since he's going to lay off the network, treat him like a reporter. Let him come on the lot. When I talked with him on the phone on the Coast the day after our meeting, I promised him I'd deliver that."

"Follow me." Jonathan rose from his stool, strode quickly over to the telephone booth, and with no wasted motion got ahold of Joe Ballantine on the Coast.

"Have Bryan come into your office," he ordered, "and tell him to pick up the extension."

When he had both of them on, he said, "Joey came back, and as you know he did a remarkable job. It did us a lot of good upstairs and satisfied the Chairman. Joey promised Morry Weinstein that he can come on the BCA lot like any legitimate press representative. He reports things as he sees them. and isn't going to hurt us. We can't control him, but by the same token, he's not conniving to take us apart. So I want him on the lot starting tomorrow."

They exchanged a few pleasantries, then Jonathan hung up.

"Well?" he asked, looking at me.

I clapped him on the back. "Thanks, pal. That's always been our strong suit. Jonathan, when we give our word, we've got to back it up."

"I just did," he said.

"Come with me, fair maiden," I said to Vera as I walked into my office, "and bring your book."

I sat down at my desk, glanced quickly through the mail and messages, then cast them aside. Vera had not given me the big cue.

"How were the ratings on *Mr. Trouble*?"

"Very good."

" 'How sweet it is . . .' I'm going to be on the private making a long-distance call. Don't let anybody disturb me. Don't let anybody walk through the door. I'll buzz you after that—I want to make some calls to the network."

"Yes, your worship."

As she started to go out the door, I called her back. "Vera."

"Yes, your worship?"

"You forgot to curtsy."

She did a quick British bob, very proper, and left.

I took out the black Madison Avenue alligator wallet and from a secret compartment selected Morry Weinstein's private number. Grabbing the phone, I direct-dialed.

A sleepy voice answered. "Hello?"

"Wake up, you silly bastard."

"Who's this?" Less sleepy. Still not friendly.

"Who the hell do you think it is?" I shot back. "Joey Bertell. Shake yourself out of sleep, kick the broad out of bed, I've got something to tell you."

His tone and attitude improved immediately. "Hey, what's new?"

"For openers," I answered, "you are on the BCA lot. . . ."

"You're kidding."

"I never kid about that sort of business."

"I'll believe it when I walk in."

"I promised you, didn't I? Morry, in my presence Johnny picked up the phone," I dramatized triumphantly, "he summoned Bryan Westgate and Joe Ballantine to a conference line, and he gave the order. You are now on the lot, as a respected reporter. Period. You and I have only one deal."

"What's that?"

"First, you're on as a reporter, and nobody wants to stop you from being a reporter. Report what you see. If you don't like a show, don't like it. If you like it, rave about it. You're on your own. Second, just don't use the pass to abuse us. Don't take anyone apart as a finger exercise."

"That's fair enough, and it's my principle."

"That's all I ask.

"You got a deal, Joey."

I knew I was giving back to this man the self-respect he had sacrificed in recent years to earn a buck. The principle he mentioned must have been hard to live up to once the discrimination and the chopping started.

450

"Morry, I'm counting on it. You've kept your word, and you've kept my confidence. You are a gentleman. I'd like to say simply that it was a pleasure meeting you, and I hope that from here on in the mutual respect grows."

"It's already there."

"A final point, Morry. I have given you *Jonathan's* word that you're on the BCA lot because I heard it with my own ears."

"I understand."

"I made only one mistake."

"What was that?"

"I should have contacted you sooner."

"That's all I've ever asked anyone to do, but you're the one who did it."

"Well, if this works out, the rest will be beating a path to your door. And now that I've seen you operate, I'll just take the liberty of saying the greatest things in the world about you, in the right places."

"Thank you." He was simple but cordial.

"Talk to you soon." *Click.*

I buzzed Vera. "Get me Virgil Esty right away."

I picked up two darts and threw them straight into the bull's-eye. I was back in stride with everything. Thank God.

The intercom buzzed, and Vera had my call.

"Virgil, Joey."

"Hi," he said, friendly but glum.

"I imagine you're worried."

"Well, sort of."

"Listen to me. I made J.J.B. promise me that you're safe."

"Makes me feel like an ass to hold a job that way. No reflection, Joey, but all I'm trying to do is the right thing."

"Virgil, don't go altruistic at this moment. The important thing is that you're there and that you stay there."

"This whole joint is in an upheaval," he said.

"I'm beginning to gather that."

"Everybody's talking about the magazine piece and how you faced up to Morry Weinstein."

"I was stupid, Virgil. I should have done it earlier."

"Maybe, but a person never can be sure about those things."

"That's bullshit. When trouble hits you in the face, you have to square off against it. The best part of this situation is he wasn't a bad guy."

"At least he delivered."

"*Now* you have the name of the game, Virgil. Okay, what's with Ted Michaels. I know him casually from the coast, but what's your opinion?"

"Everybody considers him part of a power play, and although I appreciate everything you're trying to do, he and you together can save me for only so long. I figure to go."

"Why?"

"It's Chester . . . against Bryan and Jim. Mario is with Chester, at the moment, but only because Bryan hates him. And Mario is nothing, anyway."

THE CANNIBALS

That comment made me kick myself in the ass all over again. If only he hadn't been Italian, I would never have put him in the job, no matter what Johnny said. We have an expression—you're either a *jadrool* (which is the Italian equivalent of the Yiddish *schlep*) or you're a *gavone* (which is about four steps lower than a peon). Mario Colucci had the dubious distinction of being both. He was a walking male douche bag.

Barry brought me out of the gutter. "Your interview in *Face* magazine has cut down the scuttlebutt a little bit. But I must tell you, it's all over the street that J.J.B. is going to be . . . let go."

I had to stop these rumors, fast and firmly.

"Virgil, for Christ's sake, stop falling into the bullshit. I just saw J.J.B. last night, reporting to him on a few matters, and everything is great. Don't worry about it. Tell me once, how *could* they fire him?"

"Joey, I just try to do my job. I don't know from nothing about the rumor mill."

"I'm sorry, Virgil, I didn't mean to blow."

"I understand how you feel."

Now I wanted to snap back into business. "The scripts on *The Bridge* are coming real, real good."

Silence.

"I thought the Chicago trip did us a lot of good," I probed.

The silence was conspicuous.

"Okay, Virgil. We're friends, let's act like friends. I sense something's wrong. Lay it on the line."

After a slight pause Virgil managed to answer.

"Joey, *The Bridge* is going to be canceled."

It was a stunner, but I could counterpunch.

"Why? The show's the best of anything we've ever done."

"I agree, Joey."

"Then why are we canceling?"

"All I can tell you is this. If your three scripts were like *Gone With the Wind*, we still couldn't take them."

"How good is your confidence?" I asked.

"Do you have to ask?"

"That's all I wanted to hear."

My mind was racing like a washing machine in mid-cycle. I couldn't stop it, but I had to do something fast.

"Virgil, what you're saying to me in effect is that Joey Bertell is a patsy."

"You said it, I didn't."

I had to end the conversation quickly.

"Virgil, let me get back to you, I have to make another call. We'll check again later, okay?"

"Fine," he answered. *Click.*

I put the phone into the cradle and sat back. There wasn't a chance in the world that *The Bridge* could be canceled without Jonathan behind the move. I had a decision to make. Did I call him and face up to him, or did I sit there, think about it, and play the hand as I got more cards?

I remembered an expression that my uncle told me many years ago. At this moment it was the best medicine I could possibly take—and there was no doubt I needed it, I had just been bitten by a virus. It was simple and to the point.

"Italians get mad—Sicilians wait."

I decided to wait. . . .

I buzzed Vera.

"Forget the network calls—get me Chili Monroe."

Vera buzzed twice, and I picked up the phone.

"Hello, little girl."

"I'm mad at you, little boy," she kidded. "Don't ever speak to me again."

I picked up on it immediately. "All right, you found out I was in Chicago."

"How could I possibly find that out—it was only in every paper in town."

"There was a reason, sweet baby. Can I come over?"

"Now?"

"Yeah, right away."

She giggled. "I'll leave the door ajar. If I don't answer, I'll be in the shower. You can come in and join me if you'd like. . . ."

"If I do," I shot back, "it'll only be to join you." *Click.*

I told Vera I'd be back, walked out the door, took the elevator down, and found George waiting with the car.

Standing at the curb waiting for a taxi was Harry Solomon, partner with Carroll Baer in Program Associates.

"Hi, Harry, how's it going?"

"Great Joey, good to see you."

I opened the door of the car. "Come on, jump in, and I'll have George drop you off."

"Great. Thanks, Joey."

I jargoned George. "Take me to that spot near Park. Let me off, then take Mr. Solomon to his offices or wherever he's going."

I then turned to Harry. He was a great-looking guy, good dresser, and as sharp as they came in the mental department.

"How's Carroll baby?"

"He's fine. I think he's dickering for the Empire State Building today," Harry kidded.

"My money's on him then. He'll get it."

They were a combination that had both ends covered. And they were the kind of competition I loved. It was clean in-fighting with them. They weren't part of the cannibals.

"How's Gina and the princess?"

"Absolutely great—how's Julia?"

"Fine, thank you."

George slowed down in front of the apartment, then cruised past a quarter of a block. Good old George, sharp to the last minute!

I shook hands with Harry. "See you soon, buddy."

George drove him off.

I headed up to Chili doll.

My timing was perfect. As I walked into the apartment and

shut the door behind me, Chili baby was just emerging from the shower. She had a skimpy towel wrapped around, from her bosom down to the top of you know where. A shower cap, flowered and girlish, topped the ensemble.

I took her carefully by the hand, walked her over to the big white bed, and sat her down. I pulled up a chair and sat facing her.

"For a minute," she quipped, "I thought I was going to get lucky."

"Chili doll," I said, staying serious, "some questions. I need answers and facts as fast as you can supply them."

She leaned back a little and crossed her legs Yoga style. I forced my eyes away from what this did to the skimpy towel and looked at her face. She propped her chin on her hands and listened.

"What's new? What do you know about that little cock-roach?"

"That's what I tried to call you about before I went to Chi-cago. I had some things to tell you about him."

"Anything you had to tell me then I already know. Do you know anything further—that's what's important."

"He's made twenty calls from right here to Bryan Westgate."

Bryan Westgate and Chester Plan? I concentrated. "Go on."

"They got together and pushed Tom Brady out of BCA."

"That's good news to know," I said aloud. "It means that Jonathan was in on the play. It means that Bryan had inter-ceded, and Chester was smart enough to put him on his side."

457

I ran through my mind silently the problem of why Chester would permit Ted Michaels to come in and replace Tom Brady. If anybody was ever a Bryan Westgate man, it was Ted. He could almost be called a disciple: All you had to do was say hello to Ted, and Bryan would have it five minutes later. But there'd be more to it than that. Chester was too cunning. He'd never join up with Lavender Lips without a reason.

"Has he ever talked about Jonathan?" I now asked.

"Are you kidding?" she laughed. "Do you want to hear something really funny?"

"Yeah, tell me, I need a smile."

"Do you remember he used to go to the psychiatrist three days a week?"

I nodded.

"Well, because of you, he now goes four."

"Me?"

"He feels that you left him when you started getting friendly with Tom Brady."

"He's full of shit, Chili. He's just a sulker, an undeserving parasite who doesn't deserve to be where he is. The other guy had talent, real talent—and integrity."

I lit a cigarette and puffed furiously.

"The only thing that upsets me is that Jonathan backed him, and backed him in my presence, then sawed him off at the knees. I don't understand it."

"I do. . . ."

I looked at this beautiful little girl with the apple-pie face and smile and the body that men would kill for. Was it possible that I could pick up a point of strategy from her? I could read in her face that she was about to tell me something.

In that second of silence I wondered how I could have underrated this particular part of Chili—the woman's brain. When they're sharp, they're eight lengths ahead of a man rounding into the final stretch.

"Tell me the answer, then," I hurried her.

"Your buddy is running scared."

"How do you know that?" I shot back. "You don't have a key into him."

"Chester does."

I frowned. "What do you mean by that?"

"He sees him every day, doesn't he?"

"Yes, but I see him day, noon, and night."

"Chester has spotted him running scared."

I froze. This was something I had sensed—known.

Chili knew that I realized she was right.

"Chili, did you ever hear him mention a pilot for a series called *The Bridge*?"

"You mean the one that you went to Chicago for?"

Chili was a walking encyclopedia. What a blabbermouth Chester must have been.

"Yes, that's the one."

"It's in the funeral parlor," she jargoned.

"I heard that today from Virgil Esty. That's all I wanted to know."

459

I got up from my chair, walked to the bed, and kissed her on the forehead. I drew back, looked into her beautiful eyes, and said, "One day I'll make this up to you, Chili."

She giggled in that special way. "Promises, promises . . ."

I wheeled around and left.

The last few weeks had been a sheer hell of politics and crises. This was one of the worst. I was sitting at my desk staring at the phone which I had just hung up after talking to Morry Weinstein.

Finally I grabbed the private.

As soon as the quiet voice answered, I said coldly, "I want to see you."

"Any time you want," he said lightly.

"As soon as possible." He could take that quiet voice and stick it up his ass. "I want to meet right now where we'll be alone. The alternate bar, on Madison Avenue." *Click.*

I picked up a dart and threw it with every bit of power in me. It missed the bull's-eye, but stuck three quarters of an inch into the board.

I headed out of my office past Vera, saying nothing.

"Shall I know where you're going?" she asked.

She never got the answer. I went downstairs and started to get into the car. Then I changed my mind, slammed the back door, and got into the front seat instead, next to George.

"Take me to the bar on Madison Avenue."

Not a word was spoken for two blocks. Finally George asked, concerned, "Something up, pal?"

"Yeah, something's up." But I just stared straight ahead. Nothing must mar my concentration.

Within minutes I was walking into the Winslow Hotel. Jonathan was waiting for me, sitting at one of the deuce tables in a far corner. We were alone, except for a few stragglers at the stand-up bar.

We ordered vodka martinis. In a few moments the waiter set them down. Jonathan picked up his glass. I pushed mine aside.

"Forget *The Bridge*, forget Tom Brady, and forget that miserable cocksucker out on the Coast who's your great friend." I narrowed down and stared him straight in the eye. "I want to know why you broke my word to Morry Weinstein. Nobody breaks my word. Why?"

"Joey, I couldn't help it. Bryan and Joe Ballantine wouldn't go along with it the next day."

That didn't deter me an inch. "*Why?*"

"They agreed that you did a great job and that the story he did on you was wonderful, but they feel that he's untrustworthy, and they can't take a chance. Nobody's ever been able to handle him, and he'll come on the lot and do something horrible. They don't trust him—they feel it's a trick."

"I don't give a fiddler's screw in hell who they trust. We gave our word—more important, I gave mine, and no sonovabitch alive is going to break my word."

461

Jonathan glanced around the room secretively. "Joey, there's a lot of pressure on right now. I've got to be careful."

I stood up. As I looked at the immaculate appearance, the well-groomed hair, and the studied, smiling casualness, the back of my neck prickled. I had a terrifying thought. Here was a man whom I had vouched for to friends all over the world, the man for whom I had decided to take the ultimate draw to protect, regardless of the price. And he was running scared.

I flared, and spoke straight into his kisser.

"You're yellow."

I walked out.

The weeks had flown by. It was option day.

The word "option," in any branch of the entertainment business, is the most dreaded noun imaginable. The option was designed for the benefit of, as they say in Russia, the capitalistic crowd. I couldn't knock it, because I'd had an option on anyone and everyone who ever worked for me. Now, however, it was my company that was facing one. Well, a man is entitled to switch sides.

Terry Winant was sitting *shiva* with me. "We'll be picked up." His face beamed. His bald head glowed.

"What makes you so confident?"

"It's not that I'm confident," he quipped, "but my mother is counting on it."

"And a man has to have Yankee bean soup," I supplied for him.

"When Jonathan drove with us in the car that time, Joey, didn't he tell us he'd make the show work?"

Without betraying my snag with Jonathan, I said curtly, "The show is blown, Terry, and it's a goddam shame."

"Do you really think so?"

I nodded. "It's only intuition," I said. "I'd like to be wrong."

"We've got the ratings, in spite of their interference."

"We're up against more than the ratings."

"How about the sponsors?"

"Both of them are ready to pick up the show—they've discussed it with me."

"Doesn't *that* mean we're okay then?"

"Sponsors don't run a network."

"Jonathan does. . . ."

I looked at my long-time friend and had to let him in, in some meaningful way.

"Jonathan isn't the same Jonathan, Terry."

"Do you mean all those vicious rumors are true? That he's in trouble, that he's going to be fired?"

"Terry, you're a great writer, you're my favorite novelist, and you've been my dear, dear friend. I can tell you, as sure as we're sitting here, Jonathan won't get the can tied to him."

I paused, thought of Chili's intuition and her tip, and I thought of my meeting with Jonathan at the Winslow. I added, "But he is running scared. He's going to dump us—or he's going to let someone else dump us and not look like he's a party to it."

"Would he do that to you?"

I put my legs up on the desk. "When the chips are down, I don't know."

Terry turned sentimental. "Whatever happens, Joey, you've been square with me. You've done everything you said you'd do. I don't have one complaint."

"How about your mother?"

"You're one of the few people she likes."

"You know something, Terry? Regardless of how much they killed us with their stupid junior executive interference, it's still a goddam good show. We're the top-rated New York filmed show—but we had to suffer because that variety show comes on a half hour ahead of us. It's the hardest thing in the world to get a viewer to turn away from the opposition after he's been hooked in."

"It's been a liberal education for me."

"Would you do it all over again, Terry?"

"Under the same circumstances, definitely."

"That makes two of us."

A knock on the door, and Vera bounced in.

"Your sister is on two."

"Good, I wanted to talk to her."

Terry got up.

"You don't have to leave."

"No, take the call, I have to do some things in my office. I'll stop back later."

"Okay, buddy."

I pushed down the lighted button. "Hi, Nikki baby."

"Joey, I wanted to check something with you."

"What's that?"

"We haven't been receiving our money from BCA for the last eight or ten weeks. We've been using our own cash, and we're now out of it."

"Is that standard procedure?"

"No, they had been delivering it every week. I thought they were just behind, and never brought it to your attention."

"How much do they owe us?"

"Close to eighty thousand."

"You've got to be kidding!" I screamed. "Have you called the network?"

"Yes . . . and one of your friends there said it's been held up purposely."

"Sweetheart," I cautioned, "don't mention any names on the phone—but is anything wrong?"

"Plenty."

"You're all right, aren't you?"

"Clean as a whistle, sweetheart—don't worry about me."

"That's good. That's all I care about."

"What about . . . that guy? Is he in trouble?"

Nikki was the apple of my eye. I never kidded her.

"He must be," I said, "because he's not acting like himself."

"How will it affect you?"

"I don't know, sweetheart. Keep the car motor running," I kidded.

"You mean we'll have to leave town?"

"You never can tell," I laughed. "I only wish we had something to leave with."

"Joey, I'm sorry I didn't tell you sooner about the money."

I couldn't help being bitter. "They had a lot of goddam nerve. Do you know who did it?"

"I'll tell you, but don't betray the guy, because he can lose his job."

"Thanks for your confidence, sweetheart," I said sarcastically.

"I'm sorry, Joey."

"Who was it?" As if I didn't know.

"Direct orders from Mario Colucci."

I pushed the confirmation out of my mind with a fast effort. I didn't want to get furious while I was on the phone with Nikki.

"Have you heard from Morry Weinstein?"

"He's called three or four times."

"What's his attitude?"

"He's been very sweet, a perfect gentleman."

"I forgot to tell you, Nikki, you helped me very much with him."

"How is that?"

"He commented later on the phone about how I broke off our interview when you came in, and went over to put my arm around you as if there were no one else in the room."

Three thousand miles away, I could see Nikki smile.

466

"That's the way we do it, brother."

"Well, he liked it. He digs family."

"Joey, they've never let him on the lot."

"Don't remind me. I forgot to tell you . . . Jonathan re-neged."

"Oh, no!"

"That's correct."

"How did that happen?"

"The fag and Joe Ballantine went back on their word."

"That's awful."

"It's worse than awful, honey. I can't even face the guy."

"You'll work out of it somehow."

"No, I won't. This I can't overcome. You'll realize the situation someday. For now I just can't look him in the eye. I gave my word."

"But you didn't break yours."

"I broke my promise to deliver."

Nikki was hip. She didn't comment on that, but changed the subject. "I have a little tip for you."

"Go ahead."

"The rumors on your buddy there are flying out here."

"I know, it's the same here."

"Who do you think's been giving the dirt to Morry Weinstein?"

"Do you know?"

"Yes."

"Who?"

"Bryan Westgate."

I stood up, paced away from the desk, dragging the long extension. *I knew it.* "Are you sure?" I asked Nikki.

"Positive."

"Who told you?"

"I can't tell you."

"Right, right, I understand. By the way, Nikki, from here on in—because this is war—we tighten up on the phone. *Cabeshe?*"

"*Cabeshe.* By the way, I understand . . . he has a tail on him."

"I heard that, too."

"What do you plan to do?"

"Ride it out," I said, suddenly in a good mood. "How bad can it be?"

"You have a point there. Now what'll I do about the eighty thousand?"

"Keep screaming for it—I'll do what I can at this end."

"Okay, Joey. I'll call you if I hear anything new."

Click.

After I finished with Nikki's call, I walked aimlessly around the room, hands in pockets. Back and forth, back and forth, just thinking.

The private phone rang. I picked it up. "Hello?"

"Hiya, buddy?"

"So-so. Just sitting and waiting."

"Well, why don't you meet me, and we'll talk it over."

"Obviously, that means we're canceled."

"Let's meet and talk. It's not all bad."

"Okay. Fifteen minutes?"

"At the place."

"Right." *Click.*

I walked into Le Valois, and Jonathan appeared right after me.

I shook his hand. I had a smile for him. "Good to see you, buddy."

"Double," he answered.

We sat down. With astuteness, Jean Pierre put specials in front of us and walked away.

"I want you to know that your show didn't deserve to be canceled."

I didn't speak.

"And I'm sure you realize that I had to stay completely out of this one."

I studied Jonathan's face, and I liked what I saw. Regardless of what anyone could tell me, I was positive that he was my friend.

There was something in Jonathan that people just didn't understand. I would have bet my life there was a kindness there somewhere, one that he would never display. It had been there in the *Sandstorm* meeting, which seemed so long ago

469

now. He had never liked to tell me bad news, but he had always had the guts to do it. Of course, he knew that I had the guts to take it.

"What did Ted Michaels do in the meeting?"

"He did a pitch on the show, Joey, that you'd have been proud of."

"Well, let me tell you something, Jonathan. Since he came in and personally took over, the show is the way it always should have been. Not saying that any of the earlier segments were bad."

"Well, he did go to bat."

I probed. "What else?"

"Wilson Manning went all the way."

"He's a helluva guy, too," I said. "He has some integrity in him. Had he gotten okays from the sponsors?"

"They both agreed to pick the show up. And Will was insistent on keeping it on the air. But he got outvoted. Chester and Arthur Stuart took a stand—they wanted to replace the show. So you see, you really had only the one vote, because Ted Michaels was too new to count."

I looked at Johnny, in a not unkindly way. "You know, of course, that *you* could have saved it."

"I know it," he said simply, "and I should have—if only because it's a damn good show. We kept on *MacNamara's Friends* . . ."

"You renewed that? That is the lowest-rated show in television."

"You don't have to tell me; I get sick every time I look at it. But the Chairman insisted on it, and so did Chester."

"It's amazing—good reviews can keep a show on, but a show that people watch goes off. Somebody's got to make some changes in this business."

"The changes are coming, Joey. I told you that a long time ago."

I sipped the martini and changed the subject.

"Johnny, let's talk like the two good friends we are. Regardless of what happens, we always stick together, right?"

"There's no doubt about it." His glance had that bit of kindness.

"Level with me now, however much it embarrasses or hurts you."

"I will."

"First of all, BCA has put investigators onto you. They're checking into every phase of Jonathan Bingham."

"I know that, Joey. I had a private detective friend of mine in touch."

"What are you going to do about it?"

"I went to see the Dentist yesterday. I told him that it was unconscionable, that I resented it, and that he had my resignation then and there if he wanted it. In short, Joey, I faded him."

"What was his answer?"

"The usual public corporation bullshit that they have to make an attempt to certify complaints as unfounded."

471

He took a letter out of his pocket and handed it to me. "As if I haven't got enough trouble," he said.

I glanced at the letter. It was a crank job, but signed with a name, address, and phone number. It was addressed to the FCC, and it concerned Bryan Westgate. In essence, the writer branded him as a fag, accused him of stopping good actors from working, and favoring other fags who would go to bed with him.

"What did you do?" I asked Jonathan.

"I wrote a letter topside saying that I knew nothing about his personal life, but that I considered him an extremely competent executive."

"Great. I'm glad to hear you backed him." I paused. "Now fire him."

"You know better than that."

"Johnny, we're not going to argue anymore. It's going to be soft, and it's going to be nice. He's against you. He's stabbing you in the back. He wants your job."

"Ridiculous."

"Chester has turned on you, and so has Mario. They've been back-dooring you with the Dentist. I have absolutely verified reports that they've been called up there at least seven different times. They talk, and whatever they don't know, they make up. They're turning you in."

"I'm aware of those two, Joey."

"What are you going to do about that?"

"Get rid of both of them. I'm already dickering with Len

Rich to replace Chester. I called Chester in and told him to take three months to look for a job."

Poor Jonathan. What a big big mistake he was making. I knew it was useless to tell him, but I had to try.

"Three months will give him time to kill you."

"He wouldn't dare if he ever wants to work anywhere else."

"He would dare. He's a scummy little bastard. You can't trust him for one month. He's a liar and a cheat, and he's regarded with utter contempt by everyone in the business already. But he would dare."

Johnny sipped his martini.

"I can ease anyone I want out, but there have been too many quick firings. The Chairman and the Dentist are more worried about their public image and the stockholders than they are about running the network in the right manner."

"That I understand. But you have to watch him."

"He's watched, I guarantee you."

I could tell he meant it. I lit a cigarette, took a quick puff, and got back to the crux of things.

"Let me tell you something. Bryan Westgate called me two days ago, before we had the beef. And incidentally, you and I never discuss beefs, but it's over as far as I am concerned. For whatever part I might have been at fault—for my half—I apologize."

He made no comment but he didn't have to. His look did.

"What did Bryan have to say?"

"After I scared him about all the trouble that was going on, he said that he had something to tell me personally, with re-gard to Joe Ballantine, and a scandal at the studios that BCA owns."

Jonathan perked up his ears.

"You don't have anything to do with any payola at the studio, do you?" I asked.

"No."

It was time for the sixty-four-dollar question.

"Johnny, this is what I asked you before to level with me about. Are you taking from anybody? I don't care if you are, but tell me, so I know."

"Nothing at all."

"You once gave me your word that you'd never take from anybody. Just tell me if you've kept it."

"I've kept it."

"Then what the hell can the Joe Ballantine thing be?"

"I don't know, but you've got to find out."

I got up.

"Where are you going?"

I grabbed his hand and shook it.

"Where the hell else? To find out. I'm leaving tonight on the first goddam plane out that I can get."

He spoke one word, simply. "Thanks."

California, here I come . . .

Chapter 18

There's no place like the Polo Lounge. It swings. Agents, the sharpshooters, producers, directors, actors, and those little hooker babies are all there in abundance.

I was sitting at my private table. I had nothing to do. I was really waiting for tomorrow morning, when I would be having breakfast with Bryan Westgate and trying to learn from his own lavender lips what game it was he was trying to play with me. Meanwhile, I was relaxing from all the pressures and out for fun.

Into the Polo Lounge walked a good friend of mine, Bill Brennan, one of the better account executives. He was a funny guy, but nice, and very well respected. With him was another dear friend, Milton Kellem, a songwriter, music publisher, and now an important stockbroker.

I made it a point not to wave. They saw me and motioned. Having won the first move, I gave a hand-signal invitation. They readily walked over and sat down.

"Bill baby, what's up?"

"Not too much, Joey. How's with you?"

"Fine, just sitting around."

"What are you doing out on the Coast?"

"I came out," I said conspiratorially, "with the sole purpose of starting a war."

Bill laughed. I turned my attention to Milton.

"What are you two guys cooking up?"

Milton smiled. "You don't think I'm going to tell you—you'd end up stealing it."

"How's the family, Milton baby?"

"Great, Joey. Grandma asks about you all the time."

"Grandma" was Milton's mother. It was an affectionate term that all of us in the family used with her. Milton was really like my brother. I looked at him and threw the knife in.

"You know, you're the luckiest sonovabitch alive. You write one great tune—I don't say you're not a fine publisher, but as a writer now—you write one great tune, 'Got along without you before I met you, gonna get along without you now,' and turn out to be the only man in the music business lucky enough to get Patience and Prudence to help you sell a couple of million copies. Then a few years later, with your luck, Trini Lopez makes a hit out of it all over again, and you sell another four million copies. Will you please do me a favor and tell me your formula?"

He smiled again. "Joey, you have to be Jewish."

"I'll join—I'll join."

It was fun to kid with real people.

"What are you doing?" he now asked.

"Well, I really came out to buy the Beverly Hills Hotel, because I don't like the rooms I've been getting."

THE CANNIBALS

Bill Brennan looked at Milton Kellem and shrugged.

"Trying to get anything out of him is a waste of time."

"So I see."

The drinks, which I had ordered them, now disappeared. They each took the final gulp and rose.

"I love people who drink and run. But stop in any time, it was a pleasure meeting you."

We exchanged affectionate farewells, and they left.

Andy—his name wasn't really that, but he wore the "Andrew" cigarette costume—came over and said, "Mr. Bertell, another call for you."

I didn't bother to tip Andy because I had him on a weekly allowance, which incidentally was strong, but he was a helluva nice guy, and very attentive.

I picked up the phone in a good mood. "Hello?"

"Joey, Gina."

"Hi, sweetheart. How are you?"

"Don't sweetheart me, I'm tired of this shit." She was furious. My good mood vanished. "What the hell are you doing in California?"

"I had a problem. I had to come out and take care of it."

"I don't give a damn what kind of problem you have. You've got a lot of nerve flying out there without a word. Don't you realize you've got a home . . . and a daughter—who's sitting in the other room?"

I took a drag on the cigarette, inhaled down to the tips of my toes, and exhaled slowly.

"For God's sake, Gina, not now, please!"

"Where are you?"

"I'm in Nairobi, Africa. You're calling me in the Polo Lounge of the Beverly Hills Hotel, aren't you?"

"You know something, Joey Bertell? You're a louse."

"Gina, I got real troubles. Can't you understand? Can't you be a little compassionate?"

"I'm sick of being understanding and compassionate. Do me a favor. Don't ever come home again." *Click*.

My waiter passed me, and I stopped him. "Bring me a triple martini."

I walked back to my table, and in a moment the drink arrived.

"Are you sure you wanted a triple martini?" the waiter asked.

"That's what I asked for," I snapped.

He looked a little hurt, so I added, "Yeah, buddy. I'm sorry, I got something on my mind. Forgive me, okay?"

He walked away happily.

A few minutes later he was back with a note, which I opened promptly.

Dear Joey baby:

I hope you remember me. I'm a friend of yours from Las Vegas.

Bobbi Barker

THE CANNIBALS

I looked around and saw a stunning black-haired girl sitting alone in one of the booths. She was smiling. I smiled back and waved her over.

She arrived with her drink. I rose, kissed her on the cheek, and we sat down together.

"Hello, Bobbi Barker, how are you?" I remembered her from Las Vegas, all right. A swinging chick from Hooksville. But a real winner. "What are you doing?"

"Playing the outside," she said in a provocative tone.

"You mean to tell me you don't have any dates tonight?"

"I've got eight million calls—I just checked my exchange—but I rarely work on Sunday evening."

It struck me funny. "I'll drink to that."

She lifted her glass and took a healthy sip with me.

The call from Gina had unnerved me. What stung was the harassment, not the actual words, which she would eventually retract. Wouldn't she ever realize that I loved her and the family that I was knocking my brains out to build something for?

I forced myself back into a social mood.

"What are you doing here?" I asked Bobbi.

"I've got one tentative date later, with Freddy Cabot, the personal manager of that English star. I think I may end up swinging with the star tonight."

"I didn't think those limeys split money."

"I don't know if this one spends or not, but Freddy Cabot is underwriting the situation."

479

"I'll drink to that."

We toasted again.

"Do you know Bob Massingale from BCA?" I asked.

"Yes, I've moved with him a couple of times."

"I have to go over to his room for a few minutes. You want to walk over with me?"

"Sure, why not?"

I told the waiter to keep the check open, and if I didn't come back to sign it and give himself a generous tip.

Bobbi and I strolled into the lobby, and the first person we ran into was Rosie O'Grady, a blond bundle of charm who was in the semi-pro category. She was practically a nymphomaniac and would do it for free, but if she could grab a few bucks, it always helped with the rent.

I introduced her to Bobbi, and their smiles seemed to size each other up.

Rosie had balled everybody at BCA for fun, with the exception of Mario Colucci, who she decided was singularly unattractive—either before or after, the story went, it turned out he couldn't even raise a hard-on for her.

"Guess who's in town, Rosie baby?"

"Who?" she cooed, with a twinkle in her eye.

"Bob Massingale."

"You're kidding!"

I looked around to see if heads were turning.

"For Christ's sake, don't announce it to the East Coast offices."

Bobbi smiled.

480

"Anyway, Rosie, I have to see him for a few minutes—come on over with us."

"Great, I'd love to see him."

We made our way to Bob's apartment in the west wing.

I knocked, he opened, and I walked in with the two broads in tow.

"Oh, no!" he protested. "I can't take it, I tell you I can't take it. Joey, what is this, a rib?"

"Why, no, Bob, it's just that I run into your broads all over the country. Why?"

We all sat down, Bobbi taking my hand in an extremely affectionate way, and Massingale started to make drinks without answering. The first thing a guy does when he's in an expense account room is order a bottle of vodka, a bottle of Cutty Sark, a bottle of bourbon, a bottle of rye, and about seventeen dollars' worth of mixes. Every man is entitled to feel important, especially when he's in the sales department.

Rosie had now risen and was prancing up and down, looking at Bob's crew cut and semi-potbelly, half attempting to excite him.

He stayed serious, however, and spent two minutes of business with me without so much as looking at the girls.

After the business was over, I got back to the rib, which he evidently had thought my arrival was, at first.

"Would you like Bobbi and me to leave, so Rosie and you can be alone?" I winked at Rosie.

"You're not going to believe this," he said, "but I've been

481

balling all day long. There just is no way that I could go again, or even get excited, even with Rosie."

I laughed. As I reached for my cigarettes in my inside coat pocket, I felt the stopwatch.

I always carried the stopwatch so that if I heard a special song, I could time two and a half choruses and a ride-out. You can never turn off the entertainer.

A mischievous thought hit me.

"Tell you what I'll do, Bobby baby. You say you've been balling all day?"

"That's right."

"You also say you couldn't go again?"

"Nobody could make me go again."

"I'll bet you a hundred dollars cash that you go within three minutes, with me right in the room."

"You'd have a losing bet, Joey."

"I don't make losing bets. Call it, or take it back."

"I'd be stealing your money."

"Never mind the ad libs. I'll bet you the hundred that you're off within three minutes, and we'll make it official." I pulled out the stopwatch.

He did a double-take. "You've got a bet."

I looked over at Rosie. "Don't let me down. Just tell me when you're starting."

She threw her coat off and went over to Bobby, who had been sprawled out on the bed amidst his swindle-sheet notes. With deft hands she undid his belt and pulled down his zipper.

"Now!" she yelled.

I clicked the stopwatch.

Rosie went to work on him like a trombone player in a Dixieland band.

One minute went by.

Bob Massingale laughed. "You've got a loser. I'm going to buy a hundred dollars' worth of ties."

I smiled confidently, even though Rosie, at the moment, looked like she was eating a piece of *schvat* spaghetti.

A minute and thirty seconds.

Rosie began to look like a plater in a claiming race.

Bob must have been telling the truth. He must have been swinging all day at that. It put me in a rare mood to realize that BCA was paying for this kind of conscientious staff.

Still, I couldn't stand losing any kind of a bet.

I nudged Bobbi in the ribs. "You've got half the bet. Go over and help out."

"Joey," Bobbi laughed, "you haven't changed a bit."

"Never mind the small talk. We've only got forty-five seconds left."

She dashed over to the bed, cashmere sweater and all.

Bobbi joined Rosie in playing the flute, and with her supple fingers, Bob Massingale started to hit the high notes.

I looked down at the stopwatch.

Twenty seconds to go.

The girls looked like human oil derricks. Up, down. pump, pump.

Ten seconds—and Bob screamed out, in ecstasy, "You son-ovabitch, you win the bet!"

I picked up the hundred, divided it, put it in the proper hands, and left.

I walked back into the lobby laughing. At least Bobbi didn't have a losing night, and Rosie had fifty dollars for her rent.

And I had a particular pleasure in knowing that Bob Massingale, who wouldn't go for two dollars on a fixed horse race, would put the hundred on his swindle sheet, and the Chairman would pay for a blow job, bless his little bananas.

As I walked into the Polo Lounge, I spotted the swingingest little keister I'd ever seen in my life. It was round, firm, and sat on top of two of the most beautiful legs in the world. The girl had blond hair done in a gorgeous upsweep that shone under the pink lights in a halo of pure gold. I couldn't believe my eyes. It could only be one person.

"Chili!" I yelled at the top of my voice, which seemed, in my embarrassment, to make every head swivel.

As she turned, I strode up and took her in my arms. I gave her a firm hug and a light kiss on the forehead.

"Chili, what the hell are you doing here?"

"Do you want the truth?"

"What else?"

"I got so bored with New York I just decided to get on a plane and come out."

"Chili baby, how would you like a great dinner date—go out to every joint in town tonight and get stoned?"

"With whom?" she asked suspiciously.

"With the sexiest sonovabitch who ever walked the face of the earth."

She giggled. "Business or pleasure?"

"Pleasure—but only if you're not working tonight."

"Tell me who it is," she cooed, "before I answer that one."

"What's the difference? He's a fabulous guy. You'll dig him —and you won't have to go to bed with him."

"Is he a friend of yours?"

"My very best."

"Forget it," she said, thinking I meant Jonathan. "Not a chance."

"It's not *him*, I promise you."

Chili was now on a plateau of curiosity, but she was hesitant. "The only person that I'd accept a blind date from, on the arm, is you. But at least tell me who it is."

"Are you ready?" I teased. "It's little old me."

She rose to her tiptoes, threw her arms around me, kissed me wildly on the lips, and at the top of her voice said, "My God, I don't believe it—at long last I'm going to be with you."

I must have given her arm a black-and-blue spot pinching.

"Louder, tell it to the East Coast."

"I'm sorry," she said, mortified.

"Where are you staying?" I asked.

"I took a suite here."

"Either you're with me"—I winked at her and gave her a pinch, but this time a gentle one, on the *tushie*—"or I'm with you."

"Do you want to flip a coin?"

"Let's skip all formalities," I said, "and just go out and have one helluva lot of fun. Are you game?"

She gave me that cute smile and giggle again. "You bet your you-know-what."

I waggled a finger at her. "My you-know-what's not up for grabs."

"It will be if I ever get ahold of it . . ."

I took her hand, we marched out to the doorman's station, got in a cab, and off we started.

I was trying to forget the pressure, and Jonathan, my apprehension about the meeting with Bryan in the morning, my discouragement from a talk with Sol Mack earlier, and the unhappy discussions with my sister Nikki about the eighty thousand dollars that BCA had decided to steal, thanks to that rat bastard Mario Colucci. Most of all, I was trying to forget the phone call from Gina.

When the cab pulled up in front of the Beverly Hills Hotel at four o'clock the next morning, I was totally ossified.

I had not been able to escape the pressures and the call from Gina. It now seemed to me that for some reason, whenever I needed Gina most, she failed me. Not that she wasn't wonderful, not that she wasn't naturally loyal, not that she didn't care—and I even dug her screaming at me, because I've always said that they only scream when they care—but in this case, I was fighting on so many fronts that Gina sticking with me was absolutely essential.

Through the fog of my drunken recriminations, I commenced feeling a great guilt. I couldn't blame her, because the last weeks had really been intolerable. She'd had to see me suffer every disappointment known to a man like me. The thing that really bothered her was not me—it was obvious that she cared deeply for me—but the things or people that abused me, which she hated. Her particular target during these weeks had been Jonathan.

And if I ever had to make a choice between who came first in my life, it would be, as they say in the bookmaking business, no price. Gina would be sixty-to-one to win.

I stumbled out of the cab, unable to hold myself up. Triples all over town . . . if I could have comprehended my condition, I wouldn't even have tried to make my room. As it was, I was a good bet to go to sleep in the potted plant near the hotel taxi stand.

Chili was paying the cab.

When she caught up with me, she started helping me toward the elevator. By reflex, I fumbled in my pocket for the key.

"Chili baby, I apologize for getting so stiff." My breath must have been terrible. They say vodka doesn't smell, but the amount of vodka I had consumed made the elevator a brewery.

At my floor I tripped trying to get out and sprawled in the

corridor. Chili picked me up, and somehow I managed to drape my arm across her back as she helped me to my room.

"I'm so drunk I can't even talk," I said, inside. "Call the operator and leave a nine-thirty alarm for me—I have a coffee appointment with Bryan Westgate."

"Don't worry, little boy, Chili pal will take care of you."

Reaching the king-size bed, with Chili's help, I got right under the covers.

A man can get drunk and stand up. He can consume a quart of liquor, or mix his drinks, get blind, and cover it up. But once he lies down, the room is a whirlpool, and the bed is a rowboat with an outboard motor, headed down into the vortex.

I was in the rowboat, oblivious to Chili, or the fact that she was taking off my clothes for me, or my appointment with Bryan Westgate. I was in a rowboat, and I was alone.

Seconds later there was a warm body next to me in the rowboat. The intoxicating smell of woman reached through my whirlpool brain. By conditioned reflex, I reached and grabbed the generous bundle of femininity. I pulled it close.

I put one hand under the little chin and guided her mouth to mine. I reached my other hand down and cupped the firm little *tushie*, then my fingers wandered and probed the warm, dizzying mystery.

My whirlpool was now a sexual vortex.

The woman's body was full against me, and writhing in ecstasy.

I drew back a little, in my intoxication now seeming to be crystal-clear and in full physical control. I knew I was Joey Bertell. It was Joey Bertell. It was Joey Bertell's tongue travelling hard and slow, up and down, up and down across two ripe breasts, and then up to the mouth again, the tongue against the other tongue.

I was Joey Bertell, and this was Joey Bertell's real woman, at last.

"I love you, Gina," in my intoxication seeming to pronounce every syllable perfectly. "Why the hell were you treating me the way you did? You know you're the only person in the world for me."

I continued caressing, pressing and kissing and somehow talking at the same time. It was building up, and somehow I had to tell her something before it exploded.

"Don't you know I'm knocking my brains out for you, to build for both of us? Can't you understand that I'm taking every draw in the world so that Maria has everything she ever wants? Do you think I want her to struggle like you and I had to?"

The body I was holding was as warm as fire. I had told her what I wanted to tell her, and now I could explode.

Suddenly she turned onto her side, away from me. I pressed hungrily up against the *tushie*. I put one arm underneath, and one arm over, put one hand onto each breast, squeezing in a partly sex-sadistic reflex. The breasts fit in my hands as if they were molded for me, but she was pulling away.

"That's what I mean. Goddamit, why are you turning around, why are you pulling away? Gina, everything is love for you, and let this moment have my love . . ."

The thoughts were broken now, I knew I was mumbling incoherently, and I had to let my head rest on the pillow.

The phone was ringing, jarring me out of my stupor. I groped for my watch on the table, focused on the dial, and realized this was my alarm call from the operator.

The Bryan Westgate meeting!

I jumped out of bed, dashed into the shower, and put the cold water on full blast. It invigorated me, and seemed to take away some of the stain of the night before. I gargled half a bottle of Listerine to take away the drink smell, and walked back out into the bedroom.

Chili Monroe was curled up on the couch, sound asleep!

I went over and nudged her. She opened her eyes and smiled.

"Hi, Joey baby."

"What the hell are you doing here?"

"Without me, you would never have gotten home," she answered. "You really tied one on."

I groped for a memory, but could find none. I kicked myself, figuratively. This was a great time for me to start losing my grip!

I looked at little Chili doll. "Did you protect me last night?"

She raised her eyebrows. "Well, we made every joint in town."

"I didn't make a fool out of myself, did I?"

"No, Joey," she said softly, "unfortunately you didn't make a fool out of yourself."

"How the hell *did* we get home?"

"I found a helpful cabdriver."

"Thank you very much."

"Don't thank me. I guess I was born to be a sister."

I looked at her and laughed. "Chili, you are something. I could never convince anybody in the world that you slept on my couch all night and that I was too drunk to make a pass at you."

She gave me a look. "I'll testify to it." Then, with typical Chili Monroe humor, she added, "But I'll get you one of these days."

I smiled at her warmly.

"Good-bye, doll."

I left. Next stop, Lavender Lips.

Bryan greeted me at the door.

He stretched out his limp wrist and said, "Oh, Joey, it's so good to see you."

"Hi, Bryan," I answered cordially.

He walked me inside and then through the house toward the breakfast room. On the way we passed the cage with the chimpanzee. Without Bryan's seeing me, I spit right in its eye.

A lewd thought hit me as I looked at its hairy body. I wondered whether Bryan, in one of his brighter moments, had ever made it with the animal. What a bit that would be—a pansy in a cage with a chimp. It took the curse off my real purpose in meeting with him.

We sat down, Bryan poured coffee, and I spoke without mincing words.

"Bryan, you know the trouble that we're having. We've got to know everything. You indicated to me that Joe Ballantine was in a payola situation out at the studio. Tell me about it, so that we know what the hell it is."

He blanched. "I knew that's why you wanted to see me."

I sensed he was going to renege. "Bryan, you called me, you were the one who wanted to discuss it. Of course that's why I flew out. For Christ's sake, don't piddle-paddle around now."

"I shouldn't have upset you, Joey, because I do know you have a lot of problems at the moment."

I managed not to retch. "Just tell me what the situation is."

"It's something I have under control right at the moment. Really, I would rather not spring it. But rest assured, if it gets out of hand, I'll let you know."

"Bryan baby, right at the moment, there's nothing I shouldn't know. I'm telling you all hell is breaking loose. Jonathan's getting screwed as we sit here talking."

"I've been so worried about that," he lisped.

"Worried, my ass, Bryan. Let's do something about it. If you've got a story to tell me on Joe Ballantine, for Christ's sake, tell me now. You indicated to me that he was taking money. If that comes out later, it'll be worse than if you tell me now and we plan."

492

He remained silent.

"Bryan . . . There's nothing to worry about with Johnny and myself. He's not my partner. I've never given him a dime. He's as clean as a whistle with me. It's what we don't know that's the problem."

"There are so many rumors going around, Joey. I'm so frightened. And I'm so worried for Johnny."

"Tell me what you know—I'll handle it."

What was the use? I lost my patience, changed the subject, and really turned on him.

"And what the hell was the idea of breaking your word on the Morry Weinstein thing? This guy will now nail you to the cross."

"He's a perfectly horrible man," Bryan camped. "I mean, Joey, we just couldn't trust him. Jim and I talked it over— really, we just couldn't take a chance. I mean, he's *dreadful*."

"Bryan, we're going in circles. What am I out here for?"

"It's just that I was worried. I had to talk to somebody."

"Bryan, please level with me on Joe Ballantine. He's been in New York twice."

"I know. The Dentist sent for him."

"For what reason?"

"To talk over the West Coast studio operation."

"Bullshit! When does the president of the parent company call in a vice-president of operations? Who the hell are you giving this bullshit to?"

He put his hand on top of mine and screamed, "Joey, I'm terrified!"

I should have slapped him across the mouth, but I forced myself to hold back. "You'll be terrified all right. If Johnny's your friend, try to protect him."

"Is he protecting me?" Bryan screeched.

I stared him straight in the eyes. "Goddam right he's protecing you, stronger than you can imagine."

"Nobody's protecting him," he cried. "They're all telling on him. I can't tell you anything about the studio matter, but Joe Ballantine went back and talked to the Dentist and told everything. He threw Johnny in."

I continued forcing myself to stay calm. "Who else?"

"Chester has even confided in *me* that the Dentist has had *him* up there five times, asking him all about Jonathan, his deals with the agent, and that pimp producer whom I despise —and his goddam sex life."

"What the hell has his sex life got to do with it?"

"Women talk, don't you understand that, Joey? Women talk. I'm surprised at you, I'd think you'd be the first to know that. *Women talk.*"

I looked at him in utter amazement. This stupid fairy was losing his mind.

"I'll tell you one thing, Bryan baby. If everyone goes into panic now, we're all going to be out on our asses."

"Didn't I warn you months ago," he cried, "that Jonathan should get close to the Chairman? All our trouble is the result of this. The Chairman's wife hates the snubs that Jonathan's been giving them. She goes to parties, and people think that it's Jonathan's network, not her husband's. She told a very important person that if it's the last thing she ever does, she'll get rid of him."

I had to get out of here, it was more than I could take. If I stayed any longer, I'd either stick him up the chimpanzee's ass or break his head open. Neither way would help matters.

So after a careful de-escalation of the conversation, I ducked out.

I had to call Jonathan.

The phone was ringing itself off the hook at my suite in the Beverly Hills Hotel.

I picked up the receiver and snapped a hello. The pace was quickening, and I had no time for small talk.

"Joey, this is Nikki."

That was a different kettle of fish.

"Hi, honey, what's up?"

"I got another call from Morry Weinstein, with a message for you."

"What did he say?" I asked tentatively.

"First let me tell you that he was very nice and very polite."

"Well, he's always been that way with you."

"No, but he was exceedingly nice today. The message is as follows. I took it down word for word and typed it out for you."

"Okay, honey, read it to me."

" 'Please tell your brother that I kept my word in every way with regard to laying off the Jonathan Bingham story. I feel, however, that I am no longer under any obligation because I have it on definite authority that he will be out at BCA.' "

"I hope he's wrong on that, but he's certainly right on the other."

"He did keep his word, Joey, didn't he?"

"Yes, he did, honey, and so did I. It's too bad that he'll never know I did."

"Why don't you just pick up the phone and tell him?"

"And make Jonathan look like a fool? Enemies he doesn't need right now."

"Do you think he'll get it—the ax, I mean?"

"It's just a matter of time, sweetheart, he's just not a card player."

"You can't expect him to be the gambler you are, Joey."

Nikki paused a moment. It gave me a glow. We were like two peas in a pod, and her questioning reminded me of myself.

"If he gets fired," she continued, "will it hurt him?"

The answer to that one was easy. "They'll throw parties from coast to coast," I said acidly.

"How about you?"

I tried to tease her out of her obvious concern.

"Nikki baby, I've got nine lives, and I've only used up six. Joey Bertell will be back—and heard from."

"I'll bet on that, brother."

"I love you," I said, and hung up.

The phone rang again immediately. It was like Grand Central Station.

"Hi, Joey baby," the voice cooed.

"Chili doll, how are you?"

"I've got a tidbit for you."

"What's that?"

"Everybody's being called back to New York."

"From BCA?"

"That's right."

"Are you sure?"

"I just talked to the little weasel."

"How'd you ever get ahold of him? I thought he was read-ing poetry with his broad."

"No, she attends her Girl Scout meetings in the morning."

"Touché. What'd he say to you?"

"He called to cancel a meeting with me at three o'clock to-day. I'm so damn mad—I could have used the fifty dollars."

"Never mind the hard-luck story, just tell me what he said."

"He said he had to leave right away for New York, for a very important meeting, and he made a big point of bragging to me that it would work out very well for him."

"Did he punch the line?"

"He really laid it in."

I thought back on Nikki's call, on Bryan's hemorrhaging. Now Chili baby, who was never wrong.

"Do you want to have dinner with me tonight?" she asked.

"No, I'm going to catch the first plane I can out of here."

"Back to New York?"

"No, I'm going to Florida."

"I don't believe it? Mental telepathy—so am I."

"I thought you said you were broke."

"I've got a ticket coming by wire, from a friend of mine who wants to get some sun in Miami. Do you want me to drive you to the airport?"

"No, thanks, sweetheart. I'll just grab a cab, it's easier that way. But I'll see you down there."

"Okay, Joey baby."

Click.

I walked out of the room, into the elevator, went downstairs to the travel desk, and told Eddie to get me on the plane to Miami. I gave him a ten-dollar stake and added, "Get me on the dinner flight."

"Will do."

I walked on downstairs, through the arcade, to the pay phones next to the coffee shop, direct-dialed Jonathan's private, and gave the operator my credit-card number.

He answered.

"Go to a phone you can use," I directed, "and call me back at the pay phone number that I gave you." *Click.*

I walked into the drugstore, stopped by the pay phones, and got a pack of cigarettes. I ripped off the cellophane and tinfoil corner, tapped out a cigarette, lit it, and dragged in deeply. The cigarette was half gone when the phone rang.

I picked it up.

"Yeah," said Jonathan.

"Here's the story. Weinstein says he has it on authority that you're through. Two, Bryan Westgate is a tower of shit, and I'm now going to tell you he's been knifing you behind your back. I've always known it, but you'd never let me tell you."

"Go ahead."

"Three, everyone from BCA has been called back to New York. Have you heard from Bryan today?"

"Yes, he called me right after you left him."

I smiled to myself. "I knew it. I'll bet you a thousand dollars he denied having said anything to me earlier about Joe Ballantine."

"That's right."

"This is no time for a lecture," I said tartly. "Did you get ahold of Joe and warn him?"

"Yes, I did."

"What did he have to say?"

"He said he's been suspicious of Bryan for the last six or seven weeks."

"So why didn't he open up his goddam mouth?"

"He did, Joey, I didn't listen."

The only satisfaction I could find was that the little sonovabitch Chester Plan, if it worked out his way, would at least have brains enough to get rid of the fag within six weeks. That mistake he wouldn't make. And as a further insurance policy, anyone even remotely connected with Bryan would go.

Chester Plan was an untalented man and a rat, completely devoid of any human emotion that a man could appreciate, but at least he was cunning, that much I gave him.

All of a sudden Jonathan became very bright.

"They can have this job any time they want, Joey. I'm tired of working for nothing, and I'm tired of making them all look good."

It sounded like a self-servicing statement, but it hit home.

"That's up to you, that's your ball game, Johnny. But do me one favor—and give me your word on this—if you go—and regardless of which way you go—don't let them make a Calvin Clothes out of you."

"Joey, if the chips are down, at that very moment, I'll leave. There's a million places I can go."

I picked him up immediately and gave him the backing he wanted to hear.

"Are you kidding? They'll stand in line and fight to get you. You've got to be nuts, don't even think any other way. You're the smartest sonovabitch this business has ever seen."

"How long will you be in Florida?" he asked.

"About four days. I've got two days of business, and then I might just play a little golf."

"I think you ought to," he said softly. "You deserve it."

"Johnny," I said, "I want to tell you something. Whatever the meeting is, whichever way it turns out, just know that I stand where I've always stood. I can't lie to you, because you're my buddy. I think you folded on a couple of things, but you've done a great job for this company, and, for whatever part I had in helping, I've been damn proud, not only to be associated with you, but to call you my friend."

He waited a couple of seconds, and then said, "Thanks. I know you mean that."

"Go out and have some fun tonight, then get up tomorrow and go to that stupid four o'clock meeting, and remember one thing."

"What's that?"

"*Charge forward boldly.*"

"Don't worry, Joey, I will. And we'll make it."

"You're damn right we will, buddy. Top of the goddam world!"

Chapter 19

The cold air of the ocean gave me a slight chill and woke me from the reverie. The vodka and tonic was gone; all that remained was melting ice cubes in the glass on the arm of the chair.

The shirt under my alpaca sweater was wet from my emotional strain of reliving the past. The breeze through the loose knit might have been winds off Central Park South in The City, rather than off the waves.

I snapped into action. Screw staying here, I was going back now. The time for frolicking and lying in the sun was over.

I headed away from the pool, through the hotel arcade, and walked into the Surf Shoppe, where I bought a robe for Gina.

Then I took an elevator to the upper lobby and went to the transportation desk.

"Get me on the nine P.M. flight for New York. Tonight, and first class."

"It's all booked up," he said. "We've been trying for people all day."

"Find a friend," I said, tossing a double sawbuck on the counter. "I'm going to pack."

"You'll be on it, Mr. Bertell."

I smiled and proceeded to my penthouse suite.

Dialing Intercom 8, I placed a long-distance call to Gina. After a few rings she answered.

"Honey, I'm coming home."

"How nice," she said tartly.

I ignored the tone. This was no time for petty bickering. This was going to be a real war.

The enemies were identified. They'd pounce all over Jonathan now and never let him up. He could talk from now until doomsday on "How great it's going to be from here on," but he was only kidding himself.

As strong as Jonathan was, it was a one-dimensional strength, stemming from his executive position. He lacked the power of creative talent. He would be in big trouble, and I had to get back and put some starch into that spine of his.

"Gina. Paul Power quit."

"Quit, or got fired?"

"Quit."

"Do you believe that?"

"No."

"Then why don't you level with me?"

"I just did."

She took a moment. "I can't say I'm sorry for him. I'm not —he's a first-class louse who has ruined the lives of everyone around him."

I didn't answer.

"Joey, are you so blind you don't know what's in front of your nose?"

"I'm not blind, Gina."

"I'm not going to lie, Joey. I'm *glad* he got fired. Now maybe we can have a life of our own without you jumping every time that madman calls."

"Gina, you're so wrong—I've never jumped for anyone. We live in a jungle, it's business. And also, he's my friend."

"He's nobody's friend, and I'm sick of trying to pretend he is. I'm sick of making excuses for him to people we know and work with. He's a louse, and the best thing that can happen to you is to get away from him."

"I can't turn my back on him, it's not right."

"Why not? You know he threw you in. You know he deliberately sacrificed you to try to save himself."

"That was *his* mistake."

"I don't understand, Joey. You'd never take that from anyone else—you'd chop their heads off."

"Gina, you're right. Everything you say is right, but it can't *be* that way. I held this guy out to people all over the country as my friend. Joey Bertell can't run. That's not his reputation. Not running."

"Can you get in any trouble?"

"No."

"Are you going to cause any?"

"No."

She gave a sigh. "Someday maybe I'll figure you out."

"I hope not. If you do, we'll both be on the funny farm."

That, at least, struck her funny.

"Okay, Larry Loyal, come home."

"I love you." *Click.*

I threw my clothes hurriedly into the bag, grabbed the phone, and dialed inter-room.

"Hello," came the soft voice.

"Chili, Joey. Can you talk?"

"In a way," she jargoned.

"Chase that mooch you've got in the room and meet me downstairs in five minutes. I want you to drive me to the airport." *Click.*

I went down to the cashier's cage, signed my bill, and got a hundred dollars in fives and ones. Two fives I put into an envelope marked "Maid," signed my name, and pushed it back to the cashier. From there, I handed out tips through the lobby and out to the car.

Believe it or not, Chili was in the driver's seat waiting.

"Doll, I pity the poor bastard you were with. What did you say?"

"I told him my lover was downstairs, that he was insanely jealous, that I was driving him to the airport, and we'd really have a ball tonight after he left."

"What did he say?"

"I'm here, aren't I?"

I looked her over slowly and said, "Chili doll, you sure are."

We turned out of the hotel driveway onto the airport expressway. Away from the beach, the night air was warm and soft in the convertible, and Chili looked delicious with her hair flowing. She drove left-handed, with her right hand resting easily in my lap. It got the reaction she was looking for.

"I just wanted to see if I affected you."

"You know the old joke?"

"What's that?"

"The punch line is, 'Make bigger circles.' "

She giggled, and grabbed the thermometer. It felt good. And for a change, I didn't feel guilty, because this moment couldn't turn into anything.

"What's up, Joey baby?"

I laughed.

"I mean besides *that*."

"Jonathan is out of BCA."

"And you?"

"I go with the same broom."

"I'm sorry, honey!"

That's why she was with me at the moment. Sometimes a man needs a woman just to care, even if it's make-believe. At such a time he doesn't mind being conned. The soft shoulder and bosom cures a lot of hurt. With Chili, moreover, it would never be grease.

"Will there be problems?"

"There shouldn't be . . . but there will. The press will blow it into a big story and keep it going for weeks."

507

"Why would they do that?"

"It's their job—news."

Question and answer time. "Maybe you can talk to a few of them and they'll play it down?"

"Never try to muffle the press, Chili baby. They're in the Constitution."

"What then?"

"Ride it out. There's an axiom, 'Nothing's as dead as yesterday's newspaper.' They have their rules, and I'll play by them."

"You have the answers for everything, and, honey, I hope it all works. The hell with *him*, I just don't want you hurt."

"I'll never get hurt, Chili baby, Scarred, but not hurt."

"Why don't you stay here and relax? It would do you good, and you'd be where they couldn't reach you."

I laughed out loud on that one. It was humorous to me only, but I tried to explain.

"Chili doll, for one thing, I love a fight. Second, for the first time in my life I've done nothing wrong."

I laughed out loud again. "Third, I'm going to get my jollies leading them a merry chase. Imagine those imbeciles hunting something that isn't there."

I was holding my sides now. "Everyone will have a story, everyone will have a theory. Their thieving minds won't let them believe there's nothing."

"Wonderful."

"And the great part of it is that in the hunt the penny-ante crooks and chiselers will go. Even a couple of the big fish will open their diarrhea mouths and get caught. They'll hook themselves, and have nobody to blame but themselves."

Chili had pulled up to the departure ramp. I staked the cop to a fin and told him the girl would be back in a minute.

She stayed at my side as I carried the two-suiter to the counter, got my ticket validated, then walked on. Time was growing short.

Going down the concourse to the gate, I had my last chuckle. It was from the vicarious thrill of the potbellied bastards with the black cigars looking at Chili's firm little *tushie* dimpling in her pale pink hip-huggers.

Then we were at the gate. I showed my ticket, and went to the door. Chili looked at me with just the slightest amount of moisture in her eyes. She put her arms around my shoulders, tiptoed up and kissed me with those soft lips.

"Joey, for the last time. If you ever need me, I'm yours. I still love you, and regardless of what you say or want of me, I always will."

"Thanks, doll," I said, knowing she could read the sincerity and tenderness even in my casual words. I held the easy embrace and kissed her softly on the forehead.

"And you have my word, someday I'm going to write a book about you."

She smiled with delight. "Have you got a title?"

"*The Hookers . . .*"

"Joey, you're something. Good-bye . . ."

509

I started to leave. She called me back. "Be careful—really take care of yourself. Regardless of what you say, he's still a dirty sonovabitch."

"You're right," I said, with a touch of sadness, "but he's *my* sonovabitch."

I turned toward the plane, and home.